More Praise for Warrior Monk

"Holy Scripture and unholy gun play in the same novel? Exactly - and you'll love the combination! *Warrior Monk* offers a riveting mix of action, romance, and intrigue, served up by a master wordsmith. Keating's Pastor Stephen Grant manages to wield both Bible and bullets with equal expertise. Grant is clearly in control whether in or out of the pulpit."

- Paul L. Maier
best-selling author of
A Skeleton in God's Closet

Warrior Monk

A Pastor Stephen Grant Novel

Ray Keating

Copyright © 2010 by Raymond J. Keating

For more information:
Keating Reports, LLC
P.O. Box 596
Manorville, NY 11934
keatingreports@aol.com

ISBN 1453801030

For my family,
Beth, David and Jonathan

Prelude

A few years after the fall of the Soviet Union

A suppressor never threw off his aim. But it served as a distraction while the gun rested in his shoulder holster.

He felt like the target could spot the weapon more easily. Objectively, he understood this wasn't the case below a suit jacket and trench coat. Still, it didn't feel right.

The two Americans drove on a narrow country road about an hour outside of Paris. Rain was forecasted, and the dark gray clouds appeared ready to burst. But not a drop had fallen yet.

Sunflowers populated field after field along the way. He wondered how the tall, top-heavy plants could stand so erect.

His partner on this particular assignment dropped him off around the corner from an old church, a small wood and stone structure at the center of a bucolic village. If all ran on schedule, the target, Vladimir Chenko, would be waiting in a pew.

Chenko not only had been a veteran military officer for the Soviet Union and then Russia, but also was a CIA asset. The Russian reported on the communists for years, and more recently, tried to spot any nuclear materials wandering off. Or, at least, that was his assignment from the CIA.

The nugget was money and an eventual life of capitalist leisure. Chenko retired, and was ready to be united with a bank account packed with U.S. dollars. The Russian sought a safe, preferably tropical location with America's help.

But Chenko played both sides, and it had resulted in several deaths.

One happened to be the American's mentor and friend.

By sheer luck, the agency stumbled upon evidence that Chenko had passed on information over the years from loose-lipped field operators who got too trusting, too comfortable and, therefore, sloppy. That information cost the lives of two U.S. operatives and perhaps as many as ten Russian assets who worked to undermine Soviet communism.

With the Cold War over, Chenko apparently thought no one in the West would care enough to unearth his duplicity, or that his tracks were well covered.

Chenko was wrong on each count. The Americans found out and were quite displeased.

He entered the tiny stone church, and stepped into the rear of the nave. He could smell the age and decay of the place. Like so many others in Europe, this church appeared empty – but for his target. It increasingly seemed that if you wanted to arrange a discreet meeting, a church in Europe was ideal.

He noted the side exit was open, only steps from where a man sat in the third pew, staring at the altar.

Is the bastard praying?

He paused briefly, taking another look around, then moved forward and sat in front of Chenko. The pew creaked. From the sound on the stone outside the doorway, he knew the rain had started to fall. His gaze remained straight ahead, while giving the pre-determined phrase in fluent French. "This church has seen much over the centuries."

Chenko responded in Russian, "Yes, and it, no doubt, will see more."

He turned half way around in the pew, and the Russian smiled broadly.

Chenko switched to English, "I am ready, my American friend."

Friend?

He didn't expect the Russian to be armed. After all, this was to be a happy occasion. Nonetheless, he looked Chenko over carefully.

"My wife is on one floor of a Paris hotel, and my mistress on another." Chenko laughed in delight as some do when they relish getting away with something. "Both await new lives. How are we to proceed?"

Without a word in response or to declare judgment, he rotated back towards the altar, reached his right hand inside his jacket for the Glock.

The fat, gray-haired Russian double agent moved with surprising quickness and strength. Chenko whipped a cord around his neck, cutting into his skin and cutting off his air.

He fumbled the gun as his hands reacted instinctively trying to pull away the chord. He was being hoisted back over the pew via this line of strangulation, feet just off the ground, seemingly helpless to fight back.

"I spotted the gun, comrade. Silencers make pistols so bulky," Chenko spewed into his ear.

Shit, I knew it.

Darkness and death were not far off. He snapped his left wrist back hard, allowing the tactical knife strapped low on his forearm to slip forward. He grabbed it, pressed the thumb stud to open the 3.1-inch serrated-edge steel blade, swung it around, and plunged it into Chenko's left calf.

The Russian screamed a curse in his native language, but Chenko's grip on the wire did not falter.

Son of a bitch!

Summoning the last bits of his faltering strength, he began pulling the knife up, slicing through skin and muscle, scraping against bone. The double agent screamed. Chenko's left hand flinched and loosened ever so slightly.

Finally, he had his opportunity, jamming his right hand under the wire, and spinning his body away from Chenko and onto the floor, with the bloody knife still in his left hand.

Struggling for air, he staggered to his feet. Chenko was pulling up his right pant leg, and grabbing a small revolver strapped above his ankle.

Crap!

The Russian was straightening up to fire.

One chance existed. He flipped the knife into his right hand, looked at Chenko's chest, and threw it. The knife struck home. The Russian dropped the gun. There was a strange, disturbing look of fear on Chenko's face as he turned and looked around the church briefly, and then toppled to the floor dead.

That's the first of two.

He picked up and holstered the gun; pulled the knife from the dead Russian, closed it and shoved it into his pocket; and took steps towards the side exit.

A voice from the back of the church asked in French, "Why, my son?"

He did exactly what he was trained not to do.

He stopped and turned slightly. Out of the corner of his eye, he saw a dark figure in the shadows at the back of the church. A glimmering gold cross hung from a chain around the shadow's neck, the only clear feature in the dim light.

For some reason, he answered, "It had to be done. Justice." He walked out into the hard rain.

Less than a minute later, he was picked up at the designated location. Other than an exchange on how the mission was completed, they drove in silence.

In the heavy rain, the sunflowers growing in the roadside fields drooped their heads ever so slightly.

Two hours later, he was on a commercial flight heading back to the United States.

But he felt different this time. It wasn't guilt, nor regret. There was no satisfaction, which surprised him. He felt empty.

Why risk answering that priest?

He always saw his work as having meaning and purpose. His head continued to recognize this. However, a gnawing for something more had been growing deeper inside.

The vision of the priest and that light-gathering cross kept creeping back into his thoughts during the flight. He tried to read or watch the in-flight movie, but to no avail.

What did that priest think today? Was Chenko praying? Do I care?

On that flight from Paris to New York, he realized that he did care.

Chapter 1

More than fifteen years later

Was it his church, or His church?

Pastor Stephen Grant knew the answer, but still pondered the question.

He gazed up the gentle, grassy incline at the new St. Mary's Lutheran Church in Manorville on the East End of Long Island – a beautiful Tudor-style building rising into the air.

St. Mary's differed rather dramatically from those soulless buildings inflicted upon congregations in recent times, Grant reflected. He despised the perversions of architecture that made new churches appear ready either to add a drive-up window for convenience, or to pass for a doctor's office. For good measure, on the inside, too many were designed for floorshows rather than worship. Grant bemoaned that there was little in these warehouse spaces that spoke to the majesty and mystery of God. He became convinced that architectural style and worship choices were intimately intertwined.

Grant had put so much time, energy, and prayer into St. Mary's that feelings of ownership seemed justified.

It took four years to follow through on the "Six C's," as Grant called them – concept, convincing queasy church members, cash, cow-towing to local politicians, construction and completion. The 42-year-old Grant, pastor at St. Mary's for nearly a decade, viewed getting this church built with a touch of the miraculous.

It also helped that Hans and Flo Gunderson, leaders at St. Mary's and Grant's friends, owned one of the largest construction firms on Long Island. Once all the local approvals were secured, the Gundersons made the new St. Mary's happen.

Before he got too carried away in the sin of pride, however, Stephen thought it wise to get back to the task at hand.

Grant was posting the new times for all the weekly services and activities at St. Mary's in the large roadside sign – Saturday evening and Sunday morning Masses, Sunday school, adult Bible study, Matins on Tuesday and Thursday mornings, and Vespers on Wednesday evenings. He closed and locked the Plexiglas door underneath the large white letters spelling out "St. Mary's Lutheran Church" against dark wood.

Grant still had not unearthed how this parish got its name. "St. Mary's" was pretty rare for a Lutheran church, even though that was Martin Luther's parish in Wittenberg. However, Luther's parish was named for Mary Magdalene, while Grant's was for Mary, the mother of Jesus. Stephen thought that modern day Lutherans had no clue what to do with Mary – either Mary, for that matter – so it intrigued him and actually played a tiny part in his taking the call to this church. He appreciated such oddities.

Besides, Bing Crosby in *The Bells of St. Mary's* was a longtime favorite, along with an appreciation for Ingrid Bergman as a rather fetching nun. Grant tried not to think too deeply about a Lutheran pastor having the hots for a Catholic nun.

Then again, Martin Luther married a nun, so what the heck.

It was Wednesday evening, and the new St. Mary's would be officially dedicated and blessed in ten days.

That event was scheduled to bring out a bevy of local politicians—a necessary evil Grant seemed resigned to, especially with Labor Day and the political silly season just around the corner. Grant's experiences with politicians never seemed to turn out very well over the years.

A wide array of clergy and church officials would be in attendance as well. Grant could not decide who tried his patience more – politicians or a few of his fellow pastors. Some of his collared colleagues accused him of being too liberal, others too conservative, while some would say too liturgical or even Roman, and still others labeled him too Protestant. Funny, he just thought of himself as trying – and often struggling – to get it right as a faithful, traditional Christian.

Grant had to admit, though, that he looked forward to the inevitable give and take, and needling that were to come. Bottom line: Pastor Stephen Grant enjoyed being a theological shit stirrer – tweaking those who disagreed with him along the way. He knew that this mischievous streak sometimes failed to serve his pastoral responsibilities, but he just couldn't help himself. Compared to his old job, being a pastor was so liberating. Previously, he wasn't allowed to talk about work, politics or his personal life to almost anyone. Now he could say pretty much whatever he liked, while keeping Holy Scripture, church tradition and good taste in mind.

Of course, Grant also couldn't spill the beans on what he heard in confession or during counseling – or, for that matter, any details from his previous career. Fortunately, he was trained to keep secrets.

But Grant long ago had grown accustomed to most people around him closely guarding their secrets. It took some time to get comfortable with individuals so easily spitting out the most personal and too often dark aspects of their lives, not to mention they even sought his guidance. Grant thought about some of the most bizarre confessions he heard just over the past year or so, and the ensuing problems those confessions presented.

The most sordid tales included a gruesome teenage suicide, an accusation of child molestation against a church member, and a bizarre wife-swapping episode among now former congregation members.

Stephen shook his head, and shifted attention back to the church as choir practice began on this humid summer evening. The choir was working its way into Martin Luther's "A Mighty Fortress Is Our God." *They'll never win any awards unless it's for nails on a chalkboard.* He knew that "A Mighty Fortress" was beautiful when sung well, but a poor performance inflicted an egregious injustice – particularly on Luther's original set to a bar tune, as opposed to Bach's later spruced up version.

Who am I to criticize voices singing to the Lord? After all, as his congregation discovered each weekend, he couldn't carry a tune if his life depended upon it. Grant understood many of his own gifts and weaknesses. Singing was not one of his God-given talents, a particularly unfortunate shortcoming for a Lutheran pastor.

As would become evident shortly, his life and the lives of others would depend upon gifts that Stephen Grant had perfected years ago. That was during a career quite different from a church pastor in terms of duties. But in Grant's view of the world, it was not all that different on commitment, purpose, and doing the right thing.

Chapter 2

Linda Serrano was staring into the dirty bathroom mirror in her tiny basement apartment. Her brown eyes looked sunken with heavy rings underneath. Her long dark hair was frizzy and unkempt. In her hand, she held a .22-caliber Beretta Bobcat.

It was striking how much Linda had changed from her early days at the state university. She arrived as a naïve freshman who wanted to become a nurse, and went through an education that led her in a far different direction.

Within a year, Linda dropped nursing, became a philosophy major, and joined a witch coven. But her life was fully transformed when she sat down in a "Philosophy of the Environment" class.

The professor, Andre Tyler, put all the pieces together — animal rights, the sacredness of the environment, and fighting such evils as global warming, suburban sprawl and light pollution. Linda expressed appreciation that her parents never forced organized religion upon her, but often said environmentalism filled an emptiness. She became a believer in "deep ecology."

The much older Tyler proved not only to be caring in bed, he also guided her into the cause. He described in gruesome detail how nature was being raped by capitalists, multinationals, government, consumers, materialists, SUV drivers, and worst of all, developers. Earth was overrun by people. After several months, Andre brought her into what he called a cell of the Land and Animal Liberation Army. Some people, including the law enforcement community, called LALA a domestic environmental terrorist group. Others said they just cared for the environment.

Linda carried out a variety of "missions," such as bringing down electrical lines, breaking windows at a pharmaceutical research lab, burning down houses under construction, slashing the tires on SUVs, and defacing fast-food restaurants and a butcher shop. These all were well planned – to the surprise and frustration of law enforcement.

But it was apparent that Linda Serrano only grew angrier. Now pursuing a doctorate and serving as a part-time professor at the local community college, she complained about how self-centered her students were and how little they cared about nature, or anything other than making money.

In addition to being part of LALA guerilla strikes, Linda led the public campaign to stop the construction of St. Mary's Lutheran Church in the Long Island pine barrens. Serrano often told Andre, "Sure, the pine barrens don't look like much to the average, idiot suburbanite, but those bushes, little trees, and sandy soil are obviously precious to anyone with a drop of caring." Opposing St. Mary's took much of her energy. Linda called it an "environmental crusade" – organizing protests, lobbying politicians, and working the media, with what she viewed as lazy but sympathetic reporters at local television news channels always proving useful.

She gained allies along the way. The town supervisor, Bradley Barnett, spoke out. He even received a bit of grief for starting the cry, "Find God in the trees, not on your knees," while standing in front of the bulldozers.

Eventually, the bulldozers rolled. Trees fell. A church rose.

Serrano failed to stop the building of what she labeled "that Christian monstrosity." She told a reporter, "I've tried to explain things to that self-righteous pastor, but some people never get it." She added, which did not make the evening news, "He's an asshole, and those two builders in that church are environmental rapists."

The time had come to punish that pastor, and the developer couple. She would take action. Serrano shoved the Beretta inside the pocket of her black jacket, zipped it up, climbed the stairs from her apartment and crawled inside her hybrid. It would take ten minutes to get to St. Mary's.

Chapter 3

Grant entered the church, and was hit by a blast of cool air that immediately began working to annihilate the beads of sweat on his forehead and back of his neck. He was thankful. The old church building, torn down a week earlier and with only small bits of rubble left across the parking lot, had no air conditioning.

While passing through the narthex, Stephen decided to make a quick cameo appearance during choir practice before heading to his office to work on the "freakin' sermon" — as he had come to call it – for the church blessing.

Entering the nave and proceeding halfway up the center aisle, Grant bowed before turning his back to the altar and the massive Crucifix hanging on the wall behind it.

The inside of the new St. Mary's jibed nicely with its Tudor exterior. Lining the walls was a dark wood paneling about four feet high. Rising from there up to the various points in the ceiling were off-white walls accented with wood beams. The windows and ends of each pew came to a similar pointed shape as the ceiling. Rather than stained glass, the windows featured scenes from the life of Jesus Christ etched into otherwise clear glass. Daylight was allowed to stream into the building as a result.

The largest etched window was behind the choir loft, showing Jesus as the teacher. At the other end, under the Crucifix, the altar rail closely mimicked the wood paneling and beams, while the altar was bathed in a white brighter than the walls.

Grant looked up at the enthusiastic, but out-of-key singers. The music director, Scott Larson, spotted Grant. He turned his back to the dozen voices, and looking down at Grant, combined a bright smile with a good-natured roll of the eyes. Stephen grinned and waved to the group.

Grant knew that the 22-year-old Larson was a tremendous blessing for the church. As a newly minted graduate from Concordia College in Bronxville, New York, Larson possessed all the musical skills a church needed, but Grant himself woefully lacked. Scott only recently became St. Mary's very young music director. His blond hair, blue eyes and wiry build did not fit the traditional expectations. They also contrasted sharply with his predecessor, the late Cliff Rheingold, who had become crotchety in his eighties, and scared away all but the most committed choir members. These Lutherans were too reserved to openly admit it, but soon after Cliff died, the choir numbers started growing again.

Scott actually offered a package deal. He was engaged to the always upbeat and enthusiastic Pam Carter, who also was the organist and youth group director. When he first met the couple, Grant assumed Pam had been a peppy cheerleader in high school, with good grades of course, while Scott was the All-American leading the pre-game prayer. That turned out to be exactly right.

Carter, also 22, had big blue eyes and blond hair that curved in at her neck. The hair framed a cherub-like face. She graduated from Concordia-New York as well, and now dabbled in composing. In the end, the two were a team in terms of music and youth at St. Mary's, with Scott putting his baseball and basketball talents to work with the youth and Pam helping Scott with the bell and youth choirs.

As church workers, the two earned little. Each lived with church families until they were to be married in October, after which they would move into an old farmhouse around the block from the church that had been donated to St. Mary's in the will of a late member.

Grant very much liked the couple. Though they could be a bit saccharine at times, it was rare to meet two individuals so grounded at such a young age. He could not get out of his head visions of family members one day singing around a piano at Scott and Pam's house. Grant also could not suppress the pangs of envy such thoughts stirred.

He strode back into the narthex. A turn left would have taken him down a hall to four rooms—three used for Sunday school and various church meetings, and the other for storage. He instead went down the hall to the right, which led to the budding church library and conference room, a small copy room, his secretary's office—though Mrs. Barbara Tunney more often acted like a nosy mother than a secretary—and his own office.

At first glance, Mrs. Tunney seemed like a rather typical church lady. But Dana Carvey she was not. Tunney was 70 and a widow, but she had more energy and attitude than her gray hair, glasses, sweaters and flowered dresses might indicate. She was organized; a good administrator; and once a week showed up at the church parsonage to tidy up after the single Grant. In many ways, Tunney kept St. Mary's functioning day to day.

Stephen plopped down in the plush swivel chair behind his desk. He loved his new office. In fact, it was the first real office he'd ever had. His old job required lots of travel, with Grant otherwise laboring in a cubicle. In the old church, Grant and Tunney shared the same office.

Stephen had positioned his desk in front of a large bay window, so when suffering from sermon block, he could twirl around in his chair and look out to the heavens for much-needed inspiration. He had bookcases from floor to ceiling on both sides of the window, and completely covering two other walls. They were mainly filled with tomes on theology and history, along with some historical fiction. Up against the fourth wall stood an antique wardrobe in which he hung his various pastoral garbs. One half of the room centered around his desk, with the other half looking more like a small living room, including an armchair and couch, a television/DVD combo, and an iPod docking station.

A coffee table actually was an oak gun cabinet, with a secure lock hidden from plain view. If Grant didn't tell anyone—which he didn't, not even the ever-vigilant Barbara Tunney—then no one would know that it was anything more than a place to rest oversized books, magazines and tea mugs.

In the cabinet, Grant kept a 10mm Glock 20 and a Taurus PT-25, along with his Harris M-89 sniper rifle. With both his former employer, the Central Intelligence Agency, and the Church, Grant learned enough about human nature to know that evil existed and protection was necessary. Grant kept identical handgun models at the parsonage, along with a Swiss SSG550 sniper rifle.

He occasionally left directly from church for target practice at the local sportsmen's club. An old colleague quietly arranged a membership. This allowed Grant to tell himself that his gun cabinet at church was a matter of convenience, and not a case of lingering paranoia from his old job.

Grant flipped on his desk lamp, and opened his 17-inch screen MacBook Pro. The file, recently renamed "FreakinSermon.doc," stared back, but not a word had yet been written.

Barbara called in from the copy room, "How's the freakin' sermon coming?"

"Sermon block," he grunted.

"Ah, don't worry about it. It's not like it's one of the biggest sermons you've ever given."

"Thanks for all your support. Why did I hire you again?" Grant responded.

"Actually, I was here before you, remember?"

"Oh, that's right. I keep forgetting."

Grant swiveled the chair around to stare out the window. Another prayer for inspiration could never hurt.

But a very small car pulling into the parking lot distracted him. Grant got a funny feeling in his head.

This wasn't nerves about the sermon.

It was a feeling Grant had not experienced in a very long time. He called it a "red alert" – when he felt tightness in his head and ears, like pressure building up.

It was getting darker, but he could still see someone – a woman – getting out of the car. Even though he was now a pastor and this was a church, Grant knew enough not to ignore a red alert. He instinctively closed the laptop and shut off light to see better. Grant leaned forward and watched out his bay window.

Meanwhile, the choir started taking another crack at "A Mighty Fortress Is Our God."

Chapter 4

"A mighty fortress is our God, A trusty shield and weapon..."

Linda got out of the car and walked over to the driver's side window of a silver Mercedes. Her hand was firmly on the Beretta in her pocket.

"He helps us free from ev'ry need That hath us now o'er taken..."

The window was down. "Can I help you?" Hans Gunderson asked. He was listening to the radio and getting a little paperwork done while Flo was practicing with the choir.

"I'm here for you, your wife and your pastor," Linda responded without any detectable emotion in her voice.

"What?" Hans looked at the woman standing by his car. "Oh jeez, you're that activist-professor lady. What's going on now?"

"The old evil foe Now means deadly woe..."

"I'm here to make sure you pay for your sins." Linda pulled the gun out of her pocket, held it up with both hands about three feet from Hans' head. His mouth dropped open. Linda pulled the trigger. Hans Gunderson's blood splattered the gray leather seats.

"Deep guile and great might Are his dread arms in fight..."

Linda headed into St. Mary's seeking other prey.

"On earth is not his equal..."

In the office, for a nanosecond, Grant was immobilized by disbelief. Hans shot. As the woman walked toward the front doors of St. Mary's, old instincts began taking over. Grant slipped firmly into action.

"With might of ours can naught be done, Soon were our loss effected..."

He leaped from the chair, grabbed the keys off the corner of his desk, and moved quickly to open the coffee table/gun cabinet. *Paranoia, my ass.* He picked up the Glock and loaded a magazine holding 10 rounds, sticking a second mag in his pocket.

"But for us fights the valiant One, Whom God Himself elected..."

Barbara happened to move into the office doorway, asking, "Pastor, did you hear something out...?" She froze seeing her pastor approaching with a gun in his hand.

"Ask ye, Who is this? Jesus Christ it is..."

Grant grabbed Barbara Tunney's arm, and told her in a low, commanding tone, "Call 911, and tell them we have a shooting in progress."

Tunney stuttered, "A...a...what...?"

Grant had no time to walk his secretary through this crisis. "Barbara, do it now! Call 911, and then go out the back door and away from here."

"Of Sabaoth Lord, And there's none other God..."

While Tunney stumbled to her office phone, Pastor Stephen Grant stayed low and moved quickly down the hallway holding the pistol out front. He uttered a quick, simple prayer: "Jesus, give me clarity and strength."

Part of his mind returned to a distant, yet still familiar place, but with even greater earnestness. For the coming seconds, he would be more hunter than pastor.

"He holds the field forever..."

Chapter 5

Linda Serrano burst into the church. No one was standing inside the doors. The choir still sang. Apparently, they didn't hear the gun shot. "Perfect," she whispered.

"Tho' devils all the world should fill, All eager to devour us..."

She took one of the staircases to the choir loft two steps at a time. At the top, Linda came around the corner and saw the backs of the people singing quite loudly as the organ played. A couple of heads briefly glanced her way, but no one spotted the gun hanging down at Serrano's side in her right hand.

"We tremble not, we fear no ill, They shall not over pow'r us..."

Below, Grant looked through the glass window in the door leading back into the narthex. Seeing no one, he quickly moved through it. He scanned the area, and peaked into the nave.

"This world's prince may still Scowl fierce as he will..."

Conveniently for Serrano, Flo Gunderson stood not more than five feet away in the last row. Linda moved toward her, keeping the Beretta at her side. Flo actually glanced and smiled at Serrano before turning her attention back to Scott.

"He can harm us none, He's judged; the deed is done..."

Serrano quickly raised the gun, and deposited a bullet through Mrs. Gunderson's back. It ripped through her heart.

All hell broke loose in the choir loft after the shot rang out. Flo Gunderson crumpled forward onto fellow choir members and then to the floor. She was dead before her body came to a complete rest. Half the group screamed. Others dove for cover. A few stood immobilized.

Amidst the chaos, Scott Larson tried to make his way to the shooter. The former high school sports star was not quick enough, though, as Serrano landed a slug just below his left shoulder and then a second in his back as his body turned.

At the sound of the first shot, Grant turned and sped for the stairs. With the second and third, he paused briefly at the top. He looked around the corner, and tried to assess the situation. Grant had to stop the woman who was shooting his parishioners.

As he emerged, Linda Serrano first noted Grant's gun and grabbed the person to her left and stuck the Beretta in the woman's neck. Then Serrano saw the collar. "You're the one I'm looking for, Pastor," she hissed.

Grant counted two down, and saw the shooter pointing a 22-caliber into the neck of Jennifer Brees, longtime member of the congregation and wife of Congressman Ted Brees. *Of course, grab the congressman's wife.* Just then, he realized that this shooter was the person who made his life miserable over the past few years.

Grant could see panic bubbling up in Serrano, as cries and movement among choir members distracted her. She screamed, "Get back, get back! Get away. Nobody move." She focused on Grant: "What's with the fucking gun, Pastor?"

Grant tried to sound soothing, "Let's take it easy. There's no reason for anyone else to get hurt. Why not put the gun down and we'll end all of this?"

Serrano shot back, "Shut up! I'm gettin' the hell outta here." She started frantically looking around for a way out, while ordering, "Drop the gun."

Grant ignored the demand. Meanwhile, Pam Carter started crawling out from behind the organ toward her fiancé, who was sprawled on the tiled choir loft floor in a slowly expanding pool of blood.

Linda Serrano shouted at her, "Get back where you were!" But Grant saw that Pam could not, or would not, heed the warnings. She was completely immersed in her need to get to her husband-to-be.

While keeping his gun trained on the shooter, Grant said, "It's okay. Just let her get to him." Cries continued all around.

"No, no, I said no!" Serrano shouted. She took the gun away from Jennifer's neck, in a move toward Pam. In that instant, Grant prayed silently: *God, help me.* He fired a single shot into the forehead of Linda Serrano, who fell back over the choir loft's low railing.

If the bullet didn't kill her immediately, the point of one of the pews now protruding through her abdomen finished the job. Serrano's eyes were open, vacant and lifeless.

The next line of the hymn came into Grant's head as he looked down from the choir loft:

"One little word can fell him."

Jennifer Brees looked at Grant, apparently in horror and amazement, while several streaks of Linda Serrano's blood clung to her hair and speckled her face. When the bullet had entered Serrano's skull, Jennifer's head was inches away. Yet her own pastor pointed the gun and pulled the trigger. Jennifer took unsteady steps towards him.

Grant wondered: *Is she going to call me a crazed asshole, or thank me?* She hugged him, apparently thankful.

The incident was over in a few minutes, but a great deal was set in motion.

Until that moment, Stephen Grant seemed to have existed in two completely separate universes. First, it was as a Navy SEAL, followed by time as an analyst— unofficially as an assassin – with the CIA. After a break, the second was studying to become and then serving as a Lutheran pastor. In a matter of mere minutes – excruciating minutes – the two worlds merged in a flurry of bullets, blood, song and prayer.

Chapter 6

It was apparent to anyone who looked closely that Ted Brees loved being a U.S. congressman. And he barely disguised his desire to become a senator, or maybe governor, and then, of course, leader of the free world.

In a rare unguarded moment after several drinks, Brees once confided to an almost equally ambitious member of Congress that he often fantasized about his own political career while having sex, and had admiration for a former president known to enjoy illicit sexual pleasures now and then in the White House.

Before heading off to a fundraiser, the forty-year-old Brees was intertwined with his chief of staff, Kerri Bratton, in the bedroom of his apartment on Capitol Hill. The 26-year-old Bratton had long blond hair matched by long legs that often seemed to wrap around her sexual partner like a vice. She apparently knew that the Oval Office was an aphrodisiac for Brees, as she occasionally moaned, "Mr. President."

Just as he appeared ready to reach the Oval Office, his personal cell phone rang.

No matter where Brees and Bratton were in the throes of their personal passion, both were first and foremost political creatures. Brees withdrew and Bratton waited quietly.

The congressman took a deep breath, looked at the number on the screen, and answered the phone in a voice that revealed nothing about what he had just been doing: "Jen?"

"Oh Ted! It was awful, but I'm okay ... I think." Jennifer's crying could still be heard over substantial background noise.

Ted disentangled his legs from Kerri's, and sat up in bed. "Jen, what's the matter? What happened? Where are you?"

"I'm at church. There was a shooter. She came into the choir loft, and just started shooting."

Brees slipped his feet down to the floor. "Are you sure you're okay?"

"I'm trying to keep it together. Ted, the Gundersons are dead. Scott was bleeding on the floor. They took him to the hospital."

"It'll be alright. What happened?"

Jennifer Brees shakily relayed the events to her husband. "Ted, she held a gun to my head ... If it weren't for Pastor, I might be dead." She sniffled. "Please come home. Come home now. I need you."

"Of course, baby, I'll be on the next flight out."

Congressman Brees heard his wife of eight years say again, "Ted, I need you."

He paused, glancing over his shoulder at the naked Kerri Bratton lying on the bed, and replied, "I'll be back home in a few hours. Take it easy."

"OK. I love you, Ted." Jennifer's voice cracked.

"I love you too, and I'm so glad your safe."

They said their good-byes, and hung up.

Ted Brees actually had not loved his wife for some time, and had discussed with Kerri the right political moment for a divorce. After all, as he often told Kerri, "Every decision in my life is a political one." Bratton, of course, agreed. Obviously, a divorce would have to wait until after the November election.

He turned to Kerri, "Get your clothes on, get us two tickets to MacArthur Airport, and call the district office staff. Tell them to get ready for lots of action." Ted filled Kerri in on what he knew as they got dressed. "Tell them to get information and start putting together a press statement. On the flight, you and I have to discuss how we'll handle the gun issue."

Kerri Bratton easily slipped into campaign mode. There was a reason why she was considered one of the most politically savvy staffers on Capitol Hill.

For the past three years, Kerri told her closest friends that when the time was right, political sex with Ted Brees eventually would lead to something more. After all, she noted: "We care about the same things. We're so much alike."

Chapter 7

It was 3:10 in the morning when Pastor Grant finally got back to the parsonage.

For much of the past two years, entering this empty, three-bedroom ranch put him in a melancholy mood. The six-foot, black-haired, green-eyed, athletic Grant was a very steady guy on the emotions front, but the deafening silence in each room amplified a loneliness he had increasingly experienced since turning forty.

Angst at 40 was a bit of a cliché, but it was the reality at hand.

This house simply did not feel like home. No place did.

Most nights, Grant would stay out as late as possible. When in the parsonage, without even thinking, he would flip on the television in the den. Grant would catch up on the news or sports. But it primarily served as background noise. It made the parsonage less oppressive, made it seem like someone else was there.

If unable to sleep, he'd get lost in a movie. Grant, a longtime film buff, wound up watching a lot of movies. He actually needed very little sleep since his SEAL and CIA training.

But after this day, Grant went straight to his bedroom. He thought it would take mere seconds to fall asleep after some abbreviated evening prayers.

Instead, while tossing and turning in bed, his mind worked overtime reviewing what happened earlier in the night.

The questions from the police, and later the media, were numerous, not to mention repetitive.

The big one being, "Father, why do you have these guns?"

That was followed closely by, "Father, you worked for the CIA?"

There also was a clear hint of admiration in a "Nice shot, Father" from one detective as he looked down at the dead body of Linda Serrano with the bloody hole in her forehead.

Grant knew that anyone with a collar on Long Island often was called "Father," with nearly half the Island's population being Roman Catholic.

Grant explained that he had been an analyst with the CIA – which was his title – before becoming a pastor, and that he enjoyed staying sharp by shooting at the sportsmen's club. Thankfully, no one asked if he ever killed before – in a church or otherwise. Perhaps it was just too much to imagine that a priest, or pastor, had ever killed another human being on purpose before this incident. Police and reporters otherwise seemed to appreciate the exact details he provided of the entire event.

When Rep. Brees had shown up at the police station, it was the first time Grant could recall feeling happy to see a politician. The focus shifted off Grant, and onto the congressman consoling his wife, thanking the pastor, and then earnestly working in a mini-speech on the woes of too many guns on our streets.

But Grant soon found himself being led around by one of Brees's staff members for what seemed to be photo opportunities. The feeling of happiness that came with the politician's arrival was fleeting.

As for the shooting itself, while lying in bed, he went over every detail, as trained, to determine what could have been done better.

Since coming to St. Mary's, Grant understood his job as a spiritual shepherd to his flock. But tonight, he acutely felt the failure of not being able to physically protect his members. His friends, the Gundersons, were dead. Scott was out of surgery, but one bullet had lodged near his spinal cord. Another surgery would be needed, and the doctors could not be absolutely sure if he would walk again.

Grant felt an added intensity, drive, and justification when moving against his foe this time, something that had been absent in his old missions. When he killed before, it was for country, duty, or justice – and once, in part, for revenge. But this time, it was intensely personal. He was protecting his own.

"Dear Lord, could I have done more? Moved faster?" wondered Stephen, the pastor, out loud.

But Grant, the trained killer, understood that nothing more was possible. He also knew that without his unique skills, other innocents in his church family might have died.

Stephen Grant, the pastor, started to think more about the loss of his friends, and wept. As the tears came, he could not recall the last time he actually cried. It hadn't been since his parents died.

He finally drifted off to sleep.

Chapter 8

In the morning, the story screamed across the front pages of every New York metropolitan area newspaper.

The *New York Post* naturally served up the spiciest headline: "Pistol Packin' Pastor." The *Daily News* came close with "Holy Gunfight." *Newsday* chimed in "Shootings at Lutheran Church." He flipped on the television and saw himself on News 12 Long Island, along with CNN and FOX News. Near the lead in each story was the fact that Grant, now a pastor, once worked for the CIA. Grant glanced at his laptop sitting on the kitchen table, but decided to leave to his imagination what was flying around the Internet.

He wondered if anyone from the Company would be in contact. But Grant also understood that they operated according to their own agenda and schedule. The high point of a news cycle was not the time to emerge from the shadows to talk with a former operative.

But to Grant, it seemed everybody else in the nation was interested in getting hold of the pistol packin' pastor. He wasn't ready to start answering the telephone with barely three hours sleep, and by 6:30 AM, he had wracked up 24 messages. Grant wondered if there was a message limit on his phone.

Grant was still wet from a quick shower when the phone rang again, and his message kicked in, followed by a very lengthy beep. *So, that's what happens with 30 messages waiting.* A woman's voice began, "Pastor Grant, this is Kerri Bratton from Congressman Brees's office ..." Grant moved quickly and picked up the receiver.

"Yes, I'm here."

"Oh, hello. As I started to say, I'm Kerri Bratton from Congressman Brees's office. We met briefly last night. The congressman and his wife wanted to meet with you this morning at St. Mary's."

Grant replied, "That's fine. But wouldn't it be better to meet somewhere else? My guess is that there'll be media camped out at the church."

Bratton hesitated slightly. "Ah, yes, that's no problem. Congressman Brees understands such things."

"OK, what time?"

"We'd like you to get to the church first, and be ready to meet Congressman and Mrs. Brees outside the front doors at 9:30. The three of you would proceed inside for your discussions, and then Rep. Brees will make himself available to reporters at ten. Would you also like to make a statement at that time?"

Grant worked to suppress his growing irritation. "No, that won't be necessary. And I'll be ready at 9:30. Is there anything else, Ms. Bratton?"

"No, and thank you."

"Good bye, and God bless." After hanging up the phone, Grant added: "Lord, grant me patience and understanding ... please."

He looked at the clock. Though he had Barbara cancel Matins, Stephen had to step up the pace if he was going to stop at the hospital to see how Scott was doing before getting to church. Grant called the Gunderson's daughter, Anna, who lived with her family out on the North Fork, to let her know that he would visit after meeting with the Brees's.

As he walked out the front door, his message count had reached 35, and he heard someone say she was from the "Today Show."

Katie? No, that's right. Meredith.

In his driveway, Grant unexpectedly found himself explaining his schedule as he moved past a few microphones and cameras towards his red Chevy Tahoe.

Chapter 9

Four people strode across the parking lot – with a group of media arriving to watch – as Pastor Stephen Grant waited just outside the front doors of St. Mary's.

With last night's incident providing the most powerful of reminders, Grant knew that old habits die hard. Waiting in his clerical collar, he couldn't help but assess each person that approached. He sometimes did the same thing during Communion.

The couple in front, Ted and Jennifer Brees, held hands. Though Ted's expression was solemn, nothing was out of order on his five foot, ten inch frame, from his neatly cut brown hair, to his sand-colored summer suit with a light blue shirt and dark blue tie with red polka dots, down to the brown loafers. For good measure, Brees had extremely white teeth and a slight tan. It was like watching a young, political version of George Hamilton.

Jennifer was six years younger than Ted, but didn't look like it this morning. She appeared drained – her fair skin contrasting too starkly with the blue, knee-length dress. This was quite a change from how Grant was used to seeing this smart, amusing and energetic woman.

Grant long thought that Jennifer Brees looked like the classic film actress Irene Dunne – sharp facial features, with a slightly upturned nose, and thin body. Her dark,

auburn hair was cut short. But it wasn't just her looks
that drew the comparison to Dunne. It also was her voice
that combined a touch of upper class with occasional
seductive inflections.

A few steps behind the Congressman and his wife came
another man and woman. The man was tall – basketball
tall – with small, oval-shaped glasses, slicked back black
hair with gray streaks, and a dark blue suit with wide,
bold pinstripes. The blond, Ms. Bratton, was striking,
particularly in a very short red dress with large white
buttons. But she had that almost "too perfect" look about
her – kind of Stepford Wife-ish.

I'm watching too many movies.

Jennifer kissed Grant's cheek and squeezed his arms,
and Ted shook his hand firmly. Grant thought that Brees
seemed to linger over the handshake for sake of the
media's cameras. Finally, they all went inside.

Ted Brees pointed out that Grant had already met Ms.
Bratton – they shook hands – and introduced Arnie
Hackling as his pollster and political adviser.

After they entered his office, Stephen invited Ted and
Jennifer to sit on the couch, and pulled two chairs over
from his desk for Bratton and Hackling. Stephen sat in the
armchair, and asked, "Shall we pray?"

All started to bow their heads – except for Hackling,
who asked, "Mind if I don't?"

"That's up to you." Stephen folded his hands, bowed his
head, and continued: "Dear Lord, help us through these
strange and difficult days. Please provide healing to Scott
Larson, strength to Pam Carter, and comfort to the
Gunderson family. Also, dear God, provide guidance and
love to Linda Serrano's friends and family. We pray this in
Jesus' name. Amen."

After a pause of a few seconds, Grant sat back. "How's
everyone doing, especially you, Jennifer?"

Jennifer's brown eyes moistened. "I'm fine." She fiddled with her purse strap. With a slight, forced smile, she added, "You're quite a shot, Pastor."

Ted broke in, "That's for sure. You took quite a chance with my wife."

Grant could not tell if Congressman Brees was angry or merely testing him. "Not really," Grant coolly replied, looking Ted directly in the eyes.

Congressman Brees shifted in his seat, glancing at the others.

Finally, Pastor Grant added, "I would never place Jennifer in danger. I was protecting her and the others, Congressman."

Ted responded, "You're so confident?"

Jennifer quickly broke in, saying to Grant, "And again, thank you. I guess you learn to shoot like that at the CIA."

"Certainly not at seminary," Grant replied with a small smile. "I learned a good deal working for the government."

Ted asked, "Do you feel guilty about killing that woman?"

Jennifer Brees was visibly startled by her husband's question. "Ted!?"

"No, Jennifer," Grant said steadily, "I think a lot of people wonder about that. I know I would." He turned to the congressman, "To be honest, Ted, my personal regrets about last night are not about having to, unfortunately, shoot Linda Serrano. Instead, I deeply wish that it could have been possible to do something more to save the Gundersons and protect Scott. I worry about people's spiritual well being, but last night, I ached over their physical well being as well. Jennifer was lucky. Scott, Hans and Flo were not." A lump formed in his throat.

Jennifer softly said, "There was nothing more you could possibly have done, Pastor."

"Thanks. I know that. But I wish I could have," Stephen replied.

"Well, yes, Reverend Grant, you did all you could," Ted chimed in somewhat less than convincingly. "What do you know about this Serrano woman, the shooter?"

"Congressman, I gave a rundown to the police and media last night. It apparently was in the papers and on TV today. I'm sure it's all over the Internet. She led the opposition to this church being built – protests, rallies, press conferences, and so on. Once the project was moving along, I had not seen her again ... until last night."

"So, no recent threats or contacts? Any groups that she mentioned?" Ted added.

"No, why?"

"Well, we're just trying to get a feel for how deeply she might have been involved with some environmental organizations. It would be a shame if this, ah, incident were capitalized on by certain types to turn people against the environmental movement that has benefited so many, especially here on Long Island," Ted said earnestly.

Stephen caught the slight, but unmistakable roll of the eyes by Jennifer. Pastor Grant replied, "Yes, well, we can't have that, can we? Wouldn't want to have a couple of murders, and another gravely injured victim, perhaps permanently paralyzed, reflect badly on the environmental movement, would we?"

"Oh yes, God forbid!" Jennifer added in exasperation.

Ted ignored his wife and Grant's bit of sarcasm. The Congressman actually looked pleased. "I'm going to make a similar point at the press conference outside. Just wanted to make sure you understood."

"I definitely understand, Congressman," Grant said.

"Ah, excuse me, guns, Congressman?" Kerri interjected to her boss.

"Oh yes, thank you." Ted Brees leaned forward. "I'm also going to talk a bit again about the need to do more on gun control. Obviously, as a former CIA guy, I have little problem with someone like you having a gun – though it's pretty weird given that you're a pastor." He seemed to be waiting for a response. After getting none, Brees continued, "Anyway, I'm concerned about gun ownership spreading among those who don't do law enforcement, who don't work for the government. I'll be mentioning that outside, too. OK with all of this?"

"You're the congressman, Congressman. I'm not making any statements about the environment or gun control today," Grant noted wryly. He couldn't resist adding, "But are you sure you're a Republican?"

Ted Brees chuckled. "Oh yes, but I'm no extremist."

"Yes," Jennifer said, "I cover that in our marriage."

Grant laughed. Ted Brees offered a strained smile.

As they headed out, Grant could not miss that Ted was far more interested in comparing notes with Arnie and Kerri, than with Jennifer. But once they reached the front doors, Ted smoothly moved back to Jennifer, took her hand in his, and led the way to a podium with microphones that somehow had sprung up at the edge of St. Mary's parking lot.

Grant whispered to himself, "Politicians, yuck."

The rest of his day did not improve. Grant helped make funeral arrangements for the Gundersons, and turned down dozens of requests for television and radio interviews.

Chapter 10

Shortly after seven on Friday morning, Grant walked into the diner on Montauk Highway in nearby Moriches. The owner greeted him with the usual robust smile, and enthusiastic handshake. But he quickly got more serious, asking, "Are you alright, my friend?"

"Yes, thanks. It's been quite an experience," Grant replied.

"I can only imagine. Your friends are waiting, but they were uncertain if you'd be here. Come. Follow me." He led Grant to a booth in a far corner at the back of the diner.

Waiting were Grant's two closest friends. They met every Monday, Wednesday and Friday mornings – schedules permitting – at this diner for devotions and breakfast. Or on occasion, the gathering would shift a few miles away to Rock Hill Golf Club for a round of golf followed by devotions and lunch.

Father Thomas Stone – known as Father Tom, or in this group, just Tom – was eight years older than Grant. His hair was almost completely gray, and his five-ten body now carried a notable spare tire in the mid-drift. It was difficult for Grant to think of anyone more at ease with himself and others. Stone was quick with a laugh, and his personality was laid back, as reflected by the fact that when not on official church business one could usually find him in a Hawaiian shirt and shorts during warm weather, as was the case today.

But Grant knew that Stone's attire could mislead. He was serious about the big things. Tom and his wife, Maggie, had just celebrated their twenty-fifth wedding anniversary, and they were dedicated to their six children, spread out from ten years old to twenty-three.

As for his calling, Father Tom was an Episcopal priest. Well, technically, that was no longer the case. Stone could not tolerate the sharp revisionist turn the leaders of the U.S. Episcopal Church had taken in recent times, so his parishioners at St. Bartholomew's Church voted to leave a few short years ago. As some other parishes had done, St. Bart's left the local diocese behind for oversight from a traditional Anglican bishop. In St. Bart's case, it was the Church of Uganda in Africa. Recently, it joined the newly formed Anglican Church in North America.

Fortunately, unlike many other Episcopalian parishes taking this path, St. Bart's was able to buy their church property from the local Episcopal diocese, which preferred the large cash infusion over a battle played out in public. The move invigorated St. Bart's by coming into fellowship with vibrant, traditional churches across the ocean, and by sending out a signal to a host of frustrated local Episcopalians seeking an orthodox Anglican church. Father Tom's parish had grown considerably.

The other person waiting at the table was Father Ronald McDermott, a priest from St. Luke's Roman Catholic Church and School. Father McDermott – Ron only to family and his closest friends – was ten years younger than Grant. McDermott had blond hair that was cut close, and a muscular, stocky five foot six inch body that reminded one of a fireplug. Stephen knew that Ron and Tom were close, but their personalities could not be more different.

Other than on the golf course, Stephen could not recall ever seeing McDermott without a collar in public. But that seemed completely natural. Parishioners did not call him "Father Ron." He was intense, aggressive, and possessed absolutely no reservations about expressing his opinions. Father McDermott leaned more towards theologian than pastor.

Grant often thought that if McDermott had not become a priest, he would have gone into the military. And if he had been a priest before Vatican II, Grant speculated that McDermott would have been part of the Roman-Catholics-only-go-to-heaven school, with other Christians just out of luck. But today, McDermott fell into the "New Ecumenism" camp.

Indeed, the three of them – Grant, Stone and McDermott – counted themselves in this group of traditional Christians cutting across denominations. They saw no value in the old ecumenical movement, which they felt had degraded into political and social activism. This more recent ecumenism was rooted in a shared, basic orthodoxy and increasingly found more in common with each other than with certain factions within their own denominations.

The three met about four years ago when Tom Stone sent out an invitation to local clergy to start a *Touchstone* magazine readers' club – *Touchstone* being a vehicle for Christian orthodoxy. The readers' group lasted a couple of years, but Stone, McDermott and Grant proved to be the only reliable members. Friendship, spiritual support, similar senses of humor, and a love of golf were shared, and their devotions had become part of their routine for more than two years.

Grant shook hands with each, and slid into the booth next to McDermott and across from Stone.

"Well, before we get to your adventures, shall we?" Tom asked as he held up a volume of *For All the Saints*, the prayer book they used for their devotional readings.

It was quite a contrast. In this diner of windows, chrome, and rose-colored upholstery, three members of the clergy – two in collars and one in a red Hawaiian shirt with white flowers – huddled in a booth praying.

Grant found it comforting how often what they read from this collection of Holy Scripture and prayers would speak to what was happening to him or one of his parishioners. The opening prayer for this particular Friday:

> "If ever the dark comes upon us, O God, let it be
> thy darkness. And when we hope for the wrong
> thing, let us wait in that dark until thou canst
> make us ready for what thou has promised."

Thy darkness, hope and promise? Grant thought.

After they closed the readings, McDermott turned to Grant, "So, what's the deal, after you shoot someone at church you don't return phone messages?"

Before Grant could answer, Stone jabbed, "You know, sometimes I've thought about shooting a parishioner or two, but I've never acted on it."

Ignoring Stone's comment, Grant said, "I know, I know. You guys left messages. But don't feel bad, I haven't called back 'The Today Show' either."

"Ooooh, cool," added Stone. "Katie?"

"Meredith."

"Whoops, forgot."

McDermott shifted the tone. "How are you? You managing this OK? Must be strange."

"It's toughest on Scott, Pam and the Gunderson family."

"Yes, but how are *you*?" Stone pushed. "It's not like you shoot somebody every day, even if you were with the CIA at one time."

Pastor Stephen Grant never told anyone outside a tiny circle in the Company about his work beyond being an analyst, including these two clergy.

After a noticeable pause, Stephen simply said, "Unfortunately, there was no other option."

McDermott and Stone exchanged glances across the table.

Grant caught them. "Seriously."

"We didn't think otherwise, Stephen," McDermott replied. "But you must be wrestling with this. After all, it's not like you ever shot and killed somebody before."

Well, how should I handle this with my closest friends? Fortuitously, the waitress arrived, giving Stephen a moment more to consider matters. He did a quick tally, and noted that Linda Serrano raised his body count to double figures – ten. And the second in a church.

The topic of killing or how many people he killed, of course, never came up before. Stephen decided to be as honest with his friends as he could without violating oaths. "Guys, let's just say that this was not a completely unique experience for me. And that's as far as I can go."

The three sat in silence for nearly a minute – a seeming eternity in a close diner booth – as both Stone and McDermott apparently let Grant's comment sink in.

Stone finally broke the silence in his best Sean Connery: "Well, if that's the way it has to be, Mr. Bond. By the way, do you want that orange juice shaken or stirred?"

Chapter 11

St. Mary's was overflowing for the funeral of Hans and Flo Gunderson late Saturday morning.

Grant had a wide range of experiences dealing with death during his work for Uncle Sam and for the Lord. At one end of the spectrum of reactions, the family left behind would exhibit a combination of anger and bewildered grief. They tended to be the loud ones at funerals. At the other end of the spectrum were those with an unmistakable, deep sadness mingled with hope or a peace of mind rooted in faith.

A joint funeral in a church built by this husband and wife, where they also were murdered, with their pastor killing the murderer, rated as uncharted territory even for Grant. This was one of the very few times in his life when Stephen had no idea what to expect, from the congregation or from himself.

Thus far in the service, the atmosphere was heavy, but the emotions from family, friends, colleagues, and church members were devoid of outbursts. Grant stepped into the pulpit to deliver his homily.

He took a deep breath. It was a bit uneven.

Close your eyes for a moment and think about the events of this past Wednesday. It's hard.

They might seem unreal, as if they were from a movie or television show. I'm sure I'm not the only one hoping against hope that this was all fiction, a story, a nightmare from which we can wake up.

But then as we open our eyes and look around this church, we are reminded how real and painful it all was, and still is.

This congregation, and these grieving family and friends, have been put through the previously unimaginable. A deeply disturbed individual murdered our dear friends, Hans and Flo Gunderson, while gravely wounding music director Scott Larson, for whom we pray for the Lord's healing. Many of you, no doubt, now wonder about me, your pastor, after the actions I had to take. Our new church building, a holy place, was bordered by yellow police crime tape.

But the good news in this dark time is that we don't have to pray for Hans and Flo. Their rewards are assured.

How can I know this? After all, weren't the Gundersons sinners like the rest of us? Well, of course they were. But they trusted in our Lord and Savior Jesus Christ, who through his sacrifice, death and resurrection took away our sins, including their sins, and conquered death.

Only God knows what truly lies in the heart of each man and each woman. But in the Bible, St. James spoke of faith in action. James sometimes makes Lutherans a little queasy. He shouldn't. After all, Lutherans don't buy into cheap grace. We expect to see faith in action. James wrote: "What good is it, my brothers, if someone says he has faith but does not have works? Can that faith save him? If a brother or sister is poorly clothed and lacking in daily food, and one of you says to them, 'Go in peace, be warmed and filled,' without giving them the things needed for the body, what good is that? So also faith by itself, if it does not have works, is dead."

All who cared to look could see the faith of Hans and Flo. It was not dead. It was alive.

As most of us here know, they were outgoing, friendly and welcoming. From the moment I arrived here, they showed me true hospitality. The Gundersons had me to their home at least a couple of nights each month for dinner and relaxation. We did not talk church business, but instead simply enjoyed each other's company. They are ... were ... in a sense like my family.

Grant's voice broke for just a second. Soft cries and sniffling were heard throughout the church. He cleared his throat.

Now, many people don't realize, but hospitality is a biblical virtue. Saints Paul, Peter and John all speak of the importance of offering hospitality in Holy Scripture. Flo and Hans lived it.

The Gundersons also were builders. Before it could host its first baptism, this building suffered a baptism in blood, including the blood of the Gundersons, who were the hands that built this beautiful structure.

Many people don't like builders these days, particularly around here it seems. Some don't like the change that comes with new houses. Others don't like how much it costs the taxpayers to educate the children who tend to live in new homes. The most extreme, as we apparently experienced in deadly fashion, have been so perverted that builders are viewed as downright evil. But what is it exactly that the Gundersons did? They built homes for families to live in. They built places for people to go to work. They built a church in which people could come to worship God. That's not bad. In fact, it's a calling.

Keep in mind what St. Paul said in Hebrews: "For Jesus has been counted worthy of more glory than Moses – as much more glory as the builder of a house has more honor than the house itself. For every house is built by someone, but the builder of all things is God."

And as the builders of this church, Hans and Flo Gunderson became true martyrs for Christ. We don't think of people today being martyrs, perhaps. Instead, we think of Saint Stephen being stoned, or early Christians facing the lions in the Roman Colisseum. Things that happened long ago in the pages of the Bible and history. But there are Christian martyrs all around the globe today, dying for the faith. Make no mistake, that's exactly what Hans and Flo Gunderson did, right here on Long Island, in our church.

They, no doubt, are at peace with the Lord. Prayers are needed for the rest of us left here, who need strength from God to go on without these ever-so-dear members of our family – at

least until we see them again in glory. May
Jesus Christ grant us that strength.
  Amen.

Those in the pews responded with a weak "Amen."

As Grant turned and stepped down from the pulpit,
Pam Carter started playing "I'm But a Stranger Here."
Grant sat in an altar chair, and closed his eyes, working to
regain his bearings. He looked up and stared at the two
caskets in the center aisle of St. Mary's.

Grant sang without the words registering. Instead, he
was thinking about his two dead friends, and what they
had together. They were husband and wife, parents,
friends, business partners, lovers. *Even together in death –
lucky,* he thought. *Well, perhaps being shot and killed is
not exactly lucky. But then again, they went together and in
the Lord. Many cannot say as much.*

Still staring at the caskets, Stephen's thoughts drifted
and he wondered how many of the ten deaths he had a
direct hand in were lucky.

What a journey you've taken me on, Lord.

Chapter 12

Stephen Grant grew up as an only child just outside of Cincinnati. It was a rather normal suburban, middle American childhood, though somewhat solitary. His father, Douglas, worked long hours driving a Coca-Cola delivery route, while his mother, Samantha, was a local librarian.

He was always "Stephen," not "Steve" and certainly not "Stevie," and got very annoyed when kids, teachers or any other adults insisted on changing his name.

From first grade through high school, his life was about parochial school, attending church, reading, the Cincinnati Reds and, starting in junior high, playing golf and practicing archery. But most of all, it was about the close family life of the three Grants.

After high school, Stephen went away – but not too far away – to Valparaiso University in Indiana to study history. He expanded his interest in weapons beyond the bow and arrow, and began to train far more vigorously. History came easy, which left more time for disciplining his body, improving his "warrior skills," as he liked to call them, and graduating in only three years. After graduation, his parents were not exactly surprised, but perhaps slightly disappointed and certainly worried, when he became a Navy SEAL.

About a year into his military service, the news of his parents' deaths in a car accident came. It was devastating. The core – the anchor – of his world seemed lost. While his focus in the Navy remained steadfast, the rest of his life drifted away from friends, others in his family, and church. The Central Intelligence Agency soon came knocking. Stephen Grant became a CIA analyst who specialized in skill sets that regularly got him out of the cubicle and into the field.

After an extensive period of training, one of his first "field assignments" was in Barcelona during the 1992 Summer Olympics. Grant and his mentor, Tony Cozzilino, were inserted as part of the security detail for the U.S. Olympic team.

The Olympic Games came on the heels of the end of the Cold War. The Unified Team competed in the aftermath of the Soviet Union crumbling. There were no Olympic boycotts for a change. South Africa was back in the Games, and Germany competed as one team. They were heady and hopeful times.

The 52-year-old Cozzilino was a veteran of Cold War espionage dating back before the Vietnam War. Grant learned that it was the construction of the Berlin Wall – and the deaths of East Germans seeking freedom at that wall – that made Cozzilino the coldest of warriors. His weathered face and thin dark hair actually made him look older than he was, but the rest of Cozzilino's rock-hard body was younger than his years.

Grant wondered how many Soviet threats Tony had a hand in eliminating, not to mention his role in bringing over disgruntled communists looking to talk and/or make a buck.

Over drinks, Cozzilino, the mentor, told Grant, the student, that the end of the Cold War, unfortunately, would not mean a safer world, as many pundits and politicians were proclaiming. Instead, Tony Cozzilino had the experience and foresight to understand that the demise of the Soviet's global threat would simply lead to the emergence of other threats ... other evils. That, Cozzilino proclaimed, would never change. Cozzilino said, "It's man's nature, DNA, whatever you want to call it. But it's not going to change."

Cozzilino and Grant were on watch due to reports that some former KGB agents were now in the nuclear secrets and technology business. A few at Langley were particularly worried about Middle Eastern terrorists. With the Soviets' demise, concerns lingered that Middle East terror might spread even farther than it already had.

Cozzilino was in this camp. Before heading to Barcelona, he said to Grant, "Imagine if some of those wacko Arab terrorists got their hands on a nuke. That scares me a hell of a lot more than MAD. There's a line the Reds would not cross. I'm not so sure about Muslim terrorists. Look what Israel faces. Why not the rest of us?"

His mentor helped Grant to think beyond the execution of missions, and get the big picture by tapping into and expanding his knowledge of history. Cozzilino emphasized understanding what made nations, movements, their leaders and their warriors tick.

The mission in Barcelona lacked specificity. Intelligence indicated that former KGB spook Boris Krikov might be turning up for a sales meeting. Just before the fall of the Berlin Wall, Cozzilino had crossed paths with Krikov. He did not offer details to Grant, but Cozzilino made it clear that Krikov was a formidable foe.

But Tony seemed doubtful that Krikov would turn up – or at least that they would find him. Grant later wondered if this led the two men to be more relaxed than otherwise would have been the case. Did the Soviet Union's end, the beautiful city located on the Mediterranean coast and the Olympic Games combine to generate a touch of laxness?

Cozzilino knew of Grant's proficiency in archery. In fact, he often mocked a skill that would be of no benefit in the field. Nonetheless, Cozzilino insisted the two accompany the U.S. men's team to the archery venue for practice one day. He told Grant, "You should see what real archers can do."

The morning was delightful – a sun-drenched blue sky with the air not yet dripping with humidity.

Grant and Cozzilino watched as the archers began practice. The best bows in the world made of wood, fiberglass and graphite with Kevlar strings strained in the fingers of these marksmen. Upon release, arrows of aluminum or carbon graphite streaked at some 150 miles per hour toward their targets a football field away.

Cozzilino and Grant recognized excellence.

"These guys can split an apple at 100 yards. Coz, I'm good, but not that good," Grant whispered.

"You're right about that, kid, you're not that good," Tony replied with a chuckle.

On their first day working together, Cozzilino said to call him "Coz," while Grant chaffed at "Steve" and told Coz he preferred "Stephen." Tony tried "Stephen" once, laughed, shook his head, and thereafter it was "kid" or "Grant."

While Grant became more engrossed in the flying arrows, Coz said, "I'm hitting the head." He disappeared around the end of the bleachers.

After several minutes, Grant felt a red alert for the first time since coming from the SEALs to the CIA. He followed Cozzilino's tracks around the corner of the stands, and approached the men's restroom. He pushed open the door, and heard a low voice from around the corner of the large L-shaped bathroom.

Grant reached inside his blue sports jacket and touched the Glock in his holster. "Coz?"

As he walked forward, a stall door swung out and struck him with the full weight and force of the man behind it.

Grant went down with his head thunking on the floor. A violent kick to the side of his skull caused further disorientation.

He struggled to focus. *Well, at least there's no pee on the floor.* A hand reached inside Grant's jacket and took his gun, which was then used to strike a crushing blow against his left cheek.

Two voices spoke in Russian. As his vision wobbled, Grant made out two pairs of sneakers.

The pain increased as his head was being lifted off the ground via a handful of black hair. A knife blade flipped open. Grant quickly thrust a stiff arm into the left knee of his would-be assassin. Distinct cracking could be heard, along with a curse screamed in Russian. His hair was released.

Grant then spun his body on the floor like a lethal break dancer, using his feet to topple the other Russian. While more curses were spewing forth from the Russian with the shattered knee, his partner got to his feet just ahead of Grant. Stephen received a rock hard fist into his left cheek bone again. It knocked him back into the wall, and once more down to the ground.

The bathroom door opened, and two archers entered. One asked: "What the hell's going on?" The Russians barreled past and out the door.

Grant finally saw Cozzilino on the floor at the other end of the bathroom, unmoving. Racing forward, Stephen saw the open, lifeless eyes, broken neck, and hands expertly tied behind his back with twine.

An archer came up behind him, and whispered, "Oh, my God."

Grant swelled with rage.

The Russians had taken their guns.

He ran outside and saw a car pulling away. Grant assumed that the two Russians were inside. He sprinted in the other direction, and jumped the fence into the archery range. Nobody else moved as he grabbed a bow and three arrows. Back over the fence, Stephen climbed the stairs to the top of the bleachers, while wiping blood away from his left eye. He dropped two arrows on the seat, nocked the other, pulled back the string, and found his target picking up speed after turning onto an exit road about 70 yards away. The arrow flew and hit its intended target. It punctured the front left tire of the car. The dark blue sedan skidded to a stop.

The driver's door opened, and the Russian with the bad knee struggled out of the car and pulled his gun.

Grant ignored the younger man shooting in his direction, and instead looked to the other heading towards the nearby woods. He nocked a second arrow, pulled, aimed and let the arrow fly. It struck its target in the head. The Russian tumbled to the ground.

One.

The younger assailant had stopped shooting, and staying low, was moving for cover and escape in the trees.

Grant had another chance with the third arrow. He fired, but the target hesitated for a brief moment to turn his head, and the arrow streaked just in front of the Russian. He disappeared in the tree line.

The CIA and the Spanish CESID moved quickly to clean up the situation. The importance of silence was made clear to the archers and a few others on hand. And that was that.

The dead Russian was Boris Krikov. His accomplice had disappeared.

Two years later, it was discovered that Vladimir Chenko had fed the information that Cozzilino would be at the Olympics to Krikov.

Chapter 13

Graveside at Calverton National Cemetery a few miles north of St. Mary's Church, the Gundersons' daughter Anna, with eyes wet, red and tired, whispered to Grant, "Please keep the church dedication as scheduled. Mom and Dad would have insisted."

"Are you sure?" Grant asked.

"Come on, Stephen, you knew them."

He paused. "Yes. You're right," he agreed, nodding sadly.

Later that evening, few came to the Saturday night service. Sunday's services were well attended, but subdued. On the way out the door, there was less chatting and less eye contact with Stephen than usual.

Grant wondered whether it was the murders of the Gundersons alone, his own gun play in church, or more likely, both? He had a lengthy list of church members to speak with about what happened Wednesday night. But he would start that process tomorrow.

On Sunday afternoon, Grant puttered around his office, trying to avoid going back to the parsonage too early. He decided to head to a Smokey Bones restaurant on the Long Island Expressway service road that evening to relax, eat some barbecued ribs, and catch the Reds play the Mets on ESPN's Sunday Night Baseball.

But the phone rang. It was Father McDermott inviting Grant to dinner and to watch the game at St. Luke's rectory. Though Ron was a Mets fan, Stephen quickly accepted. He promised to bring a six-pack of Heineken.

A shade before six, Stephen parked in the lot stretching between two very different buildings. On one side was the large, very 1970s-ish, tan, modern-looking St. Luke's Roman Catholic Church. On the other stood the white, very Victorian rectory. McDermott called this home, as did the senior parish priest, Father Stanley Burns.

Burns' saggy face, receding dark hair, and large, black horn-rimmed glasses made him look like former Federal Reserve Chairman Alan Greenspan impersonating a priest. But Grant could not quite peg his age. With slow movements and deliberate speech, Father Burns was one of those people who looked old for a long time. Was he 80 or 60?

After Stephen rang the doorbell, the housekeeper and cook, Mrs. Kennedy, welcomed him. Everything in the house was big – the staircase, the high ceilings, the rooms. Even Mrs. Kennedy was on the large side – short, but wide. While wiping her hands on an apron tied around her very green dress, she called up the stairs: "Father McDermott, your guest is here."

"Thank you, Mrs. Kennedy," responded Ron moving quickly down the stairs. "Stephen, how are you?"

"Good, and the beer is still cold." He held up a brown bag. Grant noted that this was one of the very rare cases where Father Ron McDermott could be caught out of his collar – in this instance, sneakers, jeans and an orange Mets t-shirt. "If I had known we were going with team apparel, I would have donned by Tom Seaver Reds jersey.

"Seaver on the Reds – not that again," responded Ron.

"Hey, for whom did he toss his only no hitter?"

"I know, I know, the Reds."

As she headed down the hall next to the staircase, Mrs. Kennedy called over her shoulder, "I'll bring you boys two iced mugs."

Whenever he visited Ron at the rectory, Grant felt much younger. Like he was a college kid visiting a buddy, and Mrs. Kennedy and Father Burns were the parents.

The rooms on the main floor in the front of the house, which served for more formal visits, included old, uncomfortable-looking Victorian-style furniture. The two men followed Mrs. Kennedy to the living area in the back of the house. Even these rooms – an area off the large kitchen with a small dining table, a library and living room – still felt, to Grant, rather impersonal. No family photos. No evidence of personal interests or hobbies.

Come to think of it. It's like my place.

They entered the living room with its dull, cream colored walls. Ron sat in a high-back, armchair, while Stephen claimed part of the rather hard sofa. Stephen poured a beer into a frosty mug for Ron, and then did the same for himself. Each had a perfect one-inch head of foam.

"Tom couldn't make it?" asked Stephen, taking a long drink and feeling the cold beer journey down towards his stomach.

"Well, you know he likes to relax with the family on Sundays after Mass," answered McDermott.

"Right."

"Besides, I didn't ask him." After taking a hearty swig of his draft from Holland, Ron asked, "Do you have any plans, Stephen, of moving from Wittenberg to Rome that I don't know about?"

Stephen was surprised. "What? Become a Roman Catholic? Are you kidding?" That came out wrong. He recovered, needling his friend. "How many times do I have to tell you, Ron, we Lutherans are the real Catholics?

We've reformed the Church, still waiting for you guys to catch up. After all, it's been nearly 500 years."

McDermott smirked, and replied, "Oh, that's right. You've mentioned that before. Sorry that we billion or so Roman Catholics around the world are so far behind you 80 million Lutherans." He took another gulp of beer, and put the glass atop a dark cherry coffee table. The coaster immediately absorbed water as the ice started melting on the outside of the mug. "The reason I bring it up is that the Vatican has contacted my bishop about you."

Grant raised his eyebrows, "What!?"

Ron continued, "Bishop Carolan called Father Burns this afternoon to see if he knew anything about you since you're local to St. Luke's. Father mentioned our friendship, and now I'm supposed to get back to the Bishop tomorrow morning to answer some questions."

"Really?"

"Yes. I didn't get any details. Any idea what this is all about?"

Grant paused to think. He picked up the mug of beer, took a sip, and placed it back down on the table.

"I have no clue as to why the Vatican would be interested in me. Unless, it somehow is tied in to what happened on Wednesday night."

"Why would the Vatican care about that?"

"Got me," Grant said.

"Could it be the papal visit scheduled for Long Island at the end of September? You know that the Pope is starting here, then traveling to various countries until Christmas. It's an unprecedented journey."

"Starts in about a month," mused Stephen, more thinking out loud than anything else.

"Do you think that's why the Vatican's calling?"

Mrs. Kennedy came in the room – still wiping her hands on that apron – and said, "Father, Pastor, please come to dinner."

Grant shrugged his shoulders at McDermott, and they both jumped up. McDermott grabbed three beers from the refrigerator, including one for Father Burns, who'd just emerged from the library.

"Good evening, Stephen," said Burns, stretching out his thin, frail-looking hand, which always provided a surprisingly strong grip.

"Good to see you, Father. I didn't know you were here, or I would have said hello."

"I was just doing a little reading." He asked Stephen, "And must I remind you again that it's Stan?"

"Right, sorry, Stan."

"Reading anything interesting?" asked Father McDermott, as he and Mrs. Kennedy filled the table with a Sunday dinner of roast beef, mashed potatoes, carrots and hot buns.

"Taking a little break from theology. I'm paging through *The Yankee Encyclopedia.*" That drew groans from both Grant and McDermott, and then a smile from Burns.

Mrs. Kennedy looked over and seemed content with the meal as presented. As she untied her apron, she said, "Fathers, you seem to be all set. Coffee is ready, and there's a coconut custard pie on the counter in the kitchen. If you don't need anything else, I'll be going home."

"Oh, aren't you staying for dinner?" Burns asked.

"No, thank you, Father. I've got to get home, so I can get Bill's dinner for him."

"Of course. So many of we men are helpless with such things, aren't we?"

"That is the truth, Father," confirmed Mrs. Kennedy with some relish. "Good night, gentlemen."

The three clergy replied in near unison, "Good night, and thank you, Mrs. Kennedy."

And she was gone.

Grace was said, and talk during dinner focused on, of course, the shootings at St. Mary's, along with some far more mundane happenings in the local community and the current baseball season, with each man's team still in the thick of their respective division races.

The table was cleared, and the dishwasher loaded. Coffee was poured for Burns and McDermott, tea for Grant, and large pieces of pie were cut. They took it all into the living room flipping on the TV just in time to see the first pitch tossed in the game.

Grant reflected that it was an enjoyable, restful Sunday evening, as Sundays should be. He was particularly grateful given what occurred over the past several days. But the inquiry from the Vatican tugged at the back of his mind throughout the night.

Since Mondays were generally pretty slow in the clergy business, all three men stayed with a good game until the Reds' bullpen blew a two-run lead in the ninth and handed the Mets a victory.

Father Burns had not brought up the call from the Bishop all night. But now that Grant was getting ready to leave, Burns asked, "Any thoughts on what the Bishop might want, Stephen, from a Lutheran such as yourself?"

"I'm a bit bewildered, Stan." Grant was being careful. "But I'm wondering if it might somehow be tied in with the shootings."

"Really?" Burns seemed a bit surprised.

"Just a feeling."

Burns declared, "Bishop Carolan indicated the inquiries were on theological matters."

Theology? OK, now I don't have a clue.

Chapter 14

Sure enough, it was all about theology.

Stone, McDermott and Grant agreed to push back their Monday devotional meal to lunch. When Stephen arrived, dressed casually in tan shorts and a white polo shirt, Tom Stone was already waiting. Today was a *Magnum PI* day for Stone – dressed in a dark blue Hawaiian shirt with white swirly flowers, jeans and white sneakers. Grant reflected that he was only missing the sunglasses hanging around his neck, a Detroit Tigers hat, and the red Ferrari in the parking lot. Stone instead drove a very sensible minivan.

While slipping into the booth across from his friend, Grant nodded and said, "Magnum."

Stone didn't miss a beat, replying, "Mr. Bond."

Stephen brought Tom Stone up to speed on the inquiries from the Vatican via the local Catholic bishop, while Tom filled Stephen in on the latest happenings in the always hectic Stone household.

After Ron McDermott arrived, about twenty minutes late, they ordered lunch, and read their devotions from *For All the Saints*.

When they closed their books, the waitress came with drinks and a small bowl of cole slaw with a crisp pickle on top for each.

Stephen looked at McDermott. "Well?"

"Stephen, I am officially sick of talking about you."

"That makes two of us," added Stone.

McDermott continued: "I was on the phone with my bishop and two of his assistants for three hours going over the theological views of my Lutheran friend. At the same time, I was e-mailing links to some of your articles, and even faxing over two in my files that aren't online. What's wrong with this picture?" A touch of annoyance was barely detectable in Ron's voice.

"Why the heck are they talking to you about me? Why not come to me directly?"

"Maybe you're up for bishop and they want to surprise you," Tom cheerfully commented.

"You're not helping," Stephen replied, giving him a look.

"Sorry."

"I didn't get to ask too many questions," Ron resumed. "But from what I was told and could otherwise figure out, they are cobbling together a thorough bio on you that will be passed on to someone in the Vatican this week. Sounded like tomorrow."

Stephen paused to mull this over. *What's the deal?* "So, what did you tell them?"

Tom jumped in, looking at McDermott, "That he's a follower of that mad monk, Luther, and believes the pope is the anti-christ, right?"

"Still not helping," said McDermott.

"Yea, I know, but I'm amusing myself." He smirked and took a sip from his Coca-Cola.

McDermott looked Stephen in the eyes. "It would probably be easier to go over what we failed to cover. We talked about your views on the Reformation; the Catholic Church; old line Protestants; evangelicals; Holy Scripture; the Eucharist; the liturgy; the current challenges facing the church in the U.S. and around the globe; the strengths, weaknesses and role of Lutheranism today; and even church music. A good chunk, though, was focused on the relationship between Christian denominations, including your take on the old ecumenical movement and the New Ecumenism among traditionalists."

"So, what did you tell them?" Stephen pressed anxiously.

"What did I tell them? I don't have another three hours to spare, my friend."

"Come on, Ron."

"I told them exactly what I've come to learn and respect about you, Stephen, over the past four years. I know your theology well, so no worries. I explained that you view the Reformation as a necessary evil. That you fall onto the Catholic rather than the Protestant side of Lutheranism. That you view Lutheranism as a reform movement, rather than a new church. That you're traditional when it comes to the Bible, worship and the culture. That you see a great opportunity for Lutheranism as a kind of bridge between Catholics and Protestants, but are frustrated by the internal squabbling among your fellow Lutherans. At the same time, though, I made clear that you're not a Lutheran on the verge of heading to Rome. And I highlighted your strong belief that traditional Christians, no matter their denomination or individual church, must become more unified in confronting the many challenges that Christianity faces and will face in the twenty-first century." McDermott paused for a sip of iced tea. "How'd I do?"

Stephen felt more at ease. "Fine, of course. Thanks Ron, and I apologize if I came across a bit edgy."

"Don't worry about it. This is all a mystery."

"And as Captain Kirk once said, mysteries give me a bellyache," Stone added, shoveling a large forkful of cole slaw into his mouth.

The waitress brought over their lunch. Each had some slightly different take on the diner hamburger – Stone with cheddar cheese and bacon, McDermott simply well done, and Grant with the traditional American cheese.

As he added ketchup and salt, Stone said, "Stephen, as easy as it is for me to say, don't get all knotted up over this. Pray, go about your ministry, and don't fret over what you cannot control."

"Good advice, my friend. Hope I can follow it."

Stone took a big bite into his bacon cheeseburger, and ketchup dripped down onto his Hawaiian shirt. "Crap."

Ron observed, "Well, that was rather un-clergy-like."

Tom grunted as he dipped his napkin in a glass of water, and tried to erase the stain.

"Well, better on the shirt than on the Ferrari's upholstery," added Grant. "After all, what would Higgins say?"

"Very funny. I'm not worried about Jonathan Higgins. It's Maggie Stone who will lecture me about getting a stain on a shirt that she always tells me is ugly and too expensive."

"Wise woman," added Ron, who seemed to be enjoying his friend's sartorial predicament as he chewed on his burger.

Chapter 15

Even for a 20-plus-year veteran of the package delivery business, the order was off-the-charts staggering. The required logistics were a formidable challenge, and the degree of secrecy unprecedented.

But Liz Crowne pulled it off, watching with great satisfaction as the last of a fleet of white trucks hit the streets of Vatican City.

About 500,000 relatively slim packages would soon start arriving at assorted Christian churches and headquarters around the globe. When asked, Liz told her staff that she did not know or care what was inside. But that wasn't quite true. From a pure business perspective, the contents did not concern her, but as a Roman Catholic, Liz did express curiosity to her husband. This job was special. Her overwhelming concern was carrying through on the promise that she and her company had made to Pope Augustine I.

The Vatican had contacted the firm's headquarters in Memphis, Tennessee, months before to see if the company could handle an enormous and historic undertaking. Assurances were made, contracts signed, and the brass brought Liz in to make it all happen. These half-a-million packages tallied up to seven percent of the seven million packages moved on an average day. She could not have been more pleased with the vote of confidence in her work and abilities.

Liz quietly amassed the trucks outside Rome, had a team inside the Vatican to run the operation, and when all was ready, the trucks moved in and were moved out as quick as was humanly possible. The entire operation was a model of efficiency.

The convoy drew attention, naturally, but once things were in motion, it no longer mattered. Incredibly, there had been no leaks. With the packages on the road, word now would spread.

The letter to be delivered to Christian leaders in all corners of the world warranted even greater curiosity than Liz had mustered. It had the potential of changing Christianity and the world. The Vatican made clear that e-mail was not enough. Personalized packages from the Pope were determined most appropriate.

By the time one of those packages reached the office of the Roman Catholic Diocese of Rockville Centre on Long Island, Bishop Peter Carolan had avoided the snippets on the news, and ignored the materials being e-mailed and faxed. Carolan thankfully had other matters to tend to, and the Bishop told his secretary that he wanted to read and digest the actual document from Rome. He knew it was central to the Pope's visit.

When it arrived at 8:50 AM on Tuesday morning, Carolan's secretary handed it to him. The Bishop asked her to close the door as she left his office.

His palms actually were sweating. There was a background buzz before and after Mass that morning at St. Agnes Cathedral. He could not help but pick up on words like "historic," "controversial," "silly," "incredible," and "critical."

Now in the quiet of his office, Bishop Carolan would read it for himself. He tore the package open, and pulled out a folder with a four-page letter on parchment-like paper clipped to the outside. It read:

Dear Peter:

"Grace to you and peace from God our Father and the Lord Jesus Christ." (2 Corinthians 1:2)

I look forward to visiting the United States, particularly Long Island, next month. Your prayers and hard work – indeed, the prayers and efforts of all the faithful in the Diocese of Rockville Centre – in service to our Savior and His Church are precious gifts from which I take great strength and encouragement.

While the logistics of my visit are being finalized among our respective aides, it is important that you understand what we – with the inspiration and support, I pray, of the Holy Spirit – are trying to initiate today, and that my Long Island visit will be the leaping off point for a global effort.

The challenges that Christianity faces and our wounds that must be healed are grave and deep. Unfortunately, much of this has been self-inflicted over the centuries. In turn, a wounded Christianity has not ably illustrated and spread the Good News of Jesus Christ. For this shortcoming, each of us will have to answer on Judgment Day.

What does the world see when it looks at the Christian faith?

Too often, it is conflict and division. We should
be saddened and ashamed that Christian unity
is so lacking. After all, Jesus specifically
prayed: "I do not ask for these only, but also for
those who will believe in me through their
word, that they may all be one, just as you,
Father, are in me, and I in you, that they also
may be in us, so that the world may believe
that you have sent me. The glory that you have
given me I have given to them, that they may
be one even as we are one, I in them and you in
me, that they may become perfectly one, so that
the world may know that you sent me and loved
them even as you loved me." (John 17:20-23)

We can – and will – debate the degree of unity
necessary, but Christians certainly must
achieve much more than what exists today.
While progress has been made, we have fallen
far short of Christ's desire.

Unfortunately, this is not just a task of trying
to bring together different denominations.
Disunity exists even within the Roman Catholic
Church, as well as within most other Christian
bodies. As a result, Christians too often send
confusing signals to the world on essential
matters of faith and morals when our message
should be clear and strong.

Like so much of our culture, Christianity
suffers from an internal erosion of the truth.
Why do Christians follow rather than inform
the culture? Too many leaders have lost
credibility due to scandals, due to a willingness
to abandon Holy Scripture and Tradition, or

because they seem far more interested in politics and social activism than in spreading the Gospel.

Some of our Lutheran friends have a point when arguing that Martin Luther's "Two Kingdoms" means that when Christian leaders or the Church do not have to speak out on a political issue, perhaps then they should not speak out. When Christians have the freedom to disagree on political and social issues, for example, declarations by the Church on such matters tend to create further strife and division. The Church must root Christians in faith and morality, and help form the Christian conscience as informed by Holy Scripture and Church teachings, with individual Christians then encouraged to act and serve accordingly in the world.

When diverging from its central mission, Christianity becomes clouded. Love, forgiveness, redemption and salvation through Jesus Christ get pushed aside. Moral authority is lost. Christianity is then unable to stand firm when it must speak out, when it needs to, when it is imperative to do so.

What are the most critical challenges faced today? Three stand out.

Relativism plagues our age. The truth of Christ has been treated as just another choice among many so-called "truths." Or the very notion of truth has been rejected. Moral verities that have served as the bedrock of civilization have

been and continue to be displaced in favor of
the latest whims and desires. Tragically and
sinfully, many Christians have joined with and
strengthened the forces of relativism.

Coupled with this is a growing and militant
secularism. God is being pushed out of the
public square. In your own country, your noble
Constitution, a document that has offered so
much for the benefit of peoples around the
world, has been twisted so that the separation
of church and state now is taken by many to
mean that the Church should never speak out
on issues carrying clear and significant moral
weight.   Indeed, especially in Europe and
increasingly in the United States, Christians
are expected to leave their faith in the pews
and in their homes when they venture to
discuss and debate in public, to cast votes or to
serve in government.   That, however, is
unacceptable. The Christian cannot, and should
not, be expected to ever leave God behind, or to
restrict the Lord to only certain realms of one's
life.   That is not what it means to be a
Christian.

Finally, in contrast to a militant secularism,
Christians, along with all of God's children, face
the grim reality of a radical arm of Islam.
While we all realize and must emphasize that
the overwhelming majority of Muslims in the
world are peace-loving, Christians and Muslims
cannot afford to ignore the dark realities of the
small, but significant extremist movement
within Islam.   From that dangerous perversion
springs   evils   of   terrorism   and   religious

persecution in our current age. While Christianity certainly has had and continues to experience dark times – "for all have sinned and fall short of the glory of God" (Romans 2:23) – the Church has left behind the mistaken path it sometimes ventured down in centuries past regarding war and persecution, and imposing the Faith at the point of a sword or gun.

Too often today, however, Christianity loses confidence, retreats and even turns inward when confronted by these grave "isms" – relativism, secularism and what has been called Islamic fascism.

The Roman Catholic Church is proposing a modest, but important first step towards enhanced Christian unity. Specifically, the proposal I am putting forth is that traditional, orthodox faithful from across Christianity come together to speak with one voice on matters of the faith and culture where Holy Scripture and Church teachings are fundamental, clear and imperative. It is necessary that Christians come together in love and brotherhood to address the culture.

Allow me to first make clear what this is not. It is not a vehicle for political and social activism to supplant the Gospel. It does not place the Roman Catholic Church in a position of leadership, but merely as one of hopefully many participants. Nor does it attempt to address the issue of the papacy itself, and the accompanying obstacles for many other

Christians. It is not an attempt to gloss over or ignore the unfortunate theological differences that exist among Christians.

Instead, this is an effort to bring much of the Christian world together to express a unified voice – where possible – on matters of fundamental morality. It is my hope that Christians across the spectrum will join in this effort; that we will meet regularly to discuss, work together in Christian love, come to agreement, and then issue clear and bold Christian declarations on issues confronting the Faith and the world.

With guidance and strength from the Holy Spirit, this effort hopefully will build, expand, and eventually bring about an even more far-reaching unity.

It is my intention to travel the globe to speak and meet with Christian leaders on this important undertaking from late September until the eve of our Savior's birth. These travels will begin in the United States, with you on Long Island on September 20, and will proceed through Central and South America, Australia, Asia, the Middle East, Africa, and Europe, ending back in Rome. Invitations will be presented for the first official gathering in this effort scheduled for the spring of next year in Wittenberg, Germany, where the Reformation started, and where Christianity can come together in order to speak with one voice to the world some 500 years later.

I have long appreciated the writings of C.S. Lewis, the great Christian apologist and Anglican layman of the twentieth century. Lewis has been adopted by all kinds of Christians around the world, from Roman Catholics to independent evangelicals. So many of his books are classics, including his thoughtful *Mere Christianity*. In that book, originally a series of radio broadcasts during the Second World War, Lewis observed:

> *"It is at her centre, where her truest children dwell, that each communion is really closest to every other in spirit, if not in doctrine. And this suggests at the centre of each there is something, or a Someone, who against all divergences of belief, all differences of temperament, all memories of mutual persecution, speaks with the same voice."*

In many ways, this is the spirit we hope to capture in this mission. That is, on many issues we need to speak with the same voice to the world – serving, empowered and inspired by that Someone.

To start, then, I call this "A Public Mission of Mere Christianity." Of course, once assembled in Wittenberg, the mission may choose another name, but this is how we will get started.

"A Public Mission of Mere Christianity" has begun today, with approximately 500,000 letters arriving in the hands of Christian leaders around the globe. However, the first on-the-ground step in this mission will start in your diocese, Peter, on Long Island.

Thank you, once more, for your willingness to serve. May God grant courage, wisdom and caring – to both of us.

Yours in Christ,
Augustine I

Bishop Carolan had been holding his breath reading the last couple of paragraphs. He finally exhaled, then breathed in deeply, and leaned back into his black leather desk chair.

He stared at the Crucifix on the wall for several minutes, lost in contemplation.

There was knock at the door.

"Come in," Peter called out.

The door opened a few inches, and Auxiliary Bishop Mark Zeller stuck his round, completely bald head in. "Done reading?"

"Yes, Mark, grab a chair," said Carolan.

"Well?" Zeller asked his superior.

"I'm excited. I think you will be as well. But it's pretty easy to see that some on the far Right, and most on the Left, will not be so happy. Here, read it yourself."

Carolan unclipped the letter, and handed it to Zeller.

The auxiliary bishop was immediately immersed. Meanwhile, Carolan opened the folder to find assorted supporting documents, including a bulletin insert summary and a copy of *Mere Christianity*.

Chapter 16

As Matins came to a close, Grant spoke the Collect for Grace from the *Lutheran Service Book*:

> "O Lord, our heavenly Father, almighty and everlasting God, You have safely brought us to the beginning of this day. Defend us in the same with Your mighty power and grant that this day we fall into no sin, neither run into any kind of danger, but that all our doings, being ordered by Your governance, may be righteous in Your sight; through Jesus Christ, Your Son, our Lord, who lives and reigns with You and the Holy Spirit, one God, now and forever."

Each time Grant uttered this prayer, he thought about the September 11, 2001, terrorist attacks. Stephen had only been pastor for a few weeks, when two commercial jets were flown into the Twin Towers a mere 70 miles away in lower Manhattan. Less than an hour before the first plane hit, Grant had said essentially the same collect – just with "thy" from the old hymnal rather than "you" or "your" from the new one.

Other than when hearing about the death of his parents, Grant never felt so helpless as he did that day. The aftermath also marked the only extended period of time when he regretted leaving the CIA to become a pastor. He had longed, once again, to take action against the terrorists who threatened the United States. That regret lingered for several weeks, and finally evaporated after much prayer, confession and guidance from Grant's bishop that got him re-centered on his faith and pastoral work.

With the shootings at St. Mary's, Grant wondered if he would be tempted once more to lose focus.

He gave the Benediction.

At the doors exiting the nave, Grant shook hands and briefly chit-chatted with the small number of worshippers – mainly, but not exclusively, gray haired ladies – in attendance. The last in line was Barbara Tunney.

"Morning, Barb," Grant said.

"Good morning, Pastor. Looks like Pope Augustine pushed you out of the news," she reported.

"What's up? I haven't heard any news yet."

"It's right up your alley," Tunney replied. "He's talking about some kind of new effort to present a unified Christian voice on hot-button issues. Or, at least, that's how Fox News was presenting it this morning."

"Really?"

"Take a look online, and I'll bring you a cup of English Breakfast tea, sweet and dark as usual," Barbara suggested.

"Sounds great. Thanks." Grant headed to his office.

As he sipped his tea, Stephen started to read one of the letters from Pope Augustine I that had been posted on a favorite Christian news Website. His cell phone rang. Grant saw that it was Tom Stone's number. "Tom?"

"Yep. Where are you?"

"In the office."

"Good. Have you read it yet?"

"If you mean the Pope's letter, I just started," answered Stephen.

"Well, get it done," Tom instructed. "Ron and I are on the way over. Be there in about ten minutes. Stephen, it's the kind of thing we've been praying for. See you in a few."

"OK. Bye."

Tom and Ron on the way? Must be some letter.

Grant turned back to his laptop, and read the letter from a Roman Catholic pontiff that would come to deeply affect this Lutheran pastor.

Fifteen minutes later, Tom and Ron were seated on the couch in Grant's office. Stephen plopped down in the armchair, putting his feet casually up on the coffee table/gun cabinet.

"Well, what do you guys think?" Grant asked.

Stone weighed in first. "Fantastic. We've each seen – been part of – various, limited, half-assed efforts along these lines. With the head of the largest Christian church on the planet getting out front, this is entirely different. And he's got the targets exactly right – relativism, secularism and Islamic radicalism."

Grant added, "You're right, of course. We've chimed in on the need for greater Christian unity, and what might be done. I think deep down, though, we – I certainly – thought it would take a monster miracle. But with Augustine emphasizing this obvious place to start, it takes all of us to a new level."

Stephen and Tom turned to the thus-far-silent Ron McDermott. Grant asked, "Well, Catholic buddy, what do you make of the gauntlet tossed down by your man?"

There was more silence, as McDermott seemed to still be sorting through his thoughts, or searching for the right words.

"He's been quiet ever since I picked him up," Tom noted to Stephen.

McDermott took a deep breath, leaned forward on the couch, clasped his hands together and let them hang down with elbows resting on his knees. He finally spoke, "You guys are right about everything you've just said. And I am downright proud of this pontiff."

"But...," Stephen prompted.

"But," Ron continued, "one thought keeps my enthusiasm in check, and another has me wondering." He paused, again.

"Spit it out," Tom insisted.

"Will this actually bring about greater unity, or even deeper divisions? You know that the revisionist lefties leading the mainline Protestant churches, and their various, often well-funded allies will go on the attack. Can you imagine the Episcopal Church signing up, Tom?"

"Absolutely not," Tom replied. "But that's no surprise. After all, this is about bringing together the traditional and conservative Christian churches and leaders."

"Are you sure about that? Will the real hard core conservative Evangelicals or Pentecostals really be able to play nice with a pope?" McDermott turned to Grant: "In fact, aren't there some conservative Lutherans, Stephen, that you can think of that simply will not come together with Christians outside their own circle? I certainly know of a good number of very conservative Catholics who will play holier-than-thou with Pope Augustine on this. They'll label him an appeaser; perhaps even calling it heresy."

"OK. You're probably right," Stephen noted. "So, does that mean we just give up?"

"Of course not," Ron retorted. "We just have to understand going in that some of the Christians who are on our side on moral issues may not be willing to work together in this way. Meanwhile, our opponents will be more than willing to team up, and reach out to groups that they've never worked with before. They are very good at forming diverse coalitions. And given what the Holy Father has laid out here, it could be a very large and powerful coalition."

Tom said, "Alright, Father Doom-and-Gloom, what else do you have that's going to bring us down?"

"Well, now that you ask, I don't think it will necessarily bring you down, but what's up with the Vatican inquiry about Stephen at the same time as this effort is being launched, and with the first stop being Long Island? Can't possibly be coincidence."

McDermott and Stone looked to Grant. Stephen said, "Yeah. I thought the same thing as I was reading the Pope's letter."

Grant shared nothing more on that topic, beyond shrugging his shoulders and declaring rather philosophically, "We'll see." But his mind was working overtime.

My theology fits. And the Vatican, along with my old friends in the U.S. national security business, would find my skill sets handy. A clergy member trained to kill could very well be in demand. Aren't too many of us around, as far as I know. If that's the case, I should be getting a visit very soon.

Chapter 17

Some 300 miles away from Father McDermott and from Manorville, Long Island – worlds away, in many respects – Todd Johnson apparently was having very similar and nearly simultaneous thoughts about coalitions. But as Johnson finished typing out a memo on the topic, his spin on Pope Augustine's proposal for "A Public Mission of Mere Christianity" was vastly different from McDermott's.

Assembling a coalition in opposition to the Pope's venture was not something regrettable or unfortunate. Johnson saw it as a fantastic opportunity, a huge potential to generate funds and activate all of those who would oppose, even fear, this mission.

Johnson was a partner with Arnie Hackling at Hackling-Johnson Advisors. The firm's headquarters was located in spacious and lavishly decorated offices just off K Street in Washington, D.C. The carpets were thick. The décor varied from office to office according to the tastes of the lobbyists, fundraisers, researchers, pollsters, media experts, and grassroots organizers employed at the firm.

What made Hackling-Johnson somewhat different – though not completely unique in a town like Washington – was that it was neither a Democratic firm nor a Republican one. It was both. Johnson had a long track record as an operative for Democrats, while Hackling mirrored that career in the Republican world. As the two were involved in competing campaigns over many years, they became friends, and found that they both viewed politics in similar fashion.

For Todd Johnson and Arnie Hackling, politics was not about ideas. It was about making a very nice living while playing a fun game. But the two played that game without any hint of emotion. Both Johnson and Hackling were pure clinicians about their politics and how they advised clients. As a result, they worked with anyone on their side of the aisle. Eventually, the two came to realize that they could boost their bottom lines by joining forces. The partnership turned out to be one of the most powerful political firms in the nation, with considerable influence in Europe, Latin America and the Middle East as well.

Domestically, Johnson served a wide array of Democrats and Democratic allies. Hackling worked with the Republicans and their friends. For good measure, the firm was well positioned to advance the assorted bipartisan efforts that occasionally cropped up through the White House, in the halls of Congress, and in various other places across the nation and around the world. All kinds of individuals, corporations and associations knew this, sought out Hackling-Johnson, and paid dearly for the firm's access and expertise.

As for the partners, they only differed in two substantive ways. One happened to be a Democrat and the other Republican. In addition, while they dressed similarly, wore small glasses, and brandished black hair with gray streaks, the 58-year-old Hackling was very tall – 6 feet, 8 inches – while Johnson at age 60 was a mere 5 foot, four inches. This often earned them comparisons to Arnold Schwarzenegger and Danny DeVito in the movie *Twins.*

Johnson grabbed copies of the memo and the Pope's letter off the printer, stapled together two packets, and headed to the partners' dining room, where he would be having breakfast with Hackling.

The memo's subject line declared: "A Gift from God."

The partners' dining room at Hackling-Johnson was far from the largest room on the floor, but it was the most important. Among the political and business elite, some said it was one of the most important rooms in our nation's capital.

Against the wall to the right was a well-stocked mahogany bar manned late in the day and evenings, through the partners' specifications, by a young, attractive, female bartender. A swinging door led to the commercial-grade kitchen. Along the opposite wall was a long table draped by a white linen cloth used for occasional buffets. The two other walls were decorated with framed U.S. currencies from various periods in history.

In the center of the room was a large, octagon-shaped table. Here was a place for a small number of powerful men and women to meet in private. They would discuss and strategize about major political issues of the day, in the U.S. and around the globe, while enjoying an exquisite meal. Usually, by the end of those meals, a lucrative contract would be sealed with Hackling-Johnson.

As Todd Johnson entered, Arnie Hackling was waiting, thumbing through *The Washington Times*. Johnson sat down at the only other seat set for the meal, directly across from Hackling.

"Morning, Arnie."

"How's life, Todd?"

"Coffee, sir?" asked the waiter softly. Johnson nodded in the affirmative. The waiter poured a cup. Hackling already had his. A small bowl of fresh fruit and an orange juice were then set in front of each, and the waiter withdrew from the room.

"Life, my friend, is wonderful. At times, it really does seem like a gift from God," said Johnson as he unfolded the cloth napkin and dropped it on his lap.

Without moving his eyes from the newspaper, Hackling replied:, "Really? Have we found the Lord this morning?"

"Well, maybe the Lord has found us. Put down that right-wing rag, and read this." Johnson slid a copy of his memo and the Pope's letter across the table.

"Actually, *The Washington Times* always has interesting op-eds." Hackling closed the paper, folded it, and dropped it on the floor next to him. He slid the memo into position on the table so he could read, and eat his fruit at the same time. "Of the countless memos you've sent me over the years, I believe this is the first with such a spiritual subject line."

"Read on, and you'll find that the idea is firmly rooted in materialism. That is, the material well being of Hackling-Johnson."

Hackling grunted through the memo, the Pope's letter and his fruit.

Once the fruit was done, the waiter appeared again. The bowls were removed, coffee refreshed, and western omelets were placed in front of each man, accompanied by home fries and toast. Again, the waiter disappeared.

Hackling smiled at Johnson across the table, and then offered his assessment. "I heard something about the Pope on the radio driving in this morning, but didn't pay much attention. This is great. Your two target lists are a good start."

"Start?"

"Yes, start. Todd, you've only got half of the equation here. All of your usual suspects are fine. We can raise money from deep liberal pockets focused on abortion, gay marriage, the environment, public education, other ACLU-type causes, social justice, and the welfare state. Hollywood will be a huge source, including assorted atheists, activist-actor-types, and New Agers. You're also right that there'll be some money from moderate Muslims – including from a few of our good friends in the Middle East – scared that this will just be another effort tarring all of Islam."

"So, what am I forgetting?"

Hackling continued, "We have to play the labor unions right. The membership gets a bit dicey on religion, but the leaders who control the money will see the potential risk here of losing a spiritual voice supporting regulation and bigger government budgets."

"Yes, we've done that balancing act before," Johnson observed matter-of-factly. "Who else?"

"The Right."

"Come on. Conservatives will eat this up. This Pope and this idea are answers to their prayers," said Johnson.

"Well, a majority will like it. But keep in mind that there are a lot of hard-core, Religious Right Protestants – including lots of fundies – who simply cannot stomach Roman Catholics and, in particular, popes. They hate the office, and whatever guy happens to be pope. Many do not even view Catholics as legitimate Christians. We've got to talk to Kenny about this, but if I am in the ballpark here, I think a fair number of fundamentalists look at anything coming from the Vatican with great suspicion. I'm sure talk of a demonic conspiracy is afoot."

"I'll check with Kenny."

Kenny Hart was the religion point person at Hackling-Johnson. While once studying to enter the Episcopal priesthood, Hart now was an agnostic, at best. He knew his stuff, and was able to talk to liberals, moderates and conservatives within Christianity, Judaism and Islam, and pretty much anyone else who believed in things they could not see. In the fashion of his bosses, Hart treated religion in a clinical, tactical manner. He not only was an associate at the firm, but also carried the title of executive director of the Faith, Trust and Freedom Foundation, which was one of a number of non-profits set up by Hackling, Johnson or both.

Hackling was on a role. "Speaking of Kenny, this is an FTFF initiative, I assume, so all the donations are tax free?"

"Of course," said Johnson.

"And don't forget there are lots of very conservative Catholics who will view this as a betrayal by Pope Augustine."

Johnson was jotting down notes now. "Got it."

"Some libertarians too. They are, by definition almost, a disorganized, often conflicted group once you get by issues like taxes, regulation and government spending. Some I've met are devoutly religious, while others are atheists and rationalists who have no use for and are bewildered by religion. They usually can't stand conservative Christians. There are some deep-pocketed libertarian-atheists both on Wall Street and in Silicon Valley."

"Good, good thoughts," muttered Johnson as he continued to scribble, while eating his omelet at the same time. He then stopped, and looked across at Hackling. "By the way, this is a massive undertaking by the Vatican. I wonder who's advising them? I never got a whiff around town."

"Neither did I," agreed Hackling.

Both men apparently assumed that some major players in Washington had to be involved.

Johnson said, "I'll have Kenny poke around on that, too."

"Good," said Hackling. "But the main thing is to have Kenny identify money names and coalition members. Then we need a basic game plan to look at by late this afternoon." Hackling was getting more animated with each sentence. "We've only got two weeks – tops – to raise funds, form coalitions, and dole out the cash. Right? According to your memo, we're four weeks out from the Pope kicking things off on Long Island. It's a plus that I'm running Brees's campaign. And I have some other contacts there that we can use. Globally, this will carry through at least to Christmas. And then Augustine wants to have the first gathering of his group in the spring in ... where?"

"Wittenberg," said Johnson. "It's in Germany."

Hackling concluded, "God, this really could be an evergreen." He smiled with glee, and took a big bite of toast.

Chapter 18

In this age of the Internet, instantaneous communications and immediate – if not necessarily well thought out – opinions, the reactions to Pope Augustine I's letters to Christian leaders worldwide came fast and furious.

Before Johnson and Hackling finished their breakfast, bloggers were blogging. Statements for the press were hitting wire services. Articles spewed forth from major media outlets. And talking heads were chattering away on every television news channel. Even CNBC had economists and money managers prattling on about the possible impact on stock markets around the globe, even though the markets seemed completely disinterested.

Johnson and Hackling's expectations – as well as Father McDermott's – were right on the mark in terms of the responses in the U.S.

The liberal side of the church aisle certainly was not pleased.

A statement from the presiding bishop of the Episcopal Church summed up what many leaders in mainline Protestant churches were saying, "The Episcopal Church is always open to ecumenical efforts that bring Christians together in the pursuit of a more just world. However, we are deeply concerned about 'A Public Mission of Mere

Christianity,' as it seems more like a mission of exclusion rather than inclusion."

The "United Faith Council," an ecumenical organization, made clear its opposition. The executive director said, "We obviously agree with the Pope's point about Jesus' call for unity, but this is not the way to go about it. In fact, it appears to be a terrible setback, undoing the healing achieved by the historic ecumenical movement with an arrogant moral absolutism and an unhealthy religious superiority."

Others were even more overt in their hostility. One leading preacher noted the unusually positive mention of Martin Luther by a Roman Catholic pope, and proceeded to hurl accusations of anti-Semitism and that Luther's "Two Kingdoms" would lead to a quietism in the church even in the face of moral atrocities.

"Catholics for Reproductive Independence" warned, "The right to abortion will be placed in jeopardy, therefore putting women's lives in peril. That will be the inevitable and tragic result if Pope Augustine and his fundamentalist forces gain any more ground."

"GLTG in the Faith" – a group representing gay, lesbian and transgendered Christians – declared, "We are worried that words like 'truth' and 'morals' signal a re-energizing of homophobic bigots within the church."

An environmental group – "Green Believers" – worried, "The idea of delinking political and social activism from the Gospel is a dangerous proposition that would lead to Christians abandoning the environmental movement, and returning to an ignorant literalism of man's dominion over the environment."

And these were just responses from fellow Christians. The non-religious Left was very displeased as well.

Beyond the negative responses from secular pro-choice, gay rights, and environmental activists, voices from academia and Hollywood, for example, were particularly distressed by any notion that Christians should inform the culture. One outraged and very famous actor-director asked, "Are we comfortable with the idea of a bunch of right-wing Christian nut cases censoring our movies, our television shows, our news, and who knows what else?"

In the political and policy realms, critics raised the specter of violating the separation of church and state. Accusations of theocracy were widespread.

But, also as predicted, some Christian conservatives were less than enthused.

Assorted, highly traditional Roman Catholic voices, who during the decades since Vatican II have played more-Catholic-than-the-pope, were distressed not just by the mere mentioning of Martin Luther, the Reformation and Wittenberg, but by the entire proposal to reach out to those outside the "true Church."

At the same time, Brother Barry Stanton, head pastor at a large independent fundamentalist church in Alabama, who also had gained an enormous following via the Internet, provided a fire-breathing rebuke that was posted on his website and YouTube with amazing alacrity. But unlike many of the videos on YouTube, Brother Barry's had highly professional sound, lighting and camera work.

A click on his rather large head – with full-bodied brown hair parted on the side, narrow brown eyes, pale skin, and a flat, large-nostriled nose – got his wide mouth moving. He spoke fast and loud, with an exaggerated southern accent. But there also was a silky-smoothness as he strolled back and forth on a large stage in a light blue bowling shirt, jeans and white sneakers.

Do you know Jesus, my friends? Well, I do. He is my friend and personal savior. I pray he is yours as well.

But there are some deceivers who claim to be a friend of Jesus or even to be like God. The

Bible warns us about usurpers and beguilers coming in the name of Jesus, but in reality, leading the faithful into the very fires of hell and damnation!

Don't be fooled! You've probably heard about "A Public Mission of Mere Christianity." It might sound temptin'. But that's exactly what it is – temptation!

It is no coincidence that this Pope chose an author named C.S. Lewis as a means for temptation. Lewis often is praised as a great Christian in some circles. I don't understand why that would ever be considered the case, however. Would a great Christian write children stories comparing our Savior to an animal, as Lewis did in his "Narnia" abominations? I think not! And this Lewis authored the book 'Mere Christianity.' I don't know about you, friends, but there is nothing "mere" about my Jesus or about my faith.

This all amounts to nothing more than another papist plot for power, and to divert each of us from Jesus. Don't follow this tool of Satan.

Remember that the Pope demands obedience to himself, rather than to God. He is a Mary worshipper, one who prays to so-called saints. He is the antichrist that is spoken of in 1 John 2:18 – "Dear children, this is the last hour; and as you have heard that the antichrist is coming, even now many antichrists have come." And remember what our brother Paul warned of in 2 Thessalonians: "Don't let anyone deceive you in any way, for that day" – Judgment Day, my friends – "will not come until the rebellion occurs and the man of lawlessness is revealed, the man doomed to destruction. He opposes and exalts himself over everything that is called God or is worshipped, and even sets himself up in God's temple, proclaiming himself to be God."

Who is that, friends, but the Pope!? This is another sign, my brothers and sisters, that the End Times are nearly upon us. Thankfully, as promised, this man of lawlessness is doomed to destruction. Amen.

A smiling Brother Barry faded out, with an 800 number and the Internet address for his Ark of Christ church fading in on screen.

Among U.S. Roman Catholic bishops, a large number were declaring their support. But some apparently were keeping their powder dry through silence.

However, a solid majority of responses from the traditional or conservative side of the Christian aisle were full of approval, hope and prayer. Various traditional Christian denominational leaders spoke out quickly in favorable tones. Assorted big name evangelical pastors issued positive statements. Practically, every traditionalist reform group within mainline Protestantism expressed support as well. And all of the major voices involved in the "New Ecumenism" made clear their near euphoria.

If one were to somehow count up sides, a solid majority within U.S. Christianity and global Christendom probably would be onboard with "A Public Mission of Mere Christianity" to one degree or another. In addition, social conservatives in politics and the advocacy community issued immediate and unequivocal support, with many noting the opportunity to strengthen the voice for traditional values in the public square.

Nonetheless, the harsh criticism from the Left and Far Right naturally was garnering most of the media attention.

Not unexpectedly, disagreement made for more entertaining news viewing.

But the media's focus shifted some when responses emerged from the Muslim community.

Most Muslim leaders clearly were skeptical. Some spoke of the obvious need to fight those who were hijacking Islam for purposes of violence and terrorism. But they clearly were not too keen on having the Catholic Church's leader bring this up. Many perceived a slap at Islam in general. There was a distinct "mind your own business" tone to their responses.

Several radical imams in the Middle East and a few in Europe, however, called for jihad against "Augustine the Crusader," and against Christians in general. Indeed, a handful of Christians were attacked and killed on a few streets in the Middle East.

Assorted Islamic terrorist groups took to the Internet to echo accusations of continuing the Crusades, and of being in bed with the "Great Satan, America."

They pledged to kill Pope Augustine I and anyone else who joined his crusade.

Chapter 19

"Allah be praised," declared Saddam Ali, as he watched a television report on the Pope's letter later that evening.

"Indeed," replied Nuri al-Dawla. "He seems to have delivered this crusader Pope right into our hands."

In their youth, the two men had fought the Soviets in Afghanistan, and then emigrated to the United States with a mission. They worked hard, never broke the law (or at least did not get caught), and now owned three grocery-convenience stores and the buildings that housed each situated around Queens, New York. But their mission was not about building businesses or families – both were married with no children – in the Land of Opportunity. It was, instead, to become a part of the community, while waiting and preparing for whatever assignment came.

They had not traveled out of the U.S. since arriving. They attended a mosque that was a model of moderation from a Westerner's perspective.

But al-Dawla was one of the most trusted Islamic terrorists in the country, with Ali his right-hand man. The two men – both in their mid-40s, in top physical condition, with dark hair, eyes and skin tone – sat in the living room of al-Dawla's home, which was perched on the service road of the Van Wyck Expressway, north of Linden Boulevard and south of Jamaica Avenue.

It was a running joke between al-Dawla and Ali that their base of operations sat on one of the busiest highways in the United States. The Van Wyck suffered from a never-ending traffic jam, and the two men wondered over the years how many American political and business leaders motoring ever so slowly to and from Kennedy Airport stared unknowingly up at al-Dawla's home. From the outside, nothing about this house would indicate that it served as a training center for these mujahideen, or holy warriors.

Even if one entered the sparsely decorated, but neat home, there would be absolutely no indication of jihadist activity. But the completely sound-proofed basement featured weapons storage and firing range, bomb-making materials, and workout and training equipment.

Nuri al-Dawla assembled the materials and facility over the course of several years, careful to attract no attention or suspicions.

The basement training center was used by Nuri and Saddam, their wives – Lama and Areebah, respectively – and two younger men who ran one of the grocery stores. On occasion, the group also used city parks in the middle of the night to expand their exercises.

The younger men, Randall al-Hakim and Abdul ed-Din, were in their late twenties. Abdul was of Arab descent born in the United States. He was short, with black hair, thick eyebrows, and round facial features. He came from Newark, New Jersey. Meanwhile, Randall was brought up in the New Jersey suburbs just 20 miles southwest of Manhattan. He had no link to Islam during his childhood, as most would assume given his bright red hair, freckles, and tall, thin frame.

They met as engineering students at college and veered off in a far different direction from their generally secular parents after 9-11. Distrust of both Jews and the U.S. government, fed and nourished on the Internet, led Abdul into a far more zealous and fundamentalist strain of Islam than his parents had ever exposed him to, and Randall Greene followed, eventually changing his name to Randall al-Hakim.

Abdul and Randall shared a basement apartment in a home not far from one of the convenience stores in Bayside.

Together, the six individuals appeared to be a unit. Nuri and Saddam ranked as experienced, complete warriors. Lama and Areebah had become skilled in close combat skills, especially with knives. And Randall and Abdul had become explosive experts. All were adept in firing a wide array of weapons.

Nuri told Saddam, "Make contact, and find out if we have the go-ahead to act. This seems ideal."

The unit that diligently, quietly trained would soon be put to the test.

Chapter 20

It was just two days since the letter from Pope Augustine I stirred up the world. Technically, stirred up that portion of the world that cared about faith or politics – or both.

To gear up the opposition, Hackling-Johnson Advisors already had gotten more than $350,000 in financial commitments from some very deep pockets. And that was just by working the phones.

Arnie Hackling and Todd Johnson had a smooth flight on the earliest shuttle out of Reagan National. They grabbed a cab at LaGuardia Airport and were heading to Manhattan's downtown financial district, with a full day of money meetings ahead. The big fish required that Arnie and Todd make personal visits.

Johnson had a list of six liberal Wall Street lawyers and bankers, with Hackling meeting libertarian types, including for dinner at the offices of a top money manager. That financier was an Ayn Rand follower who, apparently, liked to hire like-minded employees. Hackling would be making his pitch to a dozen officers and traders at the firm.

* * *

After a breakfast meeting that only netted a tentative "I'll think about it," Todd Johnson sat down for his 10 o'clock at a small conference table in the rather bland office of T. Gunther Willoughby, who served as chief counsel for the investment banking firm of Kendrick, Stark & Company for more than a decade. Willoughby was short and fat, and could always be counted on to wear a bow tie and suspenders, which only accentuated his overall roundness.

Gunther said, "Good to see you, Todd. It's been a while. Last year's DLC gathering, right?"

"Yes, Gunther. All going well? How's Arlene?"

"Wonderful. She's getting Jeremy settled at Yale. Thanks for asking. I don't mean to be rude, but I have a 10:45. Give me some more on what you have been cooking up in response to this Christian Right thing from the Pope?"

Johnson gave him the Cliff Notes version.

"Your strategy sounds spot on. I am so tired of these self-appointed moralists trying to dictate how others should live, and using government to do their bidding. The bloody Republicans are completely co-opted by these fundamentalists. I'm in church almost every Sunday but do not presume to judge others." He added, "Of course, my Episcopalianism is far different from those Bible thumpers."

Gunther leaned back so that the two front legs of his chair were raised in the air a few inches. It was a rather amazing balancing act, given his portliness. He looked at the ceiling and added to seemingly no one in particular: "My father and grandfather, lifelong Episcopalians and Republicans, must be spinning in their graves. Simply outrageous."

Gunther lingered for several more seconds in this circus-like position, then brought his chair back down on all fours. He looked at Johnson: "I'm on board, Todd. How can I help?"

"Well, we're up against the reach and riches of the Catholic Church," replied Johnson.

"Will $70,000 help?"

"Absolutely, Gunther. Your generosity will not be wasted."

* * *

Derek Stewart's money management firm occupied an entire floor fifteen stories above the very posh West 54th Street. The catered dinner was more than adequate – salad, a smoked turkey and brie sandwich, Chardonnay, and fresh, oversized cookies.

But these probably never tasted so delicious to Arnie Hackling.

Outside of major campaigns, including for the White House, Hackling never raised so much money for a cause in one day. Before taking the elevator up to Stewart's firm, Arnie was on the cell phone with Johnson, and they tallied up checks or commitments in excess of $670,000. Combined with the previous day's total, and what the D.C. office was pulling in, they were already over $1.4 million.

When the sandwiches and polite chitchat finished, Stewart stood to officially introduce Arnie Hackling.

Derek Stewart completely looked the role of the financier. The summer light tan suit, white shirt, and pink tie looked crisp and non-rumpled, as if it were the start of a new work day, rather than the end of one as was actually the case. His very blond, swept-back hair was a touch long, falling down the back of his neck beyond his shirt collar. The hair, along with his general fitness, made him look much younger than his 48 years.

Stewart stood before 13 of his employees – nine men and four women, and none of them older than 35. He strolled around the large, oak conference table, exuding confidence, if not downright arrogance.

"Thanks to each of you for staying late to hear what Mr. Hackling has to say." Derek looked at Arnie and pointed out, "We have a speaker come in one evening a month, Arnie. They've covered a wide range of topics – a good deal on economics, some foreign policy, market and industry analysis, technology, history, the arts, philosophy, so on. It's quite eclectic."

Arnie nodded.

Stewart shifted emphasis back to his employees. "But all of you are well aware that religion has never been directly on the agenda. I've made an exception tonight. Arnie Hackling is one of the nation's leading political consultants. I'm sure many of you know him, and perhaps a few have contributed to some of the campaigns he has run."

Three heads nodded in the affirmative.

Stewart continued, "Arnie is here to talk about a critical effort to counter this proposal from Pope Augustine to expand the reach of the Religious Right. Most of us here, as libertarians, have had to hold our noses in dealing with these zealots. In order to advance the case of tax relief, deregulation and property rights, for example, we've had to sign on with Republican politicians who also are in bed with the fundamentalists. It has been an unfortunate, but politically necessary marriage."

He continued to lap the conference table. "This proposal from the Pope, however, represents a dramatic and dangerous development. It's a stab, plain and simple, for a kind of theocracy. A fantastic and worrisome extension of superstition into our government and the running of our country. It is a naked attempt to obliterate the separation of church and state."

Stewart's pace was quickening, and his voice and hand motions were those of a commander speaking to his troops.

"We've had Randians here to speak to us about some of the insights Ayn Rand offered on capitalism. Rand also made several points well worth keeping in mind about religion. Just before coming in here tonight, I checked out a few online. I want to read one that, I think, is right on target regarding the current challenge."

Derek sat back down next to Arnie Hackling, opened a manila file folder on the table, and picked up a sheet of paper with quotes from Ayn Rand on religion. Stewart continued, "In an interview, *Playboy* asked, 'Has no religion, in your estimation, ever offered anything of constructive value to human life?' Rand answered this way: 'Qua religion, no – in the sense of blind belief, belief unsupported by, or contrary to, the facts of reality and the conclusions of reason. But you must remember that religion is an early form of philosophy, that the first attempts to explain the universe, to give a coherent frame of reference to man's life and a code of moral values, were made by religion, before men graduated or developed enough to have philosophy. And, as philosophies, some religions have very valuable moral points. They may have a good influence or proper principles to inculcate, but in a very contradictory context and, on a very – how should I say it – dangerous or malevolent base: on the ground of faith.'"

Stewart put the sheet back down on the table. He concluded, "I'm worried that this plan by the Pope will raise the influence of the malevolent opposed to reason to disturbing heights."

Of the employees in the room, three men and one woman were watching Stewart with enthusiastic eyes. As he read the Rand quote, they were nodding in agreement. Seven, sipping their wine, soda or coffee, looked at the table or anywhere but directly at Stewart.

But two – one man, one woman – watched Derek closely with clearly skeptical looks.

"Now," Derek added," let me turn the floor over to Arnie ..."

"Excuse me, Derek?" It was the skeptical man.

"Yes, Paul."

"I assume this is our usual format allowing for disagreement and debate," said the late twenty-something black man with a goatee. His statement was part question, part observation.

"Of course. What do you have to say?"

The seven who were staring at their glasses or the table with undeserved intensity now looked up, a few with clear expressions of relief on their faces.

Paul said, "Well, Rand had her economics basically right. She made clear the bankruptcy of socialism, and that capitalism and freedom work best. But on just about everything else, she was full of crap."

"Absolutely," chimed in the female skeptic.

Several of the silent seven looked more comfortable.

Stewart's four sympathizers turned to their leader.

But before Stewart could open his mouth, Paul continued, "I mean come on. Equating altruism and self-sacrifice to collectivism? And selfishness is a virtue? She redefined terms to fit her own purposes, which, it seems to me, was in part about public relations. It's simply sophomoric. And don't forget that not only was Rand a militant atheist, she also rejected the libertarianism that most of us here embrace. I never understood why so many libertarians almost blindly embrace her. Rand could not tolerate Christianity, but as far as I know, it's still OK to be a Christian and a libertarian."

Maria, the female skeptic, jumped in, "Right. Rand argued that conservatives failed to adequately defend capitalism because they relied on religion, and therefore abandoned reason to opponents of free markets. That assumes that faith and reason are in conflict. I would argue they're mutually reinforcing. When you look at human beings and the world around us, it is far more reasonable to see God's hand at work, than to view the entire universe being all about random chance. It seems to me that it takes a hell of a lot more faith to be an atheist than a Christian. As for conservatism, one can be a social or religious conservative, and still embrace free markets. I do.   Frankly, I think the much-talked-about conflict between social and economic conservatives is out on the fringes. That's driven home most clearly by the fact that whatever one's personal motivation in business, in order to succeed you must think of others first. Before I was able to afford my East Side apartment and Jaguar XKR Coupe..."

"Oooooo, a Jag," interrupted a couple of her colleagues.

Maria smiled. "I know, it's a nice ride. But my point is that I had to provide value to this firm and our clients first. Entrepreneurs have to create something that others need or want before they can meet their own needs and wants. Contrary to what Ayn Rand said, capitalism is altruistic."

Stewart regained the floor. "Well, I would have to disagree with both Maria and Paul. Rand's emphasis on rationality is the only ethic that makes sense. Nothing in religion conforms with reason. That's particularly true of Christianity. The individual's pursuit of happiness is the highest moral purpose, and the idea of sacrificing one's self makes no sense. It also makes no sense to abandon reason in favor of faith. Rand was right about all of this, and it's dangerous when those in government toss aside rationality and reason."

"Please don't take this personally, Derek, but you're not a parent," observed Maria. She spoke in a calm tone, with an undercurrent of authority. "Nor was Rand. I read Rand's *Playboy* interview several years ago, and it stuck with me. Rand actually called a person immoral and an emotional parasite for putting family above work. Rand only embraced romantic love, although what she called romance was self-absorbed, robotic and barren. When you have children that you love unconditionally, the idea of sacrificing for others – even dying for another – makes perfect sense. That's what God has done for his children."

The debate proceeded for another 45 minutes, while Hackling simply sat – watching and listening.

Finally, Stewart looked at his watch, and said, "Well, we will have to agree to disagree because Arnie has to head back to D.C. Anyone wanting to stop the Pope's effort can cut Arnie a check, as I have." And with a bit of show, Derek reached inside his suit jacket, pulling out an envelope for all to see and handing it to Hackling.

Stewart added, "Anyone wanting to contribute can see you on the way out, right Arnie?"

"Ah, of course, that's fine. Thank you."

That was all Arnie Hackling was able to say. A half-hour later, though, he walked out the front door of the building. His left hand was raised in the air to flag down a taxi, while his right hand held a brief case filled with another $550,000 in funding – 90 percent of it from Derek Stewart.

He got in the cab, and told the driver, "LaGuardia." Then Hackling phoned Todd Johnson.

Johnson answered, "How'd you make out?"

Arnie said, "You're not going to believe this one. More than a half-million, and I never really opened my mouth."

Chapter 21

Barbara Tunney parked her very sensible, nondescript, gray, mid-size car, and was heading into St. Mary's when Pastor Grant pulled up in his Tahoe.

When Grant caught up, Tunney remarked, "Isn't it a glorious day?"

It was late morning, the sun shining brightly, 82 degrees, and not a drop of humidity detected. A gentle breeze blew.

"Yes, it is. A little too glorious perhaps," Grant responded.

"Are we grumpy on the day this wonderful building will be blessed?"

"Not at all. It's just that perfect weather on a Saturday in late August does not necessarily bode well for people showing up at church," speculated Stephen.

Barbara said, "Don't worry. Especially with all that's happened over the past ten days, they will come. But just in case, want to pray about it?"

Stephen smiled. "Good idea."

The 3:00 church blessing was fully attended, including congregation members, friends, clergy and other church officials, local business and community leaders, and a handful of politicians, including Congressman Ted Brees and his wife Jennifer.

The service began outside the building. Emotions were raw. During the procession into the church, the choir sang "A Mighty Fortress is Our God" with tears streaming down some of their faces. At the organ in the choir loft, Pam Carter seemed to be working very hard not to cry. She played flawlessly nonetheless.

In this new church building that could seat 350 comfortably, about three dozen people wound up standing. A couple along the back wall drew Stephen's attention very briefly as he turned to the congregation. He read from the *Lutheran Service Book*:

> Beloved in the Lord, Christ Jesus is present wherever his holy Word is taught purely and the holy Sacraments are administered according to His institution. As the Lord said through Moses, "In every place where I cause My name to be remembered I will come to you and bless you."
>
> Let us pray. Almighty and most merciful God, though You are not contained in houses built by human hands, we pray that You will be pleased to dwell with us here and to make known to us Your glory. Be present in this place where we are gathered to receive Your forgiveness, hear Your holy Word, and praise Your holy name. Graciously hear the prayers we will offer to You; bless the marriages to be solemnized; comfort those who will mourn; and let harmony and peace rest upon all in this place. Bring us at last to the heavenly Jerusalem, where the Lamb is the temple, that we may unite with all the saints and angels in His praise; through the same Jesus Christ, Your Son, our Lord, who lives and reigns with You and the Holy Spirit, one God, now and forever.

The congregation replied, "Amen." When he looked up, one of the people he noted earlier along the back wall now seized his attention.

She was striking. The neckline of the white halter top dress with black polka dots plunged down between her breasts, allowing for plentiful revelation of neck, shoulders, back and unmistakably strong arms. The hemline a couple of inches above the knee also highlighted smooth and athletic legs. A shiny black belt pulled tight around the waist served as final confirmation of a beautiful shape. Her hair was long, thick and jet-black, with skin light and overly freckled from the summer sun. Her mouth featured full, pink lips, and her nose was gently rounded.

Despite being indoors, her eyes were hidden behind dark sunglasses. But Grant knew they were gray-blue, bright, and steely. In fact, he intimately knew every inch of Paige Caldwell's five feet, nine inches. It had been a very long time, but he remembered quite clearly.

She nodded ever so slightly, with her mouth turned up minutely on the sides in a subtle smile.

In those few seconds, Stephen was sucked out of church and back in time. He turned and headed back to the altar. *Paige? Knew somebody would show, but not her.* He felt a stirring, and snapped back to the present.

Grant assumed no one noticed his brief hesitation after reading the blessing, except, probably, the person who caused it.

Later, on exiting the church, the shake-the-pastor's-hand line took much longer than a typical service. It could have been worse, but fortunately most were headed to a local catering hall for the celebratory congregation dinner. Still, it was a lengthy process that seemed to slow down as Paige moved ever closer.

Most men would have been too distracted to deal adequately and courteously with each individual in the

line. Some he saw each week and others Grant had not had
contact with in months or even years. They shook his hand,
hugged him, asked what he was up to, offered condolences
regarding the Gundersons, reminisced, wondered about old
friends, introduced new people, inquired about the
congregation, and commented on the new building. Grant's
SEAL, CIA and pastoral backgrounds again came in
handy, allowing him to focus on the person talking to him
as well as simultaneously tracking the unexpected blast
from the past.

Before Paige arrived, though, his hand was extended to
Jennifer Brees. She seemed more like her old self. Jennifer
took his hand and leaned forward for a brief hug.

Grant asked, "Feeling better?"

"Getting there, yes, thanks," she replied.

Ted Brees was just behind her, and shook hands with
Stephen. "Good to see you, Pastor. I hope things will soon
get back to normal around here. If there's anything I can
do, please let me know."

"Of course," Stephen said, "and thank you."

"You're welcome. Unfortunately, I won't be at the
dinner. I have some campaign stops to make. But Jennifer,
of course, is attending. She wouldn't miss it."

"Well, I am sorry you can't make it, Congressman."
Yippee! "But I'm glad you're coming, Jennifer."

"That reminds me," Jennifer said. "We're having a small
dinner party on Friday night. If you could make it, we'd
love for you to come. It's a chance for a little calm and
sanity to kick off the Labor Day weekend after all that's
happened, and before the campaign craziness really takes
hold. How about it? Is your schedule clear?"

Stephen noted that Paige was just six people away.

"Friday night? Yes, that sounds great. Thanks very
much for the invite," Stephen told Jennifer and Ted.

"That's wonderful. I'll e-mail you the details," said
Jennifer. "Feel free to bring a date if you like."

"Ah, that's not likely."

The next half dozen in line were non-chatty regular parishioners who, mercifully, moved along.

Paige grasped Grant's hand with, Stephen thought, her typical forthrightness.

"Stephen, God, it's good to see you. Been way too long," said Paige.

"Yes, far too many years, Paige. Welcome to St. Mary's."

"Welcome to St. Mary's" – really?

She looked him up and down, and then let his hand go. "This is so weird."

"You can say that again," Stephen agreed. "Don't take this the wrong way, but what are you doing here?"

Paige ignored the question. "This is Ryan Bates. He's ... a colleague."

A tall, thin, sandy-haired man with a big head shook Stephen's hand. The serious expression on the late-twenty-something's face did not seem to quite fit right, Grant thought. Stephen guessed that Bates was new to the CIA, or maybe FBI, and trying a little too hard to fit the part.

Paige continued, "I know you've got a busy day, Stephen, but can you carve out a few minutes for an old friend? It's important."

"Now?"

"Yes," she answered firmly.

"After I finish here, I can give you ten minutes. Head down the hall to the right. My office is the second door on the left."

Paige Caldwell smiled. "Thanks, Stephen."

She strode away with Bates at her side. As he greeted others, Stephen noted the two spoke briefly in the narthex. Bates exited the building for the parking lot. Body language indicated he was not exactly pleased. Paige headed down the hallway to Stephen's office.

Fifteen minutes later, Grant stepped into the office doorway. Paige was seated behind his desk clearly looking things over. "Ahem, that is my desk," he said.

Paige smiled, stood up, moved around the desk and walked to him.

As beautiful as ever.

She placed her hands on his biceps. "It really is good to see you, Stephen." She kissed him gently on the cheek.

Still standing in the doorway, Grant realized that this might look a bit too interesting to any lingering parishioners. He stepped in and closed the door.

"Yes, well, have a seat." He pointed to the couch. *This really is weird.*

Paige sat down, pulling her dress up, revealing more leg.

Stephen removed his robes, hung them up in the armoire, and sat down in the armchair.

"Not joining me on the couch? It's been ages since we were on the couch together," said Paige, making a pouty shape with her lips.

Oh, don't do that.

"Okay, Paige. What's this all about?"

"In a second, Stephen. First, I want to know what you've been up to since you left me and the CIA for the Lord."

"Paige, you know that's not exactly how it went," replied Stephen.

"Do I? Married?"

"No. But you already knew that."

She smiled playfully. "Yes, I did. Any special someone?"

I really don't want to talk about this now, particularly with you. But Stephen also knew Paige would have an agenda to play out. "No. Not right now."

"How about anytime over the past – it has been fourteen, yes – fourteen years?"

"Paige, I really don't see how or why this is any of your business when you decide to just drop in after years of no contact," Stephen said with exasperation in his voice.

She ignored his response. "Uh-oh. Stephen, have you kept your pants zipped since the last time we did the nasty? Oh, come on. You've got to be kidding. Do you walk around with a perpetual hard on under those robes?"

"Paige, enough."

"Warrior monk, perhaps?"

"Excuse me?"

"The Knights Templar were the first Christian military order. They combined monastic discipline with skills of warriors. Came in handy for the Crusades."

She looked quite pleased with herself.

Paige continued, "Or, if you prefer a movie reference, how about *Casino Royale*, when Bond says to M, 'So, you want me to be half monk, half hit man'?   Either way, is that you these days? Monk-like with no sex, and killing a gunman – excuse me, gun*woman* – in your church. So, warrior monk?"

"History, the church and a movie. Nice."

"I thought you'd like that. Still a movie buff?"

Stephen said, "More than I'd like." *OK, this isn't helping. Let's get off me.* "Who is Mr. Bates – CIA or FBI?"

"FBI. Since 9-11, we're all friends now – CIA, FBI, NSA and so on – or at least we're supposed to be."

"And why are Bates FBI and Caldwell CIA visiting me?"

"Stephen, I'm hurt. I thought you'd be more interested in what I've been up to all this time. Aren't you the least bit curious?"

"Of course, I am, Paige. But quite frankly, I have to leave. So, let's get down to business, and leave catching up for another day."

"Fine. If you insist," said Paige. Stephen couldn't tell if her disappointment was real or feigned. But emotion now left her voice. "Your termination of Ms. Serrano ten days ago gained attention. We've had some worrisome chatter regarding Pope Augustine's upcoming visit – both international and domestic concerns. The agency and FBI obviously have been working with the Vatican. And you turn out to be the right member of the clergy in the right place. The only drawback is that you're a Lutheran pastor, not a Roman Catholic priest."

"Hence, the grilling of Father Ronald McDermott by the local bishop," Grant interjected. "You gave the Vatican a heads-up on me."

"That's right," Caldwell continued. "Your theology checked out nicely with this big initiative by the Pope. You're his kind of Lutheran, and he, apparently, is your kind of Roman Catholic."

"Yes, that would be the case. So, where is this headed?"

"Your country is asking you to serve once more."

"I don't work for the government any more, Paige. I'm the pastor of St. Mary's Lutheran Church."

"I'm well aware of that Stephen. But while you surprised me once in the past, I still know how some part of you ticks, and I find it unimaginable that you would say no to your country, especially in this case. But just in case, Pope Augustine and the president of your denomination, Reverend Harrison Piepkorn, will be extending personal invitations as well."

Stephen asked, "And what exactly am I being invited to do?"

"We want you to stick with the Pope while he's visiting the U.S."

"You're kidding."

"Not at all. It all fits together rather naturally. You've long been interested in this kind of proposal. His four days in the country will all be in the New York metropolitan area – Long Island and New Jersey. That works for you and for us. And then the Pope leaves for Mexico. We'll still be working with the Swiss Guard to protect the Pontiff there and throughout his global trip, but by then, you'll be right back here."

Grant was silent. They stared at each other for several seconds.

Lord, is this one of the reasons you put me in this particular place? Well, Piepkorn, Augustine and your country are all calling. Seems pretty clear.

Grant got up and walked to his office door. He placed his hand on the knob. But before he turned it, Stephen said, "Paige, I'm late for the congregational dinner. I'll have to let you know tomorrow. Where will you be?"

She had followed him silently to the door, and from behind, her hand joined his on the doorknob. She whispered close to his ear, "Do you have any suggestions where I might be able to stay tonight?"

He turned and dropped his hand from the door. But Paige did not let go of his. It felt like a very long time since he was this close to a woman with the hint of sex in the air. In fact, it had been a very long time. And the last time happened to be with Paige Caldwell. He had to summon a great deal of self-control.

Stephen said, "Paige, I'm sorry. And I mean I am *really* sorry. But I can't."

"Stephen, we were great." She pressed closer. "Why not?"

"I can't."

"Is there a problem, like a Viagra thing?"

"Definitely not." He chuckled a bit. "It's a God thing. Sex outside of marriage is a no-no, a sin."

Paige took a step back. She giggled seductively, and smiled. "Come, come, Stephen. I happen to have first hand knowledge that you've had sex many times out of wedlock. I could come up with a lot of names for what we did years ago, but to me, 'sin' is not one."

"Paige, our, ah, moments together were amazing. And my dreams periodically provide rather vivid reminders."

"Oh, good. Mine too. Want to make some new dreams?"

Would I like to? Sure.

"Paige, that was a different time. It's not a choice I can make now. And while it's incredibly tempting, it's not a choice, in the end, I want to make."

She turned away. "Bates and I have rooms at the Hampton Inn at Exit 63 on the expressway. I need your answer by early Monday. Preferably before."

She brushed past without looking at his face, and opened the office door. A gentleness entered her voice, as she added, "I'm disappointed, Stephen."

And Paige Caldwell left.

Yeah, Paige, me too.

Chapter 22

Professor Andre Tyler didn't seem distressed over the murders committed by Linda Serrano. Nor did the death of this woman whom he had been sleeping with on and off for some time seem to wear on him.

When asked about it by the police and by individuals around the sparsely populated late summer campus, Tyler declared he was shocked and deeply shaken. It helped that his thin, tall frame stooped some, and his slightly baggy, long face, with bushy black eyebrows and topped by voluminous white hair, gave an appearance of ongoing melancholy. The 57-year-old environmental philosophy professor remained a model of the enigmatic.

It was early Sunday afternoon. Tyler had been driving west for almost an hour from the bungalow he rented just up the street from Peconic Bay in Jamesport on Long Island's North Fork. He took no chances with such telephone calls. It would be no different this time, especially given the magnitude of this particular call. Never on his home phone. Not from his office at the university. Nor on his cell. He would randomly journey a respectable distance to use a payphone.

Tyler exited the Long Island Expressway and pulled into the parking lot of a hotel. Payphones could still be found in hotels, and they usually offered a degree of privacy. Conveniently, that was the case this time.

He had committed the phone number to memory. The area code was Philadelphia. It rang three times.

"Hello."

Andre said, "This is Wheeler. I'm looking for Robert Johns."

"Speaking. I was expecting your call, Mr. Wheeler."

"Yes. I understand you're the person for this assignment, that you have the right tools and experience."

"That's right. But for something this high profile, it's quite expensive, more money than I imagine you could muster." He accentuated the point with a short, grim-sounding laugh. "However, this especially interests me; indeed, even excites me." He was seated at a kitchen table, looking down at a picture of Stephen Grant in a newspaper story. "I'm very interested in coming to Long Island. Our mutual friend has promised 2.5 million. It will cost you another half million."

"I'll have the money in a week or two at the latest. Half wired before, and half upon completion," said Andre.

"No. Given the magnitude of the act, it will have to be full payment in advance."

Andre replied, "That's highly unorthodox."

"This is all highly unorthodox, Mr. Wheeler. Are we going to do this, or not?"

Andre paused. "Fine. I'll let you know when I have the funds."

"Then I'll start planning." Robert Johns – one of the man's numerous aliases – hung up.

Chapter 23

Grant had decided to accept the assignment seconds after Paige asked. But he elected to hold off telling her at that moment.

Stephen wanted to make sure. The return of Paige Caldwell into his life put him on guard. Was he thinking with his head, or another part of his anatomy?

Grant sat in his office early Sunday afternoon staring at the telephone. *Just when you think you're out, they pull you back in. Michael Corleone. The Godfather III. Well, the agency ain't the mob, though some think so.*

He picked up the receiver and called the hotel, and asked for Paige Caldwell's room.

"Hello."

"Paige?"

"Stephen. I was hoping you might come by with your answer. Not call on the phone. Once again, how disappointing."

"Sorry, Paige. Perhaps my answer will cheer you up."

"You're in."

"I'm in."

"I knew it," Paige remarked with some enthusiasm. "My God, it'll be good working together again."

"Well, what next?"

"Now that you've given the green light, the official invite from the Vatican will come some time tomorrow, as will the thumbs up from your President Piepkorn."

"Then what?"

"We'll let you know shortly. Good bye, lover." She hung up.

Lover? She doesn't make this easy. He looked at his watch. Two-thirty. *What now?*

Grant decided it was way too early to head back to the parsonage. He looked over at his gun cabinet, and decided afternoon practice at the sportsmen's club was in order.

Chapter 24

Monday was one of the days when Stephen Grant, Ron McDermott and Tom Stone pushed off their devotions until lunch, after a morning round of golf at Rock Hill, not far from St. Mary's.

Grant was happy to get away from all the things, including the St. Mary's building itself, that were reminding him of the Gundersons. After losing his friends, presiding at their funeral, and then dedicating the church they constructed – toss in, for good measure, his new assignment – Grant was ready to hit the greens.

Before teeing it up, Pastor Grant and Father McDermott did some putting, and split a bucket of balls on the driving range. Father Stone drove up just five minutes before their 7:20 tee time. He waved out the window of his blue Chrysler minivan as he passed the driving range, heading for the parking lot.

The clubhouse and pro shop at Rock Hill sat atop one of the highest points on relatively flat Long Island. On a clear sunny day, as this one was shaping up to be, the tenth tee lent itself to a view south of Moriches Bay, Fire Island and the Atlantic Ocean far off in the distance.

Stone walked up to the first tee right at 7:20. "How's that for timing?" he said with a smile. He then started rummaging around his golf bag for glove, tee and ball.

"Pretty good, Tom, unless you wanted to warm up first," replied McDermott, who stood next to Grant on the tee waiting for their friend.

"Hitting a bucket of balls and some putts on the practice green like you guys? Yeah, right. That's a luxury that unmarried men have. It is not a real alternative in a house with a wife and kids vying for morning bathroom time."

"Touché," said Grant.

"If you guys are ready, go ahead and hit," Tom said as the exploration of his bag had yielded a glove and tee, but not yet a ball without scuff marks.

Ron asked Stephen, "Shall I lead the way?"

"Please do."

Ron teed his ball up high. The combination of his long driver with a huge head and a flat, aggressive, inside-out swing resulted in a long draw that landed in the middle of the fairway, but continued to run left and settled just in the light rough some 270 yards away.

"Nice ball," observed Stephen, as he teed up his own.

"Thanks."

Grant showed off a smooth swing, with his high, slight fade coming to rest on the right side of fairway at a distance of 255 years.

"Even better," said Tom, who finally arrived on the tee box with a hybrid in his hand and a shiny new ball. The look of Stone's swing was not as polished as his friends'. A three-quarters back swing was followed by a hard, crushing move on the ball, with an abbreviated follow through. The result, though, was a high, straight projection that split the fairway at about 220 yards.

"And you do that without warming up," Ron observed shaking his head.

"Clean living and concentration," Tom responded.

"Really? We'll see if that clean living and concentration help you sink a putt today," said Ron.

"That will require heavenly intervention," Stephen added.

"Oh, ye of little faith," Tom replied. "I tried cross handed last night, and was jarring everything."

"Your living room carpet doesn't count," Ron countered. "You have to do it on an actual putting green."

The banter continued through the first three holes. Upon arriving at the fourth – a 160 yard par three with traps guarding each side of the large green – they caught up to two foursomes of older gentlemen. Four silver-haired duffers were on the green, while the other four waited on the tee.

Stephen said, "Apparently, all eight play golf like they're retired with nowhere to go and in no particular hurry to get there."

"Oh well, so much for breezing along," Ron observed.

The four sat down in a grassy, shady spot on a slight incline well behind the tee box.

Finally, Ron touched on the topic. "So, Stephen, anything on the Vatican, Augustine's letter, and the inquiries about you?"

"Actually, yes. Cone of silence?"

"Cone of silence," confirmed both Ron and Tom.

With this *Get Smart* pledge of secrecy, Stephen continued, "I spoke with an old friend and colleague after the church dedication service on Saturday."

Tom said, "Was that the very hot chick in the black-and-white dress who you spent some closed-door time with in your office?"

"How the he...?" Stephen started to ask. "Oh, never mind. Barbara?"

"When the wife wasn't looking, I noticed this attractive lady in church. Later, when I asked why you were running late to the dinner, Barbara said that the woman seemed very friendly, and you two disappeared into your office."

"Nothing happened," Stephen said reflexively and defensively. "Jeez, how many people did she tell that to?"

"I was there," volunteered Ron, raising his hand to emphasize his innocence.

"Maggie, too, but that was it," Tom concluded. "Mrs. Tunney seems to know who she can say such things to, and who she should not. I think she spoke to us knowing we can talk to you about such things, if necessary."

"Well, it's not necessary." Stephen's defensive tone continued.

"Okay, okay. So, who is this woman of mystery and what did she want?"

Stephen needed to talk about this. As the first foursome of senior citizens were exiting the green, a frail fellow in the second group was ever so slowly bending his body to push a tee into the ground. It appeared to be a rather arduous task, as if he were trying to insert the tee into solid concrete. After that feat was accomplished, he then faced the challenge of balancing a ball on that tee with shaking hands.

Grant decided that was going to take awhile, and he had the time to bring his two friends up to date.

"Her name is Paige Caldwell. I worked with her at the CIA. We also were ... ah ... involved."

"I knew it. This is getting good. Wish I had some popcorn. Go on," said Tom with smile.

After both Stephen and Ron told Tom to shut up, Grant went on to provide the details of the invitation from the government and Vatican.

Ron said, "You must have been very good at whatever you did for the CIA, Stephen."

"I was," Grant responded without a trace of arrogance. "And now I happen to be the right former employee in the right place at the right time with the right views."

"And with the convenience of a collar," Tom added.

"Correct."

"Have you given them an answer yet?" asked Ron.

"I'm scheduled to get an official invitation from the Vatican today, along with a blessing from President Piepkorn. But, yes, I called Paige yesterday and told her that they could count on me. This is just too important to say no."

The third elderly golfer on the tee was taking a mulligan, and teeing up another ball.

"I can't imagine how, but if I can help, Stephen, please let me know," said Ron.

Tom echoed the offer.

"Thanks, and I might take you up on that. There's one more matter in this mix that I just need to, for lack of a better word, confess," Stephen said.

"Sure," said Tom.

Ron asked, "What is it?"

"As Tom so rightly observed, Paige is very attractive."

Father Stone interjected, "I believe I used the phrase 'very hot chick.'"

"Yes, you did. Anyway, she's looking to re-ignite our old relationship."

"Really," said Tom. "If you don't mind, what kind of relationship was this?"

"It was intense. We protected each other on the job as part of a team, but we also had a powerful sexual intimacy. There was never any talk about the long run or the rest of our lives, though. It was physical and empty of any long-term consequences. Looking back, I'm not proud of it, but that was the reality. And given our work, it was not all that unusual."

Grant spoke more quickly now in order to get it all out, while the foursome in front of them drove their two electric golf carts to their four balls – none of which had come close to reaching the green. "Paige is in no way a shy girl. She makes clear what she wants. And she made it very clear on Saturday in my office what she wanted to do with me that night. And I was as tempted as I have ever been since heading to seminary. Quite frankly, I'm worried about trusting myself as I work with her again over the next few weeks."

"You guys need wives," commented Tom. "Well, not you, Ron. You're not allowed, but you should be."

"Thanks for that great insight, Tom," said Ron, with a roll of his eyes.

Tom teased, "Ron, you're a young, scrapping, good looking fellow."

"Thank you very much. What's your point?"

Tom continued: "Do you ever run into flirtatious, naughty Catholic girls seeking forbidden fruit?"

"This went unmentioned in seminary, but it occurs and far more frequently than I ever would have thought. It's not overt, but the signals are unmistakable," Ron answered.

Tom asked, "Since I assume you're not sleeping around, what do you do? How do you handle it? Prayer, a cold shower, and hope the issue goes away."

"Basically, that's it. I have to make sure that I don't send any wrong signals back."

Grant sarcastically said, "Are you guys helping here?"

"Sorry, Stephen," Ron apologized sheepishly. "Do you really think this thing with Paige is going to be a big problem?"

"I'm not sure. Paige can be persistent ... and persuasive."

"Stephen," Tom interjected, "I do have a point here."

"Could have fooled me," added Ron with a smirk.

Tom explained, "You know the drill. If you're really worried about this, I'd normally advise a person to separate themselves from the temptation. But in this case, that apparently is not an option. So, prayer and taking a shower is about all you've got. Besides, haven't you run into this over the years?"

"To be honest, not with anyone at St. Mary's. And I've only been out on a handful of dates in recent years."

Tom offered, "There is another option, you know. You've had a relationship with Paige. And I understand that she wanted to hop into bed with you on Saturday. But does she perhaps care for you more deeply than you suspect? And if so, would she be willing to play by a new set of rules that might lead to, well, who knows where?"

Married to Paige?

"Hello. Earth to Stephen, come in," said Ron after several seconds of Stephen silently looking down and fiddling with a blade of grass.

Stephen finally volunteered, "Paige never struck me as the marrying type. And even during our relationship, it just never came up and, quite frankly, never crossed my mind either."

The three men looked at each other. Ron glanced up, "Not that we've solved anything, but it's back to golf, boys. Our Champions Tour rejects are walking off the green."

They got up and walked onto the tee box.

After an unusual streak of good putting that resulted in two pars and a birdie on the first three holes, Tom had the honor. As he addressed the ball with a six iron in his hands, Father Stone said to Grant, "Stopping bad guys, beautiful women throwing themselves at you, St. Mary's and a collar. If you could carry a tune, Stephen, you'd be a strange cross between James Bond and Father O'Malley."

Bond and Bing?

Stone's six iron landed a mere twelve feet from the pin. "And today, my friends, just call me, Father Jack, as in Jack Nicklaus."

"Oh, brother," said Ron.

Chapter 25

After golf and lunch, Grant arrived at St. Mary's at 1:30. Still in his rather sweaty golf attire of a blue polo shirt and khakis, he greeted Mrs. Tunney, "Hi, Barb. Anything new going on?"

Stephen was still annoyed about having to explain Paige Caldwell's visit to the church secretary. But he would have to do so before Barbara went home today.

"How was golf?" Tunney asked, as she got up from her desk to follow Stephen into his office.

"Played pretty well – shot an 84. But Father Stone actually putted today, and broke 80 for the first time in his life. Shot a 78. There'll be no living with him now."

Tunney said, "Well, good for him. I'll send him a congratulatory e-mail."

"I'm sure he'd appreciate it," said Stephen, as he sat down at his desk, flipped open and powered up his laptop.

"I guess this is an interesting day for many. You not only got a call from President Piepkorn's office this morning, but a representative from the Vatican phoned as well." She handed Stephen the two message slips, and with a Cheshire Cat-like grin, seemed to be awaiting a rather dramatic response.

Stephen decided to play it cool. He was feeling a rather unChristian-like impulse to tweak her after what Barbara passed on to Tom and Ron about Paige's visit. "Really? Thanks."

"That's it? This is the Vatican. You know. Rome. Catholics. The Pope."

"Yes, Barbara, I'm well aware of where the Vatican is, and who lives there." He put the messages down next to his phone, and started nonchalantly looking through the items in his inbox. *This must be driving her nuts.*

It was apparent that Tunney was barely able to control her curiosity. She said rather loudly, "Pastor, what's going on?"

"OK, Barbara, if you must know," Stephen said in an exaggerated tone. He actually had not thought through exactly what he was going to tell her and the rest of the St. Mary's church family. "I got wind on Saturday. The lady I met with after the service was someone I knew from my government days. They are working with the Vatican, and she briefed me. With Pope Augustine coming to the area next month, I've been asked to be involved with the visit in some way given my views on the issues in his letter. It's a kind of ecumenical outreach."

That's the truth ... in a legalistic sense.

She seemed impressed. "That's wonderful, Pastor."

"Thanks. I'm not sure what to expect exactly." *That most surely is the truth.* "President Piepkorn and I are going to chat about what I can and cannot partake in so that some of our more isolationist brethren don't get all riled up."

After presenting some updates on church finances, Barbara returned to her office. Stephen picked up the message slips. The Vatican call wasn't a foreign exchange number. Instead, it was a 212 area code, which meant Manhattan. And the message was from a Cardinal Juan Santos.

He dialed the number. "Hello?" The voice that answered spoke English, but with an accent. Stephen recognized it as Caribbean Spanish, perhaps the Dominican Republic.

"Hello. This is Pastor Stephen Grant. I'm returning Cardinal Santos' call from this morning."

"Thank you. This is Juan Santos, Stephen. May I call you Stephen?"

"Of course, Cardinal."

"Ah, no, no. Please, I insist that you call me Juan, at least when we are speaking privately like this. Our ecclesiastical titles can be left for more official moments. Don't you agree?"

Seems like a friendly guy.

"Absolutely. And I apologize for being out this morning when you called."

"Do not worry. Your assistant told me that you were unreachable."

Probably on the 14th green, judging by the time you called.

Stephen said, "What can I do for you?"

"Actually, it is what you can do for Pope Augustine. But first, I want to pass on my condolences on the tremendous loss that you and your parishioners suffered recently. I pray that you are holding up well in its aftermath."

"That's very much appreciated, Juan. To say the least, this has been a strange time for our church."

"Indeed, it must be. And when we meet face to face, if I can somehow provide support, please ask."

"That is very kind," said Stephen.

Santos went on, "Meanwhile, the Holy Father has asked me to extend invitations to you for a private meeting with him and for the various public events that are being planned while he visits the New York metropolitan area. Stephen, I'm sure you have read some version of the Pope's recent letter to Christian leaders?"

"I have, Juan."

"Good. The Pope has become aware of your work on behalf of ... what is it called? ... the New Ecumenism, and thought you would be in agreement with his intentions and goals?"

"Most certainly. I believe it's the most important step towards increased Christian cooperation in recent memory, perhaps in some 500 years. It could open the door to more substantive progress on the theological front."

"Excellent," replied the Cardinal. "Can the Pope count on your support for this effort, your presence next month in New York, and your willingness to put all of your ... skills to work?"

Choosing your words very carefully, Juan. Perhaps worried about who might be listening. Or, perhaps you're a bit paranoid, Grant.

Stephen said, "Yes on all counts. I just have to touch base with the president of my church to get permission, and make sure a local Lutheran pastor visiting with and cooperating with the leader of the Roman Catholic Church presents no, ah, problems."

"I understand," said Juan Santos. "But I am confident that there will be no such problems."

As am I, given what's playing out here already has been scripted for us. But we have to go through the motions.

"After I speak with President Piepkorn," Grant said, "I'll let you know. You are staying in Manhattan?"

"Yes, I will be staying here until Pope Augustine's visit, making all of the necessary preparations and so on. This is my personal cell phone. So, please call me whenever necessary."

"Thank you, Juan."

"No, thank you, Stephen, and God bless you."

"And you as well."

Well, one down, one to go. Might as well get it done now.

Grant dialed the number for the St. Louis, Missouri, headquarters. Piepkorn's assistant put him on hold.

"Hello, Stephen, how are you?" The voice hinted at Piepkorn's South Carolina roots. There was confidence and firmness as well.

Grant had met Dr. Harrison Piepkorn a few times, and heard him speak on a number of occasions. Piepkorn was an upbeat, positive and gentle person.

"I'm fine, Dr. Piepkorn. I trust things are well with you."

"First, it's Harry, not Dr. Piepkorn. Second, never mind me. How is St. Mary's faring in the shadow of the shootings? We've been praying for you."

"I know you have, and thanks. It has not been easy for many, but I've been blessed with a strong congregation."

"I was planning to visit and offer support, perhaps during the dedication of your new church building. But my focus, while still on you, was redirected in perhaps an even more unexpected way. Imagine my surprise when I was contacted by the CIA, FBI and Vatican about a local Lutheran pastor."

"I'm sure it was very unexpected."

"It sure was," confirmed Piepkorn. "By necessity, I also was filled in on some of your ... well ... past experiences. I have to say, Stephen, you are the most intriguing second-career pastor I've ever come across. Once you get past this next month, we must have dinner, so you can answer some questions I have rattling around my head."

"Well, of course," said Stephen hesitatingly.

"Don't worry. I know more about you now than I probably do about any other pastor in our church. Though we've only met in passing a few times, this knowledge has fostered a high degree of confidence. Have no worries about that dinner. It's just my curiosity. I look forward to hearing about your unique journey to becoming a pastor."

"It'll be my pleasure," said Grant.

Piepkorn shifted gears. "Well, now, about Pope Augustine. Let me first ask, and please be honest, Stephen, do you have any thoughts about becoming a Roman Catholic?"

"Absolutely not. I've written and spoken on the need for greater Christian unity, but that in no way should be taken as my pondering a move to Rome."

"Good. I thought not. But I had to ask. It would not look good if my representative to the Pope's visit decided afterwards to become a Catholic. By the way, I've read your reflections on the need for a more substantive ecumenism that gets beyond the social policy focus, and for the most part, I agree."

"Thank you."

"At the same time, as you well know, we have a few strong voices in our church that are not too thrilled by efforts to reach across denominational lines. That includes some who do not agree with the effort to reach beyond Lutheranism in order to work with traditionalists across the Christian landscape."

Grant said, "I'm aware, Harry. I've received some, let's say, colorful responses to a few articles."

"I'm sure you have," replied Piepkorn. "While most of the reaction has been overwhelmingly positive, you should read some of the negative feedback I've gotten regarding my positive comments about the intentions and opportunities that the Pope's letter presents. Given that reality, we have to be very careful with your invitation to meet with and accompany Pope Augustine in New York. Don't take this the wrong way. I'm not pandering, but at the same time, I want to avoid any and all unnecessary conflict and strife within our church."

"Completely understandable, and that's exactly what you should be concerned about as president."

"Given the nature of your invitation, the reason you were selected, and the potential for certain factions to stir up conflict with a pastor working with a Pope, we need to be deliberate."

Grant asked, "So, what would you like me to do?"

Dr. Piepkorn said, "Obviously, you have a clear responsibility to undertake this task. This apparently is part of the reason the Lord has placed you in this particular place and time, Stephen."

"I believe the same thing."

"Having said that, as your bishop, I will e-mail or fax a letter of pastoral permission, making clear that it is appropriate and imperative that you do this, and that you are serving as my official representative. Unfortunately, that means I will not be attending, so you owe me." He chuckled. "That, hopefully, will shift any heat from within our own church off you and onto me. This should be treated as nothing more than you being one of many non-Roman clergy meeting with the Pope. Let's hope that allows you to blend."

"Thank you, again."

"You're welcome," said Piepkorn. "But let me add a personal note. You're being asked to do something here that could turn out to be very important to the future of Christianity. I realize that, and you have my complete support and my most earnest prayers."

"That means a great deal."

"God bless."

"Take care, Harry."

They hung up.

Important to the future of Christianity.

Grant put his head down on the desk, closed his eyes, and took a deep breath.

Chapter 26

On Tuesday afternoon, it took Arnie Hackling and Kenny Hart a little over two hours to drive from the airport in Las Cruces, New Mexico, to reach the town of Martinville.

Actually, Martinville did not yet exist, except, for the most part, in the mind and business plan of Fred Gruber. It encompassed 36 square miles. At this point, the land featured little more than brush, bushes, the occasional tree, and lots of dirt.

That is, except for two doublewide, white trailers parked at the south end of Martinville, at the T of where two two-lane roads met.

As Hart drove closer in the rented Ford Explorer, Arnie gave him a look of irritation. "You're kidding, right?"

Kenny laughed and smiled. Hart's light-brown hair, five-foot-three-inch frame, round blue eyes, round glasses and ready smile gave him a nerdish, innocent look. That look served well when trying to ingratiate himself with clients and in building alliances. Hart served as an example of appearance not always reflecting reality. He was anything but innocent when it came to the business of politics.

"Trust me, this will be worth it," Hart said.

He pulled into the dirt parking lot next to a gray Silverado. It was the only other vehicle within sight.

The two men looked up at a large billboard in front of them, positioned between the two trailers. It said: "Welcome to Martinville! A Lutheran Christian Community." On the left side was Luther's seal, and on the opposite, with his arms stretched open wide, was a cartoon Martin Luther wearing a huge smile and saying, "Come live the Lutheran way!"

Hackling stared up through the front window of the Explorer. "Hmmm. I didn't know New Mexico was a hotbed of Lutheranism."

Hart said, "It's not. But Fred Gruber plans to make it one. Or, at least on these 36 square miles."

During their flight from Washington, D.C., Hart had given Arnie the rundown on Gruber. He had made a fortune by transforming his family's German bakery in Milwaukee into a line of baked goods for grocery stores. Gruber Baked Goods was still headquarter in Wisconsin, but had a national reach.

"Trust me," Hart said again in reaction to Hackling's continued expression of skepticism.

"I am, Kenny," Hackling replied in a less-than-convincing tone.

"By the way, if it comes up, I'm a disgruntled, conservative Episcopalian."

"Okay," replied Arnie stretching out the first syllable and sounding a touch bewildered.

Both Hart and Hackling tightened up their ties. The two men got out into the hot, dry air, and stretched. Each put on a suit jacket that had been hanging from a hook over the back seat.

They started walking over to the trailer with the "Office" sign. They stopped and turned when they heard the door of the other trailer open.

Standing at the top of a short set of wood stairs was a large man. He had swept back white hair drawn into a ponytail, and a white bushy mustache below a crooked nose that looked like it had been broken at least twice. His broad, six-foot-three-inch frame, which looked as solid as a brick wall, was clothed in a red-checker shirt, and blue jeans with a large silver belt buckle featuring crossed rifles. He wore tan cowboy boots, and the ensemble was complete when, after looking up into the sunny sky, the man slipped on a pair of dark sunglasses and a large, straw cowboy hat.

Hackling whispered, "That's a German baker from Milwaukee?"

Hart ignored the comment, and gave a wave to Fred Gruber. "Mr. Gruber?"

"You bet," bellowed a deep, gravelly voice. He came down the three steps and started walking over with a John Wayne-like gait. "Kenny?"

"Yes."

They met halfway with a firm handshake. Gruber also slapped Kenny's arm with his left hand.

"After our conversations, it's great to finally meet face to face," Kenny said with his trademark big smile.

"Sure is."

Kenny said, "Fred Gruber, this is Arnie Hackling, my boss."

"Pleasure to meet you, Arnie."

"Same here," replied Arnie in a far more casual, down-home tone than he ever would have used in the halls of Washington's power elite.

Gruber added, "You've got a good man here in Hart. Hope you treat 'em well."

Kenny gave a sheepish look. "Fred, come on."

Arnie said, "Believe me, Fred, I know. It's hard to find hard workers with character these days, especially in

Washington, as you might imagine. We've been lucky with Kenny."

Gruber smiled broadly. "Good to hear."

"By the way, Fred," Arnie asked, "you mind if we ditch these jackets and ties? Can't stand them, and you seem like a guy who doesn't stand on pretentious bull shit, if you'll excuse my language."

"Get comfortable," replied a clearly enthused Fred Gruber.

Hackling and Hart removed the ties they had just tightened and the jackets they'd donned, and threw them into the backseat of the Explorer.

Gruber said, "Now, come on into the office. I'll tell you the quick history and exciting future of Martinville, and then we can get down to business on stopping this damn Pope from turning us all into Roman Catholics."

They climbed the three wood steps into the office trailer. Inside was cool and comfortable, and furnished in rather typical light-wood paneling and matching office furniture. The exceptions were the wall hangings. There were pictures of Jesus Christ and Martin Luther, a large carving of Luther's Rose, crosses, and an angel. In the middle of the room, perched atop a large table, was a model of Martinville.

Gruber led them over to the miniature town. "What do you think?" The question clearly was directed at Kenny.

"Fred, this is impressive. Your description on the phone, and what's on the website do not do justice. It's visionary."

"Thanks. It's my dream, but it's all done to His honor." Gruber pointed to one of the depictions of Jesus on the wall.

"Amen," said Kenny.

As he looked over the model, Arnie said, "Why don't you give us a rundown on Martinville? The details?"

"With pleasure," Gruber replied.

The German Lutheran baker from Milwaukee, now a man of the West, dove in with gusto.

Martinville was to be a mixed community centered around the new Wittenberg-Martinville University. The university would include a huge, gothic-style "chapel;" three large academic buildings; a dormitory; student center; indoor athletic facility; baseball and softball fields; and a sizeable football/soccer stadium.

Regarding the stadium, Gruber volunteered, "We hope to name it 'Knute Rockne Stadium.'" He waited for the inevitable response.

Hackling obliged. "Knute Rockne – the famous football coach at Notre Dame? It doesn't get more Catholic that that. Why Rockne?"

Gruber smiled smugly. "It turns out that when Rockne led Notre Dame to its first two national championships, he was a Lutheran." Gruber could not hide his satisfaction in supplying this information.

The cowboy baker continued to explain the plans for Martinville. There would be detached single-family homes, townhouses, smaller retirement homes, a medical complex (named after Luther's wife as the Katharina von Bora Hospital and Nursing Facility), the Frederick the Wise Country Club, and an industrial park. A shopping village would offer all kinds of stores and restaurants, along with a micro-brewery producing Mighty Fortress Lager.

This time Kenny Hart asked the question Gruber apparently wanted to hear. "A beer named after Luther's most famous hymn?"

"Why not? After all, Luther set 'A Mighty Fortress is Our God' to a bar tune." Again, Gruber's glee was barely containable.

Gruber finished up by highlighting four churches sitting on the four corners of a major intersection in Martinville.

Arnie asked, "Why four? Why not one big Lutheran church?" After the question was out, Hackling spotted Kenny's slight shake of the head.

Gruber said, "Yeah. Unfortunately, some of us are more Lutheran than others. That being the case, we need a few different churches for worship. We expect to have churches for ELCA, Missouri Synod, and Wisconsin Synod Lutherans, and perhaps another from one of the really small Lutheran churches."

"I see," said Arnie.

"With serious differences just between Lutherans, you get an idea of why I'm less than pleased with what this Pope wants to do," said Gruber.

Kenny seized the opportunity. "On that note, Fred, why don't we get down to business on how we can work together to stop Pope Augustine?"

"Right. Grab some seats." Gruber sat behind one of the desks in the room, with Kenny and Arnie across from him. "Lay out your plan, men."

Hart gave him the basic agenda of the diverse coalition being built, and how they would work to undermine Pope Augustine's effort.

At the mention of the "Public Mission of Mere Christianity" in Wittenberg, Gruber interrupted to declare how much that part of the plan "pissed me off."

Gruber also made clear how much he hated the idea of being involved in any way with "those wackos on the Left."

Hart said, "I sympathize. The question is: What's worse? Strategically and temporarily working with these Lefties, or allowing Christianity to get watered down?"

"Put it that way, Kenny," Gruber responded, "and it's clear what has to be done. The immediate threat must be eliminated. What was it that FDR said about some prick the U.S. had to work with? He may be a son of a bitch, but he's our son of a bitch."

Arnie said, "Yes, he was talking about Nicaragua's Somoza."

"Right," said Gruber. "Of course, FDR was a son of a bitch as well." Gruber got a hardy laugh from his own observation.

At the end of the meeting, Gruber pulled Hart on the side. "I told my wife, Jane, about you, Kenny. And how you've been finding your way back from those crazy Episcopal days. We're encouraged about our conversations. We've been praying that you'll find your way to true Christianity in Lutheranism. You know, the Wittenberg-Martinville University will be needing someone with your skills and insights."

Kenny said, "Thanks, Fred. I appreciate you lending me an ear. You've been a huge help."

Hackling and Hart left the sparse beginnings of Martinville with a $150,000 check from Fred Gruber, along with Martinville t-shirts and mugs featuring the smiling Luther saying, "Come live the Lutheran way!"

Back in the Explorer, Arnie said, "Anything I should know about you picking up and moving to Martinville?"

Hart broke into a laugh and smile. "I was a lousy Episcopalian. No way I could be a Fred Gruber Lutheran."

"So, what was all that about then?"

"Well, I might have given Fred the impression that I was thinking about Lutheranism. And that's true. I have been thinking about Lutherans. Just not becoming one."

Arnie said, "Just make sure Fred Gruber never finds out that you're a ... What are you these days?

"Agnostic."

"OK, make sure our wealthy Lutheran baker in a cowboy hat never discovers your agnosticism."

"When we're talking about $150,000 checks, that will not be a problem, boss."

Upon their return to the airport, Hackling headed east back to D.C., while Hart flew in the opposite direction.

Chapter 27

It was less than a day later, but Kenny Hart now moved in a completely different universe from the one inhabited by Fred Gruber. Hart was in Los Angeles. Beverly Hills, to be exact.

In terms of weather, Wednesday was just about perfect. Cloudless and 80 degrees. In terms of relaxation, it wasn't bad for Hart either.

Todd Johnson was out at three fundraising appointments throughout the day. First, there was breakfast with a few studio executives. Then lunch with a group of pro-choice, mainly television actresses, who also happened to be quite beautiful. And in mid-afternoon, it was drinks with a couple of documentary filmmakers focused on environmental issues. Everyone coughed up fairly nice-sized checks to stop, as one person noted, "that fundamentalist Pope and those crazy Christians."

Johnson told Hart to take the day for a little decadence, and they'd meet later for dinner.

Hart slept until 8:30. Then he took advantage of the various amenities offered at the Beverly Wilshire where he and Johnson were staying.

Kenny started with breakfast in his classic European-style suite that looked down on Rodeo Drive and out to the Hollywood Hills. The meal featured a papaya fruit smoothie, freshly brewed coffee, and a breakfast special of crab hash, poached eggs and asparagus.

Next, he entered the Italian marble bathroom and its spacious, glass-enclosed shower.

Hart had made a 10:30 appointment at the hotel's famous spa for a Balinese massage. When he emerged from the 90-minute treatment, with its aromatic oils and effleurage, Kenny Hart appeared to be as relaxed as an individual possibly could.

He returned to his room, answered some e-mail and made a few telephone calls. By 1:30 in the afternoon, Hart was at the pool bar and café enjoying a lunch of a Pimm's Cup; a Cambodian Banana Blossom Salad with grilled beef, soy sprouts, hearts of palm and hot lime dressing; while all the time watching various women in tiny bikinis in and alongside the pool.

He slipped in a short nap and another shower before dressing in light gray pants and a white cotton button down shirt with black buttons.

Arriving downstairs, he rendezvoused with Johnson, who was waiting in the hotel's CUT restaurant, dressed in black pants and a dark gray shirt with white pinstripes.

As Kenny sat down, Todd asked, "Was your day sufficiently decadent?"

"Absolutely," Hart answered with a big smile.

"Good. You've done some great work over the past week. You deserved it."

"Thanks," said Kenny.

Johnson immediately shifted to the next topic. "OK, about tonight."

Kenny's job at dinner was to bring Todd up to speed on the 9:00 gathering that night with a group of about 20 actors, directors and writers who, according to a few participants Hart had spoken with, had come to a "shared spirituality."

The starters were served. Over Hart's Kobe Steak Sashimi with spicy radishes and Johnson's Maryland Blue Crab and Louisiana Shrimp *Louis* Cocktail, Hart began, without notes, to sketch out the key guests.

Becca Roberts and Jay Storm would play hosts at their Malibu estate on the beach. Hart noted that going back about 25 to 30 years, each had received Oscar nominations for films that failed at the box office, but were considered important artistically. Since then, while aging brought fewer and smaller roles, they remained the leading activist couple in Hollywood. Becca, along with Jay to a more limited extent, served as "entertainment's unofficial left-wing guardians." Hart added, "Political thumbs up from Becca Roberts and Jay Storm is the liberal seal of approval in television and movies." Hart also pointed out that, in recent years, Roberts and Storm had been attending, on occasion, a Unitarian-Universalist congregation, which, as Kenny said, "meant that you can believe pretty much anything."

Todd said matter of factly, "I've known Becca and Jay for years."

Hart appeared taken aback. "Of course, sorry Todd."

"No reason to be sorry. Let's get to the rest of tonight's lineup." Johnson took another bite of his crab and shrimp appetizer.

Hart noted that Johnny Cartwright would be in attendance. Cartwright had become famous and wealthy playing hard-core action heroes on the big screen for nearly a quarter century. But he transformed himself several years ago into a director of films with a pacifist message. "After two of those movies were made," Hart observed, "Cartwright was suddenly in with this group. Though it's interesting to note he's never recanted his blow-up-and-or-shoot-up-the-bad-guys movies."

Shari, the single-named music and movie sensation, was going to try to attend, but as Kenny noted, "She made no promises. We talked for about 40 minutes yesterday about her becoming a spokesperson for a kind of neo-paganism, basically Earth worshipping. It was quite a conversation. She sees spirits in people, animals, plants, rocks, water and even certain intense actions." Hart took a deep breath, adding, "You know, her real name is Mary Grazinowski?"

Todd chuckled. "No wonder she went with Shari."

Hart returned to his mental list of notable attendees.

The director George Francis would be in attendance. Kenny said, "Francis, of course, is one of the most successful directors in history. It's interesting that his biggest hits lack any glaring, controversial political message. Some bloggers actually argue that he's subversively conservative. But he quietly supports liberal candidates and causes with his considerable wallet."

"Francis is too smart to piss off a big chunk of the movie-going public by shoving politics down their throats. I've tapped him before. Let's hope we can do so again tonight," observed Todd Johnson.

Their dinners arrived. Hart chose a rotisserie duckling with lavender and thyme honey gastrique, while Johnson a Wagyu beef rib-eye steak.

Kenny forged ahead.

The comedian Jackie Boswell would be there with her wife Tawny. Kenny said, "It does not surprise me that Boswell is coming, given her background with the Catholic Church. When Jackie discovered" – Hart raised two fingers on each hand making quote marks in the air when he said "discovered" – "she was a lesbian about five or six years ago, you may remember she unleashed assorted attacks on Catholicism, and how her Catholic upbringing screwed with her mind and repressed her true sexual desires."

Todd swallowed a mouthful of the Japanese beef. "Yes. She stirred up the Religious Right. Got them out to the polls. Cost two of my Democrats in Congress their seats. Fucking dike."

"Her career went in the toilet for a while. But then Jackie and Tawny went to Massachusetts to get married. That got her back in the spotlight. Now she does a stand up routine on the troubles of gay marriage."

Todd said, "Take my lesbian wife ... please." He apparently enjoyed his own joke.

Hart smiled and continued with his verbal dossier. Carl Harding also would be in attendance. Harding was one of Hollywood's top writers. He was in demand for film and television scripts. Hart added, "Harding was one of the first in Hollywood to check into rehab for an addiction to sex. He now tells anyone who will listen that he was saved by the Force."

"Excuse me?" Todd queried.

"You know. Star Wars. 'Use the Force, Luke.'" Hart smiled and shrugged his shoulders. "Not long ago in Great Britain, a push was underway to have becoming a Jedi Knight officially recognized by the government and the United Nations as a religion. Some people argued that those following the Jedi code amounted to England's fourth largest religious group. Harding's a Jedi."

Johnson paused, seemingly reflecting on what he had just heard. "When we meet, should I ask Harding how the Force got him to stop fucking around?"

"Absolutely. He'll tell you something about the metachlorine count in his blood, and how that helped pull him back from the dark side. If you look interested, don't laugh and don't mention his two ex-wives, I have little doubt he'll fork over some big dollars. Harding grew up in a staunch Southern Baptist home and town. While Boswell rails against Catholics, Harding hates evangelicals and fundamentalists."

"But many fundamentalists don't like the Pope's effort either, right?"

"Yes. But these folks tonight do not differentiate. The Pope, Catholics, fundamentalists – they're all the same."

"Good to know," said Johnson.

"The biggest check tonight should come from a non-Hollywood source – Eric Helms."

"The computer-Internet geek. Where's he been the last couple of years? I haven't heard jack."

"Well, he sold Helms Intelligence at 25, and became one of the world's youngest multi-billionaires," said Hart.

"So, what's he doing with the billions?"

"Helms believes that the mind and the soul can be made immortal through technology."

"How so?"

"I'm not completely sure. I don't think Helms is too clear on it either. He's dumped a bunch of money into a facility just outside of San Francisco where a bunch of engineers and philosophers apparently are working on the answer. From what I can figure out, Helms believes that the mind and soul can be somehow transferred into or embedded in a computer chip."

Todd said, "Maybe Helms should get together with Jedi Knight Harding."

"It doesn't stop there. Helms believes it goes in the other direction as well. He envisions computer power reaching a point where not only will independent thought develop, but so will the soul. In his view, man's ability to create will make man a god."

"So, he has no use for *the* God then."

"He's rarely seen outside his San Francisco compound. But this effort by Pope Augustine has got him all jacked up."

Johnson said, "This is some lineup, Kenny. Again, excellent work. Anyone else in particular I need to know about?"

"Just two others. First, Neil Eller has made quite a mark for himself playing leads in romantic comedies. He's also a Scientologist. Eller is somewhat unique among the Hollywood Scientology crowd in that he enthusiastically speaks in public about humans as thetans with enormous powers, living through many lifetimes, and progressing to a state of clear, that is, self realization and spiritual freedom. He also is one of the few publicly hostile to Christianity."

"OK, the other?"

"That would be Hugh Zimmer, the director. Along with Francis, Zimmer will probably be one of the most mainstream individuals you meet tonight. I don't know if you've ever seen any of his movies."

Johnson shook his head.

Hart continued, "His films actually have been embraced by some Christian critics. Each movie points to or hints at the existence of an after-life or a higher power."

"Interesting. So, what's his beef? Why will he be there tonight?"

"In interviews, Zimmer makes clear his disgust for organized religion. He can't stand any formal religious structures, but his criticisms overwhelmingly are focused on Christians, particularly on priests, pastors, and evangelists being hypocrites. Keep in mind that his mantra is the same as most everyone you will talk with tonight. They say they are not religious. Instead, they are spiritual. That's the crowd tonight – spiritual, not religious."

"Spiritual, not religious. Got it."

In a rented light blue Corvette convertible, the trip – mostly along the scenic Pacific Coast Highway – from hotel to the home of Becca Roberts and Jay Storm in post-rush-hour traffic took 40 minutes.

Johnson drove inside the front gate and parked along the circular driveway. The other vehicles were a mix of some of the most fashionable and expensive cars on the planet, along with one tiny, red-and-silver-striped "Smart" car, and two limousines.

The estate sat on bluffs above the beach in Malibu, and featured three buildings set amongst rich, green foliage.

The modernist main house was overwhelmingly white inside and out, with the rear of the home dominated by enormous windows and extensive decking. The much smaller guest/pool house and staff quarters were similarly modern.

The front door to the main house was answered by a smiling Becca Roberts, who welcomed both Kenny and Todd with light hugs and air kisses. Roberts' black hair, which had been blond during her most productive film years, fell in waves onto the shoulders of a short, white dress that tightly wrapped around her very thin body.

Becca introduced Jay as her "partner." Jay Storm was over six feet tall and fit. He had thick pepper-and-salt hair, and a face that seemed to wear a perpetually quizzical look. With white, black or some combination of the two as the overwhelming clothing choice among the guests, Storm took a bold stance with a bright yellow button down shirt and brown pants.

Becca maneuvered herself between Todd and Kenny, slipped her arms along their lower backs, and explained that she wanted them to speak to her guests first and then mingle.

Within five minutes, Kenny and Todd had glasses of wine in their hands, and were being introduced to two-dozen beautiful people.

Todd did all of the talking. In 20 minutes, he explained Pope Augustine's letter and its nefarious intent, highlighted the dangers it presented to "open-minded people," and outlined how the Pope could be stopped, but only with the financial support of the people in the house that night.

It was then time for Todd, along with Kenny, to circulate around the room. Becca easily moved the two from guest to guest. After Todd and Kenny chatted and answered questions for each individual or group, Becca — with a beautiful smile, sexually-tinged charm and a firm touch – informed each person that they should make sure Kenny received their generous support before leaving.

Johnny Cartwright, the weathered-looking former action hero and now pacifist director, wasted no time. After Becca made introductions, he immediately pulled an envelope from the back pocket of his black jeans, and handed it to Kenny. Cartwright declared, "We've had enough holy wars. They're going to bring pain. Stop the pain." He then downed the full glass of wine in his hand and placed it on the closest white table. Cartwright nodded to the group, turned, and strode across the large room and out the front door of the house.

As Cartwright was leaving, in came Shari, followed by an entourage of four very large men in tight-fitting black pants and shirts that highlighted their formidable muscles. The fifth person in Shari's group was a short, thin, very pale woman with a jet-black haircut in Dutch-boy style. Her gothic fashion statement featured boots, leggings and dress all in black with assorted silver studs and spikes. She also displayed several dragon and cross tattoos, and ruby red lipstick. The woman was Shari's personal assistant, carrying an iPhone and wearing a Bluetooth earpiece.

The black-garbed individuals served as a striking backdrop for Shari. The singer-starlet's head was v-shaped, with hairline, eyebrows, eyes, nose and mouth all pointed sharply down in the middle. Small portions of her otherwise exposed tan skin were barely covered by a white dress that draped from behind her neck and underneath long blond, tightly curled hair. The dress came down loosely in front of her breasts, lowly wrapping around her waist, with the light material continuing down in the front and back, barely covering her not-so-private areas.

Shari walked quickly towards Becca. As Shari's tall, thin but muscular, 25-year-old body gyrated across the room, anyone mildly interested in what was hidden by her wrapping did not have to rely upon imagination.

"Mary Grazinowski," Johnson whispered into Hart's ear.

"Uh ... yes," replied an obviously distracted Hart.

"I'm so sorry about being late, Becca," said Shari in a voice hinting at some kind of vague European accent, as she and Becca lightly kissed each other's cheeks.

"Oh, Shari. I'm just so pleased you could come."

"Unfortunately, love, I have to run right back out. I promised a dear friend that I would help launch his new club tonight." She turned to Hart and Johnson. "But which one of these men is Kenny?"

Hart swallowed hard and cleared his throat. "I am."

She moved her body up against Kenny's. Shari was nearly a foot taller. She took Kenny's face in her hands, leaned down and gently kissed his lips. "I never spoke to someone like you before. Our telephone conversation yesterday was so ... spiritual. We must do more. We will do more."

She smiled. Kenny stared with his mouth slightly agape.

Shari turned to Todd – "Mr. Johnson" – and extended her right hand, which Todd smoothly took and kissed.

"A pleasure, Ms. Shari," Johnson said.

"Ooo, thank you. I want to help your effort to stop this Pope and the coming attack on those of us who find our spiritual reward in nature."

Todd said, "I just made a brief presentation to the group."

"And I am so sorry I missed it."

"I would be glad to fill you in on the details right now, if you like?"

"Not necessary. Becca told me about your work, my assistant, Melinda" – Shari nodded at the woman in black standing next to her – " checked everything out, and there is, of course, Mr. Hart."

"Of course," confirmed Todd.

She turned to Melinda. "The check."

The assistant handed Todd an oversized $1 million check for all to see.

Johnson said, "My, my, your generosity is overwhelming. This will make a tremendous difference. I'm sure you know how well funded the Catholic Church is."

"My financial advisers disagree with this, but I consider it an investment." She abruptly turned her attention back to Kenny, who seemed to have recovered his faculties. "Now, Mr. Hart, would you like to come along with me tonight? I believe we can find time for some deeper spiritual explorations. If you are interested?"

"Absolutely." Kenny looked at Todd, who raised his wineglass in the air.

And off went the nerdy Kenny Hart with the barely-clothed, tall, super model-like Shari.

Todd and Becca watched as the two left, with Shari's staff trailing behind. Johnson said, "Not exactly what I expected to see tonight."

"There are always surprises when it comes to Shari."

Johnson only seemed to be half listening, still staring with a degree of bewilderment on his face. He chuckled, and said, "I gave Kenny the day off. He enjoyed the offerings at the hotel. You know – spa, rest, food, etc. I asked him tonight if he had a decadent day."

"Well, I don't know if I'd use that precise word, but given Shari's mix of the spiritual and sensual, your Mr. Hart will likely experience an entirely new level of decadence this evening."

"Interesting." Johnson broke his quasi-day dreaming. "Well, who shall we chat with next, Becca?"

She placed her arm under Todd's. "How about Carl Harding and Eric Helms? They're right over there."

"The Jedi Knight and the soul-in-the-computer magnate?"

"I know. It sounds a little weird."

"Hey, to each his own. Who is to say?"

Becca said, "That's our point. Everyone has their own truth."

Chapter 28

Recent days were almost normal. Stephen heard nothing from Paige or the Pope's ambassador. He tried to slip back into the rhythm of doing the work of St. Mary's Lutheran Church.

But, of course, there was a painful reminder that jerked him out of any true sense of normalcy. That was the absence of music, voices, and youth activities due to the continued hospitalization of Scott, with Pam at his side. And the cloud of unknown regarding Scott's outlook. The church was just too quiet.

Every day since the shooting, Grant visited the hospital. During the first days, Stephen delayed entering the room more than once as either Scott or Pam, or both, were crying. But in recent days, they worked to regain the optimism that seemed to be engraved in the very essence of each.

It was Friday afternoon. Grant checked in at the front desk of the hospital. While strolling towards the elevator, he thought about the many times he'd made this walk to visit ill members of his church, some ready to be taken home to the Lord. He also noted each time that hospitals were never as clean and sterile as most people expected.

Grant took an elevator to the third floor. As he exited and the doors slid closed behind him, Doctor Batra was coming out of Scott's room.

Batra and Grant had spoken several times in recent days. The doctor smiled at Grant. As they shook hands, Batra said, "I have some good news, Pastor."

"That's needed," replied Stephen. "What's up?"

"Scott has gained feeling and movement in his legs. That's very positive. Nothing guaranteed, of course. But the outlook has improved markedly in the last day."

"Thank God."

"Yes, indeed," agreed Dr. Batra. "The left shoulder is healing fine. We knew that. But now we are finally getting indications that things went pretty well when we removed the bullet near his spinal cord. He has much work ahead. But his chances of walking again look very good."

"Well, it's hard for me to think of two people better equipped to make that happen," observed Grant.

"Yes. In just the days that I have known them, they are quite unique. Mature far beyond their years." Dr. Batra added, "Well, I must be going, my friend." They shook hands.

"Take care, and God bless."

"I certainly hope so," Batra replied with another smile.

A majority of surgeons I've met have been pretty darn arrogant. Not Batra. The happy surgeon.

When Grant knocked and entered Larson's room, Pam Carter launched herself out of the chair next to Scott's bed. She almost skipped across the room, jumped into Stephen's arms, and clenched him tight.

"Pastor, we have good news." Tears flowed, and Stephen could see pools of moisture in Scott's eyes as well. But these were all tears of joy.

Grant could not stop his own eyes from moistening. *Stop it.*

"I heard. I spoke to Dr. Batra out in the hall."

Pam finally let go. She took Stephen by the arm and led him to the bed. Stephen leaned in to give Scott a hug as well.

Grant said, "I'm so happy things have improved, Scott."

"With God's help, I'm going to get back on my feet," Scott declared.

"How about a prayer of thanks, Pastor?" suggested Pam.

"Of course." They each folded their hands and bowed their heads.

"Father in heaven, we are overjoyed and most thankful for this news of hope brought to Scott and Pam. We thank you for the gifts of healing that you have given to Dr. Batra and his colleagues here at the hospital. And in this time of questions, mysteries, doubts, strife and suffering, we thank you for keeping us strong in faith, helping us to put our trust in your love. We pray this in Jesus' name." And they all said, "Amen."

Scott looked at Grant, "Now, I've got some instructions for you and Pam regarding the choir and bells until I'm able to get back to work."

"Yes, sir," replied Grant with a salute.

Pam said, "Wait, let me get paper and a pen to write everything down." She pulled a small pad and ballpoint from her pocketbook, and sat next to Scott on the bed.

"Okay, I'm ready," she said with a smile that positively glowed.

They looked at each other, and briefly kissed.

"Hey, enough of that," said Stephen. "Get a room."

"We've got one," said Larson.

"Do I have to leave?"

Pam laughed. "Don't be silly."

Scott turned serious again. He said, "Pastor, I don't think I said thanks for doing what you did that night."

"Nor have I said thanks for what you did, my friend."

They nodded to each other.

"By the way, when are you two good friends going to start calling me Stephen, rather than Pastor?"

Pam answered, "I'd like that. But not around others. Then, out of respect, it's still 'Pastor.' OK?"

"Works for me," added Scott.

"And me," said Stephen.

Scott continued, "Now, Steve…"

"No, no, it's Stephen."

"Yeah, I know," said Scott. "Just wanted to tweak you. Now, Stephen, about keeping my music program in some reasonable shape …"

Grant looked at the young couple. *Thank you, Lord, for these friends.*

Chapter 29

Stephen left the hospital with more than enough time to arrive at the home of Jennifer and Ted Brees. Fashionably late was not an option for the ever-punctual pastor. To Grant, an invitation for 6:30 meant arriving at 6:30.

Though Jennifer had been active at St. Mary's for a few years, this was Grant's first visit to the Brees home.

Driving south from Main Street in Center Moriches towards Moriches Bay, Grant passed houses of varying architectural styles, from small salt boxes to large Victorians. Turning onto the Brees's road, he noted that this street was far less interesting – rather typically suburban, with ranches, split levels, and a couple of colonials.

At a dead end, though, was a long row of tall, thick hedges briefly interrupted in the middle by a driveway guarded with two light stone columns and a wrought iron gate, which was open. Grant checked the house number on the roadside mailbox.

He parked curbside, and grabbed a small box off the passenger seat.

Walking past the hedgerows, Stephen entered a different world – from middle-class suburbia to the seclusion of wealth. The neatly trimmed hedges bordered three sides of more than two acres of land, with a dock on the fourth side running along an inlet that emptied to the bay.

The driveway was concrete, with triangular tiles in various earth tones laid to form large circles.

To the right was something of a mini-entertainment complex. An L-shaped built-in pool featured a waterfall streaming down from a jacuzzi. A poolside bungalow apparently allowed for a convenient change of clothes, showers and refreshments.

There also was an artificial surface putting green and sand trap for practicing the short game, as well as a tennis court. That still left ample space for a finely manicured lawn, with no crabgrass in sight.

In the water were both a sailboat and motorized mini-yacht, with four kayaks stacked on the dock.

Expensive toys.

The driveway bent to the left, and ended in a large circle in front of a Tuscany villa-style home. The tan house with its terracotta roof sprawled out to 4,200 square feet. Across the circular driveway was a separate, three-car garage, with stairs on the side leading up to a second floor. Stephen noted a dark green Volvo station wagon, a red Thunderbird convertible, and a cream colored Cadillac Escalade.

Parked on the circle was a yellow Volkswagen bug, and a black Grand Marquis.

Grant thought the grounds and buildings offered a mix of Mediterranean, American Southwest, and upscale, waterfront Long Island.

He used the iron knocker on the arched, weathered-looking wood front door. It was opened by Jennifer, who was wearing a blue-and-white, horizontal-striped blouse with straps, a pearl necklace, a pleated skirt of the same blue material coming down below her knees, and white flats.

She smiled warmly. "Pastor, welcome." She kissed him on the cheek. "Come in."

"Thanks. And I have some good news."

"What is it?"

"Scott has gotten some feeling and movement in his legs. The doctor is very encouraged."

"That is excellent news. Thank the Lord," said Jennifer.

"Yes, indeed. Oh, and for you." Stephen handed Jennifer the burgundy-colored box tied with a gold ribbon.

"Oooo, a present. I sense chocolate. Mind if I open it now?"

"Of course not." He smiled.

She undid the bow, and pulled the top off. "Chocolate truffles?" She looked at him with a mischievous smile.

"Yes. Did I do good?"

"Absolutely. Mind if we keep this between us? It can become part of my secret stash."

"My lips are sealed."

"I knew I could count on you." She slipped the lid back on the box. "Let's join Ted and the others on the patio."

She led the way past a massive family room on the right with a central fireplace, and a large kitchen on the left, including a bar in the middle surrounded by eight high stools. The décor of Southwest and the sea again somehow worked.

In the extensively-equipped kitchen, four people – three women and a young man all dressed in black pants, white shirts and thin black ties – were at work apparently preparing the evening's meal.

Jennifer and Stephen exited through a doorway onto a covered patio, with spacious, open air arches all around. "Excuse me, Ted, Pastor Grant is here," said Jennifer.

The five people seated around a large, oval-shaped table stood up. Ted shook Stephen's hand. Brees was wearing a light blue, button down cotton shirt; cargo-style, egg-shell colored pants; and brown sandals. "Pastor, good to see you again. Welcome."

"Thank you, Congressman."

"It's Ted. Let me introduce everyone. You've already met Arnie and Kerri."

They greeted each other.

Brees then turned to a man with one of the most glaringly obvious toupees Grant had ever seen. It was a black, pompadour style wig that seemed precariously perched atop the man's head. With one good gust of wind, it looked like it would take flight. He wore prescription glasses that adjusted to the light with heavy silver frames, and was overweight, with nearly every extra pound seeming to rest just above the waist, presenting a shape similar to a pregnant woman carrying triplets. He wore brown docksiders, yellowish-tan pants, a white polo shirt, and a bright green sports jacket.

Ted said, "Pastor Stephen Grant, this is Jimmy Gianelli."

They shook hands.

"Jimmy." Grant thought he looked like a character out of a mob movie.

"Pastor Grant, good to meet ya."

"Jimmy has two strikes against him, Pastor. He got rich in the cement business, and is now the Suffolk County Republican Party chairman. Be careful with this guy."

Cement business? Maybe he is in the mob.

"Hey, knock it off," replied Jimmy with a hearty laugh.

"And the better half, as they say, is his lovely wife, Brittney."

Mrs. Gianelli clearly was less than half Jimmy's age. Grant put her at 25. Brittney had long bleach-blond hair, and she apparently liked to show off as much of her dark tan as possible. She wore a red shirt that was tied together below her breasts and above her navel. The white shorts were tight, and very short. She apparently lost her footwear somewhere before Grant had arrived.

Brittney's Long Island accent was heavier than her husband's. "Oh my Gawd, I ain't never been to a party with no priest before." She extended her right hand in exaggerated fashion, while her left kept hold of a champagne flute.

Stephen shook her hand, and said, "It's nice to meet you, Mrs. Gianelli. And you still have not been to a party with a priest. I'm a Lutheran pastor."

"Really? You look like a priest." She laughed, shrugged her shoulders, and took a large gulp of champagne.

Grant said, "Please, everyone sit down."

Ted asked, "Pastor, champagne?"

The congressman gestured to the young man who had been in the kitchen earlier and was now standing next to Grant with a single flute of champagne on a tray.

"Yes." He thanked the waiter, lifted his glass towards Ted, and took a sip.

The congressman said, "I'm a bit of a connoisseur of champagnes and wines. Do you know it, Pastor?"

"Forgive my husband's crassness," declared Jennifer.

"Oh, come on, Jen. Just having some fun," said Ted.

Grant knew that the wisest course was to play dumb. But he couldn't resist.

Stephen said, "Very impressive. I don't know the year, but Krug?"

Ted Brees seemed surprised and slightly disappointed. "Correct. Very astute."

"Thank you." Grant took another sip. He sat down at the table, while Jennifer responded to the ring of the doorbell.

Four other guests arrived.

George and Joan Kraus, both in their mid-thirties, were close friends of Jennifer's and members at St. Mary's. George, a lawyer with his own firm, was a medium build, with brown hair. He wore light gray pants, and a white shirt with thin, vertical gray stripes. Joan, a math teacher at Long Island Lutheran High School, wore a navy blue blouse with white polka dots, white capri pants, and open, strapped pink shoes. But it was the combination of spiky, bright red hair, milky white skin and large blue eyes that caught most people's attention. Their two teenage daughters were spending the night at friends' houses.

Shane Wilson and Meredith Harris-Wilson were the final couple, both in their late forties. Shane's combination of oval glasses and long, graying hair, along with a button-down argyle sweater vest, gave him a certain air of sophistication, amplified by the fact that he owned a local bookstore. But dull blue eyes and a slow, methodical speaking style raised doubts about the depth of his intellect.

Meanwhile, Meri, as most called Meredith, brandished short, curly, dark brown hair, and a great deal of gold jewelry on her fingers and wrists, hanging around her neck and from her ears. A one-piece, sleeveless, black dress stopped several inches above her knees. Meri was so thin that her skin seemed translucent, barely hiding blood vessels and bones.

Meri was a television producer at a local cable television news channel. Upon introduction, she chastised Grant. "Yes, there aren't many who do not know Pastor Stephen Grant these days. Although I'm upset that you never returned our calls for an interview, Pastor."

Stephen merely replied with a smile and, "It's nice to meet you."

Grant saw how everyone neatly fit into this group.

Arnie, Kerri, Meri and Jimmy Gianelli clearly were components in Ted's political model. Brittney merely came along with Jimmy, the local Republican boss, and Shane played the part of Meri's bored husband.

Meanwhile, Joan and George fit with Jennifer.

It was Grant who felt out of place. That was most glaringly obvious in terms of his clothes. Everyone else was dressed for a casual, summer evening dinner party. Stephen still wore his black clerical attire.

After innocuous chitchat, Jennifer announced, "Dinner will be in 20 minutes. In the meantime, Meri and Shane have requested a quick tour of the house. I believe Brittney and Pastor are the only other first-time visitors. Care to join us?"

"Absolutely," replied Grant.

"Sure, me too," said Brittney. She finished her second glass of champagne since Grant had arrived, and grabbed a fresh flute from another tray brought by the waiter. "Great timing, honey," she told him.

Jennifer played tour guide. She led the small group from room to room, telling the occasional amusing story about something in the home.

Grant worked to look politely interested. But upon entering a spacious room that Jennifer referred to as her "office-den," he no longer needed to try.

Before Jennifer could say anything about the room, comments were volunteered.

Grant said, "Interesting."

Brittney commented, "Holy shit. Whoops, sorry about that, Father."

Meri declared, "Hey, I'll go along with that – holy shit."

Shane simply chuckled. "Seems a bit aggressive."

It was a large, long room set two steps down from the hallway. The walls again were light tan, with a brown tiled floor. One wall featured large windows looking out on the water. To the right was a large desk with a computer, and bookcases behind it. But adorning the wall to the left and the one through which the doorway was carved was a massive display of swords and daggers.

Grant was far from an expert, but he could see that it was quite an eclectic mix. They seemed to range from a few

originals dating back probably to the Middle Ages –
including a Crusader sword, an Italian sword, and a
quillion dagger – to recently cast replicas, to a few from
various fantasy and sword-and-sandal films.

"Apparently your husband is not just a wine collector,"
Stephen said, as he closely assessed each sword without
touching.

"What makes you think these are Ted's?" replied
Jennifer, as she twirled her pearl necklace.

"I apologize," said Stephen. "I simply assumed."

"That's alright. This is my room. It's my office. My
sanctuary, really." As Jennifer said this, she looked around
the room with a hint of melancholy passing on her face.

Shane asked, "What do you do, Jennifer, that requires
medieval weaponry?"

"The swords and daggers go back to my undergraduate
days at UNLV. I was an English Lit major, and I simply
developed an interest in the tools and weapons of the
European Middle Ages. But I eventually narrowed things
down to daggers and swords. These are a hobby. In terms
of work, I'm an economist. After digesting all I could of
Medieval literature, I earned my PhD in economics from
NYU, and went to work on Wall Street. About four years
ago, I formed a partnership with two colleagues – one in
California, one in D.C. – and we do all kinds of research
and analysis for money managers and other Wall Street
types."

"Sounds like fascinating work," said Shane.

"It is. I've been quite fortunate," replied Jennifer. She
looked at Grant, who, after taking in the swords, was now
assessing the daggers. "So, what do think of my little
arsenal, Pastor?"

"He seems very interested," commented Meri in a tone
hinting at her own lack of interest or even revulsion.

"I'm usually a bow-and-arrow guy, but you have an intriguing mix of fine replicas and notable originals here, Jennifer."

"Thank you," she replied. "Well, let's finish up the tour before dinner."

Meri and Shane stepped out of the room. Grant motioned for Jennifer to go ahead of him. She stopped, turned, looked up at him, and said in a low voice, "A sharp shooter with guns, an interest in archery, and some knowledge of daggers and swords. You're full of surprises, Pastor Grant."

She turned and walked out.

Grant briefly looked around Jennifer's sanctuary one more time. *You offer many surprises as well, Mrs. Brees. I hope your weenie politician husband appreciates it.*

Before leaving, next to the computer on her desk, he spotted an olive wood carving of Jesus and the Apostles at the Last Supper.

Chapter 30

By 7:30, the two hosts and their nine guests were seated at a long, pine table in an airy dining room. The dinnerware was clay pottery with orange and tan swirled into the color mix.

Before the dinner began, Jennifer said, "Pastor Grant, would you mind saying grace?"

"Let us bow our heads." All did so with folded hands, but for Arnie, Shane and Meri.

After a brief prayer, the waiter moved around the table filling wineglasses with Pindar's "Spring Splendor," an off-dry, light blush wine. Next came the appetizer – New Orleans style crab cakes with a remoulade sauce.

As the final appetizer plate was placed in front of Ted Brees, Brittney Gianelli broached the subject that most in the room probably would have liked to avoid.

"So, Fath..., I mean, Pastor Grant, how did you stop that wacko lady who was shooting up your church?"

"Brittney, what the hell!" said her husband. But after several glasses of champagne, and now downing large swigs of wine, Mrs. Gianelli did not seem to care very much about her husband's scolding.

Ten sets of eyes came to rest on Stephen.

Oh, great.

"Well, I'm not sure how comfortable the others are." He glanced at Jennifer, then at Joan and George Kraus.

The Krauses nodded.

Jennifer said, "It's fine, Pastor. Not talking about it doesn't help."

Grant gave a brief rundown on that evening's fatal events, sparing dinner guests the most bloody details. When he finished, there was an uncomfortable silence, with the sound of forks clinking on plates seemingly amplified.

Brittney finally said, "Crap, you must be some shot." Then she laughed.

With a piece of crab cake resting precariously on her fork, Meri offered a statement with the inflection of a question: "I read in the newspaper that you were with the CIA?"

Grant swallowed some of his delicious appetizer. "That's right. Before I became a pastor, I was an analyst with the CIA."

"Quite a career change, that," observed Shane Wilson.

Before Grant could reply, Meri added, "You must be very disturbed about the most recent news regarding your former employer?" Again, it was a statement in the form of a question.

"You'll have to be more specific, Meri. Which bit of news was that?" Grant knew exactly what she had on her mind. He took a sip of the "Spring Splendor."

Early in the week, *The Washington Post* had a lengthy front-page story about the CIA using – as one agency source called it – "aggressive interrogation tactics" in February with a terrorist leader apprehended along the Afghanistan-Pakistan border.

The story offered fodder for both sides of the debate. On the one hand, there were gruesome details as to what exactly was done to the terrorist. He had been moved to a secret location in a friendly Arab nation. The CIA's tactics included waterboarding, and the removal of two fingers. On the other hand, the information gathered led to a terrorist cell being apprehended in Paris before it had the chance to carry out a planned assault on the city's transit system, as well as the location of weapon caches in Iraq and Afghanistan.

Ted Brees said, "Meri obviously is talking about the torture reports." The congressman looked at Meri and continued, "I'm sure we're all outraged by the CIA's actions. I know I am. Even the administration did not seem to be too pleased with its own agency. Torture can never be justified. It makes us just as bad as those we're trying to stop." He looked around the table. "Am I right?"

"Naturally," volunteered Kerri Bratton.

"I should say so," added Shane Wilson. "Those acts were nothing less than barbarism."

"Well," interjected Arnie Hackling, "then perhaps half the nation ranks as a bunch of barbarians, if you believe the polls. In the latest survey I saw on the topic, I think it was 45 percent approving of the CIA's tactics, 43 percent opposed, and 12 percent basically having no clue what's going on. Though, just because the others had an opinion doesn't necessarily mean they have a clue either."

"That does not surprise me," said an indignant Meri. "Since 9-11, too many people think that this nation is free to do whatever it likes as long as it's in the name of fighting terrorism."

Jimmy Gianelli countered, "Damn right. After those bastards knocked down the Twin Towers, it's no more Mr. Nice Guy."

Meri replied, "But, of course, those particular bastards you refer to died when flying planes into those buildings."

"You know what I mean. One terrorist ain't no different from the next. As they say, the only good terrorist is a dead terrorist. I think a lot of people in this country have let their guard down, and we're gonna get popped in the mouth again if we don't get serious," Jimmy declared.

Ted stepped back into the conversation, apparently seeking to heal the growing rift at his dining room table by finding some kind of common ground. "I think Jimmy and Meri are both right, in their own ways."

Jennifer appeared a bit exasperated with her husband's comment, "How can they both be right, Ted? They hold opposing views."

"First, we obviously cannot do whatever we like in the world," Ted said. "Second, while staying within the rules of civilized societies, we also must confront the terrorists aggressively."

Grant reflected that this was not the real difference between Meri and Jimmy, but no one looked enthused about contradicting the Congressman, who also was their host for the evening.

The waiter and waitress cleared away appetizer plates. Glasses were refilled. Then a poached pear salad was presented. It was drizzled with a port wine reduction, and served on a bed of baby arugula and crumbled Gorgonzola cheese.

The discussion about torture and the CIA labored on, with George Kraus reporting on how vague the law actually was on such matters. Meanwhile, Stephen simply enjoyed the food.

The entrée came. It was grilled tuna – caught off Montauk Point, according to the servers – resting on a bed of endive and topped with herb butter. Grant took the first bite, closed his eyes, and chewed slowly. It was easy to overdo tuna, allowing it to become dry, but this tuna was grilled to perfection.

It had been quite some time since his pallet was treated this well. *It would be easy to get used to this again.*

But after a few more bites, Stephen was pulled away from his gastronomic splendor.

Joan Kraus was the guilty party. She said, "Pastor actually held a fascinating Bible study on this topic a couple of years ago."

Ted Brees said, "Really? I assume the Bible doesn't look kindly on torture."

Joan responded, "Of course not. Well, not exactly."

"Not exactly! What do you mean by that?" asked Meri.

Joan looked to Grant for help. "Pastor can explain better than me."

Brees shifted his eyes to Stephen. "OK. Pastor Grant, you certainly are a man of surprises. Are you now going to become the first member of the clergy that I have ever heard of who defends government torturing prisoners?"

"That would be newsworthy," added Meri.

This could be fun ... or maybe not.

"Well, before diving further into this heated topic, I just want to say thank you to Jennifer and Ted for this wonderful meal. It's exquisite."

Jennifer responded, "You're quite welcome. I'm just so pleased all of you could come."

Grant noted Jennifer's genuineness, and how much of a contrast that was to her husband. *Strange how some people wind up together.*

"Yes, you're welcome," added Ted. "But you're not going to divert us from hearing about torture and the Bible."

"To some, perhaps the Bible itself is a bit torturous," said Shane with an expectant smile that quickly faded when no one laughed.

"Yes, well, where to begin so that this dinner party does not turn into a sermon that bores everyone to tears?" reflected Stephen.

"I can't imagine that, but we'll interrupt if it gets deadly dull," volunteered Ted.

"The entire issue actually goes back to St. Augustine in the early fifth century. He gets credit for the Just War Theory," Stephen began.

"Can any war really be just?" asked Kerri Bratton.

Grant was a bit surprised by Bratton's question, as he did not expect her to even be listening. "That was the question many early Christians had. Could they in good conscience serve in the military? After all, Christians are supposed to turn the other cheek, and even pray for our enemies."

"That's tough. But I remember hearing that in church. What about that?" said Jimmy.

Grant chewed and swallowed another piece of tuna, and then took a sip of wine. *Ironic. I'm getting more questions here than during Bible study at church.* He continued, "Augustine wanted to make clear that Christians did not have to be pacifists, that as citizens they could serve in the military. Over the centuries, Christians have used the Just War criteria, rooted in Holy Scripture, to gauge the moral legitimacy – or illegitimacy, as the case may be – of war."

"Like a checklist to determine if a war is right or wrong?" asked George Kraus.

"Well, it's not exactly that simple. There's plenty of room for debate. Some have interpreted the Bible and Augustine narrowly, and others more broadly. Just look at the deep disagreements among Christians over the Iraq War. But in a sense, you could look at it that way, as a checklist."

George persisted, "So, what's on this checklist?"

Stephen answered, "First, the Bible affirms the state's right to wage war when necessary. St. Paul, for example, warns in Romans 13 that if you do wrong, the state bears the sword. The Just War Theory dictates that war should be in self-defense, to secure peace, to establish justice, to protect the innocent, etc. And it should be a last resort, with a formal declaration."

"All that is based on the Bible?" asked Arnie Hackling in a skeptical tone.

"Actually, yes. I can e-mail you the exact verses, and a couple of articles that explain matters in detail, if you like?"

"No, that's OK. Thanks anyway."

Congressman Brees said, "Based on what you've laid out, Pastor Grant, all of us here can probably agree that the war on terror fits as a just war."

Grant noticed that Meri looked like she wanted to disagree, but restrained the impulse to speak out.

Brees continued, "But that doesn't mean it's okay to torture terrorists."

"Ted, you bring us to part two. The Just War Theory also governs how war is waged. There are two principles at work here. First is proportionality."

Brittney chipped in: "Proportiona-what?" Her face was contorted in over-the-top fashion, as a child might when completely confused by what an adult just said.

"Proportionality," Stephen responded gently. "War should be the lesser of two evils. It also means that the force being used should be appropriate to deal with the evil at hand. It should be what's needed to establish peace and hopefully improve things, but not more than that."

"And the second principle?" asked Ted.

"That would be discrimination."

Brittney again emerged ever so briefly from what clearly had become a stupor. She said, "Oh, discrimination. That's not good."

"In this case," Stephen said, "discrimination is good. Here it means that war should only be waged against enemy combatants and military targets. Civilians are supposed to be protected."

Grant paused. He could tell that other than the Krauses and Jennifer, this was completely new ground for the rest of the dinner party. Stephen reflected that this was particularly disappointing, but not surprising, when it came to a member of Congress. Since he had been doing most of the talking, Grant was the last to finish his tuna.

As plates were cleared and the servers asked whether each diner wanted coffee or tea with dessert – and offered various flavors of each to pick from – the conversation continued.

Shane asked, "Now, Pastor, how could torture possibly fit into this theory?"

"Obviously, it generally doesn't."

"But Joan indicated that it could based on one of your Bible studies," Ted pointed out.

"You asked earlier, Congressman ..."

Ted held up a finger and shook his head at Stephen.

"Right, I'm sorry," said Grant. "You wondered before, Ted, if I was the only member of the clergy who could justify torturing a terrorist. I don't know if I'm the only one. But I'd go farther and assert that in the rarest of circumstances, it actually could be a moral imperative to, for lack of a better word, torture a terrorist."

This generated a bit of buzz around the table just as fresh berry Napoleons were being served. Strawberries, blueberries, raspberries and blackberries were layered with crème anglaise, and sprinkled with dark chocolate.

Grant knew that the banter among the others wouldn't last. He soon would be thrust back into the middle of the fray to explain his seemingly outrageous declaration. Therefore, he took the first opportunity to grab a forkful of the Napoleon. Again, it was delightful.

He managed two more mouthfuls before Meri demanded, "Reverend Grant, please explain yourself."

Well, "Reverend."

Stephen said, "Let's delve into a little Ethics 101. Consider the very rare cases of extracting information from the ticking time bomb or a terrorist leader who has information about various campaigns. The case can be made that in limited, grave circumstances where mass murder looms, aggressive interrogation tactics – yes, some kind of torture – is proportional in terms of being the lesser of two evils, in terms of the evil at hand, and as the way of furthering peace. Also, it is specifically directed against an enemy combatant. And since it's the job of terrorists to murder noncombatants, the purpose is to protect civilians."

"That's a little too neat and tidy. It's rarely that simple," said Meri.

"Indeed, I should say not," added Shane.

"I would agree," said Stephen. "And that's why I'm talking about very unique circumstances. But there are such circumstances. What do you do when a nuclear, chemical or biological weapon attack is imminent, and the authorities have captured a terrorist who quite likely has information regarding the attack, but he isn't talking? Is some kind of coercion, even torture, justified to get that information and save dozens, hundreds, or perhaps hundreds of thousands of innocent lives? Wouldn't such action be morally justified? Some say no. In fact, many, perhaps most, Christian clergy would say no. I disagree. In fact, I would argue that the clergy, in this specific case, offer an answer that is reprehensible under any moral calculus, including the Just War Theory."

It was Jennifer's turn to ask a question. "I don't necessarily disagree with you, Pastor, but how would you respond to those who say that human life is sacred, and that by sanctioning torture, we would be telling the world something quite different?"

Stephen replied, "Good thought. No doubt, this is dicey stuff. And in most instances, I would agree with that assessment. But it also is not a moral absolute. Again, I believe there are very grim instances when torture actually can become a moral imperative for a government. Remember, we are still talking about the state here. And with innocent lives on the line and the opportunity existing to extract information to stop some kind of WMD attack, then refraining from the use of torture in that unique circumstance would tell the world and one's own people that human lives are not sacred."

Other than Brittney, who was concentrating very hard on trying to get berries from her Napoleon onto a fork and then into her mouth, everyone else around the table was silent.

Finally, Joan Kraus said, "See, I told you he would do a better job explaining it than I ever could."

"Yes," said Ted. "I know I don't agree with you, Pastor, but I'm not so clear as to why any more."

"I'll tell you why, Ted," declared Meri. "You disagree because this is just another case of a right wing fundamentalist using God to justify war." She looked at Grant barely hiding her disgust.

"I think Pastor makes some good points," said Jennifer. "But while I've momentarily gained the floor, it looks like everyone is done with dessert. If you like, I thought we could take our coffee, tea or drinks out on the patio, and continue our conversation there. It looks like an ideal night, and the breeze should keep away the bugs."

People broke into their expected groupings once outside. But Stephen was surprised as Arnie Hackling sought him out. *Oh crap, not with the politicians.*

"Pastor Grant, I noted what you said about Christians disagreeing, and I wanted to get your impressions about this letter that Pope Augustine sent out," said Hackling.

But before Grant could say anything, Meri broke in, "You're asking a Lutheran pastor what he thinks about the Pope? Lutherans have no use for popes. Why are you asking?"

Grant decided to listen.

"Is this off the record?" asked Arnie.

"Of course."

"It's not really a secret, or at least it won't be next week. I'm helping to organize opposition to the Pope's agenda when he arrives here in a few weeks."

Well, well, this could be interesting.

"Really? What are you up to?" inquired Meri.

Thank you, good question, Meri.

"The Faith, Trust and Freedom Foundation is raising funds and organizing efforts so that assorted concerned groups have the ability to be heard."

"And which groups would those be?"

You go, Meri.

"You'll hear more details on Thursday, but it's actually wide ranging. Some are focused on the environment and social justice. They're worried that this could divert some Christians from their issues. Others are disconcerted by an unwarranted incursion by religion into politics. Many Democrats, in particular, are worried that this could worsen their God gap at the polls. The list is pretty long."

"Sounds like it," replied Meri. "Who else?"

Arnie said, "It's interesting to see that both liberal and very conservative churches seem less than thrilled with the Pope's call for 'A Public Mission of Mere Christianity.'"

Mental note: Tell Ron he was absolutely right.

Meri added, "What's the plan?"

"Again, without getting into specifics right now, extensive paid and earned media plans are being mapped out."

Turning to Ted Brees, Meri asked, "Are you involved at all, Congressman?"

Ted said, "This is the first I've heard of Arnie's undertakings, and I have no intention to weigh in. This is a religious matter, and it would be inappropriate for me, as an elected official, to be involved, other than to say that all sides obviously have the right to be heard." He continued, "Just between us, this is a no-win in terms of the politics. If you engage, you're bound to piss somebody off. It's prudent to just keep something like this at arm's length."

Ah, profile in courage.

Grant drifted away from the group's conversation as it wandered to Brees's reelection strategy, and was quite pleased that he was not cornered to weigh in.

For the rest of the night, Grant spoke with the Krauses and Jennifer about various people and projects at St. Mary's, including what could be done to heal the congregation after all that had happened recently.

When Stephen declared his intention to be the first to leave for the night, Meri said, "Pastor Grant, while I strongly disagree on the torture issue, you made your case well. I know you did not want to talk to us after the St. Mary's shootings."

"Don't take it personally, Meri, I didn't get back to *The Today Show* either."

"Well, that's good. But I'm wondering if you might consider being a guest on a weekly panel show we're kicking off dealing with spiritual, justice and moral issues. It's called 'Long Island Spirituality.' Wayne Walters, a local radio guy, will be the host. We're hoping to get representatives from various faith traditions for each show. What about it? Care to be a panelist once in a while?"

Stephen replied, "That's not really my thing."

"I think you'd be ideal," pressed Meri. "I really do. At least think about it some more before saying no. Here's my card. Do you have one?"

Grant gave her a card.

"Thanks, I'll be in touch."

Jennifer escorted Grant to the front door. Just before he departed, she asked, "Pastor, if you could say a prayer for me on the way home tonight, I'd appreciate it."

"Absolutely. Is everything okay?" *Stupid question.* "What happened at St. Mary's is not something easily put aside."

"You'd think that was the problem. But it's actually something else that has me worried. It could just be my imagination. I hope so. But I won't bother you with it."

"Jennifer, I'm your pastor and a friend. You can't bother me. Let me know how I can help."

"Thanks. Hopefully, it's nothing." She shifted demeanor, appearing to push aside doubt, making a decision and summoning strength. "I appreciate you coming, and hope you enjoyed yourself."

"Of course. I just hope I didn't shock your dinner guests with my musings on torture and terrorists."

Jennifer smiled. "I always welcome a lively discussion over dinner. Besides, you're absolutely right. Nothing wrong with holding a terrorist's head under water in order to stop the next attack. Anyway, good night, Pastor. See you on Sunday."

"Good night, Jennifer."

As he walked down the driveway, Grant thought about Jennifer's sudden sadness and request for prayer. *As they say in 'Star Wars," I've got a bad feeling about this.*

He began praying for Jennifer Brees.

Chapter 31

By midnight, most of the dinner guests at the Brees home had been gone for at least an hour.

Only Arnie Hackling and Kerri Bratton were left. The two were still strategizing with Ted on the campaign, which was about to kick into high gear in just four days, right after Labor Day.

Jennifer tidied up the patio a bit, and then stretched out on a chaise lounge with one of the latest books applying economics to areas not traditionally falling into the economics realm. The genre had proliferated after the success of *Freakonomics*.

Hackling yawned for a third time. Then, as a houseguest, he said his good nights and went off to bed.

Kerri Bratton thanked both Jennifer and Ted, and was set to leave.

Jennifer said, "Ted, you relax. I'll walk Kerri to her car."

"Uh ... right. Thanks for coming, Kerri," said Ted. "We'll talk in the morning."

Jennifer strolled out of the house shoulder to shoulder with her husband's chief of staff. Kerri appeared uncomfortable, as she spoke more and faster than she had all night. "I want to thank you again, Mrs. Brees. It was a wonderful evening. The food was fantastic. That dessert was particularly awesome. I hope it wasn't too fattening, or

I'll have to spend extra time at the gym tomorrow." Bratton laughed nervously.

Looking at the yellow Volkswagen bug, Jennifer ran her right index finger along the car, and said, "This is a cute little car. Seems to fit you well."

"Yes, thanks. I like it."

Jennifer turned and leaned her backside against the driver's side door, and folded her arms. She looked Kerri Bratton in the eyes. And in a calm voice, Jennifer asked, "Are you and my husband screwing around, Kerri?"

"What!? No! Why would you say that?"

"Oh, I don't know. Having a gun held to your head has a way of waking you up to what's going on right around you. Clears the mind. Makes you appreciate life more. Quite frankly, I've had a growing unease about you and Ted for some time. But I chalked it up to my imagination. Funny, I even asked God to forgive me for just entertaining such thoughts. But the more I see how the two of you interact, I feel less guilty about my suspicions. Should I feel guilty about them, Kerri?"

This time Bratton did not respond. In fact, she went from avoiding Jennifer's stare to returning it unflinchingly.

Jennifer continued, "You see, Kerri, I've learned during my eight-year marriage that Ted doesn't do well compartmentalizing. It's all or nothing with him. And from where I'm sitting, it looks like he turns to you now for campaign advice, for major career decisions, and so on. The two of you have developed a close trust that most people – other than me – probably would not pick up. I think that trust either sprang from or led to sex. Am I right?"

Several seconds passed. Bratton finally responded, "Maybe you should talk to your husband, Jennifer. It sounds like you two have issues. Now, if you'll please step out of the way, I'd like to get in my car."

Jennifer unfolded her arms, and strode past Kerri back towards the house. She entered, closed the front door, and leaned her head on it with eyes closed. She remained in that position for over a minute.

Her husband emerged from the kitchen with one of the extra berry Napoleons on a plate and chewing. "Jen, you OK?"

She raised her head, and wiped a tear from the corner of each eye.

"Actually, Ted, no. I'm not OK."

"What's wrong?"

"Well, where should I start?" She turned and faced her husband with intensity and anger on her face. "I know. How about less than two weeks after nearly being gunned down in my own church, it's become pretty clear that my husband is having an affair with his hot young chief of staff? If it wasn't my own marriage, I might even laugh about this being a caricature of a member of Congress unable to keep his own member out of his beautiful, young staffer. That's what's wrong."

Ted put down his Napoleon. "I'm sorry, Jennifer. This isn't how I wanted it to come out, especially not now. Did Kerri say something to you?"

"Fuck Kerri," fired Jennifer. "Oh, that's right, you've been doing that, you little piece of shit."

"Can't we talk about this reasonably?"

"Actually, we can't. You've destroyed our marriage. That's pretty damn unreasonable on your part. Why should I be reasonable about what you've done?"

They stood in silence, as Jennifer struggled to hold back more tears.

Ted asked, "What do you want me to do?"

"How about the truth, for a change?"

"Alright. I love Kerri, and was planning to ask you for a divorce after the election."

"And how long has this been going on?"

"Almost three years."

Jennifer took a deep breath in response to that piece of information. "Well, thank you for that one moment of honesty, Ted. Even that truth perfectly captures what you've become, what you're really all about."

"What's that supposed to mean?"

She ignored his question. "Now, there's a second thing you need to do. Get out of this house tonight."

"Tonight?" replied Ted. "It's after midnight on the Friday of Labor Day weekend. And what about Arnie?"

"Arnie, right. I'm supposed to be worried about Arnie. Take him with you."

"What? No. Not tonight. I'll make plans to leave tomorrow."

"Ted, you can go tonight under the cover of darkness and the veneer of calmness, or I can make this very embarrassing in front of your treasured political adviser. Your choice."

Ted and Jennifer Brees again stared at each other.

Finally, Ted said, "Shit! Fine!"

Chapter 32

The phone woke him up at 8:30. Grant had planned to sleep a good deal later on Saturday for the first time in months.

So much for that.

It was Joan Kraus. "Pastor, I'm sorry, but I thought I should call. Jennifer called me about an hour ago. It sounded like she had been up all night drinking. She and Ted had a major argument. Jen said her marriage was over. That Ted had been having an affair with his chief of staff, Kerri ... what's her name?"

"Bratton."

Why am I not surprised?

"Right, Bratton."

"Is Jennifer OK?"

"Well, that's just it. Jen said she had to clear her head, and was heading out on the bay in her kayak. I told her not to, or to wait until I came over. But she was adamant, said she didn't want to talk to anyone. By the time George and I got to her house, she was gone and so was one the kayaks."

"Did you call the police?"

"Well, no, I'm not sure what I would tell them. My friend might have been drinking, and she might not be in the best of shape for kayaking. Oh yes, and she's

Congressman Ted Brees's wife and I think their marriage is falling apart."

"Yes, I see what you mean. Where's Ted?"

"I have no idea. That Arnie Hackling was supposed to stay the night. But he's gone, too. I think Jen might have booted them both out during the night. She told me on the phone that Ted was gone."

"Alright, sit tight. I'll be there in ten minutes."

"George is about to take out one of the other kayaks and start looking for Jen."

"Tell him to hold off until I get there. Didn't I see a motorized boat tied up to their dock?"

"Yes, but we can't find the keys."

Once Grant arrived, they didn't need the keys to get the Sunseeker Predator 52 going. George Kraus seemed impressed with his pastor's ability to hot wire a yacht. Stephen and George started down the inlet slowly and then out to Moriches Bay, which was smooth as glass, scouting for Jennifer Brees in her kayak. They left Joan at the house in case Jennifer returned.

Considering the various directions she could have gone, they were lucky. It took them a half hour to come across Jennifer. She was leisurely paddling along in a yellow kayak, wearing a bright red, one-piece bathing suit, but no life vest.

Kraus maneuvered the Sunseeker alongside her, while Stephen peered over the side. He spotted a bottle of wine sitting between her legs. The wife of Congressman Ted Brees seemed to be in her own world, not even glancing over as the boat came close.

Grant called out, "Jennifer, are you OK?"

That broke her out of the trance. She looked over and there was a slight delay before recognition kicked in. She smiled. "Pastor Grant, what are you doing here? And why, pray tell, are you and George driving my boat?" She smiled mischievously. "Did you steal it?"

"Borrowed it."

She laughed.

Grant continued, "We were worried about you; weren't sure where you were. Joan said you and Ted had a rough night."

Her expression changed. "Ted." She sighed. "Ted is an asshole. Oh, sorry about that, Pastor." She picked up the bottle and took a slug of wine.

"No problem. I've heard worse."

The anger melted away from her face once more as she looked at Grant. "I bet you have. You've probably heard a lot of people's personal shit."

"You could say that. Why don't you climb onboard? We'll hook up the kayak, and head back to your house. Then we can all talk – you, Joan, George and me."

"No," she said rather sternly.

Oh great, she's a tough drunk.

Jennifer continued, "I'm going to have a few Mimosas and brunch at the Bayview Boat House." She pointed at the wood building with large windows on a dock about 200 yards away.

"Is that really a good idea? Why not Mimosas and brunch at your house?"

She thought for a moment. "No. I think not. I don't want to be in that house right now. So, I want to sit at a table outside the Boat House, look at the water, eat, and drink Mimosas."

Grant said, "But ..."

Jennifer interrupted: "You can either join me, if you like, or turn around and return my boat." And off she went in her kayak towards the Bayview Boat House.

As she paddled away, Grant smiled a bit.

Well, she knows what she wants.

Grant looked at George Kraus. "Any ideas?"

George shrugged his shoulders.

Stephen said, "OK, let's pull alongside the Bayview. I'll keep an eye on Jennifer at the restaurant. You take the boat and kayak back to the Brees's house. Then get Joan, and drive over here to pick us up."

George replied, "Sounds like a plan." He looked at Jennifer paddling away. "She's such a nice person. How could Ted do this to her?"

"Human beings are capable of all kinds of uncaring, unthinking acts. We're all sinners, George, but sometimes it seems that some are a hell of a lot better at it than others."

By the time, Jennifer had arrived, Stephen and George were waiting for her.

Even without any sleep and too many drinks, Grant could not help but notice her beauty and lithe movements as she climbed up the ladder, stood on the dock, and ran both her hands through her short auburn hair. She attempted a confident stride up to George and Stephen, but wavered due to the wine, and whatever else she drank.

"Gentlemen, shall we?"

"Jen, I'm going to get the boat and kayak back to the house. Joan and I will catch up," said George.

"Alrighty." She turned to Grant. "Shall we, Pastor?" Jennifer stuck her arm through his, and started walking up the dock. Grant was pulled along at first, but quickly recovered and led her to a table.

Stephen pulled out a chair for Jennifer at one of the round wooden tables with a red-and-white umbrella. She sat down a little clumsily, but recovered and gracefully crossed her legs.

Jennifer Brees looked across the table at Grant. "Let's see. I've had two unthinkable life crises over the past two and a half weeks, and you, Pastor Grant, have been around for each. Saved me once, and I bet you're trying to save me again this morning."

A waitress came over to the table.

Grant said, "I'm sorry. We came by sea rather than by land, or the front door. Is that a problem?"

"Not at all," said the chirpy, early-twenty-something brunette, who was wearing a white "Bayview Boat House" polo shirt. "I'll get you some menus."

Jennifer replied, "Thanks, but we don't need menus. We'll have two Mimosas and the brunch buffet." She looked at Grant. "If that works for you, Pastor?"

"Sure."

The waitress said to Grant, "You're a pastor? You don't look like a pastor."

Grant was wearing gray shorts and a red polo shirt. "Off duty, so to speak."

The waitress shrugged. "Right, OK. I'll get those drinks and you can head up to the buffet whenever you like."

"She's right, of course," said Jennifer.

"About what?"

"That you don't look like a typical pastor. You're too good looking."

"Some of my colleagues, I think, would take offense. And I'm guessing that there aren't too many economists around that look like you."

"I'll take that as a compliment."

"As it was intended."

OK, she's married, drunk and a parishioner. Let's take this somewhere else. Like back to her problem.

"If you don't mind me asking, Jennifer, what happened after I left last night?"

"Remember, I asked you to say a prayer?"

"Yes."

The waitress brought two Mimosas to the table, and reminded Stephen and Jennifer that they could go up to the buffet. Stephen thanked her.

Jennifer took a long draw of the cold orange juice and champagne mixture through a straw. "After the shooting at church, I started trying to sort out my life. I had suspicions, but the more I thought, it was pretty clear that Ted and Kerri were involved in more than just the campaign and politics, if you know what I mean. I decided to watch them really close last night. And I saw it. So, I confronted Kerri as she was leaving, and then my dear husband. And that was that. I threw his ass out of the house, along with his political adviser. Ted can't take a shit before checking with Arnie." She laughed at that comment, and sucked down the rest of her Mimosa.

"Time to eat," she said, jumping to her feet suddenly and knocking her chair backwards.

"Don't worry, I'll get it," volunteered Stephen.

Jennifer was swaying much more as they journeyed to the buffet table. She heaped large amounts of scrambled eggs, bacon, and hash browns onto her plate, along with a few pieces of French toast and syrup.

Where is someone that thin going to put all that food?

Stephen was hungry, but ate sparingly as he was focused on guiding Jennifer along until he and the Krauses could get her home.

While Jennifer ate, Stephen spoke. "So, do you know what you're going to do? I mean about Ted?"

Jennifer Brees responded with a mouthful of eggs, which Stephen knew she never would do sober. "Ha! I've got some interesting ideas running around this jilted head of mine."

"Nothing rash, I hope. You should take time to think things through," Grant advised.

"Maybe."

Grant saw a dramatic change in Jennifer. She looked very tired and drawn. She put her fork down, sat back in the chair, and rubbed her forehead.

Stephen asked, "Everything OK?"

"My ... I don't feel too well ... I'm sorry ..."

Oh crap, she's going to puke. Move. To the bathroom.

He got up, gently took her left arm and helped Jennifer out of the chair. But it was too late. She said, "Oh ... no." Suddenly, Grant had chewed and partially digested brunch on his shirt, shorts and right leg.

The edge of the dock was closer than the bathroom inside. When Jennifer paused to apologize – "I'm so sorry" – Grant half carried her to the water.

"It's OK, Jennifer. I've got you. Just let it out." He held her around the waist and gently patted her back.

Jennifer Brees vomited into the bay, started to cry uncontrollably, and asked, "What's wrong with me?"

"Nothing, Jennifer," Stephen told her. "Trust me, there is absolutely nothing wrong with you."

You just made the mistake of marrying a sleazy politician.

Chapter 33

Arnie Hackling had barely managed four hours of sleep. He and Ted Brees landed in Kerri Bratton's townhouse during the middle of the night. Hackling left Brees to ponder his personal life and campaign with Bratton, and went east for an appointment.

The rented Grand Marquis that Hackling was driving proved rather wide for the narrow, gravel road leading to Peconic Bay. Just after 10:00 AM, he barely made the tight turn into the dirt driveway of Andre Tyler's small beach house.

Tyler opened the screen door on the porch.

"Hello, Arnie. Did you have trouble finding the place?"

"No, no problem. How are you, Andre? Good to see you, rather than just e-mailing each other."

"I'm fine, considering everything."

"Yes. I read that you knew the woman who died after murdering those people at St. Mary's Church," Hackling said without any detectable emotion in his voice. He stood on the tiny plot of weeds that passed for a front lawn, and took a moment to look around. "Just a few yards from the water. All pretty low key. Nice."

"Not what you're used to, of course, inside the Beltway."

Arnie continued, "You were a Beltway boy once."

"True," said Andre, "but that was a long time ago. I kept my principles."

"Ah, yes, for nearly four decades now, ever since Georgetown, you've been the last principled man."

"Maybe not the last one, but damn close to it."

The two former college roommates went inside to two cups of coffee and bagels at Tyler's small kitchen table. There was no reminiscing. It was down to business. That business was a proposal from Tyler on behalf of the Our Children, Our Planet Foundation.

Despite Hackling's familiarity with Tyler and his group, Andre made the full pitch. The foundation's origins, its impressive board and roots at the state university, and a record educating the public and elected officials on numerous environmental issues, including a well-oiled earned-media machine, as well as producing its own radio, television and Internet spots. The proposal featured several Internet videos – which also would be converted into two television and radio spots with strategic buys – and a comprehensive earned media effort featuring press releases and opinion pieces.

Tyler assured Hackling that the campaign would be ready for launch by the middle of the coming week, and would run for at least the two weeks up to the Pope's arrival and the three days that Augustine would be in the United States. There, of course, would be public protests following the Pope around. Andre also outlined a domestic and international agenda that could operate all the way to the Wittenberg gathering in the spring. The entire plan came with a checklist of specific goals with accompanying dates.

By the end of the 90-minute presentation and discussion, Arnie Hackling looked satisfied. He and Todd Johnson were looking for a group to take on the Pope's proposal from the environmental angle, and this fit their agenda perfectly.

"Looks good and thorough, Andre," Hackling confirmed. "Let's do it."

He pulled out the checkbook for the Faith, Trust and Freedom Foundation, and signed a check made out to the Our Children, Our Planet Foundation for $2.5 million.

"Thank you," said Andre Tyler, and even offered a very rare smile.

Chapter 34

In the business world, Yuri Kamenev would be known as a multi-tasker.

His first job was with the KGB. After the fall of the Soviet Union, Kamenev went freelance with Boris Krikov, doing work in the nuclear secrets and assassination industries. After Krikov's death at the Barcelona Olympics, Kamenev moved deeper underground. Not only was his damaged knee repaired, but he was transformed into a new man by extensive plastic surgery.

After recuperating, Kamenev continued to be well paid for his lethal skills. Those resources allowed him to pursue a flair for writing, and he began a journalism career.

As Robert Johns, Kamenev passed himself off as a disgruntled, ex-patriot American mercenary for hire. As Roy Wallace, he was a freelance British journalist who wrote from exotic and dangerous locales around the globe.

There was the private, dark and well-paid life, and the public life of shedding light on many parts of the world. Editors around the world came to like Roy Wallace. He provided clean, accurate copy, and worked cheap.

Sitting in an apartment in Syria on September 11, 2001, Kamenev clearly enjoyed watching death rain down on the Americans.

He spoke to the screen, "The Americans will respond, perhaps against places like this." He glanced out the window. "Perhaps it is time for Roy Wallace" – he slipped into a British accent – "to take a job somewhere safe." He continued to stare at the screen. "Like in the U.S. Americans just love Brit journalists." He laughed. "Ironic, right under their noses."

So, with an impressive international portfolio and a bargain price, Roy Wallace became a reporter and columnist with the *Philadelphia Sun.*

Roy Wallace quickly grew as a respected journalist in the Philadelphia area, while gaining some attention in New York and Washington, D.C. circles as well. His columns were all about coldly assessing the politics and strategy of his topic, and that occasionally included religion. His penchant for pithiness, and that flawlessly manufactured Brit accent, even made him a favorite guest on local talk radio.

No doubt, Roy Wallace, Robert Johns and Yuri Kamenev were the same man, just doing dramatically different jobs depending on the day.

On this particular Sunday morning, Wallace was sitting in a Roman Catholic church in Philadelphia, listening to a homily about Pope Augustine's upcoming visit and waiting to interview a few parishioners once Mass was over.

Chapter 35

Pastor Stephen Grant brought the cup up to the lips of a kneeling Jennifer Brees.

"The blood of Christ shed for you."

The last thing you probably want today, Mrs. Brees, is wine.

He continued down the Communion rail during Sunday's early service, as Jennifer blessed herself, stood up, bowed, and went back to her seat.

Later, on the way out of church, Jennifer spoke softly, "Pastor, I apologize for yesterday. It's embarrassing. I haven't been that ..." – she paused, glancing over her shoulder, and shifting closer to Grant – "... sick from being drunk since college."

Grant replied, "No worries. How are you feeling?"

"I've got dry mouth and a nasty headache. But when it comes to you-know-who, I think I've already moved from sadness to anger. Don't know if that's good or bad." She lowered her voiced to a bare whisper. "I'm plotting my revenge."

Grant raised an eyebrow.

What does that mean?

"Don't worry," said Jennifer. "Nothing drastic. Just a lesson to be taught." She smiled, but quickly grabbed her forehead as if the smile made her headache worse. "But right now, I'm going home to drink some iced tea, take a few more aspirin and go back to bed."

"Don't drink iced tea. Gatorade's better."

"OK, thanks." Off she went, gingerly putting on her sunglasses before hitting the bright sunshine outside.

After the late service, no one lingered on another warm, late summer day. Grant changed into blue shorts, and a gray Cincinnati Reds t-shirt. Sipping on a cold Coke in his office, he had the laptop open and was tuning in to the Reds-Cardinals game via MLB.com.

His mind wandered, worrying about Jennifer Brees. But he was jerked away from his thoughts.

"Are your Reds winning?"

Grant looked up to see Paige Caldwell leaning in the doorway. She was wearing a yellow bikini with white flowers, and a white, mesh sarong wrapped around her waist. Her feet were bare.

Whoa. He swallowed hard.

"Game's just starting."

"Can I tear you away, Stephen? I need to bring you up to date on Augustine's visit."

"Sure, but how about a little heads up next time? And you don't exactly look dressed for a meeting, particularly at church."

"Do you like this? I bought it yesterday." She spun around with her long black hair swinging. "What do you think?"

He watched with appreciation. "You look beautiful, as always, Paige."

"Thank you, Stephen."

There was a short, awkward silence.

"Sit down. Bring me up to speed," said Grant.

"No, not here. We're going to the beach. I want sun, a swim in the ocean, and something to eat. I'll bring you up to date along the way."

On the water with another woman?

"Paige, I don't know. I have to ..."

She folded her arms, and interrupted, "Stephen."

Oh, what the heck. Pretty sure Paige won't puke on me.

"OK, let me throw on some trunks." He opened one of the drawers along the bottom of the armoire, and pulled out a red bathing suit with white striping.

Paige sat down in the armchair, crossed her legs and smiled. "Please do."

"I'm changing in the men's room. Be right back."

She was driving a white Ford Mustang convertible, with the top down.

Grant threw a small gym bag in the back seat, with a towel, the blue shorts, a white polo shirt and a pair of underwear inside. "Nice ride. The agency upgrading its rental deals?"

"Somebody cancelled, and I wound up with this." She started the engine, and asked: "Where are we headed?"

"Depends. We can stay close at Smith Point beach. Or, if you want to drive a bit, we can head out to Montauk, and hit the beach at Hither Hills. There are some great spots for food."

"How long of a drive?"

"Dicey on Labor Day weekend. Without traffic, it'd be a little over an hour. We might luck out if people are already where they want to be on Sunday afternoon."

She pulled up to the STOP sign at the bottom of St. Mary's driveway. "We've got GPS. You know my driving skills. The top's down. It's a gorgeous day. Think I can take Montauk in 75 minutes?"

"Go for it," said Stephen.

Paige smiled, hit the gas, and fish tailed as she turned, leaving tire marks in her wake.

Though not behind the wheel, Stephen was enjoying the ride in the convertible. Besides, the driver was pleasing to his eyes, and brought back a flood of memories.

The conversation heading east on Route 27 was all business, namely, Caldwell briefing Grant.

She seemed to be methodically going down a mental checklist. Pope Augustine would arrive at Kennedy Airport in 17 days, on a Wednesday morning. He would stay and have his meetings at a sprawling retreat house on the north shore of Long Island in Nassau County. Originally built by a wealthy businessman after the Civil War, the layout fit nicely for security purposes, and had more than ample space to host the various invitees from parts of American and Canadian Christianity.

That first day's afternoon would feature a Mass and meeting with various cardinals. Day two would be about the first "Public Mission of Mere Christianity" ecumenical gathering, followed by a larger press conference and then a smaller group of select journalists for a more intimate Q&A with the Pope. There would be a Mass at the Meadowlands football stadium in New Jersey on Friday, with Augustine flying out to Mexico City late that afternoon.

Grant's job was to stay as close to the Pope as possible – starting at Kennedy Airport, staying at the retreat house, being at the various gatherings and backstage at the stadium Mass, and then accompanying Augustine to the airport for his departure.

As they sped eastward and spoke about what was expected from Grant during the Pope's visit, St. Mary's Church not only shrank in the rearview mirror, but in Stephen's mind.

Grant knew that Pope Augustine would be one of the most well-protected people on the planet during his global journey. Stephen understood that his role was to serve as another layer of protection, offering unique value in that any troublemakers would not necessarily suspect that one of the guys in a clerical collar near the Pontiff would be a trained killer.

Paige made excellent time – weaving in and out of some angry drivers, while managing not to do so when a local town police car lurked. Slowing down to roll through the village of East Hampton, she reported that there was a group of concern in Queens.

Coming to a stop at a red light, she said, "It's a tremendous opportunity for us. The FBI flipped someone on the inside who now regularly passes along information. They've been training for a number of years. But given their location, we're waiting to hear if the Pope's visit activates them."

"A little dangerous letting a cell like that hang around, don't you think?"

"Not given the intimate role of our mole."

Soon this stretch of the South Fork of Long Island narrowed down and the traffic evaporated. Caldwell sped by summer homes with large windows, seafood restaurants, and a few hotels on the ocean dunes.

Grant instructed, "At the fork, bear right and slow down."

"Yes, sir."

Caldwell turned onto Old Montauk Highway.

"Just up here, you can make a right into Hither Hills."

The state park was a campground on the beach. Grant handed Paige money for the parking fee, and they made a right into a nearly full parking lot.

Paige said, "Time for a little R&R. No more Pope talk."

She brought the roof up. They each grabbed their small bags of clothes and towels.

Grant asked Paige, "Want me to see if we can get chairs and an umbrella from the office?"

"No, I brought a blanket."

"Sounds good."

Over the dunes and onto the beach, they chose a spot at the left most point within the lifeguard boundaries, and spread out the blanket by the edge of where the ocean rolled up the sand. The waves were peaking at about three or four feet.

Paige stood looking at the ocean made blue by the sky. At the same time, Grant took in Paige's hair blowing in the wind, the additional freckles that had popped out during their drive with the top down, and the fitness of her body.

As she turned, Grant shifted his own gaze to the water.

"I'm dying to dive in," she said. She unclipped and dropped the white sarong on the blanket.

"Let's do it," Stephen replied. He pulled his shirt off to reveal a muscular chest and flat stomach.

"Very fit, Stephen. You're still pretty hot, well, for a man your age." Grant was five years older than Paige.

"Very funny. It's not easy with so many church dinners involving white sauces."

Paige flashed a brief hint of displeasure with the comment, but quickly recovered. "Shall we?"

They ran to the water, both plunging into a wave just before it broke.

The crisp cold of the water engulfed all of Stephen's body. It was invigorating. He swam under the surface for several yards, and then came up for air. Paige broke the surface about two yards in front of him. Drops of water glistened in the sun as they rolled down her face and fell from her nose and chin.

The two swam and floated. Beyond the remote chance of prying ears, Grant asked about some of the people they had both worked with at the agency. Paige provided rather thorough updates. And they laughed about joint and individual mistakes of the non-deadly variety.

A little sunbathing followed, then a stroll down the beach while admiring a few homes up high on the dunes. And finally, another swim.

After Paige declared her hunger, they hit the showers to change for dinner.

Stephen quickly tugged on the polo shirt and shorts. When he came of the men's room, Paige already was waiting in tropical print shorts, and a white and blue tie-dyed cardigan. Her hair was pulled back in a ponytail.

"Took your time?" she asked.

"I love a hot shower after swimming."

"Mmm. If only they were co-ed, we could have enjoyed it a lot more."

"Don't be bad."

"Why not?"

Grant redirected the conversation. "Any preferences for dinner?"

"You seem to be the local expert."

"How about the best New England clam chowder around, and excellent lobster salad?"

"Perfect."

A few minutes later, Stephen directed Paige to pull into a parking lot of stones.

"Really, this is it?" said Paige. "What's with the big lunch sign?" The roadside, brown-and-white wood building had bright red, white and blue awnings. A large blue sign with white letters sitting atop said, "LUNCH," and under that "LOBSTER ROLL."

"Trust me on the food," Stephen assured her.

After waiting twenty minutes, they were seated at a wood table positioned in front of a screened window. The décor was all from the sea – nets, mounted fish, and a shark jaw.

Paige told Stephen to order. He didn't even look at the menu. It would be a crock of New England clam chowder, a lobster salad platter, and a Samuel Adams beer for each. Once the chowder arrived, crammed with potatoes and large pieces of clam, Paige took a spoonful and was won over.

Grant decided this was the time to move the conversation away from the local charms.

"The other day, you teased me about not wanting to hear about what you've been up to since I left the company."

She broke the infatuation with her soup only long enough to say, "Yes."

"You've pretty much brought me up to date on the work front. What's been going on in your life, Paige, beyond the agency?"

"I know you'll disapprove, Pastor Grant."

Stephen could not miss the tone when she said "pastor."

Paige continued, "But my work is my life. That used to be the case with you as well, Stephen."

"Still is. It's just that my work has changed."

"There was a time when you thought the work I do – that we did – was important."

"I still believe that, Paige. If I didn't, I wouldn't have signed up for the assignment with Pope Augustine. But I was called to move on."

"Ah yes, the call." She made air quotes when saying "call." "I remember when you first told me that you felt a calling. Are you still sure about that, even after what's happened over the past two-and-a-half weeks? Haven't you felt the pull in recent days, back to our work? And, I have to ask, Stephen, what did you do after 9-11?"

9-11. Knew that was coming.

"Paige, 9-11 was … was hard. It was the only time I doubted my decision to become a pastor. I nearly returned to the company in the following days."

"What did you do?"

"I thought about where I would do the most good, and the answer became clear, eventually."

"And now?"

"I don't think these last few days have been about bringing me back to the CIA. I think I've been put in this position regarding the Pope's mission and visit for a reason, for a purpose."

"Do you think God put you in this spot?" The tone verged on mocking.

"Sure do."

The waitress brought each a large platter with lobster salad resting on a bed of lettuce, along with cole slaw and french fries. Grant watched Paige taste her first forkful.

"How is it?"

"Delicious."

They ate in silence for a few minutes.

Stephen finally spoke. "Paige, being a pastor is where I'm supposed to be. You made me feel like I was supposed to apologize to you for making this decision. Are you ever going to accept and be at peace with this?"

"When you told me that you were entering the seminary, I was angry. But after you left..."

"Actually, I believe you were the one that walked away."

Paige ignored his interruption. "I got back to work. I thought about you now and then, but after a while, it became a passing regret. But when the director called me in about you on this assignment, I started thinking more about seeing you again, and how good we were together. I've never worked so well or made such wild love with anyone else. I realized I missed that, and wondered about getting it back."

"I can't go back to that work, Paige, and there has to be more than sex in a relationship. No matter how great that sex is."

Paige took a sip of her beer. "The kind of relationships normal people have are not an option for me, Stephen."

"Why not? People at the CIA have spouses and families, Paige. You know that."

"Spouses? Families? Are you kidding?"

"No, I'm not."

"Of course, a lot of people at the agency have families. But you also know that most people that do my job – what you used to do – do not have families."

"But how much longer are you going to do that job? Don't you think about what's next? Don't you wonder if there's something more?"

"No, I don't. This is who I am, and what I want to do."

Well, no surprise.

"It's different for me," said Stephen.

"As much as I hoped otherwise, Stephen, I knew, I felt, this would be the result. But at the very least, I thought we could stoke some old fires."

They finished eating in silence. The check came, and Paige beat Stephen to it. "I was going to pay for a beachside room tonight, but that's not in the cards. Is it?"

"No, it's not."

God, give me a break. I haven't had sex in ... too depressing to count.

"So, Pastor Prude, I'll just pay for dinner."

The waitress took the check and her credit card.

"Now it's all business, Stephen?"

"Come on, Paige. Everything we've been through, 'just business' doesn't cut it. I still care about you. Why not friends?"

Did I really just give the "just friends" line to Paige?

She looked at her bottle of beer, and drank down the last few drops. "Just friends with someone that I've already had unbelievable sex with is new for me."

"Me, too."

"I guess friends it is, lover boy," said Paige.

"Fair enough," said Grant.

Stephen knew that it would not be that simple given their past and Paige's personality. But he promised himself that after this mission, he would not lose contact with Paige Caldwell again.

"At least, for now," Paige added with a seductive smile and tilt of her head.

Lord, help.

Chapter 36

"I received word this morning. We have the go-ahead," reported Saddam Ali, quietly. He and his wife, Areebah, had just arrived at the home of Nuri and Lama al-Dawla.

Saddam gulped down half of his tall glass of lemonade on an overcast, humid day.

"Excellent," said Nuri al-Dawla. He was standing over a gas grill, turning chicken breasts.

In the very tiny backyard to the house on the Van Wyck Expressway, the al-Dawlas and Alis, along with their employees Randall al-Hakim and Abdul ed-Din, appeared to be enjoying the Labor Day holiday. Nuri made sure that the neighbors and local customers saw the two couples celebrating the holidays of their adopted country.

Lama and Areebah were casually leaning on the fence, talking and laughing with members of the Rodriguez family that lived next door. Lama was the shorter of the two, with shoulder length dark hair and large round eyes that seemed on the verge of popping out of her head. Areebah was tall and thin, with much darker eyes and long hair that reached the small of her back.

Abdul and Randall sat across from each other under a blue-striped umbrella at a picnic table playing a game of chess.

It was exactly as Nuri instructed. The outward appearance could not possibly give away anything about the cell's preparations to launch an assault as payback for America's allegiance with Israel and participation in the oppression of the Palestinian people, for Afghanistan and Iraq, along with its countless offenses against Islam by average Americans in their day-to-day lives.

When the food was ready, they sat around the picnic table with a very American-looking feast of chicken, corn on the cob, fruit salad, and baked beans. But the conversation focused on their plan for assassinating Pope Augustine I after his arrival in New York City.

Nuri and Saddam had agreed that getting close enough to the Pope for death to come via a knife, gun or even a bomb would not be possible. So, they would roll the dice. The group of six would split into three teams. Two would be watching from one of the highest rooms in one of the tower hotels just outside Kennedy Airport. They would relay which route the Pope's motorcade would take exiting Kennedy Airport for the drive to Long Island's North Shore. Two routes were the most likely options.

One route was eastbound on the Belt Parkway. Saddam had rented – and had to pay a highly inflated price for – the top floor of a two-story commercial building with perfect site lines close to the highway.

The second, ironically, was the second floor of the al-Dawla's own home and training facility. The Van Wyck Expressway ran directly from and into Kennedy Airport.

If the authorities decided to take a more circuitous route for security purposes – for example, by heading towards Manhattan and then doubling back via the Brooklyn-Queens Expressway – then the teams would be mobilized to three predetermined locations – two on overpasses and the other along the service road – closer to the Pope's destination.

Nuri noted that the Van Wyck route was preferable. The house sat well above the highway, offering the best strategic position to launch the attack. The Al-Dawla home, quite simply, offered the high ground. However, the building along the Belt Parkway offered a better angle.

If the motorcade took a different route, the chances for failure increased. Each team had to be prepared, Nuri emphasized, to improvise to carry out the mission. Nuri and Saddam understood quite well that even failure could be transformed into victory.

The attack would be carried out with shoulder-launched armor piercing missiles. They had acquired two dozen West German Panzerfaust 3s a few years ago. The team along the Belt Parkway would have half of the launchers ready for firing, with additional missiles available for reloading, if time somehow permitted. The Van Wyck home team would have the remaining launchers and ammunition loaded and ready.

The strategy was to take out one of the lead vehicles to stop the convoy, and then focus the remaining firepower on the Pope's armored limousine. They counted on the missile fire to be overwhelming.

Escape routes were laid out, though the team actually launching the attack faced a dubious future. But such a death in the name of Allah, Nuri reminded each, undoubtedly would pave the way to paradise.

Chapter 37

About the same time that the terrorist cell in Queens was plotting the murder of Pope Augustine I, similar barbecue fare was being served some 64 miles east on green grass stretching behind of the rectory St. Bartholomew's Church in the village of Eastport.

Tom and Maggie Stone began hosting an annual Labor Day barbecue when they arrived at St. Bart's. Over the years, with the number of Stone children growing to six, it became a running joke that the party celebrated sending the kids back to school.

Since it was open to the entire congregation, and given St. Bart's recent growth, this was the largest Stone back-to-school gathering yet. More than one hundred guests were expected throughout the afternoon and early evening.

Father Ron McDermott and Pastor Stephen Grant were among the attendees. And while Tom and Maggie played hosts, Ron and Stephen volunteered to handle the grill. Hamburgers and hot dogs were on the menu, in addition to chicken.

Stephen welcomed the opportunity to be away from the main flow of the party. He was able to just cook, drink a few beers, talk with Ron without being overheard, and watch.

After his experience with Paige the day before, Grant's attention was drawn to the interactions of the families.

Many young people were in attendance. Friends of the Stone children ranged from pre-teens to recent college graduates. But there also were a few couples with babies and toddlers.

He watched married couples who immediately went in different directions after arriving.

Other couples congregated together in familiar groupings.

Some parents hovered over their children. The contrast was clear between those operating in sync, and those who disagreed over the most basic child-rearing issues.

Still others all but ignored their kids. Those seemed to be the children causing the occasional, minor trouble.

Two families arrived, said their hellos, and then largely kept to themselves. The children stuck close to the parents, and the parents mainly spoke with each other and their own kids.

Ron interrupted Stephen's reflections on family life. "You're pretty quiet. Can't even get you talking about the Reds still being in the race for the National League Central."

"Sorry, Ron," said Stephen. "Lost in thought."

They each took slugs from their respective cans of Budweiser. On the eight-foot-long and three-foot-wide massive grill, Stephen flipped the burgers and rolled the hot dogs, while Ron was in charge of chicken. One St. Bart's family – parents and three kids – approached the food tables with empty plates, and each went away having to carry their bounty with two hands.

Stephen watched as the mother aided the youngest, and the father directed the brood to a free table.

"And what exactly are we pondering, Stephen?" asked Ron. "Pope Augustine's visit?"

"No. That's not it."

Stephen pulled a couple of burgers and a few hot dogs that were ready to the side of the grill, away from the hot coals.

"Are you going to tell me, or shall we just barbecue in silence?"

Actually, Ron, you're probably the best person to talk with.

"Do you really want to hear about my female angst?"

Ron said, "Well, since you don't want to talk baseball, and otherwise have chosen silence, I guess I have no choice. Just throw me another beer first."

Stephen opened the large white cooler a few feet away, reached into the frigid mix of ice and water, and pulled out two beers. "Hey, I found two Beck's. Stone's apparently hoarding the good stuff."

"Not any more. Let's drink them," whispered Ron with a grin.

They popped the bottles open, and sipped the German brew.

"All right, now I'm ready for the roller coaster love life of Pastor Stephen Grant."

"Very amusing. You've been hanging around Tom too long."

"True enough. So, what's up? Is this junior high, and you want me to tell someone that you like her?"

"Sometimes you're a schmuck."

"Thank you, Pastor."

"You're quite welcome, Father." Stephen took another sip of beer. "Actually, I went to Montauk after church yesterday with Paige Caldwell."

"Ah, yes, the beautiful old flame."

"We went over some details on the upcoming papal visit. But then we hit the beach, and caught up with what each of us has been up to."

"And?"

"It was a great afternoon, and we went to the Lobster Roll for dinner."

"Love their New England clam chowder," Ron chipped in.

"Me, too. Anyway, I found myself pondering what we had talked about at Rock Hill the other day."

"Which part?"

"If Paige was interested in something more than sex."

"Oh, right. You know, most clergy aren't wrestling with how to deal with the beautiful spy who wants to jump their bones."

"You really are hanging around Tom too much."

"It's the beer talking."

Stephen continued, "The bottom line is that she really is not interested in anything more than her current life. The pastor and the spy do not have a future together."

"I'm sorry, Stephen."

"I can't say that I expected anything different, and I'm not sure that I really wanted anything more with Paige." *Is Jennifer a different story?* "Even if I did, Paige's priorities would have had to have changed dramatically."

"Yours apparently did at some point."

"True. But hers did not. Some people in places like the CIA, FBI and NSA simply cannot imagine doing anything else, and have a difficult time making room for much else in their lives. That's Paige."

They dealt more burgers, hot dogs and chicken.

Stephen said, "Ron, how do you deal with knowing that you will not have a family of your own? Is it somehow easier when it's simply not an option?"

"During seminary and immediately after being ordained, I never gave it much thought. But after just a few years of parish life, looking around at the various families and experiencing the sometimes intense loneliness, regret and envy creep in on occasion. The party line, of course, is that we're better able to serve Christ and the church without our own families. Blah, blah, blah. But I've come to think that many priests would do far better work for the Lord with the love and support of a family. And no, I don't think it makes it any easier knowing that a wife and kids are not an option. There is resignation, sometimes a lack of hope."

"I see."

"Actually, I don't think either of us fully understands what we're missing. Look at Tom." Ron pointed at Tom across the yard. He was throwing a baseball around with two of his sons, along with a couple of other kids. The look on his face was one of joy and contentment.

"Until you find a non-spy to settle down with and have some kids, and for the rest of my life, we certainly can care for, and even love, others. We can give advice to the families in our parishes, and feel like we're part of some of those families. And in a sense, we might be. Of course, I also have four siblings, and my parents are still around. I know you remember your mom and dad with love. But I don't think any of this captures what a parent feels towards his own child. I suspect it is a completely different kind of love and acceptance. It's on a level that we can speculate on and intellectualize, but not truly grasp without being parents ourselves."

They were silent for a while, with just the sound of the occasional flame flaring up to make meat sizzle.

"You are a wise man, Ron, beyond your years," said Stephen.

"Yeah? Or maybe it's just the beer talking."

Chapter 38

Areebah and Saddam Ali pulled into the parking lot behind a two-story building in Flushing. It was a little after 9:00 PM on Labor Day.

The first floor of the two-story, brick face building hosted an electronics store, with the couple's apartment a flight up. Their building was sandwiched between two others, which also had stores at street level and apartments above. Across the street was a hospital.

After entering the two-bedroom apartment, Areebah said, "I ate too much. I need to go for a run."

"Fine," said Saddam flatly, as he sat down in an armchair, grabbed the remote, and powered up the television.

Areebah changed into shorts, t-shirt and running shoes. As she headed to the front door, Saddam called from the living room: "Don't get too tired, Areebah, we are overdue, and tonight is the night."

"We'll see," she responded.

"No, we will not see," he shouted. "It has been too long."

She closed the apartment door, quickly moved down the stairs, and stretched her muscles just inside the door to the street.

Areebah stepped out onto the sidewalk, and started running north on 168th Street.

Even though she lived in Queens her entire life, Areebah Ali had covered a lot of ground during her thirty years.

While attending public schools, she grew into an attractive young woman. But her strict parents always hovered and controlled. The family attended a mosque that quietly pushed a radical strain of Islam. Outside of school, she was immersed in hatred of Jews and Israel, suspicion of Christians, and distrust of most of the Americans around her.

College was never an option. Instead, Areebah's eleven-year marriage to Saddam was quietly arranged by her father. She never showed any indications of resentment. Instead, Areebah enthusiastically responded when her husband eventually revealed the role that he and Nuri were playing in advancing Islam.

She trained vigorously, and became an expert in a variety of weapons and in hand-to-hand combat.

But the more moderate mosque the couple, along with the al-Dawla's, attended in order to ward off any unwanted suspicions from the authorities gradually had an effect.

When she first contacted federal authorities a year ago, she told them, "Things have changed. I finally understand what life and Islam are about, and it is not what I was taught."

For a few months, she looked for openings indicating that her husband might consider a new way of thinking. But she finally admitted to her handler four months ago that there was no hope.

From that point forward, she largely continued with her normal everyday life. Only two things changed. One was that Areebah avoided having sex with her husband. She manufactured medical excuses, but his anger and frustrations were growing. The other was that she regularly passed on information about the cell to the FBI.

Using a pay phone in the shadows of a gas station, Areebah gave the exact details of the plot against the Pope to a concerned but very appreciative Agent Ryan Bates. He told her that they likely would be moving against the cell within a day or two. She would get the signal via her cell phone from a predetermined number. Once she saw that particular number, Areebah would have five minutes to extract herself. If she missed the message or for some reason could not get out, all teams would have clear instructions to secure her safety. Keep in mind, Bates told her, that it would most likely be in the middle of the night.

She jogged back to the apartment. Areebah took the key out of the sport case hanging on a necklace, and entered the building that soon would no longer be her home. Another key opened the apartment door.

Saddam was still watching television in the living room.

She went into the bathroom, turned on the shower, and undressed. Areebah stood under the hot water with her eyes closed for a couple of minutes.

The shower curtain was pulled open by a naked Saddam.

"I'll join you, my dear."

"No," she responded. "I mean, I still do not feel right. I'm sorry. I don't know what's wrong. But no."

"It is not a request, Areebah."

Saddam stepped into the shower, and tried to grab her. She pulled away, and slapped his face. They stood facing each other with mutual looks of surprise and water pelting down.

Saddam's expression and voice became more menacing. "Don't ever do that again."

He forced himself upon Areebah, who avoided having their lips meet, and kept her eyes tightly closed.

Chapter 39

After finishing the Tuesday Matins service, Grant spent time checking and returning e-mail, making a few phone calls, and going through a small stack of mail and notes.

Just a few minutes after ten, Barbara Tunney knocked and entered Stephen's office. "Just got a call from Joan Kraus."

"What's up? Anything important?"

"She said we should flip on News 12. Apparently, Jennifer Brees is going to be on in a few minutes. She's holding a press conference."

"Uh-oh." Grant picked up the television remote, and clicked on the local news channel.

Is it lesson time for Congressman Brees?

* * *

"Thanks, again, you guys for being here," said Jennifer Brees.

"Jen, we're your friends. We're here for you, honey," replied Joan Kraus, standing next to her husband George, who was nodding in agreement. "But are you really sure about this?"

"Absolutely, and stop asking me that."

They were standing on an expansive lawn outside the building housing the local cable television news station. About 30 feet away waited a podium, a News 12 camera and microphone, three additional mikes for radio stations, and a half dozen reporters, including scribes from *Newsday*, the *New York Post*, and the online *Long Island Sentinel*.

On Labor Day, Jennifer had contacted the handful of reporters, editors and news producers she had developed a relationship with through her economics work and by being married to a U.S. congressman. In exchange for keeping the press conference quiet, Jennifer promised headlines and a very limited number of media invitees.

"Wish me luck," Jennifer said to the Krauses, as she strode towards the podium and small band of reporters.

Jennifer unfolded a sheet of paper, placed it on the podium, and read. "Thank you for coming. You don't know how much I wish we weren't here. I discovered over the holiday weekend that my husband, Congressman Ted Brees, has been having an extramarital affair with his chief of staff, Ms. Kerri Bratton."

Mumbles came from the reporters gathered.

"Ted told me that he loves Ms. Bratton, and had planned to ask for a divorce once his reelection race was over. By making this public announcement, some people might doubt that I am a private person. They would be wrong. I am. I take no pleasure in disclosing my husband's adultery. In fact, I am deeply hurt and embarrassed."

"Then why do it?" called out one reporter.

Jennifer plowed ahead: "The reason I have decided to hold this press conference is that I'm not about to stand meekly by, as too many others have done in recent years. I'm tired of seeing good little political wives standing quietly next to, and tacitly supporting, their two-timing politician husbands, in essence playing enablers and excusing irresponsible behavior. Throughout their careers, too many politicians have someone around to clean up, cover up or gloss over their wrongdoings. That's not for me. Unfortunately, my husband has changed, or he never was the man I thought he was. He has become a caricature. He talks about family values, but has destroyed our marriage by fooling around with a young, pretty member of his staff. For Ted now, it's all about his own selfish desires, which are focused on getting reelected and getting laid."

There was silence. Jennifer folded the paper and placed it in the right pocket of her blazer.

"Any questions?" she asked.

* * *

"Excuse me, Pastor, but, holy shit," declared the clearly stunned Barbara Tunney.

"You can say that again, Barb," replied Stephen.

Ha, good lesson, Jen. The jerk deserved it.

* * *

"Fucking bitch, fucking bitch, fucking bitch!" screamed Congressman Ted Brees at the television set in his campaign office in Riverhead.

Once they heard about Jennifer's press conference, Kerri Bratton had shuttled Ted into his office and closed the door.

The Brees rant continued for another minute or so, while Kerri waited patiently in a chair with her back straight and hands crossed in her lap. Once Brees appeared to finish spewing obscenities, she said, "We have to respond, Ted. And quickly."

"I know. I know. Get Arnie on the phone."

* * *

Congressman Brees's response featured a brief apology to his constituents, with the rest being a gently worded criticism of Jennifer choosing to air personal business in public, and how "unfortunate and regrettable" that was.

State and local Republican leaders had talking points that this was a personal matter that would not affect the wonderful job Congressman Brees has done for his constituents in the First Congressional District.

Meanwhile, the Democrats had seen Brees's strength in the polls, and decided to run a sacrificial lamb. After retiring from a state government job, the 76-year-old Martha McGraw had been an anti-war, green, pro-choice gadfly for nearly a quarter century. She had practically no money to run a campaign, and about a dozen campaign volunteers. When called by the media for a comment, Martha simply said, "That's none of my business."

By the end of the day, the news stories inevitably carried the Shakespeare line from "King Lear" that "hell hath no fury like a woman scorned."

Chapter 40

Tom Stone asked, "Is there anything else that can possibly happen at your church?"

At their Wednesday morning diner devotions, Stone held up the cover of the *New York Post*. "In case you missed it," he said to Grant, who just sat down in the booth.

The front page featured a photo of Congressman Brees and Kerri Bratton walking next to each other. It would have been an otherwise innocent picture if not for the accompanying "Getting Reelected ... Getting Laid" headline.

Almost all of the news stories, analysis and commentary were positive towards the woman who had almost been killed two weeks ago, and now discovered her famous husband's infidelity.

"I bet Barbara that the *Post* would use the phrase 'getting laid' on its cover," said Stephen. "She owes me a buck."

Stephen, Tom and Ron ordered breakfast, and read from *For All the Saints*.

The food arrived quickly, as they all were eating relatively light.

Ron sprinkled a little sugar on his oatmeal. "Did you know that Mrs. Brees was going to do this?"

"No," said Stephen. He ate a forkful from his bowl of fruit, and wiped the corners of his mouth with a napkin. "She vaguely mentioned something when drunk on Saturday, and told me on the way out of church on Sunday that she was going to teach the Congressman a lesson. I really assumed it was her hurt, the alcohol and hangover talking. Apparently not, as it turns out."

Tom observed, "You don't sound too distressed."

"Distressed? Why should I be?"

Tom was spreading cream cheese on a bagel. "Well, is this really the best way to deal with the breakdown of a marriage?"

"Normally, I would not recommend it."

"But it's alright in this case?" Ron asked with a hint of indignation.

"Yes," said Stephen. "Congressman Sleaze-Bag deserved it. Jennifer Brees is a nice, smart, genuine person. And she was right about those hapless political wives who make it easy on their political husbands. That list is disturbingly long. What's up with that anyway?"

Ron responded, "Perhaps it's called forgiveness."

"Or maybe it's about enabling, relativism, and/or power couples getting used to the rewards of politics."

"Maybe," Ron said, watching Stephen closely.

Stone was glancing at the *Post* story. "Besides being a nice person, Mrs. Brees also is loaded. Says here that she comes from gambling money. Over the years, her father built and sold three casinos in Vegas, and now runs two more – Casino Beach and The Twenties. Plus, her economics firm is very highly regarded among Wall Streeters."

"Really?" said Stephen. "I knew the Brees's were well off, but didn't know the source of their wealth."

Ron added, "Now that Paige Caldwell is not an option …"

"Wait," Tom broke in, "what happened with Paige?"

Ron said, "You were busy with guests on Monday. Stephen gave her the just-friends line on Sunday."

"The just-friends blow off to an exciting, beautiful woman like that. Very impressive, Stephen. And do you now have interest in the wealthy, pretty, soon-to-be-divorced Jennifer Brees? Throw in your assignment, and all of a sudden, you are living a very exciting life, Pastor Grant. I can't keep up with all of your adventures. Ron and I live vicariously through you."

"Remember, Tom, envy is a sin," said Stephen.

Chapter 41

2:05 AM, Flushing, Queens

Her cell phone, set on vibrate, rested on the night table next to the bed.

Since turning out the light at 10:30, Areebah Ali had gotten up once to use the bathroom. Otherwise, though not sleeping a wink, she had not moved. Her back was to Saddam, and her eyes were set on the cell phone.

The call came.

The vibration caused the phone to move slightly. But the sound was barely perceptible.

She glanced over her shoulder. Saddam's snoring continued.

Areebah quietly opened the phone, shielding the screen light from her husband with her body.

She stared at the number. The vibration stopped.

Areebah had less than five minutes to get out of the apartment without waking Saddam.

Dressed in panties and a gray t-shirt, she got up and moved to the chair where shorts, white ankle socks, and running shoes waited.

She dressed quickly, and finished tying the second sneaker. The clock now said 2:08.

The floor creaked as she stood up.

Saddam stirred. Areebah froze.

He opened his eyes, and squinted at her in the darkness. "What are you doing?"

She whispered, "Going for a run. Can't sleep at all."

"What time is it?"

"Don't worry about it. Go back to sleep," she said in a soothing voice.

Saddam looked at the clock just as the digital "8" turned to a "9." He said, "It's after two o'clock in the morning. We have to get up at five. Get back to bed."

"In a few minutes." She walked out of the bedroom.

"No," Saddam declared. He rose from the bed. "It is too late."

Areebah continued moving down the hall, and opened the apartment door.

She was halfway down the stairs, with Saddam appearing behind her at the top, when the front door to the walk up burst open and tear gas canisters broke through the back and front windows of the apartment.

Areebah didn't look back, but heard Saddam yell, "You bitch!"

1:55 AM, Bayside, Queens

Two sets of stairs led to the basement apartment shared by Randall Al-Hakim and Abdul ed-Din – one from the tiny backyard and the second from inside the home.

FBI agents in body armor, gas masks and night vision goggles secured the main floor and removed the elderly homeowners. Unfortunately, the couple was awake, and the wife screamed at the invasion of their bedroom. The noise made it necessary to move immediately, rather than waiting for the scheduled 2:10.

Fortunately, even after the two doors were broken down and tear gas fired through the basement windows, Al-

Hakim and ed-Din were groggy, and had no idea what was happening. The two men were secured.

2:05 AM, three stores around Queens, and a commercial building along the Belt Parkway

At each of the three convenience-grocery stores owned by Nuri al-Dawla and Saddam Ali, four FBI agents and four New York City police officers from the city's anti-terror task force pulled up in official, unmarked vehicles. The intelligence from Areebah Ali made it clear that no one would be at each of the stores at this time. But no chances were taken. According to the plan, each store was to be picked apart during the early hours of the morning.

Meanwhile, given the purpose of renting the top floor of the building near the Belt Parkway, a slightly larger, more heavily armed and protected group of law enforcement was assigned there.

2:09 AM, Jamaica, Queens

Outside the al-Dawla home, FBI agents were in position – not only on the ground, but also on the partial first story roof outside the second floor bedroom windows. Special Agent Ryan Bates was at the front door. He looked at his watch. At 2:10 AM precisely, he gave the signal.

The front and back doors of the home crashed in, and tear gas launched through the windows.

Lama bolted up in bed.

Nuri grabbed the cell phone under his pillow and opened it.

FBI agents came through the bedroom windows.

Nuri's right thumb hit a button that brought up a list of numbers. His thumb moved again, dialing the number at the top.

The call bounced off cell towers on its way to seven different cell phones.

Nuri and Saddam had agreed some time ago that their efforts might be detected by American law enforcement. Despite such failure, they must be able to deal a blow.

So, the two men, unbeknownst to Lama, Areebah, Randall and Abdul, wired each location in which they lived, worked and operated with C-4 explosives.

The cell phones served as the detonators, and were carefully wired into each building's electrical system to maintain power. Well hidden, each phone waited like an amoral soldier, devoid of compassion, for its orders. And those orders came at precisely 2:11:17 AM EST.

* * *

The empty commercial building along the Belt Parkway erupted.

A couple, who had arrived in the U.S. nine years ago from Jamaica, occupied the neighboring house just across a narrow driveway, with their two children. No one survived what turned into a smoldering wreckage.

A 69-year-old mother of three, and grandmother to five, had arrived with her husband of 46 years on a late flight into JFK from Los Angeles. Their daughter picked them up. They drove east on the Belt Parkway, heading out to Long Island. As a brick from the explosion streaked through the air and the car moved at 58 miles an hour on the parkway, the timing was, unfortunately, perfect. The brick entered the open front, passenger side window, and ended the grandmother's life by striking her in the temple.

Far more lucky, the team of 12 anti-terror officers – eight FBI and four New York City police – were not yet in position due to an earlier traffic snarl. They saw and felt the explosion, but none were seriously injured.

* * *

The al-Dawla-Ali grocery store on Northern Boulevard in Flushing was detached from other buildings, surrounded by a parking lot.

Just a few minutes before, the police had prodded a homeless man, asleep and propped up against the front of the building, and moved along six high school teens drinking in the back parking lot.

The eight federal and local law enforcement agents probably never knew what had killed them.

* * *

The convenience store in College Point was on a desolate street that only grew active during daytime business hours, though, at this time of night, some transactions in the underground economy – namely, drugs and prostitution – were not unusual.

Tonight, the usual suspects could not disguise their amazement. First, the police only gave them a quick warning and sent them on their way. Second, they were knocked over by the massive explosion, and when looking back, saw nothing remaining of the cops.

* * *

One block away from the Long Island Railroad station in Jamaica, the devastation expanded.

The grocery store claimed the ground floor of a four-story apartment building. On each side were three-story buildings, also with stores on the ground level and apartments above.

In the three buildings, there were a total of 22 apartments. Four sat vacant, and in another three, the residents happened not to be at home. Once the shock of the immediate blast subsided, 28 people were dead, and another seven struggled as life gradually slipped away in the huge pile of rubble.

On the street, four FBI agents and four police officers had died.

* * *

Another four FBI agents and two police officers were meticulously poking around the Bayside apartment, while four other agents had taken Abdul and Randall up the back staircase and were escorting them around the house.

The cell phone behind a false closet wall in the Bayside basement apartment received its call to action.

Of the two home-grown terrorists, the 11 FBI agents, six New York City officers, only the two cops who had escorted the elderly homeowners to a friend's house down the street survived.

* * *

Areebah Ali looked at the masked faces of the armed FBI agents.

She was commanded to stop and move against the wall. As armored individuals streamed past her, two others pulled her out the door.

Shouts could be heard from the building as she moved towards a large, dark SUV. But it wasn't quick enough.

As was the case with 24 of the 28 FBI and police personnel on the scene and the six individuals living in the apartments in the adjacent buildings, various parts of Areebah Ali mixed with the dirt and debris generated by the explosion. Only the two FBI agents on the roof of the hospital and the two in the armored prisoner van survived.

Across the street, windows were shattered and walls shaken at the hospital.

* * *

"Put your hands up where I can see them," shouted one of the agents who came through the window.

Lama raised her hands in the air.

Nuri put down the cell phone, and placed his hands on the top of his head.

While the house sitting along the Van Wyck Expressway was fully loaded with explosives, Nuri had removed the detonator shortly after he and Saddam had installed it and the C-4.

Nuri never told Saddam.

The al-Dawlas were searched, bound and moved to the FBI prisoner transports.

As the doors closed on the vehicles, Agent Bates answered his cell.

"Bates." He listened to the desperate, emotional report from the street outside the former home of Areebah and Saddam Ali.

Bates said, "Oh, dear God, no." He ran up the steps of the al-Dawla home, shouting: "Everybody out! Get the hell out! Now! The place is rigged to blow!"

By the time all personnel were out, the nearby houses evacuated, vehicles moved away, and local traffic stopped, the extent of the other attacks had started to come together. More than 60 law enforcement likely dead. The number of murdered civilians would bring the total dead above a hundred.

Bates tried to find out from Nuri and Lama al-Dawla if their own home was wired to go up, and if there were other targets.

Lama appeared shocked by the reported explosions. She would not look at the agents, nor would she look at her husband.

Nuri was calm, silent.

Chapter 42

Grant was in a deep sleep.

In a dream, he was resting in a chaise lounge next to the pool at the Brees home. He had a writing pad and book open on his lap. It was the Bible. Grant's attention was drawn to Jennifer in the pool. She was floating, looking at him, smiling and laughing.

He felt comfortable, very much at home.

A phone was ringing.

"Don't bother," Jennifer said. "Let the machine get it."

But it was next to him now, and continued ringing, growing louder...

Grant woke up. His phone actually was ringing.

Crap.

He was not pleased about being pulled out of his dream. The clock taunted him, saying it was 4:34 AM. He picked up the receiver.

"Hello."

"Stephen, turn on your television."

"Paige?"

"Remember that cell I mentioned in Queens?"

He immediately brushed away the cobwebs of sleep. "Yes."

"Well, the FBI and New York City's finest moved in a little over two hours ago. It all went to hell. The bastards had the places wired. We lost 63 law enforcement, and at least 46 civilians."

Dear God. No.

Stephen asked, "What about the terrorists?"

"Our mole is dead, along with three of these shits. But we've got our hands on two, including the ringleader. They're scheduled for enhanced interrogation."

Grant knew what that meant. He watched it once, and would never forget. Even though he still defended its very limited use, as he had at the Brees gathering less than a week ago, Grant never again wanted to witness it.

Paige continued, "We'll be in contact later."

She hung up.

Grant flipped on the television. The reports were on nearly every channel. The city was locked down – roads, trains, air travel. The news anchors knew less than he did.

Chapter 43

By the time the house along the Van Wyck was secured, both suspects already had been whisked away from the scene without most agents and officers on hand realizing it.

The husband and wife were gagged, bound, hooded, and placed in separate black, armored Suburbans. But they were taken to the same place, so that whatever information offered or extracted could be compared and confirmed.

Agent Ryan Bates directed the team to a secluded horse farm in northern New Jersey.

All records showed that the farm had been bought in 2002 by a married couple named James and Kathleen Kelly. In fact, Jim and Kay, as they were known locally, did live on the farm and raised thoroughbreds. But the Kelly couple, who before retirement traveled extensively for business, had a long relationship with the CIA. The U.S. taxpayers indirectly paid for the farm. It doubled as an emergency location to bring terrorists and other national security risks captured in New York City and surrounding metro area for the purpose of gaining information.

Hidden below an indoor riding ring was a multi-room, high-tech complex featuring both time-tested and newly developed tools for information extraction.

Bates reported Lama's reaction to the news that her husband had blown up their colleagues to his superiors. He highlighted the shock on her face. She might be ready, Bates argued, to turn under gentle prodding. If not, interrogation tactics could be beefed up later. And given the number of agents and police who were just murdered, there would no shortage of volunteers willing to push the prisoner much harder. His superiors agreed.

It didn't take very long. The questioners focused on the deaths of Areebah, Saddam, Randall and Abdul, all by Nuri's hand. Yet, they pointed out, Nuri was unwilling to make the same sacrifice. His cowardice, the interrogators asserted, was obvious, and raised doubts about everything Nuri had said and done.

Lama's feelings of betrayal quickly surfaced. It became clear that she knew nothing about the wiring of the explosives, and was particularly wounded by the death of Areebah Ali. Once Bates convinced her that the best he could do was a promise to avoid the death penalty, Lama spilled everything she knew about the planned attack on Pope Augustine, and the cell's longtime operations.

Unfortunately, it was nothing that the FBI had not already gotten from Areebah. Nuri al-Dawla had been very careful, even with his own wife.

Meanwhile, in another part of the sub-equestrian facility, Paige Caldwell watched through a one-way mirror as two FBI agents went through the motions of questioning Nuri al-Dawla.

Nuri seemed oblivious – whether the queries came softly, shouted out, or with slaps meant to inflict pain but cause no internal injuries. Over more than three hours, when uttering any sounds at all, Nuri answered only with chanting.

But various blows to the head and stomach were coming with increasing enthusiasm. The agent running the Nuri interrogation, Rich Noack, stood expressionless next to Caldwell. He turned to an agent by the door, and sent in the stop order.

Noack said to Paige, "This guy's not going to cough up information this way. Judging by what we know of his history" – he was scanning a print out on al-Dawla's background – "he's no nonsense. But he obviously isn't all that interested in martyrdom. That's our advantage. It's time to get more serious. We need to know if others are targeting the Pope, and quickly, not to mention whatever else we can get from this bastard in terms of his puppet masters, his network, the entire operation."

Paige added, "It won't take long after this incident for any others in the country to start moving."

"That's sure as shit."

Though in his late forties and a bit out of shape from too much time at a desk, Noack still cut a powerful, six-foot-six figure, especially with his bald head. The jacket to his dark blue suit was off, the top button on his white shirt open, with a red-blue striped tie tugged down slightly.

Noack ordered Nuri moved from the sparsely furnished room featuring a metal table and two chairs. The terrorist was roughly escorted down a hallway. A heavily insulated door was opened.

Three individuals – two male and one female – were waiting in white lab coats. Their titles – to the very few who knew of their existence – were Enhanced Interrogation Specialists. In addition, three very large men in red jump suits stood ready to spring into action.

The room looked like it could be in a hospital, dominated by white, easily washable tile, three metal gurneys, and assorted medical devices, surgical tools, IVs, and drugs. The temperature was a very cool 50 degrees Fahrenheit.

A large machine featuring a long, clear tube in the center dominated the room, with a control panel on one side and a set of stairs on the other leading up to a small platform and long table with straps atop the cylinder. It was known simply as "the tube."

Caldwell and Noack entered an anteroom above that looked down on the entire scene through large windows.

"I'm guessing the Vatican would not approve of the measures you're about to use to protect the Pope," Paige said.

"I leave the saving souls business to them. They should leave the fighting terrorism and national security work to us," Noack replied.

"Couldn't agree more," Paige replied. "The tube is an interesting bit of hardware. I wonder who dreamed it up."

"Unique it is. From what I've heard, there are only a half dozen in existence. Three in the country, and three in strategic spots around the globe." He added, "It's supposed to be easier on the interrogators. You know, limit the potential negative mental and emotional effects that water boarding can have on agents."

Paige smirked while looking down at the room and the tube. She said, "Hmmm. I guess I'm an old-fashioned, hands-on type of girl."

Noack looked at Caldwell, with an arched eyebrow.

In the room below, the two agents who had been interrogating Nuri handed him over to the three large men in the red jumpsuits. They roughly stripped al-Dawla naked. It was apparent that the room's coolness took immediate effect. They dragged him up the stairs on the side of the tube, and strapped him down to the flat surface on top. Nuri was completely immobilized.

A jump-suited individual descended the stairs to make room for one of the men in a lab coat. In less than five minutes, he placed 40 small, sticky diagnostic scanners over most of al-Dawla's body. A computer image of Nuri's body, along with his vital signs, popped up on a control panel screen. The female specialist seated at the panel did a quick check of the data. She gave a thumbs up.

That signal was returned by the specialist next to Nuri, and by the third, who stood by the machine ready to monitor what would soon occur within the tube.

The specialist on the machine's platform leaned down inches above Nuri's face. "You have a choice. You can either give us what we need now, or you will do so after experiencing complete helplessness and horror. After what you did today, I personally want you to get the full experience. Which will it be? Who are you working with? Who else is targeting the Pope? And we want to know how many of your comrades are in the U.S., and where they are."

Nuri had his eyes closed, and resumed his chanting.

The specialist declared, "I was hoping that's what you'd say." He looked down at his two colleagues, waved his right hand back and forth in the air, and said loudly, "Green light."

The woman at the console flipped a switch. The table that Nuri al-Dawla was strapped onto was lowered into the glass tube, and rotated so Nuri eventually was facing down, though firmly attached to the cold metal slab. As he hung there, a cover then slid across the top of the tube. Nuri was completely enclosed, and his eyes were now wide open.

Once the specialist hit a large green button, high-speed water jets filled the tube with cold water. Nuri barely had time to take in a small amount of air. His muscles fought against the restraints, but to no avail. The terrorist was completely helpless.

The entire tube filled with water in less than four seconds. Al-Dawla's eyes darted around as his fear and panic mounted, while the specialist standing outside the tube watched Nuri's face calmly. At 24 seconds, al-Dawla's mouth reflexively opened seeking air, but only taking in water. The specialist on watch quickly signaled to his colleague at the controls with a hand across the throat, and a loud, "Red light." A red button was hit, and the water was completely sucked out of the tube in five seconds.

Al-Dawla spat, gagged, regurgitated. He was rotated onto his back. The cover slid open, and he was brought up. Nuri immediately began shivering.

The man in the white lab coat stepped forward. He screamed in the terrorist's face. "Are you ready to talk?"

"No, please, no ..." said Nuri quietly.

"Did you say no?! You want more. That's fine with me," said the specialist. He took a step back.

Nuri yelled, "No, I mean I'll talk." He began weeping. "I'll talk."

And he did.

Chapter 44

Nuri al-Dawla coughed up five other cells that reported to him in the U.S. They were in Los Angeles, Chicago, Milwaukee, Miami, and just outside Washington, D.C., in northern Virginia.

He also fingered his network contacts in Iran, Iraq, Afghanistan and France.

In addition, Nuri claimed to know nothing about another planned attack on Pope Augustine.

A second round in the tube yielded the same information. Nuri was told that if everything did not check out, the consequences might make him long for the tube.

It was information that Agent Noack forwarded to the director of the FBI, and Paige Caldwell passed on to Langley. Once confirmed, action would be swift. In fact, by 3:30 EST on Friday afternoon, the Los Angeles, Milwaukee and Chicago cells, which already had been under limited surveillance, were taken into custody. The Miami and D.C. groups, however, had already evacuated, and left little behind to pick up their trail.

As for the international information, the French were appreciative, and moved immediately. Iraqi security forces also acted with speed and severity. And the Afghanistan and Iran information were shared between the CIA, NSA and the Pentagon.

After the primary work was done on al-Dawla, Noack, Bates and Caldwell were drinking coffee, relaxing in a lounge-like room below the New Jersey horse farm.

Bates asked the other two, "Were you surprised that al-Dawla talked so quickly?"

Noack merely answered, "No."

"Why not?"

"Was this your first time seeing an enhanced interrogation, as we like to call it, Agent Bates?" Noack responded.

"Yes."

"I've seen several." Noack looked at Caldwell.

She said, "Me? I've participated in several – both sanctioned and a few on the fly."

Noack turned back to Bates. "Two things. First, somewhere along the way in the U.S., doubts about dying for his cause obviously crept into the mind of Nuri al-Dawla. I'm sure he rationalized it all, but it was no mistake that his house did not explode like the other buildings. The explosives were set. But the trigger either was never put in place, or at some point, it was removed. Quite simply, while willing to sacrifice, or murder, others, he himself did not want to die."

Noack took a slug of coffee, and assessed a small tray of donuts on the table until he found a cruller. He continued: "Second, that being the case, I knew Nuri would crack because the tube is all about the immediate and intense fear of dying." He took a large bite out of the cruller.

Caldwell remained silent, watching the two FBI agents.

After swallowing, Noack said, "Have you ever experienced water boarding, Caldwell?"

Bates looked surprised by the question.

Paige replied, "I haven't. My experiences left permanent scars."

Noack said, "Several years ago, I took one for the team. A few of us involved in this business were asked to experience what we might have to dole out one day. That was a controlled experiment with people that I knew were not going to kill me. Yet, the reaction of intense fear is automatic. It's instinctual. I don't know if anyone could actually control it. I certainly couldn't."

Noack finished the cruller, and took another drink of coffee amid silence in the room. "So, Agent Bates, that's why I was so confident that al-Dawla would talk."

"But what about the possibility of just telling us anything, not the truth?" Bates responded.

"There's certainly a chance," Noack said. "Lord knows, it's happened. But in my view, it's more likely with the zealots who have no fear of dying. He might serve up lies to stop the immediate discomfort, while thinking that it's OK if he must become a martyr at some point in the future. But the guys who don't want to die are less likely to take that risk. It's really only a question of how many water boarding – or now tubing – treatments are needed. One or two." Noack looked at Paige, and asked, "Would you agree?"

"For the most part," she said.

Bates said, "What's next for al-Dawla?"

Noack replied, "Kept alive long enough to be useful. Then he'll face a military tribunal, and be shipped off to hell."

Paige said, "But after tonight, and until his most deserved execution, he will, no doubt, avoid any cruel and unusual punishment. And that's a damn shame."

Noack asked, "Is that the old-fashioned, hands-on girl talking?"

She nodded.

Noack raised his cup to her.

Chapter 45

Pastor Grant closed his laptop after finishing the main draft of Sunday's sermon.

His sermons were usually done by early Friday afternoon, followed by a few edits on Saturday morning. But today, it dragged on to nearly 4:30.

Stephen had talked about the bombings during the Thursday Matins service, and a special Vespers gathering later that night. They were the largest turnouts for mid-week services since the 9-11 attacks, except perhaps an Ash Wednesday here or there. Pastor Grant learned from those earlier acts of terror, however, not to expect the spike in attendance to last.

After the country's most deadly day of terror, church attendance at St. Mary's had jumped by about 50 percent. But roughly a month later, it was back to normal. People came to church in the aftermath of the attacks saying that they sought answers and comfort. Whether finding what they wanted or not, they again stopped coming – except a few more come back on Easter and Christmas.

At first, Stephen felt responsible, blaming his own distractions and doubts about his pastoral call and desire to get back in the fight against terrorists. He never fully shook off that sense of guilt. But after hearing about and reflecting on the same phenomenon at so many other churches, Grant largely concluded that it wasn't about him. Nor was it about whether people did or did not find what they came looking for. Instead, he saw a combination of short attention spans, widespread desire for the quick fix, everyday duties once again crowding out the Lord, and people generally looking to God only during the worst times in life. And even then, for many, it was an occasion to question God, rather than seeking out His comfort. Grant came to see that each person had to decide what really mattered. His job was making the case that God was the ultimate priority.

The impact on Grant this time around was different. No doubts materialized about his calling. Nor was there the near-overwhelming wish to get back in the game. But Stephen also realized that his job helping to protect Pope Augustine may have quenched any lingering subconscious thirst on that front. After all, he was, to some degree, in the game.

Stephen tried to come up with a sermon that helped people sort through their feelings and responses to the devastating bombings. The usual query he heard in similar times and during natural disasters was: How could God let this happen? Grant wanted them to ask two different questions. First, why do I only come to God in bad times? Second, if I think about God in bad times, shouldn't I be making time for him in good times as well?

He pushed his chair away from the desk, and turned to look out the window.

The phone rang. Barbara had already left, so Stephen picked up. "St. Mary's Lutheran Church."

"Pastor Grant?"

"Yes."

"This is Meri Wilson-Harris. I told you I'd be calling with an invitation to be a guest panelist on Channel 15's new show. Well, 'Long Island Spirituality' tapes its premiere a week from today."

Before he had a chance to open his mouth, Meri plowed ahead undaunted. "Now, before you say no, I told our host Wayne Walters about you, and he very much wants you on. Wayne is very insistent on having balance. Real balance, not that Fox News stuff. Given your rather unique views, yesterday's terror attacks somehow linked to the Pope's visit, those allegedly responsible, and the fact that you are representing your church during Augustine's visit, Wayne wants you to know how important he believes it is to have you on the show."

Grant wasn't sure why he responded the way he did. Perhaps it was part of that subconscious thirst. Or maybe it was her use of the word "allegedly." If he was the show's balance, another part of him clearly did not want to leave another media venue without a traditional Christian voice. He simply said, "Meri, I appreciate the invitation, and would be happy to come on the show."

She was clearly taken off guard. "Really? Well, that's great. Thank you. You'll need to be in the studio by 1:00 on Friday, so we can start taping at 1:30. The show will air on Friday night at 7:30, and then again on Sunday morning at 11:30. I'll e-mail all of this to you. We're still finalizing the other three guests."

They exchanged e-mail addresses, and finished their conversation.

It wasn't until after he hung up that Stephen started to wonder if a television talk show was the wisest decision given his task for the government. Just then, his cell rang. He flipped open to see Paige Caldwell's name and number.

Coincidence?

"Paige?"

"Stephen."

"What's the latest on the bombings? Learn anything?"

Paige said, "One gave up without a fight. It took a bit longer with the leader. But it was pretty clear that he wasn't the martyr type. So, after one session under a new technique, he coughed up all kinds of information. Stephen, you should see this new technique. It's not my preferred way of doing business, but it takes water boarding, and ..."

"Paige," Grant interrupted her growing enthusiasm, "I really don't want to know."

"Oh, right, sorry about that, Pastor."

Stephen noted the sarcastic emphasis on "pastor" once again. "Did this guy know if there would be anything more on Augustine's visit?"

"He hadn't heard that anyone else among the Islamic extremist set also had been tasked with murdering the Pope while in the U.S. Of course, given what Augustine wrote in that letter about the threat of radical Islam, we're assuming others will be lurking. At the very least, if not in New York, most certainly elsewhere as he globe trots."

"Absolutely," agreed Grant. "What does this mean for my assignment?"

"Everything gets cranked up, of course. We'll need you all of Monday to walk through the security for the entire visit, including each venue. I trust that's doable?"

"Sure."

"I thought it would work. After all, Sunday's your busy time."

"Since you brought it up, what do you do with your Sundays? Why not come by St. Mary's on Sunday morning? Helps to put things in perspective."

"Stephen, that's not the invite I've been waiting for from you. Our next get together will have to wait until Monday morning. Be at the Federal Building in downtown Manhattan by 7:00 AM sharp."

"Sounds good."

"Bye bye, lover." She hung up.

I really wish she didn't call me that.

Chapter 46

A small, unobtrusive black iron sign with gold lettering said this was the right place: The St. Ambrose Retreat House.

Grant's Tahoe seemed to barely squeak through the narrow opening in the tall wrought iron fence. Following a few other cars, Grant drove along a gravel path past a two-story brick gatehouse, through thick woods, over a stone bridge spanning a small stream, and then out across a vast expanse of lawn.

He pulled into a parking lot that sat in between two massive stone buildings, at least 200 hundred yards from each. On the other side of the structures was more lawn extending to cliffs overlooking the Long Island Sound.

Grant was several minutes early, as usual, for the 11:00 AM briefing and discussion for those who would be attending Pope Augustine's "Public Mission of Mere Christianity" gathering in a dozen days. Today, some would be at St. Ambrose's in person – or their representatives would – with others tuning in via the Internet. Stephen had never been to St. Ambrose's before, so he checked out the facility's Website to get a little background the night before.

The buildings originally were two homes constructed not long after the Civil War by Xavier Puddleworth, considered the baron of the buggy whip business. After he completed an 18,000 square foot gothic style house, his wife, Penelope, found that it failed to meet all of her needs. So, Xavier built her an even more impressive, 29,000 square foot castle just a few hundred yards away.

Shortly after Xavier passed away, the Puddleworth's son, Norton, took over the business just as it was becoming clear that the horse and buggy, along with the buggy whip, would give way to the internal combustion engine and the automobile. The Puddleworth estate slowly decayed. Eventually, the increasingly distraught Norton committed suicide.

Norton's wife, Isabel, however, possessed far greater pluck and business acumen than her late husband. She also happened to be a devout Roman Catholic. Through strategic investments, Isabel rebuilt her family's fortune, and restored the two homes. But as the tax burden rose, she donated the entire 95 acres on Long Island's Gold Coast to the Roman Catholic Church. She lived out her remaining days in California, dabbling with dollars in the budding movie business.

Over the years, the Catholic Church used the facilities for a variety of purposes, including a seminary, a convent, and an all-girls high school. Finally, the gothic home became an abbey for a small number of monks, who recently gained some prominence with a line of barbecue seasonings. Grillin' with the Monks had grown into quite a success, including a recent expansion into barbecue utensils, hot pads, cookbooks – their new book was titled *Search for the Holy Grill* – and aprons, along with a weekly cooking show on Long Island's Catholic cable television station.

Meanwhile, the castle became a retreat house, as well as a much sought after location for weddings, corporate events, and political fundraisers. Special barbecues with the monks were becoming particularly popular. In fact, those tuning in to the briefings through the Internet would not only miss a tour of the buildings and grounds on this day, but also one of those delightful Grillin' with the Monks barbecues.

After the estate was declared an historic landmark, the diocese proved quite adept at lobbying federal, state, and local elected officials for a rather steady stream of taxpayer grants for the upkeep and improvement of the facility. The latest government grant made the entire estate a WiFi hotspot.

Monks with taxpayer-funded WiFi and a cable cooking show. Can't make this stuff up.

As he walked towards the castle, Grant noted a drawbridge spanning a mock moat with a fountain. Grant strolled across to be met just inside the building by a woman who introduced herself as Sister Elizabeth McCoy.

More "Flying Nun" Mother Superior than Ingrid Bergman.

She checked off his name, and gave Stephen directions to the meeting. All he had to do was join the stream of mainly men in collars or suits heading through a massive archway off the right side of a huge central room that featured marble, tapestries portraying assorted saints, and a massive staircase. The stairs split halfway up at a seemingly life-size statue of St. Ambrose, and then arched around to meet again at a second floor balcony that wrapped around the room some 18 feet above the ground floor.

Did Ambrose actually look like that, and how would we know?

Grant slowly proceeded down a wide hallway and past two massive rooms, then turned left and followed the flow of traffic past another three. Each space apparently had a specific theme or purpose, including a library and a relaxed sitting room with large screen television.

The monks' barbecue show must look good on that baby.

A meeting room with tables arranged in a massive square, with microphones, media plug-ins, and leather chairs at each station had a UN-ish feel to Grant.

As he passed a formal sitting room, Stephen thought of Jennifer Brees, given the knight armor with swords standing erect in each corner.

Then came a large open solarium at the back corner of the building. As Grant entered, to his left were doors leading to his ultimate destination – an auditorium stretching across most of the back of the castle. The gently rising rows offered 750 seats looking down at a stage positioned in front of 20-foot-high windows. The view across the lawn to the Sound and over to Connecticut was striking, especially given today's clear, sun-drenched sky.

As Grant took a moment to absorb the scene, someone stepped next to him and said, "Beautiful, no?"

"Absolutely."

Stephen turned to see a Roman Catholic cardinal in red and black attire. He was a few inches shorter than Grant, very thin, with thick black hair and goatee that accentuated an angular face.

"Pastor Grant."

"Yes." They shook hands. "Cardinal Santos?"

"It is good to meet you face-to-face."

"Same here."

Santos lowered his voice, and moved closer to Grant. "I also feel better knowing that you will be staying close to the Holy Father, Stephen, with these terror attacks. I urged him to call off this entire endeavor." He shook his head. "But he insists on going ahead."

Grant whispered, "Juan, the Pope is right. Many people, many interests, both violent and nonviolent, would love to see Pope Augustine abandon this effort. If he backs down, they win."

"Who is that talking, Stephen," Santos' voice was now barely audible as the two men huddled closer, "the pastor or the old CIA man inside you?"

"Both, and neither has any doubts about the reality of the situation."

"You Americans rarely have doubts."

"Juan …"

"That was uncalled for. I apologize, Stephen. Your country has done everything we've asked, and more, in the work to keep the Pope safe."

"Stay focused, Juan, on what the Pope is trying to accomplish; on what it can accomplish for Christianity and the world. Do the work Augustine needs you to do, and let the security professionals do their jobs. Most of all, of course, stay focused on Christ."

Santos took a deep breath. "You are correct. Thank you." His smile indicated a bit of relief.

A priest approached with four individuals in tow. Grant pegged them as press. His voice returned to its normal level. "Thank you, Cardinal Santos. God bless."

They shook hands. Santos said, "And God bless you, Pastor Grant."

Grant dropped back several steps allowing Santos to get back to work. Stephen recognized the lone woman in the group as a religion reporter from PBS. He also noted that one of the men seemed to be watching him. Grant nonchalantly lingered. It was only a few seconds, but the man's gaze clearly was pointed in his direction. Finally, the interest in Grant gave way to Cardinal Santos when the priest introduced the man as Roy Wallace, a columnist with the *Philadelphia Sun*. Wallace's greeting came with a British accent.

Grant did not recognize him or his name.

Must have me pegged as the pistol packin' pastor.

Wallace was tall and fit, with swept back red-blond hair, a protruding chin and nose, and rectangle-shaped, gold-framed glasses. Over his shoulder hung a black laptop bag.

Grant overheard that the other two were a radio talk show host and an Internet blogger, respectively.

Santos said, "Did Father Alou also fill you in on Pope Augustine's affinity for zobo from his Nigerian homeland?"

Each of the four members of the media said no. Father Alou apologized.

Santos explained, "Given that you four are being given special access to the Pope, for a more intimate conversation about his 'Public Mission of Mere Christianity,' he will offer each of you a glass. This has become something of a tradition when his Eminence hosts guests. Zobo is a favorite drink from his homeland of Nigeria, made from a herb and mixed with water, sugar, juice, ice, and usually some soda water as well."

"Yes," said Wallace, "I read about it. I was wondering if we might be treated to this African fare."

"Indeed, you will, Mr. Wallace," replied Cardinal Santos. "I trust this does not present any dietary problems for anyone? If so, we can arrange to have something else on hand."

All four reporters presented no reservations about accepting zobo from the Pope.

As Santos continued to recap seemingly mundane items, Stephen moved away and up the aisle to get a view of the entire room.

Within a few minutes, more than 110 people were seated as Cardinal Santos approached the podium and microphone.

Grant was distracted by three monks in light gray robes outside the windows. They were firing up large gas grills. What they might be preparing for lunch, however, remained a mystery as a massive screen came down from the ceiling behind Santos, completely eliminating the view of the green lawn, blue water, and Grillin' with the Monks.

The thought of the barbecue made Stephen's mouth water. He had left the parsonage without having breakfast.

"A Public Mission of Mere Christianity" came up in huge letters on the screen, and the rest of the room went dark.

Chapter 47

After the late service on Sunday morning at St. Mary's, Stephen changed into jeans, sneakers and an olive-colored t-shirt. He had two stops on his Sunday afternoon schedule.

The first was to bring Communion to Scott Larson in the hospital.

Grant grabbed a gray leather case with a white cross on the cover off a bookshelf in his office. He sat at his desk, and opened the portable Communion set. Inside were a small bottle, a bread tray, and four small chalices. Each was silver plated, with the chalices also gold lined. He poured wine into the bottle, and placed a few wafers in the bread tray. He would wait until he got to Scott's hospital room to offer the words of institution, and consecrate both. Stephen sealed the bottle, placed the cap on the tray, and put both back in the case. He snapped it closed.

His second stop would be at the firing range at the sportsmen's club.

Stephen moved across the room, and unlocked the oak coffee table/gun cabinet. He removed the 10mm Glock 20, and his gun cleaning tools.

Grant noted how easy it was to slip back into the old habit of efficiently and quickly disassembling, cleaning and reassembling a gun without really thinking about it. When finished, he opened a cushioned gun attaché, placed the pistol and six magazines inside, and shut it.

He went back to his desk, and put down the gun case.

At the sight of the silver metal weapons case next to the leather Communion set, Grant paused.

Am I supposed to feel conflicted, Lord?

It was nothing more than a mental exercise in the rhetorical. Pastor Stephen Grant felt no conflict whatsoever.

He picked up the gun attaché case in his right hand, wedged the portable Communion set between his right side and arm, and strode out to his SUV.

Chapter 48

"Thank you, dear. Now, if you could leave us to business."

Bradley Barnett summarily dismissed his wife. That was his style.

During five years as Brookhaven town supervisor, Barnett had earned a reputation among his colleagues and the local media as the most arrogant politician they'd ever met. And that was saying something in politics, especially in New York.

In a tight-lipped, clenched-jaw style, the short, handsome Barnett, with light brown hair and blue eyes, regularly lectured other council members how to vote, and instructed newspaper reporters and columnists how to cover issues.

For a 31-year-old man, Bradley Barnett wreaked of old-money establishment in a way that fewer and fewer still did in the early twenty-first century. And while Barnett was about old money – as well as new – the family business was anything but establishment.

According to the official line from the Barnett family and friends, they amassed wealth from the work of Bradley's grandfather and father. The grandfather started a fertilizer business after returning from World War II, and diversified into assorted other endeavors, including a construction firm, a restaurant, a catering facility, a local radio station, and a used car dealership. His sons joined, expanded and eventually ran the assorted businesses. That is, except for Bradley's father, Peyton. Peyton Barnett became a successful defense lawyer, including representing some of the most notorious figures in New York organized crime.

But that career choice was no mere coincidence. The largest chunk of the Barnett family fortune was generated over nearly forty years from gambling operations from Portland, Maine, down to the Florida Keys. But with the spread of casino gambling in the late 1980s and early nineties, the business took a hit. So, the Barnett network diversified into distributing a wide array of knock-off and smuggled products, including cigarettes that had become extremely profitable as states and localities jacked up excise taxes. With the spike in the popularity of poker on television starting in the early 2000s – especially Texas Hold 'em – the Barnetts capitalized by sponsoring, organizing and running poker parlors in cities and suburbs up and down the East Coast.

While his grandfather and father were now dead, their work kept paying sizeable dividends to Bradley. In the underworld, the Barnetts did not fully fit in, and were known as the WASP mafia.

Bradley Barnett was never much interested in any aspect of the family business – legitimate or otherwise – except to the extent that it kept him living in his accustomed lifestyle. He never had a job in high school, and traveled much of the world for two years after graduation. While earning a political science degree from Yale, Bradley finally found his cause, and subsequently set his sights and pocketbook on advancing the environmental movement and a career in politics. His wallet and environmentalism made him welcome in the Democratic Party, with many willing to ignore his father's work in defending gangsters, not to mention Bradley's own annoying personality.

Barnett's political supporters often pointed out, "Why should the son have to pay for the sins of the father?" And Barnett affirmed this by very publicly disowning his father's work not long after Peyton's death from a massive heart attack during Bradley's senior year at Yale.

The sprawling, white-shingled-and-stone home on three secluded, wooded acres in the exclusive community of Belle Terre was built by his grandfather. And the maple-wood library in which Barnett now sat with his guest was his father's creation.

They were sipping after-dinner brandies – Grappa from Italy – poured by Mrs. Barnett before she was excused.

Bradley sat in a brown leather armchair. Andre Tyler was in the matching chair just a few feet away.

Barnett said, "Now that we are free from my wife, let's get down to business."

"Certainly," replied Tyler.

"You have raised the half-million for Johns?" Neither Barnett nor Tyler had met the chosen assassin. Robert Johns had come highly recommended as having the skills and experience to pull off this seemingly impossible job, and then somehow disappear.

"Yes. But if anyone were to take a close look, it might be hard to hide where such a significant chunk of money went."

"Don't worry about that. Make a half-million buy with my radio station for ads against the Pope's agenda. I've brought in funds from elsewhere for Johns."

"That works for me."

"I'm sure it does."

Barnett checked his watch, and finished his Grappa. "Now, Andre, it's time for you to play drop man."

"Excuse me?"

Barnett reached down and tapped a wide, black leather, legal attaché case. "This is Johns' $3 million. He has checked into or is about to check into the Marriott in Islandia. You're simply going to the front desk, and requesting that this be put in the hotel safe for Mr. Robert Johns. Make up some name for yourself. I don't care what it is. Just make sure it cannot be traced in anyway. Take a receipt, and leave. Understood?"

"Perfectly clear."

An hour later, Andre Tyler was driving east on the Long Island Expressway, and the man known as Robert Johns had picked up his payment for services to be rendered, while canceling his hotel reservation.

Chapter 49

For such an early appointment, Grant decided to drive into Manhattan, rather than taking the Long Island Rail Road.

He left the parsonage a little before 5:00 AM, and pulled into a parking garage a couple of blocks from the Federal Building at 6:30. He didn't bother to grab a cup of coffee, knowing the FBI would have plenty of black, high-octane sludge on hand to get everyone jumpstarted for the day.

The downtown Jacob K. Javits Federal Building was pretty much what one would expect of a government building built in 1967. The architecture was stylistically challenged.

Waiting at the security entrance was Paige, dressed in a simple, double-breasted, black pantsuit with a white shirt. Her long hair was pulled up into a bun in the back. Grant recalled how much he enjoyed when she wore her hair up in anticipation of later seeing it come undone. In fact, that scene had popped into his dreams since their jaunt to Montauk.

Move on, Grant.

With Paige was Ryan Bates, dressed in standard FBI-issued blue suit, white shirt, and dark tie.

As Stephen approached, Paige said, "I told Ryan you'd be early."

With Bates and Caldwell, Stephen passed quickly through security. But not as quickly as would have been the case when he was with the agency in the early 1990s.

A few minutes later, he was shaking hands with various individuals from assorted security and police departments in a rather bland conference room. Grant sensed the sadness and anger looming not far below the surface after losing so many FBI agents and police just five days earlier.

In fact, Stephen himself was feeling a bit conflicted. His instincts as a pastor were to try to console, comfort and provide hope – even speak of forgiveness. But given his recent experiences of having to kill Linda Serrano, the re-acquaintance with Paige, being drafted by the government once more, and the terrorist roundup and attacks the previous week, Grant also sympathized with the impulse not to forgive. While usually preaching a good game on forgiveness, Grant had a very tough time living that particular message. He understood the desire to strike out in the name of justice, even if that justice was accompanied or even driven by a hearty dose of vengeance.

Grant – dressed in a light gray suit, white shirt and red tie – was introduced as a pastor and former CIA agent. He knew that neither aspect of this odd combination would sit well with a good number of people in the room. In Grant's experience, the FBI and other non-CIA, law-enforcement types rarely trusted the agency – referring to anyone with the CIA derisively as a "spook." Sometimes that mistrust was justified. But in Grant's view, it was more overly active imaginations and misunderstandings, rather than actual actions by the agency that generated this trust deficiency.

Meanwhile, his experience as both a pastor and an agent taught him that too many on the frontlines of keeping the American people safe carried an unwarranted burden of guilt. Because of actions taken on the job, they often felt somehow not good enough to attend church or even to be loved by God. As a church pastor, Grant had the opportunity to help various local police officers work through and get by such mistaken beliefs. He even gained a couple of families as members at St. Mary's as a result. Grant wondered if the CIA, FBI and other federal security agencies had improved their efforts in providing spiritual support since his days on the job, especially post-9/11.

FBI Special Agent Rich Noack strode to the front of the room to speak to the half-dozen FBI team leaders that would be in charge of Pope Augustine's security while in the U.S., along with another seven representatives from the CIA, NSA, Homeland Security, and local police departments.

After getting everyone settled, Noack gave a rundown on the day's schedule. Those in attendance would be split into three groups. They would head in different directions, but by the end of the day, all the points on Pope Augustine's visit would be covered by each group, including Kennedy Airport, the St. Ambrose Retreat House, and the Meadowlands in New Jersey, where Augustine would celebrate Mass before leaving for Mexico. Everyone would meet back in the same conference room in the late afternoon to compare notes, and deal with any questions that came up.

After covering the logistics, Noack shifted focus and tone. "Listen, I recognize that we haven't had time to mourn, or even to fully absorb our losses. Funerals started on Saturday. But we'll miss a couple today. Tomorrow will offer additional opportunities to honor our dead." He paused, and looked down for a moment. "Most of us don't like to dwell on such matters, but we're not invincible. So, don't be a schmuck. If you need help, get it. None of this is easy, but this is what happens in war. And houses rigged to blow is what happens when those we're fighting screw the rules. Anyway, we have a job to do. And don't think that because this particular terror cell is no longer in operation that we can relax. None of us in this room can afford to rest. At least not until Pope Augustine is safely out of the U.S., and on to his next stop. God help us."

Noack looked around the conference room. And his gaze stopped on Grant.

"Speaking of God, all of you know that we have a team member on this assignment with a unique background, to say the least. Stephen Grant is a Lutheran pastor, but he also served this nation proudly as a Navy SEAL and with the CIA." Noack now addressed Grant directly. "Pastor, though we haven't actually met yet, I hope I'm not out of line if I ask you to say a prayer for those who have lost family, friends and colleagues, and for our efforts over the coming days?"

Grant stood up. "Yes, of course, Special Agent Noack." He walked to the front of the room, and stood next to Noack, who given his height, size and bald head stood as an imposing figure. "Let's bow our heads." Stephen noticed that Paige and a couple of others did not do so.

"Dear Lord, thank you for these brave men and women who serve and protect the people of this nation. St. Paul noted the role of government as protector. He wrote: 'Then do what is good, and you will receive his approval, for he is God's servant for your good. But if you do wrong, be afraid, for he does not bear the sword in vain. For he is the servant of God, an avenger who carries out God's wrath on the wrongdoer.' As agents of our government, grant all of the people involved in maintaining the safety of Pope Augustine the wisdom, compassion, courage and discernment to serve properly as the bearers of the sword. We also come before you, Lord, asking that you grant healing and provide comfort to the individuals who lost friends, family members and colleagues at the hands of those who kill innocent human life in some perverted idea of religion. We pray this in the name of Jesus. Amen."

The 15 people were split into teams of five, and moved downstairs into three black Chevy Suburbans. Grant was with Caldwell, Noack, Bates, and a lieutenant from the Nassau County police force named Mel Dwyer.

The starting point for Grant's group would be the Meadowlands, so they headed to the Holland Tunnel. Bates was driving, with Noack riding shotgun. Dwyer and Caldwell were in the second row, and Grant wound up in the back third row.

Dwyer reminded Grant of a mischievous Irishman in his early thirties. He had short, curly, reddish-brown hair, and beard and mustache of the same color. Dwyer was turned sideways, with his head leaning against the window, looking at Grant in the seat behind him.

"So, you're a pastor?" asked Dwyer.

Grant noted that he smiled easily. *Here it comes.*

"Yes, the Lutheran variety."

"I'm a Catholic. But other than the big holidays, I ain't been to Mass regularly in a hell of a long time. Probably a half-dozen years."

"Ah, you're an 'EC' Christian," Grant responded.

"EC?"

"Only in church on Easter and Christmas."

"Yeah, I guess." Dwyer chuckled a bit. "Don't get much out of it. You know what I mean? But Karen, my wife, she takes the four kids every Sunday. And the three in school, they go to Catholic school, too."

"Good for her ... and them."

"Yeah, but I just can't do it. Like I said, don't get nothing out of going to church."

"I hear that a lot."

"I bet you do. What do you say?"

The other three in the SUV were quiet. Bates was driving, and both Noack and Caldwell were looking out the windows. Grant couldn't tell if they were listening or trying not to.

"Depends on the person, but sometimes I ask: What do you expect to get from going to church? What's the purpose?"

"What do you mean?"

"Well, do you actually listen to what's being said? Have you ever asked why certain things are done? What's the purpose, the meaning? Or, is it that you're really not that interested, or too lazy to get up on Sunday mornings? I'm not saying this is the case with you, Lt. Dwyer, but in my experience, the 'I don't get anything out of it' statement sometimes serves as a respectable excuse in certain company for not caring or just being lazy."

Dwyer smiled and said, "So, you don't screw around; don't beat around the bush. I like that. OK, you're right, sorta. When I'm off, I like to sleep in on Sundays. Besides, like I said, the kids go to Mass, to Catholic school, and that's the main thing, right?"

"Maybe," Grant said. "But if I may ask, why bother sending them to parochial school? After all, what's the point if you don't get anything out of it?"

Dwyer responded, "I want them to believe in God. Shit, I believe in God."

"Don't get me wrong, I'm not telling you what to do. You have to make your own choices. But as you said, I try not to beat around the bush. And I always thought that police officers appreciate the direct, no-nonsense approach."

"I'm not a bull-shitter, and don't want others to bull shit me. Excuse my language."

"No problem. That being the case, what message are you sending your kids?"

"Message? That they have to go to church."

"But on the one hand, you sacrifice to send them to Catholic school. On the other hand, what are you telling them when you sleep in on Sunday morning while the rest of the family heads off to church?"

Grant thought he caught part of a smile on Noack's face in the front seat. He could not see Paige's face. She sat unmoving, still staring out the window.

"Yeah, I got it," said Dwyer. "Guilty of 'don't do what I do, do what I say.'"

"Basically."

Dwyer smiled again. "I like you, Grant. You're not a bull shitter either."

"Thanks, and I like you, Lt. Dwyer. Now, get your ass to church on Sunday."

From the front of the SUV, Noack said, "It's nice that you guys like each other. If you're done with Sunday School, it's time to get back to the job at hand."

Chapter 50

"Have you ever seen a coalition like this?"

Jim Hunter, the pudgy, rumpled, frog-like newspaper reporter sitting next to Roy Wallace, didn't wait for an answer. Instead, he went on to speak the names of the groups and individuals scheduled to appear at this press event held at the Hotel Pennsylvania in New York City, right across Seventh Avenue from Penn Station and Madison Square Garden.

After he finished going through the list, Hunter observed, "Funny. Only hatred for the Catholic Church could bring together a group this diverse. Some of these guys don't want to be seen in the same state together, never mind the same room. Yet, here they are. What do you think, Wallace?"

Roy Wallace remained focused on his laptop screen, and dismissively replied, "You'll know that when you read my column."

The grizzled Hunter shook his head. Just loud enough for Wallace to hear, he said, "Asshole Brit."

"Ever charming, James," replied Wallace.

At the front of the meeting room was a stage with a podium and a screen above on the wall. About three-quarters of the chairs were filled with media and other interested parties.

Among the assorted non-media individuals in the room was the FBI's Ryan Bates, trying to look very non-FBI-ish.

In addition, at the request of Stephen Grant, Fathers Thomas Stone and Ronald McDermott were in attendance. Stone and McDermott just happened to be in the seats directly behind Hunter and Wallace.

Grant wanted to know who was there and what was said, but felt he might be pushing his luck by attending himself, especially given that he already was going to appear on television on Friday. Stephen knew that Ron could be counted on for an accurate recall of what was said, while Tom would provide an excellent feel for the event, picking up on some of the subtleties of the gathering.

As they sat waiting for the press conference to start, Stone tilted his head toward McDermott and whispered, "It's like we're Rick and TC helping Magnum."

Ron asked, "And who am I, Rick?"

"Well, you're short like Rick, but I can't see you running the King Kamehameha Club. You're too stuffy. I'll have to be Rick."

"Rick was kind of shady, and TC had the helicopter, correct? I'm okay with that. And it's become easier in recent days to think of Stephen as Thomas Magnum."

"Our friend is full of surprises lately," agreed Stone.

At the mention of Grant's name, Roy Wallace paused at his laptop.

At 11:00 AM, a line of fifteen individuals walked onto the stage.

Jim Hunter was not happy. "Oh, crap. How long is this going to take? They'll say each person will only speak for two minutes, but that never happens. They're supposed to show TV and radio spots, then Q&A. This'll take two hours."

"Stop bitching, James," said Wallace.

"Screw you, Roy."

Becca Roberts stood at the podium. Over her left shoulder stood her partner, Jay Storm, still looking quizzical. Over Roberts' other shoulder was actor Neil Eller, a thin, gangly fellow with hair that seemed to have never met a comb. Eller was best known for playing easy-going leads in romantic comedies, and lately for his Scientology affiliations.

Roberts was dressed simply in light gray pants, with the collars of a white blouse and blue blazer turned up. She brushed back some of her long black hair, and spoke in a confident tone. "Thank you all for coming. My name is Becca Roberts. I'm an actor, writer and concerned global citizen. Before you is a very diverse group of people, who disagree on many issues. But what brings us together is our mutual concern regarding Pope Augustine's so-called 'Public Mission of Mere Christianity,' and that the first stop on the Pope's journey around the world pushing a close-minded agenda will be here in the New York City area next week. Each person will make a brief statement of no more than two minutes."

Hunter smiled, shook his head, and whispered, "Yeah, sure."

Roberts continued, "You'll also have the chance to take in a few television, Internet and radio spots. And again, you'll see that the individuals and groups coming together here today can hold strikingly different views. In fact, we have diverse reasons for opposing the Pope's effort. Nonetheless, we've come together now in a show of unity. Let's get things started by introducing a dear friend of mine. Most of you know him from his many popular films. Mr. Neil Eller."

Roberts took a step aside to allow Eller to claim the podium. The actor had "aw, shucks" mannerisms, presented an easy, slightly crooked smile, and spoke softly. He said, "Thanks so much, Becca. I'm humbled to be on a stage with so many impressive individuals, all of whom, I must point out, have far more important jobs and are much smarter than this silly actor. But I'm honored that whatever fame – hopefully not infamy – I might have acquired due to my films can bring some attention to this effort. So, Becca, Jay and I got to work with director Hugh Zimmer to produce this public service message. Please have a look."

The lights in the room dimmed, and everyone on stage turned and looked up at the screen. The commercial began with a fade in. Seated on three stools were Neil Eller, Becca Roberts and Jay Storm, against a simple, dark gray background.

Eller began, "It speaks well that we are such a spiritual nation."

The camera cut to Becca, "Almost all surveys show that we are among the most spiritual people on the planet."

Then to Jay, "Our nation also is a diverse one. A place of many faiths."

Eller continued, "People are free to worship as they please. That's their own private choice."

Becca said, "Unfortunately, we and many other Americans are worried about Pope Augustine's 'Public Mission of Mere Christianity.' We certainly respect the beliefs of Roman Catholics, and all Christians."

Over to Jay, "But when the leader of any faith starts talking like he has some kind of a monopoly on truth."

Neil, "Or that his church should inform our culture."

Becca, "Or a person of such enormous influence attacks our constitutional separation of church and state."

Jay, "Or goes out of the way to condemn a peaceful religion due to a few extremists."

Neil, "Well, that's when we have to stand up, and say something is wrong."

Becca, "The Pope calls this a 'Public Mission of Mere Christianity.' But unfortunately, it looks more like another case of fundamentalist intolerance."

Jay, "Please stand up against intolerance."

Neil Eller concluded, "Join us. Make your voice heard by adding your name to a petition supporting religious freedom, an independent culture, and the separation of church and state on the website of the Faith, Trust and Freedom Foundation."

The web address appeared on screen, running below the three smiling Hollywood faces.

Part of the room erupted in applause. McDermott and Stone were not among the pleased.

Father McDermott was visibly annoyed. "Give me a break," he said to Stone in a failed attempt at whispering. "What a load of distortions. What about freedom of speech for Christians?"

"I know, Ron," whispered Tom. "Calm down. We're not here to debate. We're ... well ... on reconnaissance. Besides, weren't you the one that predicted this kind of offensive would be launched?"

"Yes, I was," replied Ron. "But it still bugs me."

The lights came back up. Becca Roberts introduced the Reverend Donna Nicks-Simpson, executive director of the United Faith Council and a Methodist pastor. A mousy lady of 75 years with hair dyed blond pulled a box out from underneath the podium, and stepped up to the microphone.

Rev. Nicks-Simpson said, "Thank you for being here. As Ms. Roberts said, I'm Pastor Donna Nicks-Simpson. I'm retired from parish work, but have served as executive director of the United Faith Council for eight years now. The United Faith Council started out many years ago as a Christian ecumenical organization. Today, we count among our membership churches and individuals from across Christianity, along with Jewish, Muslim, New Age, Hindu, Buddhist, Native American groups and individuals, and people representing additional belief systems. As you will hear in this public service radio announcement, we are very worried that Pope Augustine is not really interested in bringing people together, but instead looking to cause greater division and conflict. That, quite simply, is not the true mission of Christianity or any other compassionate belief system. Please listen to this."

Nicks-Simpson stepped back from the microphone, and the radio spot was piped in over the sound system. With choir voices faintly heard in the background singing a nondescript song, a smooth feminine voice said, "Since its creation nearly a half-century ago, the United Faith Council has been about bringing people of good faith together. We've worked to find common ground between many different spiritual bodies. That's why we were so disappointed to discover that Pope Augustine's 'Public Mission of Mere Christianity' seems to be all about dividing us, rather than uniting us. This mission makes Christians look arrogant, when people of faith should be humble. It makes spirituality appear to be about superiority and prejudice, when we should be about welcoming others on their own terms. The Pope has said that one voice is needed on faith and culture. We respectfully disagree. What we need is to be united in our diversity. That's what the United Faith Council is all about. Please become active by contacting the United Faith Council." A web address and 800 number followed.

Father Stone chuckled and said, "'United in our diversity' – got to love that one."

McDermott's irritation seemed to be growing. "What does that mean? Does that make any sense to you?"

"That doesn't matter. What matters is how it sounds, and how it makes people feel. It's not about thinking things through. It's not about understanding one's faith. It's about feeling and emotion."

"That's for sure," replied Ron.

Wallace turned halfway in his seat. In a hushed tone, he said, "Gentlemen, pardon me for overhearing. But you made it rather hard not to do so. When on reconnaissance, you're supposed to make yourself inconspicuous. Like that FBI agent several rows back."

Wallace nodded towards Ryan Bates, with both Tom and Ron turning to see. Bates ignored the glances.

Wallace continued, "I heard you mention Pastor Grant. I once met your friend, but I don't think he'd recall me. But I certainly saw the stories about the recent shootings at his church out on Long Island. Tragic, but it was a compelling news story."

Tom asked, "And you are?"

"Roy Wallace, with the *Philadelphia Sun*. And you gentlemen are?"

Stone glanced at McDermott. "I am Father Tom Stone, and this is Father Ronald McDermott."

"Nice to meet you."

Wallace turned his back on Stone and McDermott, who shrugged their shoulders at each other.

Becca Roberts was at the podium for the next introduction. "It is now my pleasure to introduce Sister Elizabeth Peters, who leads Catholics for Reproductive Choice, and runs a crisis pregnancy center in Beverly Hills."

Tom whispered to Ron, "Crisis pregnancy center in Beverly Hills? Is she kidding? What's the deal with Sister Peters?"

Ron said, "She's been a liberal gadfly around the church for a long time. But Peters' radical pro-abortion activities led to her being defrocked about ten years ago. She didn't seem to care very much. Still goes by 'sister,' and look, still wears a habit. Wait'll you hear this. She's a pro at ginning up outrage."

A pugnacious, flat-faced, hefty woman in an off-white habit and dress grabbed both sides of the podium. Sister Peters gave the impression that she was more than ready to fight off anyone looking to wrest that podium from her.

Peters leaned close to a microphone she clearly did not need. "This Pope is no different from most of his dictatorial predecessors. He's a close-minded fundamentalist. He wants a few close-minded Christians to tell others how to live. That's what this so-called 'Public Mission of Mere Christianity' is zeroed in on. And as misogynists, they want to control the lives and bodies of women. Obviously, a top objective is to advance the anti-choice agenda by outlawing abortion. You know, there's an old joke that if men could get pregnant, abortion would be a sacrament. But since they can't, women are stuck fighting for their rights. Augustine is just another pain-in-the-ass papist."

Becca Roberts took a step forward, and leaned over to whisper in Peters' ear. Before Roberts got a word out, Peters said, "Yeah, yeah, I know, honey. Move the old controversial broad along. Well, here's a message from Catholics for Reproductive Choice."

A young woman's voice came over the sound system, "I'm a mom of three and a practicing Catholic. My husband and I juggle work and family, just like so many other families. We do soccer practice and are active in our local parish. And we are so proud of our children, who attend parochial school. But before getting married, I got pregnant. We were in college, and clearly not ready to become parents. There was just no way I could have cared for a child, and still completed my education and gotten my career off the ground. I had the option of terminating the pregnancy at an early stage. Thank God I did. Being able to plan meant that my husband and I were fully prepared to provide for a family. Like so many other members of Catholics for Reproductive Choice, I understand the importance of women being able to make their own choices about their own bodies. While as a Catholic I respect Pope Augustine, I'm worried about the loss of independence and choice. The church says that each one of us should have the freedom to make our own choices according to our conscience. That goes for women and their reproductive rights. Please join Catholics for Reproductive Choice, and help protect our most basic rights."

Ron declared, "Knew what was coming, and it still pisses me off. The name calling, the over-the-top rhetoric, the manipulation, the inaccuracies, and the arrogance – that's the usual package for so-called Catholics for Reproductive Choice."

"I know," said Tom softly.

"A commercial about a woman aborting her baby due to inconvenience? That's it – the best they can do? Well, at least it's accurate in terms of the usual reasons. And did she actually thank God for having abortion as an option? And then there's the ridiculous implication that following one's conscience means whatever decision you make is OK. What relativistic crap! How about a morally-formed and informed conscience?"

Tom Stone said, "Ron, I'm on your side, remember?"

Next up at the microphone was Andre Tyler, in attendance as director of the Our Children Our Planet Foundation. His bushy eyebrows and untamed white hair clashed with a tidy, dark gray suit.

Tyler said, "The Our Children Our Planet Foundation is an educational organization focused on educating the public, governmental officials and the media about issues affecting our environment today, and the environment that will be inherited by our children and grandchildren. Our concern about Pope Augustine's global project is that it would redirect churches and many Christians away from concern about our environment, and from engaging in the work to protect our planet. We have worked together with the group Green Believers to produce this television and Internet video public service announcement."

The music was deep and dire, with a grainy, black-and-white picture on screen. The scenes flashing by included smokestacks, burning foliage, a polar bear struggling to get on a floating chunk of ice, and massive traffic jams. An NFL Films-like voice spoke in an ominous tone: "As hard as it is to believe, there was a time when churches and religious bodies in this country did not see it as their responsibility to speak out in defense of God's creation. They simply did not care what damage was done to the planet, arrogantly thinking they had dominion over land, water and all living things. That changed in recent times, with many churches becoming more environmentally conscious, speaking out against the raping of our world. They mobilized to stop water and air pollution, the destruction of the rainforest, the loss of open space, the destruction of species, and the advancement of manmade climate change. Unfortunately, now Pope Augustine's 'Public Mission of Mere Christianity' seems to be a mission to turn back the clock; to pull Christians away from social activism; to, in effect, silence voices of faith when it comes to our environment. Our children and our planet cannot afford such reactionary religion. Instead, we need an open-minded spirituality that embraces our environment."

Roberts went on to introduce individuals representing assorted faiths, political views and philosophies. A leading atheist, for example, complained about God being inserted further into politics and society. An imam accused Pope Augustine of stoking further distrust against Muslims. The leader of an ultra-conservative, anti-Vatican II, breakaway Catholic group accused Pope Augustine of "syncretism."

Brother Barry Stanton from the Ark of Christ in Alabama made the journey to speak. He not only lambasted the Pope, but almost everyone else participating in the press conference for not being sufficiently committed to Jesus and the Bible.

By the time all the statements were made, videos seen, audios heard, print ads read, and questions answered, it was a couple of minutes after 1:00 in the afternoon.

Jim Hunter leaned over and whispered to Roy Wallace: "Told you – two hours."

"Get a life, James," replied Wallace.

Chapter 51

Once every couple of months, Stephen Grant, Tom Stone
and Ron McDermott indulged themselves by meeting for
dinner at a place several steps up from the typical Long
Island diner.

They were seated at a table in front of a gas-fueled
fireplace for an early dinner on Tuesday evening at
Tweed's Restaurant & Buffalo Bar in Riverhead. The small
bar and restaurant was located on the old town's Main
Street in an historic 1896 building that first housed the
John J. Sullivan Hotel.

Each was enjoying a bowl of Long Island clam chowder,
while also splitting a bottle of Chamarre's Cabernet
Sauvignon. A particular favorite of Ron's, the Long Island
clam chowder was lighter than either its Manhattan or
New England brethren, but still had a spicy bite to it. The
broth was clear, with the taste of large, tender clams
shining through. In fact, Tweed's chowder was award
winning.

The soup bowls were taken away, and replaced by two
appetizers they agreed to share. The carpaccio of bison
tenderloin with white truffle oil was meltingly delicious, as
was the sliced smoked duck with fruited chili sauce.

Stephen asked, "So, what was the deal at the press
conference today?"

McDermott gave a detailed rundown on the speakers, and the major points hit without referring to any notes.

As he was wrapping things up, their dinners arrived. Stephen had the Aquebogue Duck Two Ways, pan seared and in a blackberry reduction. Tom seemed especially pleased with the arrival of a massive bison burger. Ron chose the hearty Bison Cowboy Steak.

"Impressive account, Ron. You could have been in the surveillance business," Stephen observed.

"Well, don't grant your man McDermott double-O status just yet," said Tom.

"Why is that?"

"He was less than inconspicuous in terms of criticizing some speakers. Actually, strike that – criticizing every speaker."

Ron said, "I wasn't that bad."

Stone rolled his eyes.

"Anything that we didn't know going in?" Stephen asked.

Tom said, "Two things struck me, besides being present to hear all of the over-the-top rhetoric. First was the obvious discomfort among those on the far Left and on the far Right standing on that stage together. It was pretty funny. In order to get the likes of Brother Barry Stanton; pre-Vatican-II, holier-than-the-pope Catholics; the green movement; and a pro-abortion, former nun on the same stage opposing the same thing speaks volumes about the fear and anger Pope Augustine has generated. It's quite astounding."

Stephen said, "And second?"

"The money."

"Money?" Ron asked.

"There's the cost of producing all of those video, radio and print ads. But when they announced where all of those ads and commercials would be running – including the New York City-area market – it just blew me away. With

Maggie in public relations, I've picked up on some of this over the years. And we're talking several million dollars."

While eating their meals, they kicked around the topic.

Stephen summed up, "So, we've got big money that's scared and angry."

"That sounds about right," Ron responded.

Tom added, "Almost forgot. Ron's ramblings on the speakers drew the attention of a reporter sitting in front of us. He said that he met you briefly, but you probably wouldn't remember."

"Who was he?"

Ron answered, "Roy Wallace. Said he was a columnist with the *Philadelphia Sun*."

"Yes. We weren't introduced. But he was at St. Ambrose's when we got the rundown on Augustine's visit. He was watching me for a bit. Kind of odd given he was being introduced to Cardinal Santos at the time. I figured it was about the shootings."

"He did mention recognizing you from the news," said Ron.

There you go.

Stephen said, "Guys, thanks for taking the time to go into the city, and sitting through that press conference. The very least I can do is pick up dinner."

"That would be the least," added Tom with a smirk.

After taking care of the bill, Grant looked at his watch. "I have to get moving. It's 6:45, and I've got a church council meeting at 7:30."

"Oh boy, lucky you," said Tom.

"We still on for golf in the morning?" asked Stephen as he got up from the table.

"Six-thirty at Rock Hill," said Ron.

"Works for me. Gives me enough time for my noon Bible study," Tom added.

"Good. It'll probably be my last bit of sanity until Pope Augustine leaves," said Stephen. "I'll see you in the AM, gentlemen."

In unison, Tom Stone and Ron McDermott looked over their shoulders, saying, "Gentlemen? Where?"

"That never gets old, guys."

Chapter 52

Stephen made it back to St. Mary's with fifteen minutes to spare.

The council meeting was held in the conference room/library, which was dominated by cherry wood – the walls, the bookcases, and the long conference table in the center of the room.

Grant was starting to fully realize how much of the costs of this church his friends the Gundersons actually ate.

On this night, church staff expected in attendance were only Barbara Tunney and Stephen. Grant doubted Pam would be there, with fiancée Scott still recovering from his wounds. But Grant would announce the good news received the day before that Scott was out of the hospital and at home, while still rehabbing.

Given his penchant – or obsession – with time, council meetings often were a test for Grant. With his SEAL and CIA experience, he knew the importance of being patient. His past work often required the discipline to remain quiet, to not move even, for hour upon hour. Patience could mean the difference between the success or failure of a mission; and on occasion, between life and death.

In more recent times, there were plenty of opportunities for silent prayer and reflection.

Yet, a lengthy church council meeting, with conversations circling around and around and getting nowhere, often put Grant to the test. He could grow downright antsy.

The meeting was brought to order by the congregation president, Everett Birk, who tipped the scales at over 300 pounds. His blond hair cut in a flat-top style was accompanied by a thin beard and mustache. When first heard, his gentle voice didn't fit the man. He was a tenor in the choir.

During church meetings, every time Everett sat down on a metal folding chair, Stephen wondered if it would hold.

Birk asked Grant to open with prayer. Everyone bowed their heads and folded their hands.

Grant first read a passage from Scripture – Psalm 23: "The Lord is my shepherd; I shall not want. He makes me lie down in green pastures. He leads me beside still waters. He restores my soul. He leads me in paths of righteousness for his name's sake. Even though I walk through the valley of the shadow of death, I will fear no evil, for you are with me; your rod and your staff, they comfort me. You prepare a table before me in the presence of my enemies; you anoint my head with oil; my cup overflows. Surely goodness and mercy shall follow me all the days of my life, and I shall dwell in the house of the Lord forever."

He paused a moment. It was quiet.

Grant continued, "Let us pray. Dear Lord, we thank you for bringing us together this evening. Please give us the wisdom and clarity of thought to carry out your will. Guide us through these troubling times. We ask comfort for all of us who have suffered loss, and those who perhaps are struggling with all that has happened in recent weeks. And please grant healing to our music director, Scott. We pray this in Jesus' name. Amen."

Amongst the mumbled responses of "Amen" came a loud, "I'll say Amen to that."

Everyone in the room turned to see a smiling Scott Larson seated in a wheel chair in the doorway, with Pam positively beaming behind him. The room erupted in joy, including a few tears.

Scott and Pam – though mostly Pam – provided a quick rundown on Scott's recovery and rehabilitation. She concluded, "Technically, Scott should not be here, but he insisted. He's much farther along at this point than any of the doctors had predicted."

Scott said, "Watch."

Pam responded in a voice rich in worry and warning, "Scott..."

"Just this, don't worry." He slowly lifted the lower part of his right leg, so the entire leg extended straight out. He lowered it, and then did the same with his left.

This generated another eruption of emotion from members of St. Mary's church council, including smatterings of "Thank God!"

After a little more catching up, Scott interrupted, "Okay, I think Pastor wants to get this meeting back on track." He looked at Grant smiling, "We all know how big you are with keeping on schedule."

"I think I can live with a bit of tardiness given the situation."

Room was made at the table for Scott, with Pam taking a seat next to him.

Each committee leader or staff member offered a brief update, including education, youth, evangclism, buildings and grounds, finance, fellowship, and worship. Even Scott chipped in with the new schedule for St. Mary's various choirs, with the adult choir resuming practice tomorrow night, though under the guidance of Pam for now. It all seemed like the usual fare for a council meeting at St. Mary's.

Then came Grant's "Pastor's Report." After dispensing with the mundane, he moved on to the two big topics that, no doubt, were on the minds of most in the room.

"I've spoken to each of you individually about what happened nearly four weeks ago. It's been extremely difficult for all of us, with the loss of Hans and Flo, obviously, and Scott being injured." Grant nodded in Scott's direction. "And just seeing this dreadful event play out here in our own church is very emotional and trying. The majority of us here tonight were present that night. And then there's the media attention it brought the congregation. I know that some of you were contacted with questions about St. Mary's, the Gundersons, and me. I appreciate the support you've shown. And I hope the meetings, and other times here and there, that some of us have had – just to talk and pray – have helped. But since our last council meeting was in mid-August, I thought it important to see if members of the council think there's anything we need to address as a council, or as a church, in a more official manner in the aftermath of everything that's gone on?"

As he expected, the initial response Grant received was silence. "Anything?" More silence. "Come on, really nothing?"

"Well, Pastor, now that you mention it." It was Nicole Foreman, who led the church's education committee. Nicole was normally happy and flighty; a disposition that seemed accentuated by her short, bouncy black hair, bright green eyes and wide smile. But now she was clearly nervous and unsure.

"Yes, go ahead, Nicole," Stephen said in his most soothing pastor voice.

"Well, I was kind of surprised that you had a gun – well, I guess, guns – in your office. Is that a good idea? After all, this is a church."

Before Grant could respond, Sean McEnany spoke. "If he didn't have the gun, Nicole, how many more people would be dead? How many people in this room right now would not be here?"

Grant knew many Seans over the years. McEnany had moved smoothly from serving as an Army Ranger to a firm that did corporate security work. He was a vice president for both sales and strategy. Though he was out of the Army for a decade, Sean McEnany still had the look – blond hair in a very short, near-crew cut, and neat, crisp suits on his muscular, fit, five-foot-ten-inch frame. He came across as confident, but not arrogant. Sean also had a low, raspy voice.

Ever since the shootings, Sean had mentioned during brief conversations heading out of church that he wanted to sit down with Grant to discuss what happened. Grant had not thought much about it, however, considering it nothing more than one of those vague, polite invites that neither person winds up following through on. Sean had only been a member of the congregation for a bit over two years. His willingness to volunteer, and his organizational skills, got him onto the church council within a year of coming to St. Mary's. Grant knew a few basics about Sean, but in no way did he truly know the man.

Scott chipped in, "I certainly would not be here."

"Well, I hadn't thought of that," Nicole said, still nervous and unsure.

Stephen said, "I understand your concerns, Nicole. No doubt, others have similar worries. But let me reassure you that everything was under lock and key, and stored properly. And my top concern always is safety." He looked directly in Nicole's green eyes. "You have no worries."

Nicole looked down. "I'm sorry."

"Sorry? You have absolutely nothing to be sorry about," said Grant. "Someone in this room should have asked that question, and you did."

McEnany said, "I do have a question on the outreach front." Sean led the evangelism committee. "We might want to step up getting word out to the locals on all of the activities going on here at St. Mary's – worship, youth, music, education, and so on. Just so people get back to thinking of us as a church active in the community. Not just the church where those shootings happened."

"Or the church with – how did the *New York Post* put it? – the pistol packin' pastor," said Scott with a smile. Most in the room managed a brief laugh.

"Thanks for that contribution, Scott," Grant said.

"You're welcome." Scott shrugged.

Everett said, "Sean, that's a great idea. And since you brought it up and head up evangelism, can we get you to draw up a quick action memo and e-mail it to each of us?"

"No problem. You'll all have it by the end of the week." He entered a reminder on his BlackBerry.

"Quite frankly, I'm far more worried about this Pope thing, than about your guns," said Suzanne Maher in a stern and dismissive, yet squeaky voice.

Maher was the church vice president. But Grant also had a private nickname – only shared with Tom and Ron – for Mrs. Maher: "St. Mary's enforcer of doctrine."

Maher had a tendency to come across as one of those compassionless, nit-picky individuals who turned people away from church. While Grant viewed doctrine as critically important, and loved to debate and discuss points on theology with almost anyone, he understood that guiding parishioners needed a gentle hand. In her self-appointed enforcer role, Maher was anything but gentle. During a Bible study or other church gathering, if someone strayed ever so slightly from Lutheran doctrine, Suzanne Maher pounced like a ferocious cat on her prey. She even challenged Grant on a sermon point now and then on the way out of church. As much as it irritated at times, Stephen was in a position to laugh it off. Many parishioners, though, were unsure of how many angels might be able to dance on the head of a pin.

At the same time, though, Maher's generosity went beyond most anyone else at St. Mary's. She not only gave of her time and treasure – which was considerable – for the church, but Suzanne Maher also supported individuals and families at St. Mary's when they hit troubled times. At one moment, Maher could be chastising you for failing to grasp Martin Luther's points on law and gospel, and at the next, writing checks to help pay your mortgage or rent if you were out of work.

Right now, Grant knew, it was time for the nit-picky enforcer. The 70-year-old widow with light gray hair, and baggy skin that seemed to barely hang onto her bones, sat perfectly straight and unmoving in her chair.

Grant said, "This Pope thing, Suzanne?"

"Yes. I think we should be concerned as a council and a church as to why you are involved in this visit of Pope Augustine and this so-called mission of his. What is he calling it?"

"A Public Mission of Mere Christianity," Grant volunteered.

"Right. Why are you involved in this?"

"First and foremost, I was asked to do so by President Harrison Piepkorn. He's the president of our church body, Suzanne."

"Yes, I'm well aware who Reverend Piepkorn is, unfortunately," said Maher, barely hiding her disgust.

"Second, I am very excited about this effort. And as a congregation that emphasizes and embraces traditional Christianity, our entire congregation should be enthused."

Maher quickly replied, "I don't see why we should be enthused by anything any pope does."

"Let me explain what Pope Augustine is looking to achieve. He wants to bring together traditional Christians from across denominations in order to present to the world a unified voice on some of the most critical challenges confronting Christianity today. For example, he cited relativism, or the idea that there is no absolute truth as one of those challenges facing us. Isn't relativism the exact opposite of what Christians should believe and teach about Jesus Christ?"

Grant did not wait for an answer. He forged ahead. "The Pope also spoke about the need to fight against those pushing the idea that the church should not speak out on any issues in the public arena. You know the attitude: feel free to worship however you like, but don't be speaking out in the political arena, even on issues like life and marriage. And the other challenge mentioned by the Pope was Islamic radicalism, and what that means in terms of not only terrorism, but also religious persecution."

Sean McEnany asked, "What's wrong with that?" The question clearly was meant for Suzanne Maher.

But Stephen did not want this to slip away from him, and cause strife and hard feelings. "We obviously have disagreements with other Christian denominations. But they are still our brothers and sisters in Christ. And while some of our differences are pretty big, we have so much more in agreement. What the Pope has proposed is simple: It would be a tremendous benefit if as many Christians as possible can come together to speak out on issues where the Church has a clear imperative to speak out. In such instances, the Church should inform, rather than follow, the culture." He paused for effect. "This is important stuff, and something that a church like St. Mary's should be standing for, and firmly so. We're fortunate that the Pope has chosen to kick off this global effort locally."

JoAnn Brown raised her hand, and said, "I would like to make a motion."

Grant wondered if others in the room were as surprised. It was hard enough to get JoAnn to make her treasurer's report each month, never mind actually offering a motion.

Everett said, "Yes, JoAnn."

She brushed several strands of her straight blond hair away from her oval glasses and pale, washed out face devoid of any makeup. "I propose a motion stating: 'St. Mary's Lutheran Church endorses the goals of "A Public Mission of Mere Christianity," and is pleased that our pastor, the Reverend Stephen Grant, will be involved in this important effort while Pope Augustine is in the area.' In addition, Pastor Grant should provide an explanation of what 'A Public Mission of Mere Christianity' is all about for the Sunday bulletin and the church newsletter."

Grant loved it. *Perfect.*

The motion was seconded and quickly passed, with only Suzanne Maher voting no.

Chapter 53

Wednesday had been a good day for Grant. He played well during the early round of golf with Ron and Tom. After not breaking 80 all year, he finally did so today – along with Tom Stone doing it for the second time in a row, and the second time in his life. Their performances left Ron even more perturbed with his own 93, punished by an errant driver resulting in his worst round of the year.

The afternoon in his office was amazingly quiet. No phone calls. No unannounced visitors. As a result, Stephen was able to get ahead on a good deal of work that would otherwise have been neglected in the final days before and during Pope Augustine's visit.

He felt at ease preparing for Vespers.

Stephen knew that prayers at the close of a day should not launch a person on a spiritual roller coaster ride. Nonetheless, that's what often happened to him with Vespers.

During the service, he usually found a degree of serenity. Vespers allowed him to place the day – no matter what had happened – into perspective; that all was in God's hands. This didn't always happen, of course, but it seemed to occur more often for Stephen during Vespers than most other times of worship.

Stephen particularly liked singing Psalm 141, as laid down in Philip Pfatteicher's *The Daily Prayer of the Church*: "Let my prayer rise before you as incense; the lifting up of my hands as the evening sacrifice... Set a watch before my mouth, O Lord, and guard the door of my lips. Let not my heart incline to any evil thing; let me not be occupied in wickedness with evil doers."

When feeling particularly "high church," Stephen would even burn some incense before the service, so the smell lingered in the sanctuary. Incense during the actual service would just be seen as too Roman for some Lutherans at St. Mary's.

It would all come together for what should be a peaceful end to the day.

And sometimes that peace took Stephen all the way to his bedtime prayers, and sleep.

But on other nights, the loneliness waiting at the parsonage felt almost overwhelming. Those were the truly late nights when he found a movie or two to distract.

Following Vespers on this particular Wednesday night, choir practice was scheduled to resume for the first time since the Gundersons' funeral. In fact, of the nearly two-dozen people attending Vespers, almost half were choir members.

After the service, Stephen shook hands and spoke with those leaving the church. He then stopped to chat with some choir members before they ascended the stairs to the loft for practice, including Everett Birk, Suzanne Maher, Nicole Foreman, Joan and George Kraus, and Jennifer Brees.

Stephen had not seen Jennifer since her press conference announcing Ted's infidelity. She seemed to be back to her old self, perhaps even a little more outgoing than typical.

Pam started working the organ a bit, which was the signal for the choir stragglers to get upstairs.

As she drifted towards one of the staircases with the Krauses, Jennifer turned. "Hey, Pastor, are you hanging around while we're practicing?"

"Yes, I was planning to get a little work done. Maybe put the ballgame on the computer."

Jennifer stopped, while Joan and George continued. "Mets or Yankees?"

"Originally from Ohio, so it's the Cincinnati Reds."

Jennifer folded her arms. "You're kidding, the Reds?"

"Do you have something against my Reds?"

"As a Cardinals fan, I sure do."

"St. Louis? Oh, no. Why?"

Pam's organ playing stopped, which meant Jennifer was officially late. She started walking backwards towards the steps once again. "We can pick this up later. I've invited the choir members back to the house for a late night Cobb Salad, a little wine and some dessert. Not sure how many are coming. Care to join us?"

"Despite your allegiance to the Red Birds, yes, I'd like that. Thanks."

"Great. I'm late." She turned and quickly went up the stairs.

Stephen was about to head to his office, but paused. He thought about going up the same staircase, and offering some words of encouragement to the choir. But he stood and listened. All seemed normal. Chitchat among members died down, as Pam started to go over the hymns they'd be working on, and voices were soon raised to the Lord. They weren't any more in tune than previously, but Stephen thought it sounded beautiful. No, not exactly beautiful. It sounded reassuring.

He turned and headed to his office, satisfied that, at least in terms of St. Mary's choir, life was moving ahead. As it relentlessly did, no matter what happened day to day.

An hour and a half later, just past nine, Stephen found himself in the spacious kitchen of the Brees home, cutting chicken into small pieces to be mixed in the salad. With it being relatively late in the middle of the week, few of the choir members took Jennifer up on her invitation. Joan and George Kraus were also helping in salad preparation.

Glenn Oliver was given the task of opening the wine, and pouring glasses for all. Glenn was a widower. He was a short, thin, easy-going black man in his late fifties, with many specs of gray in his black hair. Glenn had a long and successful career as a compliance officer on Wall Street, which he noted made him as popular as internal affairs officers were with other cops. When his wife, Dana, was diagnosed with cancer four years ago, Glenn gave up the work and the commute, retiring to take care of her. She died two years ago. After emerging from a four or five month fog that Stephen helped him get through, Glenn had become far more active at church, and was now slated to take over as the chairman of the buildings and grounds committee with the death of Hans Gunderson.

Stephen noticed that Jennifer did a little bit of everything to pull the meal together, including warming some bread, while making everyone feel at home.

Ted Brees is an asshole.

The five diners filled their bowls with salad and dressing, grabbed their glasses, and ventured into the dining room, where the bread and more wine waited on the long pine table.

The conversation moved along amiably, and fairly innocuously.

Stephen found out that Jennifer received her Cardinals fandom from her mother.

Jennifer said, "I grew up in Nevada, but my mom was from Missouri. She used to take me back to her family home not too far outside St. Louis for a few weeks every summer. We used to go to 10 or 12 Cardinal games every year. She loved the pace and rhythm of baseball and its season. She infected me."

"That's interesting," said Glenn, "becoming a baseball fan through your mother. The story is usually from the dad or grandfather."

"My father was always very busy with work. Still is."

"What about your mother?" Stephen asked.

"She died many years ago."

"I didn't know," said Stephen.

"Long time ago, or at least it seems so." After a short lull, Jennifer said, "I trust each of you to be honest with me. What did you think of my press escapade regarding Ted?"

"'Escapade' – do I sense some regret?" asked George.

"It depends on what time of the day it is. Sometimes I'm still quite confident it was the right thing to do. But at other times ..." She let the sentence hang, and took a sip of wine.

"If you really want honesty," started Glenn.

"I do," assured Jennifer.

"Well then, I think you did the right thing. I'm tired of these freakin' politicians who think they can get away with anything. I'm sorry. I know he's still your husband, and you obviously loved him. Might still, I don't know. But knowing you, Jennifer, and thinking about what he did." Glenn shook his head, and took a slug of wine. Then he looked at Jennifer and said, "Your husband, Mrs. Brees, is an asshole."

Jennifer laughed, and so did everyone else.

Hey, that's what I was thinking.

Jennifer said, "I've been talking to Joan several times a day since the shootings at church. So, I know what she thinks, not to mention her husband: Both are supportive, but doubtful. What about you, Pastor?"

"I'm with Glenn. Ted's an asshole."

"Hey, I can get away with that," said Glenn. "You're a pastor. Aren't you supposed to have something more constructive, or at least kinder and gentler to say?"

"Not if we're abiding by Jennifer's request for honesty," said Stephen. "Look, I certainly do not take adultery and the end of a marriage lightly. Anything but, in fact. And I've worked with couples who are trying to get through tough times, and truly want reconciliation, forgiveness, want to save their marriages. But I have little tolerance for self-indulgent individuals who abandon their spouses."

Stephen stopped once he spotted a tear coming down Jennifer's cheek.

"I'm so sorry, Jennifer. I didn't mean to hurt you."

"Hurt me? Don't be silly. You and Glenn are absolutely right, and you've reassured me that I did the right thing."

"What's wrong then, honey?" asked Joan.

"Just thinking about the decisions we make, despite the lessons we supposedly learned. My father wasn't the greatest dad, and as I recognized in high school and college, he was a lousy husband. I found out that he cheated pretty regularly on my mother, on us. When I spoke to her about it, I can remember being so stunned that she knew about it. Yet, she did nothing ... for various reasons." She stopped, and refilled her wine glass, while the other four waited quietly. She continued, "I swore that I would never marry someone like my father. And then I recently discovered that I did." Several more tears fell. "After I emerged from my drunken, self-pity binge," she looked at Stephen, " I decided that I would not let Ted get away with it, the way my mom let my father off the hook."

Glenn said in hushed tone, "Good for you."

Jennifer wiped her eyes, and sniffling nose. "Maybe. But aren't we supposed to forgive? As Christians, that's what we're supposed to do, right, Pastor? I'm having a very tough time with that forgiveness thing right now."

"Me too, Jennifer. It's easier to preach about forgiveness, than it is to actually forgive," said Stephen. "I don't think God will hold it against you right now."

"I hope not." Jennifer took a deep breath. "OK, enough of that. It's time for dessert."

"We're going to have to pass on dessert," said Joan. "Have to make sure that everything our high school junior and sophomore just assured me on the phone happened actually did happen."

"Come on, Joan, your kids are great," said Jennifer. "Probably the most mature, responsible teenagers I've ever met."

"They certainly were among the best behaved when in confirmation," chimed in Stephen.

"Thanks."

George added, "But they're still teenagers, and they experience periodic brain farts. So, we need to get home."

Jennifer tempted, "We've got chocolate cheesecake for dessert."

"Cheesecake?" said George.

"Come on, Mr. Kraus," urged Joan. "You don't need the cheesecake, and what about those brain farts you just mentioned?"

"Oh, right," said the now reluctant George.

"I'll walk you out," smiled Jennifer.

"I think we know our way by now," said Joan.

After the Krauses left, Jennifer, Glenn and Stephen sat in the living room with cheesecake, coffee and tea.

They wound up talking about the new church building and reminiscing about the Gundersons.

Jennifer observed, "Hans and Flo – they had the real thing, didn't they?"

"They sure did," agreed Glenn.

"As did you and Dana, Glenn," added Stephen. *Probably shouldn't have said that for either of their sakes.*

A few seconds of silence allowed for sips of coffee or tea, and bites of cheesecake. Jennifer asked, "How do you two handle being alone? If you don't mind the question. I mean … I'm wondering … Oh, forget it. It's none of my business."

"Jennifer," said Glenn, "it's okay. Taking care of Dana, I didn't have time to think about being alone. Actually, I put it out of my head. Didn't want to think about her dying, or me being alone. Afterwards, our three kids helped. Most days, I'm fine. Rarely bored. Early on, Pastor helped me get by the toughest stretch."

Glenn and Jennifer looked at Stephen.

"Well, I'm not sure if I'm the right person to answer this question right now," said Stephen.

"Why?" asked Glenn.

"With friends and the flock at St. Mary's, I can't say I'm truly alone."

"But," pressed Glenn.

"But ... while it never used to bother me, it's been harder ..." He looked at Jennifer. "Never mind. Not the time."

"Pastor, please, go ahead. Don't stop on my account. I asked."

Her dark brown eyes seemed to reach inside Stephen, pulling out the truth.

Grant said, "I've lived alone for a long time, since leaving the Navy. Never thought much about it. It certainly never bothered me. At least, it never used to. It's been different the past two years, though. Tougher. I actually try to avoid returning to the parsonage too early most nights."

The stare between Stephen and Jennifer lingered just a moment longer.

"I didn't know, Pastor," said Jennifer.

Those eyes. That voice. Smart. Caring. She really does have the beauty and presence of an Irene Dunne.

"This is the last thing you need to hear. It's just one of those points in life to get through. More an annoyance than anything truly serious. Just need to keep it all in perspective, especially compared to what's gone on lately, especially to you, Jennifer. Nothing worse than a whiny pastor."

But Stephen could not pull his eyes from hers. *Where are you, Glenn? Jump in any time now.*

"Besides," Glenn said, "Jennifer, you are not a woman who will be alone long."

She laughed. "Not too sure about that. But thanks, Glenn."

"Have no doubts. And on that more upbeat note, I have to get going," said Stephen.

"Me, too," added Glenn.

Outside a few minutes later on the circular driveway, Glenn asked, "Pastor, you sure you're okay?"

"Yes, thanks, Glenn. I just hope I didn't make it worse for Jennifer."

"Don't think so. She's had a tough time, to say the least, over the past few weeks, with more to come as she slogs through the feelings of a failed marriage. But she's strong, and will get through it."

"I agree."

"Yeah. I kind of thought you would. Good night, Pastor Grant." Glenn Oliver smiled what appeared to Stephen as a knowing smile.

The two men shook hands, got in their cars, and drove out the front gate of the Brees' driveway.

What did Glenn mean by "I kind of thought you would"? And that smile. Was it that obvious?

Chapter 54

Ryan Bates and Paige Caldwell were now scheduled to drop by for a brief visit after Matins on Thursday morning. The meeting had not been on Stephen's agenda for the day, but Paige called early to arrange it.

When they arrived a shade after nine, Barbara showed them into Stephen's office. She offered coffee or tea, with everyone declining. As she backed out of the room, Mrs. Tunney gave Stephen a rather stern stare, very much, Grant thought, like a mother signaling that the son better behave himself. *What does she think is going to happen?*

After a few niceties, Bates, again dressed in standard FBI blue suit, cut to the issue. "Is appearing on television to discuss the Pope's visit the wisest choice, given your role?"

"Oh, so that's what this visit is about."

"Yes, Stephen," said Paige, "our worry-wart friends at the FBI apparently are concerned about what you might say."

Grant said, "I can't be trusted to keep certain things quiet? Is that it, Agent Bates?"

"No, not exactly."

"Well, then exactly what is it?" pressed Grant.

"It's just that agreeing to such a show seems to be an unnecessary risk."

"In what sense?" Grant noticed Paige's sly smile. She was enjoying this.

"Why put yourself in the position of possibly, inadvertently, revealing something about Pope Augustine's visit and security?"

"That, of course, would bring us back to the idea that the FBI thinks I lack the discipline to govern my tongue, wouldn't you say, Paige?"

"Certainly appears that way, Stephen," Paige gleefully added.

Bates threw a glance of annoyance Paige's way. "It's simply an unnecessary variable to throw into this mix. My superiors request that you not do the television show."

"I appreciate the FBI's concern, Ryan. If I were in your shoes, I'd probably be pretty annoyed with me as well. But I'm not in your shoes, and while I have agreed to do a job for this Pope, my faith, and my country, I respectfully decline the FBI's request. I have greater responsibilities in terms of being a Christian and a pastor, and this opportunity to go on television is something that I should do, especially given the purpose of the Pope's visit. And in terms of my cover – if that is the right word for it – doing this television program fits quite neatly. I'm a participant in this historic effort, and I bring a supportive point of view to it. So, how could I not accept the invitation?"

That was pretty good for just thinking it up.

Bates seemed to be processing what Grant told him. "I see your point. But ..."

Grant interrupted, "No buts about it. I feel a responsibility to do the show. It reinforces the role that the Vatican and the U.S. government have asked me to fill. And with my experience with both the CIA and the church, there should be no issue about my ability to keep certain information confidential."

Grant and Bates looked at each other.

Paige said, "The CIA is satisfied, Ryan. How about the FBI?"

"Given that we do not apparently have a choice, I assume it will be fine."

"Great," said Grant, "anything else?"

"No, that would be it," declared Bates somewhat coldly.

Grant shook hands with Bates and Paige, who held the grip a bit longer than necessary.

And as Stephen held open the office door for the two federal agents – Ryan exiting first then Caldwell – Stephen had to stop from letting out a noise as Paige pinched his ass as she brushed by.

Bad girl.

Chapter 55

At the parsonage late on Thursday night, Grant lay staring at the bedroom ceiling.

He felt like a high school kid. Two women swirled around his head.

He knew Paige so well, and could easily slip into "knowing her" – in the biblical sense – once more. Gorgeous and seductive, and as Stephen remembered, strong and limber.

Then there was Jennifer Brees. Smart, wonderful to be with, caring, direct, and an elegant beauty. *And what's the deal with the weapons? Could make for an interesting evening.*

But unlike a high school boy working to figure out how to be with a girl he has become infatuated with, Grant struggled to get both out of his head.

Despite their conversation in Montauk, Paige was either still looking for fun, meaningless sex, or she was mercilessly teasing him. Stephen knew Paige enjoyed the tease, and if he weakened, she certainly would be open to the sex. Stephen concentrated on not weakening, and therefore, finding a better way of dealing with Paige's attention.

As for Jennifer, there was the not-so-little matter of her being, at least for a while longer, a married woman.

Kind of tough to get around that reality. And even when she's finally divorced from the asshole congressman, dating a parishioner is very risky, especially if things don't work out. Tom calls me James Bond. 007 would have no problem with any of this. He'd simply sleep with both.

Grant laughed to himself.

You're also arrogant even to assume Jennifer is or could be interested.

He was wide awake.

OK, movie time.

Stephen looked at his bedside clock. 12:37 AM.

He went into the kitchen, and grabbed a Vanilla Coke from the refrigerator. In the living room, he opened the DVD cabinet, and ran his eyes across the hundreds of titles. "My Favorite Wife" jumped out at him.

Is that going to help? What the hell.

He settled in to watch the 1940 comedy starring Cary Grant, Irene Dunne, Gail Patrick, and Randolph Scott. Stephen had long appreciated this light, amusing fare. Cary Grant's character, Nick, marries Patrick's Bianca, believing that his first wife, Dunne's Ellen, and mother of his two children was dead, being lost at sea seven years ago. Ellen, of course, returns on the day of the wedding, leaving Nick to sort out the mess; and Bianca trying to figure out her new husband. Also in the mix is Scott's Steven Burkett, who was with Ellen on a tropical island for those seven years.

As he sat watching the movie, it was no longer escapist comedy.

How did I get into a position whereby a classic screwball comedy speaks to my life?

But he also could not take his eyes off of Dunne throughout the film. And when it was over at 2:30 in the morning, he sat in the dark thinking about Cary Grant sorting through his conflicting emotions and strange circumstances to arrive at – or return to – the truth that he only loved Irene Dunne.

Life is not an old-time Hollywood romantic comedy. You should know that, given everything you've done and seen.

Chapter 56

The usual Friday morning devotions and breakfast were on for Grant, Tom Stone and Ron McDermott at the local diner. It would be the last AM gathering for the three friends until Pope Augustine left town.

About halfway through their respective meals, Tom observed, "You know, I seem to eat with you guys as much as I do with my family. What does that mean?"

Ron replied, "Since Stephen and I are single, it does not say much about us. But you? Frankly, it does not speak well of your responsibilities as a husband and father."

"Thanks," Tom said.

Stephen added, "It's true. Tom, is everything OK at home?"

"And thank you as well, Stephen."

Ron and Stephen laughed.

Ron asked, "So, I assume we are all preaching on the Pope and 'A Public Mission of Mere Christianity' on Sunday?"

Both Stephen and Tom nodded in the affirmative, Stephen sipping some Earl Grey tea, and Tom coffee, sweet and light.

"It'll be easy for me, obviously, but how are you guys going to preach from Lutheran and Anglican pulpits about the Pope?" asked Ron. "I'd pay to see some of the faces in those pews."

"Well, I have the C.S. Lewis angle to please my Anglican parishioners," said Tom.

Ron said, "That is, assuming they know who Lewis was."

"If they listen to my sermons, they do."

"That's right, you work Lewis, and even some of his Inklings buddies, in now and then."

"What about your Lutherans, Stephen?" Tom queried.

"On Wednesday night, the church council passed a resolution endorsing 'A Public Mission of Mere Christianity' and supporting my involvement."

"Impressive," observed Ron.

"The vote fell one short of unanimous."

"The enforcer?" asked Tom.

"Of course. But there will be raised eyebrows, no doubt, from others on Sunday. I'll make the case in my sermon, and pray that most will be onboard in the end, or at least not make a big stink."

"To be honest, the real wildcards in my parish, and I assume yours as well, Stephen, are the ex-Catholics," said Tom. "Given that such a big chunk of the Long Island population is or was brought up Catholic, I'd guess that about 20 percent of the members at St. Bart's are former Roman Catholics, and more than half of those are rather angry ex-Catholics."

"At St. Mary's," Stephen said, "it could be one in three, and two-thirds of those are pissed off at the Catholic Church. And you're right, Tom, they will be the unknowns on Sunday."

Ron shook his head. "What's the deal? I'm curious as to what you guys hear from those who left Rome – pissed off or otherwise."

Tom said, "It seems a good number were not firmly committed to the Catholic Church in the first place, or they married an Anglican, Lutheran or some kind of Protestant, and the spouse's faith becomes the family's faith, or they make a compromise choice. There's also the divorced who feel shunned."

"I'd agree," said Stephen. "Among some of the generally pissed off ex-Catholics, it seems like it can be as simplistic and petty as disliking some priest or nun along the way, or as complex as people feeling disgust and deep betrayal because of the priest pedophilia scandal."

"Well, I can understand the last point, especially given the cover up by various bishops," Ron said. "It's an ongoing embarrassment."

Tom added, "Take solace, my friend, in the fact that the Catholic Church in this nation is still growing a bit, or at least holding its own. Neither Stephen nor I can say the same about Lutherans or the Anglican-Episcopalian grouping. We're declining."

"Good point, Tom," said Ron with a smile. "I do feel better."

They got back to Pope Augustine's visit, sharing a few points that might be worth highlighting in their respective sermons.

"By the way, Stephen," said Tom, "Ron and I have a little surprise."

"What's that?"

"Turns out both of us will be attending the Thursday gathering with the Pope."

"I thought Ron might be in attendance," said Stephen.

"I think Bishop Carolan felt bad after the grilling I was given about you," said Ron.

"How did you weasel your way in Tom?" asked Stephen.

"Weasel? You wound me."

"Yeah, right," said Stephen waiting for his friend's explanation.

Tom continued, "It was decided – with some well placed seeds I helped plant – that it was important to have a few voices representing traditional Anglicans from North America at the 'Mere Christianity' gathering. In turn, that inclusion would give a boost to those traditional Anglicans. My Ugandan bishop, who happened to know Pope Augustine when he was a cardinal from Nigeria, got involved, and next thing you know, I'm in the door."

"Everyone benefits?" said Ron.

"Absolutely," replied Tom. "There was no way I was going to miss an historic event like this in my own backyard."

"Glad you're both going to be there," said Stephen.

Chapter 57

Grant parked his Tahoe in the gravel parking lot at Channel 15.

After signing in at the front desk a couple of minutes before 1:00, Meri Wilson-Harris quickly appeared. "Pastor Grant, hello. I must say that I was a bit surprised you agreed to be on the show after your initial reluctance."

While it was the same woman he met at the Brees dinner party – again wearing a very short one-piece dress and an overabundance of jewelry – Meri now put forth an unmistakable no-nonsense air.

"To be honest, I was a bit surprised I agreed as well," said Grant with a smile.

"Yes, well, this way please. We'll get you into the green room for make up, and then onto the set. Our other panelists should be here shortly."

Make up? Ugh.

She led him down a narrow hallway with fake light wood paneling and drab beige carpeting to a small room.

Both outside and inside, Grant noted that the building offered striking contrasts. High quality, top dollar, state-of-the-art video and sound equipment were integrated into a structure that appeared to be held together by not much more than chewing gum and duct tape, while also housing rugs, chairs, tables and other props that, upon close inspection, were cheap. Pressed wood seemed to dominate the décor.

The "green room" actually had the same ugly carpeting and paneling. There were two small couches, and a barber shop-style set up along one wall, with a large mirror, a shelf upon which assorted grooming tools were laid out, and chair.

Libby, a tall slim woman with long dark hair pulled back in a ponytail, large glasses, tight jeans, white t-shirt, and a black smock, was applying make up to a man sitting in the chair.

Meri said, "Wayne, our first guest is here. Pastor Stephen Grant." And with that, she turned and left.

"Pastor, thanks for being a guest on 'Long Island Spirituality,'" called Wayne Walters from the make up chair in a strong, smooth voice. "I think we're going to have an interesting first show."

"I'm looking forward to it."

After the final touches were put on Walters, the radio-turned-television host rose from the chair and extended a handshake to Grant. Wayne Walters had the right look for television, Grant thought. He was on the short side – about five foot six – but his blond hair, blue eyes, slight tan, and perfectly white teeth seemed specifically designed for television.

Forget radio, Wayne, television calls.

Grant was the next victim in the make up chair. And while being worked on, he heard new voices in the hallway. After emerging powdered and quaffed, Grant met a gentle-looking, gray-haired rabbi named David Levy. The rabbi was called to the chair, but made it clear to Libby to do nothing more than take the shine off.

Behind Levy was a surprise – *Philadelphia Sun* columnist Roy Wallace.

Wallace immediately said, "Ah, the pistol packin' pastor, that is, according to the *New York Post*."

"I was so pleased with that headline, as you might imagine," Grant responded sarcastically.

They shook hands, with Wallace gripping especially hard, Grant noted.

"No doubt. I met your recon team on Tuesday at the press conference."

Grant feigned ignorance, "My recon team?"

"Two priests. I overheard your name, and told them to say hello. I spotted you previously at the St. Ambrose Retreat House. You had been talking with Cardinal Santos until our media group interrupted."

"Oh, yes. My friends mentioned you passed on greetings."

Wallace continued, "If you're wondering, I'm a last-minute fill in for an imam who is MIA. They had trouble reaching him over the past day or so. I've known Meri, Ms. Wilson-Harris, for a few years, and she knew I was staying local for the Pope's visit. So, here I am."

As Rabbi Levy got up from the chair, Wallace was next for make up work.

At the same time, the last panelist arrived. Father Jack Kim was a second-generation Korean American. The thin 34-year-old had jelled black hair, dark brown eyes, and as Grant immediately discovered, an outgoing personality.

The five men eventually were seated around a rectangular table – more pressed wood, Grant noted – with Walters at the head, Grant and Levy on one side, and Wallace and Kim on the other. The set also had cheap carpet, but in a bright royal blue. And behind Walters, spelled out on the false wall was "Long Island Spirituality," along with a host of religious symbols.

Each guest was hooked up with a clip-on microphone, and asked to check the spelling of their names and affiliations on screen. While Walters flipped through some notes, Meri reminded the panelists that the half-hour show would be dedicated to the terror attacks in New York City by the radical Islamic cell, and the Pope's visit.

Meri said, "Gentlemen, please keep your comments brief and to the point. No filibusters. And try not to talk over each other." She paused as if rethinking her instructions. "Although, if you guys decide to mix it up a bit, that can make for good television. And don't forget to look in the camera when being introduced, and when thanked at the close of the show. Otherwise, it's a conversation, so look at Wayne or to whomever you're directing your comments. Good. Questions? No? Good." She turned to Walters, "Are we set, Wayne? Anything else you need?"

"Just have Libby come in for a final look," Wayne responded.

Libby, already waiting in the shadows behind a camera, dabbed Walters make up, and put a few strands of blond hair back in place with a light touch of a comb. A brief shot of hairspray followed. She gave a perfunctory glance at the others around the table, and left.

One-thirty arrived, and Grant could hear Meri, now in the control room, screaming through Walters' earpiece that was slightly dislodged from his ear. Walters' expression never changed, and he smoothly slipped it fully into his ear.

One of the cameramen announced, "Quiet please. Five seconds."

Grant heard music playing in the distance, and then a deep voice declaring, "Because your faith matters, it's time for 'Long Island Spirituality' hosted by Wayne Walters."

The red light on the main camera sprang to life.

Walters said, "Welcome to the premiere of 'Long Island Spirituality.' We're going to be here each week with you because, unlike many in the media, we realize that faith matters. We'll ask some tough questions, and we're going to work very hard to provide balance. We want to hear all views."

Wayne Walters went on to introduce the panelists. Each one offered a nod of the head and a small smile for the camera – except for Wallace.

Walters then ventured into the first topic, recapping what happened in Queens, the number of buildings blown up, how many lives lost, and identifying the terrorists, noting that four of the six were born in this nation, and all seemed to be model citizens until this event. He continued, "It has been reported that the cell's true target was to be Pope Augustine I during his upcoming visit to the New York area. Blowing the buildings apparently was some kind of back-up plan if their plot was foiled, which it was by law enforcement."

In the control room, Meri instructed the engineer to move to a wider shot of the entire table.

Walters looked from one panelist to another. "Gentlemen, this terror cell was rooted in radicalized Islam. What are the broader implications of Islamic terrorists, not only again murdering American citizens, but also apparently targeting a Roman Catholic Pope who recently highlighted Islamic radicalism in his now-famous letters sent to Christian leaders around the world? Some might ask: Was the Pope asking for this? Let's start with you, Father Kim?"

Father Kim said, "Asking for this? Absolutely not. The Holy Father's idea for 'A Public Mission of Mere Christianity' is to bring Christians together on issues of mutual concern. It is not about dragging down anyone else's faith. Now, ..."

Roy Wallace interrupted. "I think many people might find that interpretation hard to swallow, Reverend Kim."

"Excuse me?" Kim seemed taken off guard.

Wallace spoke in calm, cool fashion. "Well, it is clear that Pope Augustine is looking to take on what he perceives as three major evils. He is attacking what he calls 'moral relativism,' 'militant secularism,' and 'Islamic fascism.' And given Roman Catholic history – namely with the Crusades – no one should be surprised by a backlash. The Pope has taunted them, stoked the fires of radical Islam."

Time to jump in.

"Mr. Wallace, first, your statement on the Crusades is simplistic. Rather than applying a twenty-first century mindset to the Crusades, you might try to understand the very different assumptions about life and what was important, and the worldviews prevailing from the eleventh to thirteenth centuries. For good measure, the assumption that the Crusades should somehow play into the twenty-first century world is ridiculous. It's an excuse to justify actions that cannot and should not be justified. It's also a way to create some kind of moral equivalency between the radical, terrorist factions in Islam to some part of Christianity when no such equivalency exists today."

Before Roy Wallace could respond, Walters said, "I'd like to get Rabbi Levy into the discussion. What's your take, Rabbi?"

Levy said, "I agree with Father Kim, Pastor Grant, and yes, Pope Augustine. The three great monotheistic religions share much, including, to a significant degree, a common moral code. All of us can and should be concerned about an erosion of values and an effort to push religion out of the public square. That's one of the reasons why I was excited about this show, Wayne. It puts religion in the public discussion."

"That's exactly what we want to do," replied Walters.

Levy continued, "But each of these faiths has had failings at various times in our respective histories. And sometimes those failings were injustices inflicted upon another faith. But at this moment in history, it clearly is Islam that must find a way to, for lack of a better phrase, play nice with others. And I'm not just talking about dealing with the terrorists that have attacked America, but the Islamic Arabs who oppose the mere existence of Israel. Many of the Jews living in Israel might disagree with the idea that most Muslims just want to live in peace."

Wallace said, "That's grossly unfair, especially given the Palestinian situation. Israel is no innocent. And one might use the Israeli-Jewish-vs.-Arab-Islam conflict to make the counter point to the Pope's mission and what you are saying here. Namely, that religion should not be in the public square. That it only means trouble."

"It depends on what we're talking about when it comes to religion getting involved in politics or political issues," said Grant.

"What exactly do you mean by that, Pastor?" asked Wayne Walters.

"It's very much a matter of degree. At one end is theocracy, and what Islam, for example, teaches about the mix of religion and government. On the other end is the more traditional Christian position. That position says, as Pope Augustine basically has pointed out, the Church itself speaks out on issues only when there is a clear Scriptural or moral imperative, and otherwise influences public policy indirectly by informing the conscience of the Christian in the pews."

Father Kim said, "Of course, there's a vast expanse in between. That includes a long tradition of social justice within the Catholic Church, not to mention among many Lutherans, notably in the Evangelical Lutheran Church in America. Many Christians believe that the church should be weighing in on a host of issues that impact not just the spiritual, but the material well-being of individuals, especially when it comes to the poor."

"True," said Grant. "But the Pope wisely and specifically said that he is steering clear of that social justice – or social gospel, as some Protestants call it – agenda. It would defeat the purpose of pulling traditional Christians together to speak with one voice on the clear challenges."

Walters said, "Let's get to some specifics. What issues are we talking about?"

"Knowing where the Pope and the Catholic Church officially stand," said Wallace, "it will be the hot button issues embraced by the Religious Right, including abortion, stem cell research, euthanasia, and opposition to gay marriage. Ironically, of course, that's not an agenda that brings Christians together. Instead, it winds up doing the exact opposite of what Pope Augustine says he wants. It will divide Christians."

"I'm obviously in no position to be speaking for Christians," injected Levy, "But if I may? I believe you are missing the point of the Pope's efforts. It seems to me that he is not trying to bring together *all* Christians. Although I'm sure he'd like to do that. But, instead, he seems to be trying to unite Christians who agree on these topics in the public arena."

"I think that's correct, Rabbi," said Grant. "But the implications go deeper. Even though we can and do disagree on certain matters of interpretation, what this effort says is that these are traditional Christians who have deep respect for, and seek guidance from, Holy Scripture. That common recognition provides something more fundamental to build upon."

"Did you say 'fundamental'?" asked Roy Wallace. "Many would say that you are talking fundamentalism. Taking the Bible as something that was dictated by God, and should be blindly followed."

"That's an interesting debating tactic, Mr. Wallace," said Grant. "Labeling your opponent with a word that has negative connotations. In reality, Holy Scripture is the inspired Word of God. And it serves as the foundation of the Christian faith. Again, traditional Christians might have some differing interpretations here and there, but unlike liberal Christianity, you don't get to just pick and choose what you want from the Bible."

Wayne Walters said, "OK, we only have a few minutes left. Let's wrap up this show with two key questions, and I'd like quick answers from each of you. Number one: How do we get the world to focus on Islam as a religion of peace, rather than on being known by the fanatic fringe? Roy, you first."

Wallace said, "It seems to me that the onus rests on the non-Muslim world to understand that Islam is a religion of peace, and that non-Muslim leaders – namely, Christians and Jews – must play a part in educating their flocks in churches and synagogues."

Wayne said, "Father Kim?"

"Well, Mr. Wallace is partially right on the idea that we all have a part to play. But it's clear that change is needed to alleviate the circumstances that tend to breed radicalism and generate terrorists, such as poverty and hopelessness."

"And your thoughts, Rabbi Levy?" asked Walters.

"With all due respect, Mr. Wallace and Father Kim could not be more wrong. It's not, for the most part, about understanding or education among Jews and Christians, nor is it about poverty relief. Instead, it's about Islamic leaders overcoming the violent aspects of their faith, including the fact that the founder of Islam, Mohammed, was a warrior."

Grant noted that Walters suddenly looked very uncomfortable. In fact, Grant thought he spotted a few beads of sweat forming on the host's forehead.

"Well," Walters said, "that would seem to require another full show to debate." He looked to Grant with an expression that not-so-subtly said, "Help."

No help here, Wayne.

"As politically incorrect as Rabbi Levy's comment might seem to some, he is on the right track." Grant could see

Walters deflate just a bit in the shoulders. "While most Muslims obviously want the same things as the rest of us – including peace – Islamic leaders need to get far more serious about excommunicating, if you will, the radical fringe, and undertaking a far deeper reformation than anything that Christianity went through."

Walters said, "Yes, well, just so the viewers know. We were scheduled to have a local imam on the show, but he could not make it. But we will try again to have him on the next show, so we can get another take on such matters and achieve some balance." He paused and looked down at the papers in front of him on the table. "My second question is about Pope Augustine's mission: What do you think the Pope will accomplish? Let's go back around the table. Pastor Grant?"

"Depending on how it is welcomed, organized and executed, it could turn out to be the most important juncture for Christianity in nearly five hundred years. If the Pope brings traditional Christians together in a formal process to make their voices heard in the public arena, that would be a monumental accomplishment."

Wayne said, "Rabbi Levy?"

"I would agree with Pastor Grant. It would be quite an accomplishment, and if it stays focused on core moral issues, benefits will accrue to those of us who are not Christian, but share those values."

"And Mr. Wallace?"

"I'm always very skeptical about grand efforts like this one. There are too many variables at work. One simply never knows what might happen to derail the plan. What might go wrong."

Grant could have sworn he saw a slight smile briefly pass on Roy Wallace's face. *Odd.*

"And finally, Father Kim," said Wayne Walters.

Kim smiled broadly. "I'm very optimistic about the Holy Father's undertaking. As Pastor Grant indicated, it has transformative possibilities – not only for Christianity, but for the entire twenty-first century culture. On a variety of major moral issues, it is crucial that the world hear a clearer, more unified Christian voice."

"On that optimistic note," said Wayne Walters, "I want to thank each of our panelists."

Chapter 58

Word about his television appearance quickly spread among St. Mary's congregants, and among those with a stake in the activities of Pastor Stephen Grant.

After "Long Island Spirituality" aired on Friday evening, he received numerous congratulatory texts and e-mail, including from Scott and Pam, the Krauses, and most of the church council – with the exception of Suzanne Maher. Grant lingered over two e-mail in particular, for very different reasons – one from Bishop Peter Carolan and the other from Jennifer Brees.

The Roman Catholic bishop simply wrote:

Pastor Grant:

I believe the Holy Father would be pleased.

Thank you, and Christ's blessings.

Peter Carolan

Jennifer's said:

Pastor:

Saw you on television. Impressive. You looked and sounded good.

But here's my question: How could someone be so right on such important theological matters, yet so wrongheaded when it comes to baseball? ;)

Take care.

Jennifer Brees

Grant again felt like an infatuated teen re-reading the e-mail from Jennifer.

"Looked and sounded good," hmmm? You're so sad, Grant.

Phone calls came in as well, including from Tom Stone, Barbara Tunney, Ron McDermott, and a particularly intense Sean McEnany. In fact, McEnany seemed very intent on finally meeting Grant for a quick beer or two, pushing for tonight. His curiosity peaked, and given another excuse to get out of the parsonage, Grant agreed.

They met at a local pub at 9:30, and ordered two drafts from a local brewery – Blue Point Brewery's "Hoptical Illusion."

"Nice job on television," said Sean, after popping a peanut in his mouth and taking a sip of the cold beer.

Grant thought the dark lighting in the bar fit with McEnany's low, raspy voice.

"Thanks. It was an interesting mix. I don't know if you could notice on television, but the host, Wayne Walters, was getting a bit, let's say, squeamish when Rabbi Levy and I offered our respective views on the problems faced by Islam."

"No, couldn't tell on TV."

"After the show was over, the producer was pretty displeased. From what I could tell, particularly worried about what kind of feedback she might get from certain corners. I could hear her screaming at somebody to find out what happened to the imam who was supposed to be on, and to get him, or another Muslim representative, on next week's show. I've got a feeling that the rabbi and I will not be invited back anytime soon."

"You never know."

Each man drank some of their "Hoptical Illusion."

"Well, I'm glad we're finally able to sit down and talk one on one," said Grant. "Can't get into much before and after a council meeting, or when filing out of church. This is overdue."

McEnany said, "Definitely. As I said a couple of times in passing, I've wanted to get with you since the shooting – one on one."

"Why particularly since the shootings?"

"Curiosity."

"About?"

"As a former Army Ranger and doing corporate security for a while now, I was impressed that you took the shot at Serrano and hit your mark dead on."

"Lucky, in part. I've always scored high as a marksman."

"I'm sure that's true, Pastor. But we both know that what you did that night was overwhelmingly about skill and an exceptional – dare I say, professional – coolness under pressure. For good measure, though we touched on it at council the other night, you have quite a little arsenal in your church office. Makes me wonder what you might have at home."

How did I get this guy in my congregation?

Grant drank from his beer, choosing not to volunteer anything, at least not just yet.

McEnany was evaluating Grant. He continued, "I hope you don't mind. But I did a little checking on you."

"Excuse me?"

"It's part force of habit, and part that curiosity thing."

"And what did you find, Sean?" Grant offered a look and tone of bemusement.

"Like some others at church, I knew you had been a SEAL and worked as an analyst with the CIA, even before the media reports started breaking. I'd always found your history interesting, but didn't give it a whole lot of thought until the Serrano incident. After that I admit that I did a little deeper digging – on my own and through a friend in the government."

Oh, great.

"And?"

"You served our nation well as a SEAL," Sean said, taking two large gulps to finish his beer.

"Thank you."

"As for the CIA, you seem to have had a dull few years at the agency. In fact, the records I saw indicated one of the most mundane CIA careers ever. Had to be tough going from a SEAL to a CIA desk jockey."

"It's not Jack Bauer, Sean. Dull overwhelmingly is the intelligence business. You should know that, given what I know about your work." *And I'll now make sure that I get a complete background, Mr. McEnany.*

"You're right," said Sean. "Another beer?"

"Sure," replied Stephen.

Sean grabbed both mugs, and took them up to the bar. While McEnany was away from the table, Grant decided that he would push his parishioner. McEnany returned with the two beers.

"Sean, I've been away from the CIA for a long time, and am kind of rusty on trying to figure out what people are really saying while saying something else. So, let's go direct. Why exactly are you poking around in my past?"

"You're right. I apologize."

Grant could not read Sean's face well enough to figure out if the apology was real or not.

Sean continued, "Again, it's purely my own inquisitiveness, or nosiness. Like I said, there was the expertise of your taking down Serrano. But then, within a few days, you became a relatively last-minute representative during next week's visit by Pope Augustine. And apparently, you'll be at the same places as the Pope throughout his New York visit."

McEnany let his observation stand, turning back to the peanuts and his beer.

"Sean, I'm not sure where you're headed here. But rest assured, I am no longer on the CIA's payroll, nor any department of the U.S. government. I'm a pastor, have been for some time now, whose interest in a new kind of ecumenism got him invited to a special gathering of Christians." That was the truth – as far as it went.

"Of course," said McEnany. He drained his beer. "Pastor, this was ... interesting. I've got to head home. By the way, I e-mailed the memo to everyone on council earlier tonight about the evangelism effort with the local community."

"Thanks for doing that."

"No problem." Sean got up from the table. "I want you to know, Pastor, anything the church needs, and anything you need, just let me know. I very much want to be a friend." He pulled out a business card, and placed it on the table in front of Grant. "Again, sorry about my little investigation."

"No worries."

"Good night, Pastor Grant."

"Have a restful night, Sean."

Sean McEnany left the pub, leaving Grant staring at the business card and wondering.

What the hell was that all about?

Grant pulled out his cell phone. "Hello, Paige. I was wondering if you could do a little digging on someone for me?"

Chapter 59

A missing person's report had been filed. The board of trustees and staff at the Eastern Suffolk Muslim Center had been frantically trying to track down Dr. Ahmad Faqih. His wife was inconsolable.

When a producer from Channel 15 called the Faqih home on Saturday morning, her tone of irritation quickly melted away when hearing that Dr. Faqih was missing. She offered her sympathies and hopes.

Since retiring as a college physics professor nearly a decade before, Faqih could usually be found in one of two places – at the center or at home. As of Saturday morning, he had not been seen at either location for nearly three days. And no one could find a trace of Faqih, or any evidence of foul play. He left the center after lunch on Wednesday for a brief walk around some of the streets of Riverhead, as he often did. And had not been seen or heard from since.

It would be over a year before what remained of the body of Imam Ahmad Faqih would be discovered by teenagers wandering through some secluded woods east of Riverhead on the North Fork. The police would never figure out that the two bullets professionally deposited in his skull were delivered due to a local television panel show.

* * *

Grant was late getting to his sermon. Fortunately, though, the topic was not only near to his heart, but fresh in his mind, given his moonlighting for the federal government.

After finishing up a new member class, Grant flipped on the computer a little after eleven on Saturday morning. The sermon was written and edited in just over an hour.

As the document was printing out, his mind, led by a growling stomach that had not yet been fed, wandered to ideas for lunch. Grant decided that this would be one of his days to be "bad" at lunch. His mind was set on a massive hero sandwich crammed with breaded chicken cutlet, American cheese, bacon, lettuce, tomato and mayo, served hot. It was done particularly well at a local deli.

With mouth watering, he climbed into his Tahoe. His cell phone rang. Grant looked at the numbers on the screen.

"Hi, Paige."

"Hello, lover."

"Please stop calling me that."

She ignored his request. "I've got the scoop on your Mr. McEnany."

"That was quick."

"I'm always ready to meet your needs. You know that Stephen."

"And the rundown on Sean? Can we do this over the phone?" Grant started up the Tahoe.

"Actually, yes. What McEnany has told you about his experience and work all seem to check out. The Rangers. His position with CorpSecQuest checks out, as does CorpSecQuest itself."

"You sure? Who are his friends in the government?"

"It turns out that CorpSecQuest doesn't limit itself to private sector work. A subsidiary is GovSecQuest. It does a great deal of work with the Pentagon."

"Interesting."

"McEnany is a regular visitor to both Capitol Hill, and across the river at the Pentagon."

"But nothing more? Nothing unusual?"

"No. Appears to be pretty standard lobbying and Pentagon contract work. Apparently, GovSecQuest has a handful of former or retired military and CIA, and the Pentagon has a contract to tap their insights and expertise on various projects – from hot war zones to policy strategy in areas that might get hot."

"Sean never mentioned the Pentagon work to me."

"And he had no reason to do so. That's part of his job," Paige reminded Stephen.

"Right. Anything else worth mentioning?"

"Not really. He's got plenty of friends on the Hill and in the Pentagon that would not have had to dig much to get what he had on you. After all, it was hardly thorough in terms of your time with the agency."

"Unless, of course, he was holding back."

"Always a possibility. Spook-military types are such pains in the ass, aren't they? Any other members of your congregation you want me to run background on?"

"Funny. Thanks, Paige. I owe you." Grant immediately regretted throwing in that last line.

"Well, I can dream up all kinds of ways for you to pay me back. Hmmm. Remember what we did that night in Calgary while waiting for ..."

"I was thinking lunch."

"You're no fun."

"Yes, you've told me. Talk to you later."

Chapter 60

Even though it had been a few years, Father Tom Stone still periodically reflected to his wife Maggie, as well as to Ron and Stephen, his amazement that the congregation was able to stay in St. Bart's. Tom would comment: "Interesting what a few million dollars buy, even in the church."

St. Bartholomew's Church itself was a beautiful, historic stone building that resembled a mini-castle. Another building comfortably housed church offices, a large room for congregational meetings, dinners and events, classrooms and storage. And the large, six-bedroom parsonage was made of the same materials as the church. All of this sat on four acres on a lake in Eastport.

As the congregation at the 10:00 AM Sunday Mass finished singing "Onward, Christian Soldiers," Father Stone climbed the few stairs into the pulpit that featured carvings of the four Gospel authors around the outside, along with St. Bartholomew, one of the twelve Apostles.

Stone said:

Brothers and sisters, grace to you and peace
from God our Father and the Lord Jesus Christ.
Amen.

I'm guessing that as time passes fewer and fewer churches sing the hymn we just did. The concern seems to be that "Onward, Christian Soldiers" might offend modern sensibilities. They cannot fathom that the words "Christian" and "soldiers" could possibly go together. It just makes no sense to them.

However, this point of view assumes that there is nothing that the Church and Christians must fight for or against. We here at St. Bart's understand firsthand that this is simply not the case. We had to stand up and fight for the authority of God's word, and the long Tradition of the Church, with the gifts of faith and reason from God.

Indeed, it was only with strength and illumination from the Holy Spirit that we were able to serve as faithful Christian soldiers during our struggles with the Episcopal Church. It took a heavy toll on this parish. And we, together, eventually decided that we could in good conscience no longer remain Episcopalian, but that we needed to find a way to remain within traditional Anglicanism. That, too, was a wrenching process. But as we sit here today, the members of St. Bart's have emerged from this fight as far stronger and more dedicated Christian soldiers.

And now I want to talk about the gathering that I will be attending this week. As you all know, Pope Augustine I is coming to Long Island, as he launches a global effort to foster a more unified voice among traditional Christians on issues upon which the Church should not be silent.

This is not another case of the so-called
social gospel replacing the Holy Gospel. We've
seen where that leads. Nor is it an effort to
place the Pope or the Roman Catholic Church
in some kind of position over other Christian
churches.

Instead, if it's done right, this should be a
positive, much-needed effort to create unity
among traditional Christians on some very big
issues where Christians should be speaking as
one. That includes, for example, genocide;
abortion; marriage; terrorism, especially terror
in the name of religion; euthanasia; ethics in
science, government, business, and yes, the
church; efforts to push God out of the public
arena; a culture that degrades rather than
uplifts; a wide array of other matters important
to the family; and so much more that springs
from a creeping and expanding moral
relativism.

All of us here should be concerned about
Christian unity. In the media, churches like St.
Bart's that decided to leave the Episcopal
Church have been portrayed as creating further
division within the church. But as I kept
reminding this congregation throughout that
ordeal, we were not the dividers. To the
contrary, by remaining faithful to God's word,
we were maintaining a unity with Anglicanism
and the larger Church.

Now, we might have another chance at
working and unifying with our Christian
brothers and sisters, and exhibiting that unity
quite clearly to the world. And as Anglicans, we
should take great hope – and yes, be pleased –
that Pope Augustine decided to call this effort

"A Public Mission of Mere Christianity." Of course, that comes from the book *Mere Christianity*, which was written by C.S. Lewis. And as everyone at St. Bart's knows – due in part to my ramblings – C.S. Lewis not only was the greatest defender of the faith during the twentieth century, he was an Anglican.

If "A Public Mission of Mere Christianity" is to make a difference, then we will have to realize that we are part of a war. Not necessarily a war with bullets and bombs – though, make no mistake, that is the case in some parts of the world – but a war nonetheless that affects the lives and souls of all. And we have to be prepared to serve as Christian soldiers.

As the hymn says: "Brothers we are treading where the saints have trod. We are not divided, all one body we, one in hope and doctrine, one in charity." That is how we should be, and what we should strive to be.

And the hymn continues later: "Onward then, ye faithful, join our happy throng, blend with ours your voices in the triumph song; glory, laud, and honor unto Christ the king." That's right – "happy throng."

In the end, we are to be happy, joyful Christian soldiers. It might be hard to see it that way when considering what we are up against at times. But we are doing this in service to the One who died for all of us, and conquered death for our salvation.

In this sinful, fallen world, very few things are easy. But as St. Paul wrote in Ephesians: "Put on the whole armor of God, that you may be able to stand against the schemes of the devil." And what more could we possibly need "with the cross of Jesus going on before."

As I attend this gathering of Christians, please pray for me, and for the entire effort. It distresses God that when the world looks at Christianity, it often sees division, disputes and squabbling. Sometimes division is necessary to remain faithful. But it is nothing to be celebrated. And serious efforts to bring greater Christian unity in a true, loving and faithful way should be embraced and supported. It is my hope and prayer that this is what "A Public Mission of Mere Christianity" will turn out to be.

At the same time that Father Tom Stone was making his call for Christian soldiers in Eastport, quite a different sermon was being preached on the upper East Side of Manhattan.

The church was much larger and perhaps even more majestic than St. Bart's. And like St. Bart's, it was built by Episcopalians and claimed links to the Anglican Communion. However, the rector and congregation at the Episcopal Cathedral of St. Francis were happily Episcopalian.

This Sunday, a guest was delivering the sermon. The mouse-like, septuagenarian Donna Nicks-Simpson, Methodist pastor and executive director of the United Faith Council, slowly ascended the many stairs to the pulpit that hung high above the pews. The 50 or so worshippers in attendance – a little more than half the number who sat in the pews at St. Bart's out on the East End of Long Island – seemed far fewer given the enormous size of the church.

Any doubts that this tiny woman would not be heard in this grand cathedral were quickly put to rest. Her voice was at the same time strong and soft, and it echoed amidst the relative emptiness.

Nicks-Simpson said:

The Pope is coming to town this week. He's kicking off something called "A Public Mission of Mere Christianity."

Pope Augustine, of course, should be welcomed and given the appropriate respect as the leader of the globe's billion or so Roman Catholics.

Unfortunately, as a Christian who values ecumenism and diversity, and sees value in and accepts all faith walks, I am deeply worried about what Pope Augustine is trying to do. There is much to fear here.

But aren't we told not to fear? In 1 John 4:18, we hear: "There is no fear in love, but perfect love casts out fear."

But I cannot find any love in what Pope Augustine is proposing.

I fear that he is trying to push biblical literalism at the expense of love.

While speaking of unity, I fear that the Pope is trying to lead Christians down a path of close-minded fundamentalism.

I fear that he believes that Christianity is superior to all other belief systems. Such attitudes do not breed love.

Instead, I fear he wants to do serious damage to those other faiths.

I also fear he wants to advance a kind of theocracy around the world.

I fear that the Pope is attempting to undermine the important work that churches do in trying to stop exploitation, to help the helpless, to feed the hungry, to protect God's creation, and to accept all.

I fear that he wants to roll back the clock, to a time when Christians said it was okay to hate gays, lesbians and the trans-gendered, to a time when homophobia seemed to be a sacrament.

I fear that this Pope wants to put men back in charge of what women can do with their own bodies. I fear that he wants women to be silent and submissive.

Many of these things, of course, might still be the prevailing view among the leaders of the Pope's church. But I can tell you from my own experiences, this is not the reality for the Roman Catholics I know on the ground. The ones who love each other and all that God has created.

I fear that he wants fundamentalists to control the media and the arts.

I fear that he wants to turn Muslims into boogey men in order to advance his own church. Call it the Neo-Crusades, if you like.

I fear that cloaked in the rhetoric of unity, the Pope is planting the seeds of division.

While Christianity should be all about love and compassion and inclusion, I believe what the Pope is pushing will result in conflict, even spurring hatred and hate-filled acts. Whether he intends this or not, I do not know. I certainly *hope* not.

Whether intended or not, this is the harsh reality that we face. I hope you will not sit idly by while the rights all of us enjoy are put at risk.

If you would like to become active, please see me after church about the work we're doing at the United Faith Council, and how you can get involved.

Please do not sit on the sidelines while this thinly veiled fundamentalism marches forward.

Chapter 61

Roy Wallace's column ran in Monday's *Philadelphia Sun.* It drew attention in political and religious circles, and generated seemingly countless hits and comments online. The piece raised possibilities that few liked to consider.

The Pope and His Enemies

Roy Wallace, Philadelphia Sun *columnist*

Will Pope Augustine I regret launching his effort to create greater public unity among conservative Christians around the globe?

Augustine is not a man who shies away from controversy. Nor is he a stranger to personal danger. As Alexander Usman, he had to face threats and challenges during his time as a priest, bishop and cardinal in Nigeria. Indeed, there was at least one attempt on Cardinal Usman's life.

Many have speculated that his courage in the face of both physical and religious threats earned him election to the papacy. Some also saw that since Christianity and Islam are both vibrant and growing on the continents of Africa and Asia, the Roman Catholic cardinals were making a statement to the world, and to Islam, by electing Usman to the papal office.

Pope Augustine seems to be following this playbook. By specifically citing a radical strain of Islam in his letters announcing "A Public Mission of Mere Christianity," however, the Pope has stirred talk of a new Crusade, and several cases of violence against Christians and their churches have been reported from the Middle East.

There is more, though, in terms of potential violence than just attacks from Islamic terrorists.

The Pope has not pleased all conservative Christians, by any means, with many fundamentalists viewing any pope and any papal actions as the work of the so-called devil. Are there some amidst this group willing to pick up the sword, if you will, in order to take on Satan?

At the other end of the philosophical spectrum, atheists and secularists are very wary, with many viewing this as a bid by the Vatican to exert control over national and international politics and policy. This particularly concerns advocates for family planning and abortion rights in many parts of the world. Would the threat – real or not – of a theocracy limiting individual rights spur some to violence?

The environmentalist movement is worried that "A Public Mission of Mere Christianity" signals a step back from and even a cracking down on the social justice, or social gospel, movement within the Roman Catholic Church. Leading environmentalists have made clear that they are deeply opposed to the Pope's plan, fearing that they would lose some of their Christian supporters and activists. Much the same can be said of animal rights activists.

Keep in mind, that some of this nation's leading domestic terrorists are from the fringe of the animal rights and green movements.

All it would take is one person from any of these camps to strangle the Pope's mission in the cradle.

Civilized people throughout the world should debate, criticize and defend "A Public Mission of Mere Christianity" – and even do so forcefully and passionately, but always peacefully. Let's hope that peace reigns over the coming days.

Only Wallace himself could appreciate the irony of the column.

Chapter 62

At 4:00 PM on Monday afternoon, Grant was seated in the U.N.-like meeting room in the castle at the St. Ambrose Retreat House. The big chamber, large square of tables and assorted media bells and whistles seemed a bit much for the purposes of this meeting. Though Grant was appreciative of the very comfortable leather chairs.

Along with many other visitors this week, St. Ambrose would be Grant's place of residence until Friday, rooming with the Grillin' Monks in the accompanying Gothic abbey across the large lawn. He had arrived and stowed his gear in his assigned room. The accommodations were a strange amalgam that might be best described as lavish barracks.

The meeting was for those involved in maintaining security during the Pope's visit. Among those in attendance were representatives from the FBI, including Rich Noack and Ryan Bates. Grant spotted Mel Dwyer among the local police contingent. Paige Caldwell, and no doubt others, were present for the CIA's observe-and-advise roles. The Pope's Swiss Guard naturally was represented. And Cardinal Juan Santos was present apparently to oversee, and make sure everything at least appeared in good order.

Barring any last minute changes or surprises, this was review time. Everyone already had gone over the security

plans and options several times. As for the FBI and local
police, the number of reviews ran into the dozens. They
would reassure each other that nothing would be left to
chance. Among those who knew better, however, the
unspoken reality was that accident, luck or the near-
perfect plan could circumvent even the tightest security. It
was that last point – the near-perfect plan – that pushed
these men and women to go far beyond what most thought
would be necessary.

As this final, detailed walkthrough of the week's
security proceeded, Grant's mind was ping-ponging.

At one time, he was thinking like the CIA operative he
once was, running each point of the plan through
alternative scenarios, trying to figure out how they might
play out.

At another point, he was reflecting as a pastor and
theologian on this historic event. Would this be a turning
point for Christians in terms of their ability to work
together, and perhaps lay the groundwork for further unity
down the road? How far and deep would the roots run?
Would it have staying power beyond Pope Augustine and
other leaders involved in the launch?

As the meeting proceeded, Grant was developing two
sets of mental notes – one on his role in securing the Pope,
and the other regarding the potential implications of "A
Public Mission of Mere Christianity" for the Church.

He found himself focusing more on the theology, and
less on the security. That's only natural, Grant reflected.
After all, he left the CIA behind to become a pastor. He
was serving God. But didn't he decide that being placed in
this current situation was no mistake, that God put him
here for a reason, using his experiences as both CIA agent
and pastor?

Just then, Tony Cozzilino, his mentor and friend from
the CIA, invaded his thoughts. It was a cold reminder of
what happened the last time he let his guard down.

Stephen Grant refocused, deciding he could not afford to short-change either half of his mission.

There would be times in the coming days requiring him to be more theologian than security agent, and other moments when it would be very much the reverse. Right now, it was time to be the CIA agent he once was.

But just as he put an end to the ping-ponging in his mind, the security meeting was over.

On the way out, Dwyer grabbed Grant's arm from behind.

"Hey, Lt. Dwyer, how are you?"

"It's Mel, and I'm doin' good. How 'bout you?"

"Well. Thanks."

Dwyer said, "I'm on the go. But just wanted to let you know, you got me thinkin', and I'm getting' my ass out of bed now on Sunday mornings going to Mass."

"That's great."

"My wife says to tell you, thanks."

Chapter 63

Dinner was under a huge blue-and-white tent set up a mere ten yards from where the grass ended at a short stonewall running along the top of the cliffs overlooking the Long Island Sound.

Grillin' with the Monks presented a marvelous late summer Long Island clambake for the 40 to 50 security and church personnel preparing for the Pope's visit. In addition to lobster, clams, mussels, and grilled corn on the cob, there was potato salad, cole slaw, and fresh corn bread. Dessert featured strawberries marinated in Grand Marnier served over sponge cake and topped with a dollop of homemade whipped cream.

After getting his clambake bucket, along with potato salad and bread, Grant was waved over to a table by Father Stanley Burns, the senior parish priest at St. Luke's. Grant knew or recognized everyone. In addition to Burns, Bishop Peter Carolan, Auxiliary Bishop Mark Zeller, and Cardinal Santos were seated at the table.

It was time to be the theologian.

"Pastor Grant, please sit down and eat with us," said Burns.

"Thank you, Father," replied Stephen. Everyone stood and shook Stephen's hand.

Grant added with a wry smile, "But are you gentlemen really sure you want a Lutheran at the table?"

Cardinal Santos declared, "Of course. That is what this mission is supposed to be about, correct? Perhaps greater unity in the public square starts with eating meals together, eh? I understand that eating dinner together helps families, and what are we Christians supposed to be, but of the same family."

"Besides," Bishop Carolan added, "You're more Catholic than many Catholics I come across, Pastor Grant."

Stephen replied, "Well, don't let some of my Lutheran brethren hear you say that."

Bishop Zeller asked, "Would it really cause problems?"

"You don't really want to hear about arcane Lutheran politics and struggles."

"Actually, I would like to learn more," said Zeller. "Since the Holy Father's announcement about this 'Public Mission of Mere Christianity,' I've noted my own ignorance regarding our Christian brothers and sisters in other denominations. What little I know of modern Lutheranism is that it seems that there are some significant divisions, right?"

Stephen said, "That is more correct than you probably realize." He looked at the four faces at the table. When not cracking lobster claws or scooping clams from shells, their attention was on Grant. So he decided to forge ahead. "OK, if you don't mind me eating and talking at the same time, I'll give you the quick Lutheran 101. The Evangelical Lutheran Church in America, or the ELCA, is the largest Lutheran church body in the country. But I would argue that in terms of its leadership, at least, it is perhaps the least Lutheran entity. It has descended into a very liberal Protestantism, with the social gospel crowding out the Holy Gospel, and cultural trends too often overriding the authority of Holy Scripture. At the same time, though, there are many faithful, traditional Christian pastors and laity within the ELCA, and they are struggling over what to do given the direction of the national church."

"That is quite a dilemma," said Father Burns.

As he ripped the tail off the lobster, and broke open the shell, Stephen continued, "It is. As for me, I'm a pastor in the Lutheran Church-Missouri Synod, or the LCMS, which is the second largest Lutheran church body in the U.S. We're much more conservative or traditional – depending on the pastor and congregation – than the ELCA. I'm happy to say that the LCMS works hard to stay faithful to Holy Scripture, and does not let politics, or the latest social causes or cultural trends push it off track."

"Good for you," said Carolan.

"Yes, but we have our challenges as well. There are battles over worship and liturgy, the role of women, church structure, who is eligible to receive communion, and the do's and don'ts when coming together with other non-LCMS Christians due in particular to a very conservative wing that, at least in my own view, verges on isolationist at times."

"Well, it sounds like Lutheranism in the U.S. faces many of the same challenges that Roman Catholicism does," Zeller said. "We have many of the same, or at least similar, challenges or factions, but all under the umbrella of Roman Catholicism."

"No doubt," said Stephen. "I think most denominations do today. And while I joked about your comment, Bishop Carolan, you hit the nail on the head in noting that perhaps I'm more Catholic than some of those who actually are Roman Catholic. As various people much smarter and more insightful than myself have argued, this points to the growing reality that traditional Christians across denominational lines often have more in common with each other than they do with the liberals or revisionists within their own church body."

Cardinal Santos said, "And hence, we have 'A Public Mission of Mere Christianity.'"

"Right," said an increasingly excited Pastor Grant. "And that's why so many of us see this as a great and historic opportunity. But I'm preaching to the choir – a most distinguished choir. I'm sorry, gentlemen."

"Sorry?" said Carolan. "Why? What you've said, and your obvious enthusiasm, is reassuring and contagious."

Zeller added, "Might I ask another Lutheran question, Pastor Grant?"

"Of course, Father."

"You mentioned that the ELCA was descending into liberal Protestantism."

"Yes."

"What's the general view among Lutherans as to your Protestantism, if you will? I've heard in passing some contradictory things, including that some Lutherans do not consider themselves to be Protestants. That's perplexing to this Roman Catholic who takes it for granted that Lutherans are Protestants. After all, didn't Martin Luther launch the Protestant Reformation?"

"Ah, even here we Lutherans disagree. In addition to the liberal-conservative-traditionalist wrangling among Lutherans, many, myself included, see Lutherans breaking out as Protestant Lutherans and Catholic Lutherans. The Protestant Lutherans, whether liberals or more conservative, tend to shun the liturgy and de-emphasize, to a certain degree, the sacraments, and embrace the Protestant label. In contrast, the Catholic Lutherans – sometimes called evangelical catholics – tend to be more liturgical and sacramental, and embrace the idea that Luther never intended to start a new church. But he only sought to reform what we now call the Roman Catholic Church."

Bishop Carolan queried, "And you fall into the Catholic Lutheran group, I assume?"

"Yes, I do. And I know that no one else at this table will likely find this amusing, but I joke with some Catholic friends that we Lutherans are the real Catholics."

"You're right, Pastor Grant, we don't find that amusing at all," said Bishop Carolan with a straight face, that quickly broke into a smile and laugh, with the rest of the table joining in.

At the close of dinner, Carolan said, "The cardinals and other dignitaries will be arriving tomorrow afternoon, and as far as I know, each of you are, or can be free, in the morning?" He looked around the table at four nodding heads. "Good. We're doing Matins in one of the chapels at 6:00 AM. So, I invite each of you to be ready at 7:00 in the morning in the parking lot. There will be a van there for us. Dress is very casual. No collars, etc. Wear sneakers if you have them."

Cardinal Santos said, "Might I ask what we'll be doing?"

"This idea just occurred to me, and if you don't mind, your Excellency, I'd like to keep it a surprise," replied Carolan.

Chapter 64

With Pope Augustine I's flight due to touch down at Kennedy Airport the next day, activities among the media, interest groups, blogs, talk radio, and television talking heads had reached frenzied levels. The advertising battle was running hot via television and YouTube, with radio ads and full-page newspaper purchases swirling into the mix as well.

The Our Children Our Planet Foundation was particularly active pitting the Pope's initiative against the environment, and therefore against current and future generations of children. The foundation's offensive included educational efforts via radio, YouTube, a New York metropolitan television buy, and a full-page ad in the *New York Times* signed by national, state and local members of the green movement that carried the title "Why Is the Pope Trying to Turn Christians Against the Environment and Our Children?"

Pro-choice groups cranked up the vitriol. Catholics for Reproductive Choice seemed to drop any concerns they had about a group with "Catholic" in its title attacking the Pope. Sister Elizabeth Peters appeared on MSNBC and referred to Pope Augustine I as "a monster" because he did not care that babies would be born in his homeland of Nigeria in severe poverty and disease.

National, state and local politicians on the left-of-center side of the political aisle were trying to strike a balance between lining up with their political allies, while trying not to go too far in alienating many Catholic voters. Supervisor Bradley Barnett certainly was playing that game. He appeared with a leading East End environmentalist on a Channel 15 news spot. When an anchor challenged an accusation made against the Pope, the activist declared, "Did you read Roy Wallace's column on Monday? Read it on the *Philadelphia Sun's* website. He wondered if the Pope was inviting violence with his agenda. One has to wonder if such a narrow-minded and ultimately hateful plot actually deserves some kind of violent response?"

Barnett pounced, "That's simply outrageous. I in no way want to be associated with these irresponsible comments. I am just as concerned as anyone else about the Pope's wrongheaded ideas. But this can in no way justify violence."

Chapter 65

Roy Wallace spent most of Monday and Tuesday doing radio and television interviews regarding his column on potential violence against the Pope. He deftly walked the line of not advocating violence, but simply raising the possibility as a reality that must be faced. During one interview, he said, "The world, after all, is a dangerous place, filled with people willing to do things that most of us would view as unthinkable. Americans were supposed to have learned that years ago on 9-11."

He made sure that no interviews would be on his schedule after 7:00 PM on Tuesday night. Wallace told his editors at the *Sun* that he would be using that time to finalize research for the Pope's arrival and his interview with Augustine.

In reality, though, in a comfortable room at one of Long Island's most luxurious hotels, Yuri Kamenev put aside his British Roy Wallace persona in order to finalize the details of the unthinkable act he was preparing to commit as the American mercenary, hired assassin Robert Johns.

Johns cracked open his encrypted laptop, entered the necessary security codes, and pulled up his plans for the coming days. If all went well, Roy Wallace would be able to continue his journalism work. But if his identities were revealed at any point along the way, his escape hatches would allow for a stealth getaway, with offshore access to the funds amassed from this job and earlier work.

Plan A would give new meaning to the phrase "poison pen." Johns performed a final test of his creation. In two four-color ballpoint pens, he replaced three of the ink cartridges with precise measurements of a poisonous cocktail using the juice extract from yellow jasmine, a flowering vine found throughout much of the southern United States. Using yellow jasmine – or *gelsenium sempervirens* – as the foundation, Johns' supplier, a longtime concocter of handy poisons, engineered the dosage and effects.

Another double cartridge pen would include a far heavier dosage for Johns to inject into whatever juices Augustine would use to sweeten the zobo, thereby throwing suspicion off anyone in the room and onto those who acquired, stored and brought in the ingredients for the Nigerian drink.

At the high dosage, immediate speech loss would be accompanied by vertigo, slowing heartbeat, labored breathing, muscle contraction and weakness, with death coming within five minutes due to asphyxia. Most victims, however, would remain conscious until the end, when pupils would be dilated and fixed, and the panic and fright of looming death fixed upon the face.

In his role as journalist Roy Wallace, he would add the poison while aiding in the distribution the Nigerian drink during the exclusive media session set up for four select journalists. One of the four-color pens, marked by three scratches, housed the high dosages. The other carried low dosages that would not bring about death for several hours.

Johns would use low dosages on himself, and on one other lucky journalist in the room. While gambling some, he counted on quick action by the medical teams on hand and at the hospital to save him via gastric lavage and follow-up counteragents. The other two journalists and the Pope would not be so fortunate.

All of the pens would remain unnoticed by the tight security at the St. Ambrose Retreat House – before and after the poisoning – with each reset to the ink cartridges.

His poison pens were ready.

If the situation failed to let Plan A play out, Johns' Plan B would have him move with the Pope to Mexico City. One of the venues for a Mass set up nicely for a sniper shot that few men, other than Johns, could be sure of pulling off. Johns had done it before with his German Heckler & Koch PSG1 sniper rifle. And extraction via his escape route would be relatively easy.

It was obvious, though, that Johns was counting on a successful poisoning of Pope Augustine I. If achieved, his personal addendum to Plan A would mean cleaning up bits and pieces that might lead back to him, followed by a quick mission of revenge.

Chapter 66

On Tuesday night, Stephen Grant also was preparing for Pope Augustine I's arrival. But in quite a different manner than Yuri Kamenev.

In fact, the entire day was starkly different from what Grant himself would have done in years past, before he had become a pastor. At that time, it was all about checking and re-checking the plan and his weapons. All stray thoughts and emotions would be banished, with the exclusive focus on the work.

This morning, however, was very different. Prayer began during Matins led by monks. That was a first for Grant.

And then it was time for Bishop Carolan's surprise.

It turned out that Carolan came from a rather well-off North Shore family with a small – that is, small for Long Island's Gold Coast – two-story gray-shingled house sitting on the harbor in Oyster Bay. The Bishop reported that he grew up there, and now it was home to his sister and brother-in-law. But he still had an open invitation to stay, and sail whenever he liked. Carolan specifically noted that the 32-foot sailboat docked at the home was his, and they would be taking a relaxing, though relatively brief, sail into the Long Island Sound.

So, after a hearty breakfast of cinnamon oatmeal, blueberry muffins, coffee, tea and juice prepared by the Bishop's gracious sister, four Catholic clergy and one Lutheran pastor set sail. They headed up and out of Oyster Bay, and into the Sound.

While playing deckhands under the captaincy of Bishop Carolan, the five men shared some of their backgrounds – where they came from, and how they wound up in the ministry. Grant's journey gathered the most interest and questions.

The roundtrip sail lasted a bit more than three hours. They were back at St. Ambrose's before noon.

The afternoon and evening were consumed by introductions of and amiable chitchat with a dozen U.S. cardinals, three Canadian cardinals, a few bishops and a handful of other Christian leaders who would be staying at St. Ambrose. Most out-of-towners would be rooming at hotels in the region, mainly in Manhattan.

After a cocktail party under the big tent, the conference attendees headed into the castle for dinner. Grillin' with the Monks meant a choice of grilled Long Island duck with an apricot glaze or barbecued chicken in a smoky Bourbon sauce.

Grant reluctantly pulled himself away from the fascinating conversations with some of the nation's pastoral and theological leaders. He journeyed to the second floor of the castle, which served as base of operations for the security personnel. It provided clear views of the lawns stretching out from both buildings, and housed high-tech surveillance equipment, weapons ranging from side arms to rocket launchers, and sleeping quarters for those tasked with protecting the Pope and everyone else in attendance. With heavily-armed teams spread out around and outside the St. Ambrose House grounds, enhanced by the best in technology and good old heavy armor, this facility of the Roman Catholic Church was as secure as a fortress.

Grant was pleased with that reality, since after this day of sailing, and both intellectual and spiritual enrichment, he had to work in order to concentrate on shifting from theologian mode to security mode. He stopped partway up the massive, ornate staircase in front of the statue of St. Ambrose, and looked around at the portrayal of various saints on the hanging tapestries. He took a deep breath.

Upon entering the security areas, there was the added distraction of agents and police taking note of his collar, even though all were briefed on his background and current role. But Grant finally got down to the job at hand. He spoke to Agent Noack, who had nothing new to report.

Grant moved to his footlocker where his compact Taurus PT-25, with magazines, and his old, trusty tactical knife, were stored. He made sure all were in working order, put them back in place, and locked the case. He would be back early in the morning to strap the gun under the pants on his left leg not far above his shoe, and the knife strapped to his right.

Well, that's that, I suppose.

He had another look around, and decided it was time to descend from the security area. Grant exited the castle, slowly walked across the grass under a crystal clear, star-filled sky, and entered the abbey.

The Puddleworths' sensibilities when erecting this gothic-style building back in the nineteenth century made for an ideal abbey. The family's original small chapel still served for private prayer. After taking over the facility, the Catholic Church merged another four rooms on the ground floor into the facility's main chapel.

The windows along the north side of what was called the Holy Family Chapel long ago were replaced with stained glass scenes from Acts. Stephen found that interesting. He could not recall being in another church or chapel with scenes from the Book of Acts. These included the Ascension, Matthias being chosen to replace Judas, Pentecost, Peter and John on trial, Philip and the Ethiopian Eunuch, Paul's conversion, and Paul preaching in prison.

But Grant's attention was drawn to the window between Peter and John, and Philip. That was the martyrdom of Stephen. Grant, in fact, was specifically named by his mother after St. Stephen, the first Christian martyr. So, this was a scene Grant was familiar with – Stephen gazing up at Jesus at the right hand of God the Father, the Holy Spirit as a dove shining the power of faith down on Stephen, all while an angry crowd threw stones to kill Stephen.

Hope that's not prophetic as well.

He turned to the altar, behind which was a wall of statues of saints, with Mary and Joseph atop looking down lovingly on Jesus as a baby. Grant loved his Catholic brethren, and even admired various aspects of the Roman church, but he had a tough time with the Catholic view of and emphasis on saints, especially in worship spaces like this. But he slid into one of the pews, even though Vespers would not begin for another half hour.

Grant's main preparation for tomorrow was to just sit and pray, asking God to enlighten, to provide love and forgiveness, and to protect and watch over all of the faithful that would be working in the coming days to strengthen His Church.

Chapter 67

The Pope's plane – actually an Alitalia jet set aside for papal travel – touched down at Kennedy Airport on Wednesday morning at 9:40.

In addition to Pope Augustine I and the flight crew, others onboard the commercial jetliner were Vatican officials and security, and 55 members of the international media. Add in those already in the country that would be covering the Pope's visit, and there would be 95 members of the media on hand for Thursday's first gathering of "A Public Mission of Mere Christianity" and the follow up press conference, as well as Friday's Mass in the Meadowlands. Today's meeting with cardinals would be private.

Much of the press, being largely liberal, and either agnostic or atheist, simply did not know what to do with Pope Augustine. They loved the idea that this pope came from Africa, and was not an old, European white guy. But they were repulsed by, in their eyes, his conservative, fundamentalist or archaic beliefs. Yet, as he met with the media, strolling about the airplane and speaking comfortably and with humor in a variety of languages – something one of his predecessors, John Paul II, often did – even some of the most hardened and cynical reporters found themselves liking this man. While many reporters and columnists were opposed to and did not trust his intentions regarding "A Public Mission of Mere Christianity," they respected his courage in the face of personal danger. And during those moments of personal contact, it was easy to see on their faces that many media representatives were drawn to this tall, thin, balding 60-year-old man, with dark skin, an easy smile, a firm handshake, and a keen intellect.

Pastor Stephen Grant was introduced to Augustine by Cardinal Santos on the tarmac, standing outside an armored Chevy Suburban with bullet-resistant glass.

Augustine shook Grant's hand, and pulled him close. The Pope whispered, "Ah, a Lutheran with a license to kill. Should I be worried?"

Grant was not sure what to say, until the Pope's face broke into a broad smile and a robust laugh followed. But Grant was taken off guard again, when the Pope slapped him on the back.

A few more introductions were made. The Pope waved to the people watching from terminal windows. Everyone was shuffled into vehicles, with Grant in the third row of the Pope's Suburban, behind Augustine and Santos, and the caravan of several black Suburbans and assorted vans moved out.

The journey to the St. Ambrose Retreat House began on the Belt Parkway heading east. The vehicles went by the remnants of the building that had been rented by Nuri Al-Dawla and Saddam Ali. Grant reflected that, if they had been good, the spot probably would have been ideal to launch a missile attack on these vehicles. *One for the good guys.*

Grant sat quietly in the back seat, while Santos briefed the Pope on what had been going on at St. Ambrose in preparation for his visit.

Stephen noticed that Cardinal Santos left out yesterday's sailing excursion. When they had a private moment, he decided he would have to tweak the Cardinal a bit.

Chapter 68

Pope Augustine I's initial meeting was at 4:00 PM, and held in the U.N.-style room where Grant had attended a security briefing earlier in the week.

But Pastor Stephen Grant would not be sitting in on this gathering. It was exclusively for the upper strata of the Roman Catholic hierarchy of North America – American and Canadian cardinals.

Word was that Augustine would be making brief comments to the cardinals, and then open it up for a Q-&-A session. The Pope had gained a reputation for running dynamic sessions with certain audiences, and was very open to addressing questions and even complaints frankly and forthrightly.

Pastor Grant, along with other security and clergy, would be positioned outside the room. A pre-dinner cocktail party also was under way in the solarium. Round tables with chairs were scattered around the windowed room. Grant decided to seat himself at one of the tables closest to the windows on the north side of the room. From there, he could watch everyone who entered and exited the room.

So easy to fall into old habits.

In addition to the security detail and the three monks who oversaw the food, the room was populated by personnel of both the clerical and lay varieties from the Vatican and the U.S. Catholic Church.

Most chatted amiably, or checked their mobile devices – or did both at the same time.

Grant periodically circulated about the room, sipping on a Coke, offering brief introductions and not lingering long in any one conversation. His purpose was to get a read on as many as possible in the room. He also wandered up and down the wide hallway outside the room where the Pope was holding his meeting.

Grant felt comfortable with the situation. He stopped at the bar for another soda, and returned to his well-positioned seat.

It was about 5:15 when Grant noticed a new face entering the room. He was a priest roughly Grant's age. The medium-built man looked a bit disheveled. His light brown hair was unkempt, with parts matted from sweat. His thick framed glasses were off a bit, so that the right lens sat higher on the face than the left. The priest also avoided looking at anyone in the face. He moved to the buffet table, and filled up a plate mainly with crackers, layered cheese and *pâté de foie gras*. He came away from the bar with a glass of water as well.

The priest sat down at the table next to Stephen's, and proceeded to spread the *pâté* onto crackers. After each cracker was topped, he put the knife down and took a sip of water. As he sat, he would periodically bow his head slightly, in prayer Grant thought. The man was clearly uncomfortable, nervous.

Grant decided to introduce himself. When the priest opened his eyes and looked up from praying, Grant said, "Quite a moment for the Church. Very exciting."

The man seemed surprised by the interruption, jerking his head in Grant's direction. "I suppose. Seems more like a time of uncertainty, perhaps even doubt, Father."

Grant smiled. "Actually, I'm not a 'Father,' per se. My name is Stephen Grant. I'm a Lutheran pastor here on Long Island."

"Lutheran? I see."

Grant picked up an undertone of annoyance.

"Yes. And you are?"

For the first time since entering the room, the priest made direct and extended eye-to-eye contact with someone. Grant saw more than annoyance, perhaps anger behind those eyes. The man sternly declared, "I am a Catholic priest. Father Armand Buklis. I am an aide to Cardinal Cox." The man was dismissive, and turned back to his water.

"I see." Apparently, this was no fan of the Pope's mission. Grant decided this was not the time for a debate. He tried to change the subject. "What do you think of the monks here at St. Ambrose's? They've made quite a splash with their Grillin' with the Monks venture."

"Rather self-indulgent and self-aggrandizing for my tastes."

Just then Pope Augustine entered the room with the cardinals in tow. Grant observed, "Ah, the man of the hour."

Grant watched Augustine as he moved into the room, and began talking with the guests. The Pope's considerable personal magnetism was only magnified by his being the tallest person in the room, but for one FBI agent.

Stephen was so caught up in watching Augustine smiling and, in effect, working the room that it took a moment longer to recognize the funny feeling in his head, the sudden and growing feeling of tightness and pressure.

A red alert?

Grant looked around, and saw the back of Father Buklis heading across the room toward the Pope. Grant looked down at the table where Buklis had been sitting. *Water. Crackers. Pâté. No knife. Crap.*

Grant moved after the priest. He noticed that while Buklis's left arm swung naturally, the right arm was pinned at his side, like he was hiding something.

Buklis was two strides from Augustine's back when he pulled out the knife, and screamed, "Apostate!"

Grant yelled, "Knife," as he bolted towards the murderous priest.

No one else in the room could do anything more than turn in the direction of the shouts. Buklis started to bring the knife down towards the large target that was Augustine's back. Before the blade could rip through the Pope's robes and skin, Grant, flying through the air and focused on the hand clutching the weapon, was able to divert the knife thrust. And like a defensive end trying to make a lasting impression on an opposing quarterback, Grant maneuvered his body and forearm so that when he came crashing down on the priest, Father Buklis's face bore the brunt of the fall as they hit the floor.

The knife tumbled harmlessly out of the priest's hand, and Pope Augustine I was still standing, unharmed.

Chapter 69

Grant was always a bit surprised when any government entity – even a security or law enforcement agency – moved with speed and efficiency.

But within minutes, Buklis was moved to the second floor security area, with his boss, Cardinal James Cox, soon being hustled in as well.

Grant was able to observe as FBI Special Agent Noack questioned Buklis. The priest swung wildly between crying for forgiveness and lashing out that he had to act as Augustine clearly was a tool of the devil trying to destroy the one true Church of Christ.

Buklis explained that he at first disagreed with the Pope's mission, but eventually came to understand that it was dangerous, concluding it was "satanic." He insisted, though, that it did not occur to him what had to be done until he sat spreading *pâté* on crackers in the solarium. Buklis said, "I looked at the knife, and understood that I would be the only one who could stop this. It was up to me. I had to act. And I did." His face crumpled from intensity into horror. "God forgive me," he said among the sobs.

Grant did not know if Buklis was asking forgiveness for trying to murder Pope Augustine, or for failing to achieve his objective.

Either way, he's freakin' nuts.

After the questioning of Buklis was done, he was whisked away by the Nassau County police.

As for Cardinal Cox, the man obviously was bewildered, appalled, saddened by and innocent of his assistant's attack. Cox reported, "I know he was skeptical of this 'Public Mission of Mere Christianity,' even a bit troubled. I thought having him meet the Holy Father would be a tremendous benefit. Dear Lord, I never dreamed anything like this could ever happen ... that Armand was capable of anything like it."

There apparently was some debate if the incident should be kept quiet. It seemed settled that the incident would be made public after Pope Augustine had left for Mexico, so as to not take away from the effort at hand. But Cardinal Santos delivered a clear message to public relations staff that the Pope would not stand for any kind of delay or misinformation.

So, the news was put out in simple terms by the Vatican and law enforcement – that the Pope was attacked by a disturbed priest who was now under arrest; the attack was foiled by a member of the security detail; and the Pontiff was unharmed and his schedule would not be altered in any way. The only detail withheld was that Pastor Stephen Grant was the person who stopped the Pope's murderer.

By the time everything was wrapped up from a security standpoint, it was nearly 11:00 PM. Grant was ready for bed.

He left the castle to head over to his room in the abbey. He paused in the cool night air, and looked up. The sky had started to cloud up, but many stars were still visible. Tomorrow's weather promised rain.

Stephen usually found that star-gazing put him in the right frame of mind for prayer. The sky at night revealed the awesomeness of God's creation. At once he felt the humility that comes with insignificance, and the warmth of knowing that despite his insignificance and unworthiness, the Lord loved him. Like the earth under his feet, and the massive, magnificent stars countless light years away, he was created by God. But even more wondrous, God became man – Jesus both divine and human – died for him, for all, conquered death, and offered love, redemption, salvation and eternal life. It was with this understanding that Stephen, face uplifted to the sky and eyes peering into space, thanked God for allowing him to be here and to help save Augustine.

Ever since he watched the 2003 film *Luther*, with Joseph Fiennes portraying Martin Luther, he closed many prayers the way Luther was advised to pray in that film: "I am yours. Save me."

Grant made his way to the abbey. After passing through security at the door, a voice from the darkness declared, "I've been waiting for you, Stephen."

Cardinal Santos rose from a chair and emerged from the shadows.

OK, Juan does look a bit creepy with the black hair, goatee, and dark robes in this light and setting. Central casting would have made him the murderer, as opposed to the geeky priest with the crooked glasses.

"Juan. You startled me."

"Stephen, I think not. I saw what you did today. Your movements were almost catlike. Forgive me, but I do not think that much startles you, my friend. You were obviously very good at whatever it is you did for the CIA."

Grant glanced around to make sure they were alone. "The old training and instincts never completely leave."

"I am sure you must be very tired. Can you spare a few moments before bed, however?"

"Of course, what is it?"

"The Holy Father would like to thank you, personally."

"That's not necessary."

"But it is. And he insists. Please, this way."

Grant followed Santos up a flight of stairs. They stopped at another security checkpoint. But as at the front door, Grant was treated like a hero, not a risk.

Santos knocked on a door, and a voice in the room beyond said, "Please, come."

The room was a large, ornate bedroom that fit into the gothic style of the home. On one side of the room was a very large canopy bed. On the other side was a sitting area featuring a chair and couch.

Pope Augustine I was sitting on the couch, looking, to Grant, very un-pope-like. Gone were all of the papal garb. Here was a man in a green, terrycloth robe over a set of tan pajamas. On his lap was a stack of papers. In his hand was a pen. And on his nose were a pair of reading glasses. He looked like any other person catching up on some work late at night.

The Pope plopped the papers down on the couch next to him, placed his glasses on top, and rose to his full six feet four inches. "Ah, the man who saved my life today." He strode across the room, and extended his hand to Stephen. "Thank you, Pastor Stephen Grant."

"Of course, sir, you're welcome. But I was doing ..."

Augustine held up a hand. "Do not say that you were just doing your job, Pastor Grant. After all, I am fairly sure that the job of a Lutheran pastor – ex-CIA or not – does not include saving the life of a pope. Please, accept my deepest gratitude."

Stephen felt an immediate affinity for this man. "Of course, sir, you are most welcome."

"And please stop calling me sir. When amongst my non-Catholic clergy brothers, I find it easiest if we all go with the title for shepherd. After all, that is what we are all striving to be, shepherds to our flocks, each other, and the world. Is 'pastor' alright with you?"

"Absolutely."

"Good."

A monk from the abbey brought in a tray with tea and two cups. He withdrew, and with a nod from Augustine, so did Cardinal Santos.

Grant found himself sitting in an abbey with a pope whose life he just saved.

Weird.

"Can I pour you a cup of tea? I have found this decaffeinated black currant tea has a relaxing effect before bed."

"Yes. Thank you."

"How do you take it?"

"A small amount of milk, one sugar."

And now the Pope is making me tea. Weirder still.

Augustine sat back on the couch, and took a sip of the tea. "Cardinal Santos has told me a bit of your story, Pastor Grant. It seems to have been a diverse and fascinating journey for you, no?"

"Yes, very much so."

"If you do not mind the question, how did you go from working for the CIA to becoming a Lutheran pastor?"

"I don't mind at all, Pastor." *"Pastor" for this man doesn't sound right.* "I believed in the work I was doing at the CIA, and still see the critical importance of it to this very day."

"After today, I see it as well," Augustine added with a smile.

Grant smiled as well, and sipped his tea. "After my parents died, I lost touch with the Church. Eventually, though, I found myself back in the pews, getting more involved when I could, and feeling very much at home. Then I started to wonder if what I was doing was the best way to help people. In a sense, a debate emerged in my mind and heart. As I look back, God was calling me in one direction, while I was still pulling in the other. I started thinking about my career saving people from the evils of this world, versus playing a more direct role in eternal salvation. It was not easy for me to let go, even to be sure that I *should* let go. After all, as a Lutheran, I'm a big believer in the jobs each of us take being vocations – actual callings, not just job choices. But there was just too much pulling me to become a pastor. And here I am."

"And apparently, the Lord is putting you to work on both fronts these days. You are here on the part of your church body as a theologian, and you are here due to your background and skills as a government agent. Interesting how the Lord works, isn't it, Pastor Grant?"

That's what I've been thinking. "It is indeed, Pastor."

"May I ask what the theologian thinks of 'A Public Mission of Mere Christianity?'"

Grant shared his excitement about what the Pope had proposed. The two men spoke for nearly an hour about the opportunities at hand and the obstacles. Neither denied, nor attempted to minimize, the issues and challenges that separated, for example, their respective Catholicism and Lutheranism. But at the same time, the two agreed on the need for the Church to speak to the world with a unified voice on many issues, as well as working towards greater unity in general, especially given Jesus' own prayer for unity in the Gospel of John, Chapter 17.

Augustine I said, "I know you know the verse, Pastor, but it is a powerful reminder of where humanity has failed Christ's church." He closed his eyes, sat back, and recited verses 20-23: "I do not ask for these only, but also for those who will believe in me, through their word, that they may all be one, just as you, Father, are in me, and I in you, that they also may be in us, so that the world may believe that you have sent me. The glory that you have given me that I have given to them, that they may be one even as we are one, I in them and you in me, that they may become perfectly one, so that the world may know that you sent me and loved them even as you loved me."

Chapter 70

Grant made his way back to his room just after 12:30 AM.

He knelt bedside the bed to pray. As he read the now-previous day's devotional readings from *For All the Saints*, his mind kept wandering. He resorted to reading aloud to help his concentration. But that failed as well. Even as he read the words, part of his mind kept journeying back to the attack on the Pope and their subsequent one-on-one.

He laid down in bed, but quickly acknowledged being too keyed up for sleep.

No late-night movies at the abbey.

Grant took out his Bible, and turned to John 17. Before he came to the verses spoken by Augustine, Stephen was reminded of "being in the world, but not of it." He first heard that during confirmation class. He read what Jesus prayed, "I have given them your word, and the world has hated them because they are not of the world, just as I am not of the world. I do not ask that you take them out of the world, but that you keep them from the evil one. They are not of the world, just as I am not of the world. Sanctify them in the truth; your word is truth. As you sent me into the world, I have sent them into the world."

We're in the world, have a responsibility to the world, yet we are sanctified – set apart by being under God's Word.

Grant reflected some more about the remainder of what was known as Jesus' "high priestly prayer," including that great and formidable emphasis on unity. That was not something that could simply be ignored, Stephen thought, as far too many clergy and churches chose to do. As he continued to read, his commitment to the mission of bringing a more unified Christian voice into the world was only being strengthened, as was his enthusiasm for the leadership of Pope Augustine on the matter.

Before closing his Bible for the night, Grant's eyes moved to the previous chapter. He noted at the end of Chapter 16 that Jesus told his disciples that the time was here when they would be scattered, when they would leave him, and that they would face "tribulation" in the world.

Disunity, turning away from God, troubles in the world – and those were Christ's disciples. Actually with him. And yet, there it was. The chapter before Jesus prays for unity, most of his disciples flee, abandon him, and deny him. How much more can we expect today – two millennia later?

A vibrating phone interrupted his ruminations. Grant looked at the screen, and debated for a moment whether to answer or not. It was Paige.

He answered. "Grant."

"You big fucking stud. I am so hot for you right now."

Readjustment time. "Who is this?"

"I'll ignore that because you stopped that nut-job priest from killing the Pope, and the CIA is basking in the glory because you're one of us."

"Was one of you."

"Details, details. How do you feel?"

"Well, to tell you the truth, I haven't had too much time to really think about it."

"Well, what did the Pope say during your meeting?"

"How did you know about that? I just ..." Grant caught himself. "Oh, never mind. We actually wound up talking theology."

"Too bad."

"I was wondering where they were stashing you since I got here. What have you been up to?"

"The assistant director decided to give me a couple of official days off in order to do some unofficial poking around on the groups that are protesting the Pope's visit."

"Ah, checking up on law-abiding citizens. I thought that was a no-no for some time now."

"It is. But this is my own, personal work being done at a local business that, of course, has no ties whatsoever to the government."

"Come to think of it, where are the local marchers, chanters and sign wielders?"

"For security purposes, not to mention some pressure from those very wealthy Gold Coast residents, they have been corralled into a designated area about a mile-and-a-half from the retreat house."

"Like they did at the Master's golf tournament a few years ago?"

"Exactly."

"That must be driving them crazy."

"It is. But the media has been more than accommodating in taking up their cause, and splashing videos and photos everywhere. So, they're probably getting more attention than they otherwise would have. And trust me, once you start crawling inside these groups, and find out who is behind them, they deserve something far different than positive media coverage."

"Okay, let's move on from this topic before I find myself hauled before a Senate committee someday. Wouldn't look too good for St. Mary's."

"Suppose not. Besides, you'd probably be very disappointed as to who is in bed with whom."

"Disappointed, yes. Surprised, not so sure."

Chapter 71

By 9:30 on Thursday morning, all of the attendees for the first gathering of Pope Augustine I's "Public Mission of Mere Christianity" had passed through the narrow gates and doors at the St. Ambrose Retreat House. With a few minor questions here and there, the guests had also passed through the expansive security checks. Given that just about a thousand individuals would be in attendance, the speed at which this was accomplished was a credit to all of the security agencies involved.

With news of the attempt on the Pope's life by a disgruntled priest spreading across the globe, requests for additional media credentials flooded the Vatican's press office. The flood, however, was turned back. But for three exceptions, no additional credentials were issued, given the limited space, the security requirements, and the fact that the allotted press slots were filled over two weeks prior. The exceptions were the three U.S. evening broadcast news anchors – who were not originally planning on being in attendance. The news divisions had discussed it, but failed to see how the gathering was newsworthy. As one network news decision-maker said, "Does anybody really care about a bunch of right-wing Christians talking about how to impose their views on others? In fact, *should* anyone care? Leave it to the cable and Internet guys."

The line among some of the press corps covering the event was that the networks were granted special dispensations for their earlier sin of arrogantly ignoring this global event occurring in the backyard of their New York City headquarters.

Roy Wallace had no trouble entering, with his background thoroughly – or so it was assumed – checked as one of the media involved in the special sit-down session with the Pope. His three multi-ink pens – resting in a tray in seeming innocence – passed through the X-ray machine without notice. Wallace took his tweed sports jacket off the conveyor belt, slipped it back on, and took his change, BlackBerry, and three pens from the tray. Wallace put the pens, loaded with poison, into the inside, left pocket of the jacket.

Since the previous day's events, the three networks also had tried to get in on the select-access session – or better yet, set up their own one-on-ones with the Pope – but they were gently rebuffed on those requests, with the promise of setting up such sit downs at another time. The limited access session would still have the Pope meeting only with Wallace, PBS religion reporter Kathleen Tanglewood, Internet blogger Devin O'Neal, and talk radio host Brett Buck. Tanglewood was known for being impartial, O'Neal for covering all matters Christian, and Buck for often coming to the defense of Catholicism against what he referred to as "a media establishment with an anti-Catholic prejudice."

The schedule for the day had the Pope addressing all of the attendees at 10:15 AM, followed by Augustine answering questions written out on cards, and selected and asked by an individual from the Holy See press office. That was expected to last roughly two hours.

While attendees then would move to lunch under the tents, the Pope would shift to a neighboring room for a press conference where he would field questions from all of the media in attendance for another half hour. This would be, to say the least, an historic occurrence, and the Vatican's press office impressed upon the credentialed media just how rare it would be, and that if everyone did not perform in a professional, civilized manner, it might not occur again. Or more accurately, that some media outlets might not be invited back if this were to occur again. It was an open question if such a thinly veiled threat would actually stop a grandstanding reporter from making his or her mark by trying to embarrass a pope while being watched by people around the globe.

Next, Augustine would shift to another, smaller room on the second floor for the meeting with the four selected members of the media. This was billed as a more intimate, conversational gathering, allowing for a unique give and take between four members of the media with the head of the Roman Catholic Church on what he was about and why he was launching this "Public Mission of Mere Christianity." That was slotted for one hour.

After this nearly four-hour marathon, Pope Augustine would retire to his rooms in the abbey for some much-needed nourishment and rest.

Meanwhile, attendees would be breaking into discussion and strategizing sessions during the afternoon, with everyone coming back together for fellowship and an early dinner.

Tom Stone and Ron McDermott had traveled together to the event, and were lingering outside the doors to the auditorium trying to spot Grant before the Pope's address.

After Matins, Grant spent time in security briefings focused on how the circle would have to be further tightened around the Pope in light of the previous day's knife attack. After receiving numerous one-on-one kudos, FBI Special Agent Rich Noack acknowledged Grant's actions before leaders of the security effort, who responded with applause.

Though the talk was serious, Grant could feel that both the sense of urgency and the level of concentration had fallen off ever so slightly since the previous day. A loopy priest's attempt to murder Augustine had been stopped. And that had come on the heels of a foiled terrorist plot to take down the Pope, though with significant loss of life, including FBI brethren.

What more could possibly happen? It was only human nature to assume the worst was behind them.

But Grant also knew that even slightly distracted, these men and women would never get sloppy, and they would continue to offer Pope Augustine the best protection available.

In the end, it was decided that four more personnel would be added to the detail assigned to moving around the facility with Augustine.

As he moved towards the auditorium, Grant's mind again was working on two tracks. His eyes still scanned for anything out of synch. But increasingly his mind was centered on John 17, and what "A Public Mission of Mere Christianity" might look like and how it could work.

He put those musings on hold when spotting Tom and Ron.

"Glad you guys could make it," said Stephen.

"What the heck, nothing better to do," quipped Tom Stone.

"Right," replied Stephen.

"Did you see what happened with the attack by Buklis?" asked Ron McDermott.

Grant paused, deciding, again, what he could and should tell his friends. He glanced around, leaned in closer, and whispered, "Let's just say, I was involved, and leave it at that."

Tom said, "You stopped him, didn't you?"

Grant's slight tilt of the head and silence provided the answer. Stone smiled. McDermott shook his head.

Stephen looked at Ron. "And guess who I had a chat with late last night?"

"Oh, please," said Ron. "Give me a break."

"What can I say? By the way, your boss is a nice guy."

"Really?" said Ron, "I wouldn't know. Apparently, though, my Lutheran friend does."

Tom added, "Now, now, Ron, envy not only is a sin, but it's unbecoming."

Grant noted more security personnel entering the atrium room. He turned back to Tom and Ron. "Go ahead in, and grab your seats. Time to take in some history."

They entered the auditorium. McDermott went up the stairs for his seat in one of the back rows. As a representative for his Anglican church body, Father Stone sat midway up. And Grant had a seat to the left of the stage, with his back against the wall. It allowed him to watch Pope Augustine I, as well as nearly everyone else in the room.

Chapter 72

Pastor Stephen Grant was not, as he occasionally put it, a "touchy-feely" Christian.

As was the case with his Navy SEAL and CIA experiences, Stephen learned to be a bit wary of emotions driving his faith. It wasn't that he shunned emotion. Nor did he try to ignore his feelings.

And his faith was not a purely intellectual undertaking. But he tended to tilt in that direction. In fact, a seminary professor reminded him that it was not enough to simply know that God was there, that God existed. There had to be a relationship, faith in God's grace and in his power to redeem, save and transform.

For Grant, as time passed, it was all about balance. He worked to balance the mind and the heart; reason and emotion; and the desire to know and understand more with the humility to accept the mysteries of God and faith. It was not always that simple for him.

But right now, Pastor Grant was swept up in a rare instance of spiritual and emotional euphoria.

He listened to Pope Augustine's address to the first gathering under the umbrella of "A Public Mission of Mere Christianity." The Pontiff's description of what Christians needed to do, together in the world, was inspired. The response from the nearly 800 people in the room reflected that spiritual reality.

Stephen could, well, feel it. He wondered when the last time such unity existed among so many Christian leaders gathered in one place.

And this nearly euphoric feeling continued throughout the Pope's historic press conference. The questions, though politely put, reflected the usual ignorance and bias Grant had come to expect from so much of the media.

Theocracy?

Imposing your religious views on others?

Doesn't the church have enough problems of its own?

Given the Crusades, Inquisition and pedophilia scandals, why should anyone listen?

And so on.

But this Pope – no, Stephen reflected – this man, flawed and sinful like any of us, answered each question calmly, thoughtfully, and with disarming kindness. And with a mix of principle, faith and humor, Pope Augustine I gained a kind of attentiveness among members of the media that few, if any, in public life could have even hoped for, and many politicians would have killed for. Congressman Ted Brees came to Stephen's mind.

Grant was now following the Pope, his aides and security entourage up the staircase in the castle's main lobby.

Augustine stopped at the statue of St. Ambrose, and gazed at it. As this continued for several seconds, a silence descended in the large chamber. The Pope said, "He was interesting, St. Ambrose. During a tumultuous time of disagreement in the latter part of the fourth century, he tried to keep peace among Christians in Milan. And he was not even baptized when clergy and the people called for him to become the bishop. He did not want the job, but finally acquiesced, was baptized, and eight days later became the bishop. He would be one of the great Latin

Doctors of the Church. And as we talk about the Church's role in the public arena now, it is worth recalling that Ambrose previously was a lawyer and politician who came to be a powerful voice in the Church for celibacy and voluntary poverty. If that happened today, few, I think, would doubt the transformative power of faith in our Lord." The Pope smiled, and most everyone else joined in with his infectious laugh.

That would be a miracle.

With Cardinal Santos leading the way, the Pope continued up the stairs to the left of Ambrose. At the top, various members of the entourage moved to their respective assignments. Santos and Augustine made a u-turn, walking along the second floor railing, heading for the last room on the right, still accompanied by the expanded number of personnel guarding the Pope. Grant was trailing the pack.

Waiting inside the room were the four members of the media for the more intimate discussion with Augustine – a "get to know the Pope" session, as some billed it. The ground rules had been straightforward. No audio. No video. Not even computers. It was meant to be a conversation between a public figure and members of the media, who would be armed with only pad and pen.

The four were paired off in conversation. Roy Wallace towered over the 27-year-old, short, thin Kathleen Tanglewood, whose shoulder-length, light brown hair fell slightly down the right side of her face. It managed to highlight, rather than hide, her large, bright blue eyes and pale skin. Wallace and Tanglewood's chat was casual, with a touch of flirtation.

Meanwhile, Devin O'Neill and Brett Buck were immersed in part discussion, part debate over what the Pope's initiative would mean for Christianity. O'Neill was a five-foot, eight-inch 30 year old, weighing in at a rotund

230 pounds, with a thick head of black hair and a mustache.

The 52-year-old Buck, in contrast, was long. It seemed that every part of his body had been stretched beyond their intended measurements. He was a thin six feet, three inches, with a vertically extended, balding head, and long arms, fingers and legs. It was all finished off with size 15 feet.

Outside the door, Cardinal Santos and Pope Augustine were immersed in a private conversation. It ended with the Pope telling Santos, in Spanish, "This will be done as I originally insisted. I will meet alone with these four people. Look around, my friend, there is no reason for concern."

"As you wish, Holy Father," replied Santos, with a ring of unpleasant resignation.

"Thank you," said the Pope, as he patted Santos on the shoulder.

Pope Augustine I looked around at those in the hall. Upon spotting Stephen, he offered a broad smile, and a nod of the head. Stephen returned both.

With that, the Pope entered the room for his media sit down, and Cardinal Santos closed the doors behind him.

Santos walked over to Grant. "The media. I feel like I am feeding the Holy Father to the sharks."

"From what I have seen today, the Pope knows what he is doing. He had them eating out of his hand at the press conference. I don't think you have to worry."

"Yes." Santos seemed to be only half listening, as he stared at the door that he had just closed. "He should have someone else in there with him. Someone on his side, so to speak."

Grant smiled at the Cardinal's over protectiveness.

Inside, Pope Augustine I moved to the middle of the long room to greet each person. Five, high back chairs were set up in a circle at the room's center. On a table to the right were the ingredients for zobo – the red concentrate from the hibiscus herb mixed with sugar and water; fresh orange and pineapple juices; soda water; sprigs of mint; a bucket of ice cubes; and glasses.

After brief introductions and greetings, the Pope said, "I know we do not have much time. But allow me the indulgence of serving a drink from my native Nigeria. Zobo can be quite refreshing. Yes?"

Each agreed, as had been agreed to days earlier, and selected a juice flavor.

As the Pope turned towards the table of ingredients, Wallace said, "Your Eminence, might I do the honors? I often made zobo when I stayed in your country several years ago on an assignment."

Augustine brightened. "You know zobo?"

"Yes, quite well."

"That would be wonderful. All of the times that I have presented it outside Nigeria, no one has known the drink. Please, be my guest."

Roy Wallace mixed three glasses of ice, red zobo syrup, orange juice, and soda water, topped off with lethal doses of poison from a pen. Two more glasses also had ice, zobo syrup, and soda water, but with pineapple juice and nonlethal – at least if treated in timely fashion – doses of poison. The pitcher of zobo concentrate received another dose of the poison, and each drink was topped with a sprig of mint.

Wallace took the tray of drinks to the Pope and the three other members of the media. The Pope, Buck and O'Neill were handed the zobo mixed with orange juice, while Tanglewood and Wallace took the pineapple mix.

Seated, the four from the media looked to the Pope. Augustine raised his glass. "Thank you, Lord, for the bounty you have bestowed upon your children." He paused, seemingly searching for a word. "What is it that you Americans say? Cheers?"

The four news people replied, "Cheers."

They drank from their glasses, with Roy Wallace delaying ever so slightly, being the last one to let the poisonous concoction pass his lips.

The effects were nearly immediate. Efforts to speak led to nothing but brief gurgling noises from the throat. Glasses fell silently onto the carpet, followed by bodies and chairs.

O'Neill had tumbled to the side and rolled onto his face. His last moments of life were spent staring into a deep green carpet.

Buck was the only person that remained upright. He helplessly watched those around him fall. He died watching others die.

Tanglewood had tumbled backwards. She lay on her back, with hands at her throat, looking up at the high ceiling with its ornate carvings. That fall onto her back, and immobilization, would haunt her dreams for the rest of her life.

Pope Augustine I had fallen to his right. He lay on the floor, head resting on his bicep. He stared at Wallace who lay across from him in a mirror-like position, head on his left bicep. As life began to drain away, through the paralysis brought on by the poison, Pope Augustine I managed a slight smile.

The Pope had been holding the drink in his right hand. As he fell, the glass was launched, and began to roll. As is often the case with old buildings, this floor slanted. Augustine's glass continued to roll on its side in the shape of a large arch, until it hit and came to rest at the door.

Outside the room, Grant stood directly across from the door with Cardinal Santos. Each was in thought. Grant was absentmindedly staring at the larger-than-typical gap between the door and the floor when he saw something hit and come to rest against the door inside the room.

What the ...?

As he walked to the door, he felt the tightness in his head, and the feeling of his ears closing up.

Red alert?

As Grant approached the door, he bent down to have a better look. When he straightened up, he saw FBI Agent Ryan Bates standing a few feet away, watching. Grant waved Bates over.

Grant pointed to the bottom of the door. "Look."

Cardinal Santos suddenly appeared next to Grant. "What is it?"

"A glass rolled up against the inside of the door. I don't ..."

But before Grant could get another word out, Santos pushed passed Bates. With everyone's attention in the hall now, Santos knocked forcefully on the door, and without waiting for a reply, he opened it. "Excuse me, Holy..." He immediately slipped into Spanish, and cried out, "Dios Mio, por favor, no!"

Grant saw the bodies on the floor in the middle of the room. As security rushed in with guns drawn, he drew his Taurus PT-25 from under his pant leg, and followed.

Grant saw no one else was in the room, and no evidence that anyone else had been in the room. Other than the door all had just rushed through, the only other way in and out was via four windows. And all were closed tight.

Santos yelled out, "The Pope, he is dead! He is dead!"

FBI agents called out that two were still alive. Emergency doctors and other medical personnel were in the room within a minute.

The quick diagnosis was poisoning.

Efforts on Buck, O'Neill and the Pope were fruitless.

But the stomach pumping began on Tanglewood and Roy Wallace. A doctor declared, "These two might have a chance. Get these people moving."

Grant felt immobilized as the action swirled around him. His right hand hung down at his side, clutching the gun. Finger still on the trigger. His head bowed down. A rage built inside.

Who did this?

Stephen Grant wanted to shoot the culprit. If the person were standing in front of him at that very moment, even unarmed, Grant felt like he would have pulled the trigger.

He looked up, just as one of the doctors moved away from the Pope's body.

Grant was transfixed by the look on Augustine's face. No hint of fear, horror, confusion, or even anger could be detected. Instead ... *Is that a smile?*

Chapter 73

Wallace and Tanglewood, accompanied by an FBI agent and a county police officer, were whisked away to a local hospital.

Once deemed secure, again, the laborious process of treating the entire St. Ambrose facility as a crime scene got under way, with everyone questioned.

The FBI and local police added more personnel, and jointly interviewed and ran backgrounds, again, on every person in attendance. Members of the media proved to be the most difficult to interview, as they were more inclined to ask, rather than answer, questions.

But the primary focus fell on those involved in preparing and delivering food and beverages, given zobo's emergence as the chosen murder weapon. The Grillin' Monks, along with the temporary staff brought in for the Pope's visit, were each isolated, and placed under the closest examination. But the interrogators came away with no information, though they never before experienced so many blessings and prayers at a crime scene.

Throughout this process, Grant drifted. He had gone from feeling euphoric, to extreme anger, to deep sorrow, and now ... to feeling nothing. He listened to some of the interrogations of the monks and other food preparers. But nothing struck him. Nothing jolted and pulled him out of the fog into the clarity of action.

Eventually, he wandered towards the atrium room off the auditorium. Upon entering, it was like being blindsided by a wave at the beach, getting knocked over, and struggling to get control over one's body so that feet could find the relative stability of sand.

In front of him stood a sea of mostly men, more than half dressed in black with a small square of white showing in the collar. Catholics, Anglicans, Lutherans, Methodists, Baptists, Presbyterians, evangelicals, and other assorted Christians were joined together in prayer. A few members of the media had put aside their work for the moment to participate.

Some looked skyward. Various heads were bowed. Others simply stared straight ahead. Many had tears in the corners of their eyes, or rolling down their cheeks.

After being interviewed by law enforcement, some simply had left the St. Ambrose Retreat House. But others, without any prompting, found their way into this room. A few began praying, and then it built.

To Grant's right, Bishop Carolan was leading the prayers.

Stephen spotted Ron, standing with hands clasped together and head bowed beyond Carolan. He knew that Tom was somewhere in the room as well.

Stephen's mind told him to enter and join in. That's where he should be.

But he was still wavering, trying to steady himself. The power of what was going on in this room took Stephen off guard. He'd already ridden his emotions to vast heights today, and now was fighting to not get dragged down by an emotional undertow.

He turned away.

As he walked down the hallway, Grant decided emotion could not be shed or quelled. So, he decided to choose anger over sorrow, for now. Grant could use anger, in particular a righteous anger.

Giving in to sorrow would make him relatively useless. And it might have overwhelmed Grant given his sense of failure. He was part of the Pope's theological and security teams. Security obviously, somehow, failed. Pope Augustine I stood ready to make religious history, and now he was dead. Grant would push away the sadness, and embrace the anger. That would feed his pursuit of justice.

He made his way up the main staircase, passing St. Ambrose, heading back to the security areas.

Grant spotted Paige sitting at a computer, with Rich Noack leaning over her shoulder looking at the screen.

As he approached, Paige rose and took two steps towards him. She lightly touched his left arm. "I just got here. I'm so sorry, Stephen."

He tried not to look into her eyes beyond a quick glance. "Me, too. What do we know?"

Grant listened to Paige and Noack. He even pitched in with a few thoughts and ideas. But, at this point, they knew very little.

We don't have shit.

Chapter 74

As news of Pope Augustine I's murder escaped and spread around the globe, those protesting "A Public Mission of Mere Christianity" melted away, for the most part. When prominent opponents were tracked down by members of the media, they expressed their sympathies, but with an unmistakably defensive tone.

The Internet was rampant with news and analysis. But given the World Wide Web's ability to empower the ignorant and small minded, rumors, conspiracy theories, baseless accusations, and comments of celebration and approval flew as only they can via high-speed, broadband networks.

In his maple-wood library, Bradley Barnett seemingly could not absorb the information of the Pope's demise fast enough. He read and clicked at a furious pace.

He came across a video interview with the actress Becca Roberts. She was crying and saying, "No one, of course, would ever want something like this, something so horrible, to happen."

"Pathetic," mumbled to Barnett to himself.

Next he found news footage of small groups in a few Middle East hotspots dancing, chanting and firing guns in the air. That made Barnett smile.

He clicked over to Microsoft Word, and read the press statement he had typed out:

> "Pope Augustine I's apparent murder is a heinous, despicable act that deserves widespread condemnation. I disagreed with the Pope's perspective on a variety of issues, including the implications that his recently announced project might have for protecting the environment. But violence should not be condoned in any way. My deepest sympathies go out to Catholics in the Town of Brookhaven, across the nation and around the world."

Barnett saved the document, and attached it to an email to his assistant with instructions to put the statement out on the wires and send it to their internal media list immediately.

Barnett's wife came into the room. She was trembling. "Brad, isn't it terrible?"

"Yes, darling, it certainly is. Come on, I'll fix us each a drink."

Just as he slipped an arm around his wife's waist, the phone rang on his desk.

"You go ahead into the family room. I have to answer this quickly. I'll be right in to mix those drinks." His wife wandered away, and Barnett picked up the phone. "Yes, Bradley Barnett."

"Barnett, he did it!" The voice on the other end was an enthused Andre Tyler.

In a low, deliberate tone, Barnett said, "Professor Tyler, I am not sure what you are talking about. You're not getting carried away with your work, are you?"

"Whatever do you mean? ... I'm looking at the television, and ... and ... Oh, yes. Of course. I mean no, I'm not. Sorry."

"We'll talk soon, perhaps sometime next week about that project." Barnett had been around mobsters long enough to know what should and should not be said, especially since there was the chance – even though it might be quite slim – that someone else was listening to your telephone conversation.

Tyler stumbled, "Yes, right, take care."

Barnett hung up the telephone, and looked down at his open calendar on the desk. He looked at his next day's schedule, and in a late afternoon slot, he wrote "Call about AT."

He went into the family room, and mixed a White Russian for his wife, and a Scotch on the rocks for himself.

They sat together on a plush couch, and watched the large, flat screen television on the wall. CNN was showing Catholics holding prayer vigils around the world, mourning the loss of their Pope.

* * *

Meanwhile, south and east of Barnett, another politician, Congressman Ted Brees, sat with his feet up on his desk in one of his district offices, television clicker in hand, flipping from news channel to news channel.

He smiled broadly at his lover and chief of staff Kerri Bratton, who was sitting on the office couch in a pulled-up short dress with her long legs crossed. Brees said, "The press statement went out?"

"Yes, Ted. Fifteen minutes ago. I sent everyone else home."

"Good. Good. I think we hit the right tone of sympathy and outrage at the Pope's murder, and the need for justice."

"Absolutely."

Brees continued, "And I told you it would pay off not getting involved by saying anything about that agenda the

Pope was pushing. Sure, it got us a bit of brief grief from a few of the abortion and enviro activists. But that decision could not have turned out better given what's happened now. I'll even score some points with Catholic voters who actually care about their religion."

Bratton nodded, "You made all of the right choices."

Ted looked directly into Kerri's blue eyes. "'You'? Don't you mean 'we' made all of the right choices, Ms. Bratton?" He smiled again.

"Thank you, Ted."

"I don't think we've forgotten anything, have we?"

"Well, there is one thing." Kerri put the pad and pen she was holding on a side table.

"What did we miss?" asked Ted.

"Apparently, when I changed earlier, I managed to forget something." She unfolded her legs to allow Congressman Ted Brees to see her absence of panties. "There's no one in the White House, Mr. President, and the door is locked."

Ted Brees joined Kerri Bratton on the couch, and with the television screen flashing images of prayers and mourning around the globe, they indulged each other in their own world.

Chapter 75

His BlackBerry was vibrating, again. He looked at the screen. It was St. Mary's.

No doubt Barbara, again. No time. She'll have to wait.

Grant was lost in trying to pull apart the plot ending in the murder of a pope and two journalists, with two others only surviving due to quick actions by the medical teams on hand.

He had stayed with Paige, Noack, Bates, and other investigators at the St. Ambrose Retreat House since the poisonings. Each grabbed short stints of rest during the overnight.

At one point, to get re-energized, Grant went over to the abbey, grabbed a very quick shower and put on his civvies.

All of his attention and energy was focused on justice.

At least, that's what he told himself: *Justice.* But a certain part of him, a part Stephen was trying to keep at bay, knew this was not his pursuit. Nor was his anger purely righteous. He allowed his motivations to descend into revenge.

Grant continued to envision finding the murderer. And with no one else around, pulling the trigger, and sending him – Stephen was sure – straight to hell.

The investigation had produced little. The poison had been identified as a derivative of yellow jasmine. It had been mixed into the juice flavoring for the zobo, and wound up in each person's glass. It seemed that the difference between life and death turned out to be little more than a few drops, according to the FBI's forensics team.

But, in general, the investigators were running into nothing else but dead ends. Nothing was found to link the poison to anyone. In fact, they could not figure out where the poison had come from, nor how it got into the zobo. Every theory the group could come up with failed to pan out. And their "individuals of interest" weren't all that interesting.

Grant's phone vibrated once more. He glanced at the screen, and hit "Ignore."

Agent Noack said, "It's not even 9:00 AM, and you must have gotten nearly ten calls, Pastor. And yet, you have not answered one."

As they worked together through the night, titles had been dropped in favor of first names. But now Noack had returned to "Pastor," with emphasis.

Grant stared at Noack for a long moment. "Yes. Why?"

"Quite frankly, while I understand your passion here, I was wondering if those calls were from your parish?"

Grant thought: *Who the hell do you think you are?* But he said, "Excuse me?"

Noack responded, "I could not help but wonder if members of your church have been trying to get a hold of you." The big and bald Rich Noack said it all rather casually.

"Well, Agent Noack, I'm not sure how that is any of your business."

Noack kept looking at Grant while taking a sip of his black coffee. "Well, in one sense, it's not. After all, how you run your church is your business. However, at the same time, I do have some say in how this multi-agency, international murder investigation proceeds, and you have, more or less, inserted yourself into that investigation."

Paige was listening. "Wait a minute, Noack, ..."

At the same time, Grant started, "Hold on ..."

Noack put a hand in the air before either could proceed any further. After a bigger gulp of coffee, he continued, "Now, don't get me wrong, you've been a plus here. Putting some things in the mix that the rest of us might have missed. I appreciate that. But I also understand that this is not what you do, at least, not for some time and not any more. After all, you're a pastor. In my position, I have to assess where resources are put to best use. Given what's happened, and your rather unique, dual role during Pope Augustine's visit, it's rather easy to get caught up in what we're doing here, with old instincts kicking in no doubt. But you need to ask yourself, are you putting your resources – your time, energy and efforts – to their best use right now? Or, do others need you more, quite frankly, than we do?" He leaned back in his chair, looking at Grant and finishing his coffee.

Grant knew Noack was right, but he was angry at the FBI agent for bringing it up. And glancing at Paige, she was less than pleased with Noack as well.

All Grant could muster was, "I need a break." He exited the back of the castle, and walked out to the stonewall that ran atop the cliff sweeping down to the Long Island Sound. He shoved his hands inside the pockets of his jeans, and stared out at the water and the cloudy sky above.

Paige came up beside him, and slipped her left arm inside his right. "What does Noack know? FBI agents can be such assholes."

Stephen smiled slightly. They stood there quietly for a couple of minutes, just looking at the water.

Paige broke the silence, "Talk to me, Stephen. What are you thinking?"

"What am I thinking? I think that Noack is absolutely right. But I'm pissed off that he's right. Nearly every fiber of my being wants to stay here, figure this out, and hunt down the bastard or bastards who did this. But I have responsibilities elsewhere, and they're big ones. And so far today, I've been ignoring those responsibilities. And quite frankly, I might have gone on ignoring those responsibilities, but for Noack's little intervention. I've been very good at rationalizing, but playing agent with you again since Augustine was taken down has been self indulgent."

They continued to look across the Sound amidst more silence.

Stephen finally added, "Quite frankly, the last thing that I want to do at this exact moment in time is go back to my pastoral duties at St. Mary's. God forgive me. But that's exactly what I should do. And I know that's probably not what you wanted to hear."

He turned to Paige, and saw that her eyes had moistened. "Paige..."

While still staring out at the Sound, she interrupted, "You're right, Stephen. That's not what I wanted to hear. But it is what you need to do. I know that now."

"You do?"

"Yes. Our trip to Montauk did clarify things, provide closure, turn the page ... whatever sappy cliché you want to use ... for me." She turned, slipped her arms around his back, pulled him closer, and looked into his eyes. "My dear, you are stuck being a pastor. That means you will not have access to this beautiful, toned body for romps in the sack as you once did long ago. And that, as you well know, is your loss. But I will not let you forget it because I will continue to flirt and arouse you without mercy."

"Oh, you will?"

"Yes." She pushed her body up against his groin ever so slightly with a mischievous smile. "Well, at least until you find some respectable woman to play the role of pastor's wife, then I'll stop."

"How civilized of you."

"I know. Stephen, you are done being a government agent, and it's time for you to get back to being a pastor. I still don't get the whole church thing. But you do, and that's where you belong now."

She reached up and cradled Grant's head in her warm hands. She pulled his face down, leaned up, and lingered in a kiss on his cheek. Still holding his head and gaze, Paige whispered, "And now we both have to get back to work."

Paige pulled her eyes away from Stephen's, turned and walked back to the castle. She called back over her shoulder, "I'll let you know when we've got something." There was a pause. "Now get back to church, lover boy."

Grant stood in silence as he watched Paige Caldwell stroll away.

Chapter 76

After packing up his gear and leaving the grounds of the St. Ambrose Retreat House, Grant was soon speeding along the Long Island Expressway heading east in his Tahoe.

He called Barbara Tunney and apologized for not getting back earlier. He brought her up to speed on his experience with the murders, and started to give some basic instructions for pulling together a last-minute prayer service tonight at St. Mary's.

But Barbara interrupted, "Both Father Stone and Father McDermott have been trying to get a hold of you since very early this morning as well."

"Yes, I know. They're on my list to call."

"Well, don't bother. I've been trying to reach you for the same reason. Your two priest friends have decided that a joint prayer service is in order tonight, and they've selected St. Mary's as the location."

"Oh, they have. But how can we ...?"

"Father Stone and Father McDermott reached me at about eight, after missing you, to see if St. Mary's calendar was clear. I told them it was, and we all agreed that you would agree this would be something important to do. Father McDermott pointed out that it would be powerful if the new local Lutheran church would host such a service for a murdered Catholic pope. They again agreed that you would agree, but before anything got rolling, obviously, I said I needed your okay."

"Thanks, Barbara. You were all correct. I think it is important that we take this opportunity, but you obviously were right to check in first. Where did you leave it with Ron and Tom?"

"Father Stone's wife drew up a one-page invitation with all of the information. I just got it in my e-mail. You just need to review it, and we can all spring into action."

"No need for my review. Go with it."

"Are you sure?"

"Absolutely."

After the call, Grant flipped on the radio, and listened to a news station for the latest information and reactions on the Pope's murder. The news people knew less than he did.

Chapter 77

By mid Friday afternoon, Roy Wallace was well out of danger, but still in a weakened state. Against doctors' recommendations, he was checking himself out of the hospital.

While Wallace was slipping on his sports jacket, a baby-faced doctor of Japanese descent urged him to stay through the weekend. "Mr. Wallace, you really should remain here to make sure there are no additional reactions to the poisoning."

"Doctor, you did say that I am out of danger, correct?"

"Well, yes, in terms of dying. But you're weak, and I can't rule out that your body might react in some other way. And we're not 100 percent on everything at work here. I'd like to keep you for observation."

"I appreciate the concern. But I am part of one of the biggest news events in recent times, and I have a job to perform. In fact, given my own brush with death, I consider it a duty." Wallace stepped out of the room, and into the hallway.

The doctor said, "Can't you write from here? With a laptop and so on?"

"From a hospital bed? Please, I do not think so. This is far too important. I have to clear my head and be in the right setting. I'm sure you understand." Wallace glanced into the room next to his, where Kathleen Tanglewood was lying in the bed asleep. "And you're sure Ms. Tanglewood is going to be fine?"

The doctor seemed to resign himself to Wallace leaving, and shifted his attention to the television reporter. "She should be fine. Her body, for various reasons, reacted more harshly than yours did." He paused. "Though obviously, you both fared better than the Pope and the other two victims." His voice trailed off, as he looked down at the clipboard he was carrying.

"Indeed," said Wallace.

The doctor looked up. "Ms. Tanglewood will take a bit longer to get back on her feet than you, Mr. Wallace."

Wallace turned to the two FBI agents and three police officers who were talking just a few feet away. "Gentlemen, against doctor's orders, I am leaving to get back to work covering this tragedy. Are there any other questions I can answer?"

All five shook their heads, with an FBI agent saying, "No, thanks, Roy. Your thoroughness was much appreciated. When we have more, we'll call."

One of the police officers added, "Do you want us to drop you somewhere?"

"No need. I've already called for a taxi. Thank you."

After taking a few steps, Wallace stopped in front of the doctor. "Might you do me a favor, doctor?"

"Yes, of course. What is it?"

Wallace pulled out a business card, and reached inside his jacket pocket to take out a pen. He clicked.

The doctor took note. "A multi-color pen. Haven't seen one of those since I was a kid."

As he wrote on the back of the card, Wallace replied matter of factly, "I use them all of the time. You can order them online. The different colors allow me to do a better job making changes and editing. Funny thing, though, the three other cartridges in this pen are out of ink." He shook the pen, and shrugged his shoulders at the doctor.

Wallace handed over the business card. "If you could give this to Ms. Tanglewood when she is feeling better, I would be eternally grateful." He winked and walked away.

The doctor looked at the card, noting Wallace's position with the *Philadelphia Sun*. He flipped it over to read what was written. "Let's compare notes over dinner. Call me."

The doctor shook his head.

One of the FBI agents came over. "What is it, doc?"

"Mr. Wallace gave me his card to pass on to Ms. Tanglewood. Apparently, in the midst of this mayhem, he's looking for a date."

The FBI agent took the card, and read Wallace's message. "Huh. I'm not sure if that's smooth or repulsive."

The doctor said, "I'm sure."

* * *

Wallace paid the driver, and got out at his hotel. Shortly after entering his room, his cell phone rang. The call had been forwarded from the phone for Robert Johns.

He lost the British accent, and replaced it with an American one. "Johns."

"It's Barnett. We have a problem."

"Yeah?"

"Tyler seems a bit too excited. I don't trust his mouth."

"OK. There will be an additional clean-up fee."

"That's not a problem," said Barnett.

"Good. We have to move fast. I don't like to meet face to face, but I can be to you by eight."

"That will be fine."

"Will you be at home?"

"Yes, I live ..."

"I know where you live."

There was a pause. "Naturally. I'll be expecting you."

Wallace hung up the telephone. He had a lot of work to get done in a very short period of time. A column had to be written, and weapons needed checking.

Chapter 78

Nearly all of St. Mary's choir members had shown up. Scott and Pam had made sure of that. Pam was at the organ in the choir loft, along with Scott who had graduated to a cane.

At 8:00 PM, the choir began the procession into the nave, while leading a nearly full St. Mary's in singing "In Christ There Is No East or West."

Stephen and three other local Lutheran pastors followed. Among those in the pews were Tom Stone, Ron McDermott, and a dozen other clergy from various churches in the county.

* * *

Yuri Kamenev smoothly transitioned back and forth between acting as American assassin Robert Johns, and as British journalist Roy Wallace.

Right now, Robert Johns took center stage.

After driving slowly up the road, Johns parked the rented, black Ford Flex in the driveway of Bradley Barnett's home. He looked around the secluded, wooded grounds, assessed the home, and walked carefully up to the front door. He rang the bell, and again surveyed the area while waiting for the door to open.

It was answered by a woman who welcomed him, introducing herself as Mrs. Barnett. She offered to take him to the library where her husband was awaiting his arrival. She turned to lead the way. Johns pulled out a Russian PSM pistol with a suppressor attached and deposited a bullet into the back of her head.

Given the relatively small size of the pistol and the silencer, there was little noise. The woman even crumpled to the carpeted floor quietly, just missing a thin glass shelf, and the door to the room where she was headed was closed.

"Convenient," whispered Johns.

He slipped the gun back in its holster, and pulled the dark jacket he was wearing closed. He walked down the short hallway, and knocked on the door.

*   *   *

Stephen led the service. But he was pleased that Pastor Jed Raft from Holy Trinity Lutheran Church had called in the early afternoon to see if Stephen wanted someone else to offer the homily. He quickly took Raft up on the offer. It freed Stephen up to make a few calls and drum up information on developments related to the murders.

After the Gospel reading and a singing of "The Church's One Foundation," Pastor Raft ascended into the pulpit. Actually, he waddled to and hoisted himself up into the pulpit. Raft was a short, wide man in his late thirties with thin dark hair. His cheeks draped down so far that they hid any neck that might exist. And rather than hanging down, his arms seemed to rest on his spherical torso, with elbows sticking out to the sides.

Before he could begin, Raft dropped the top sheet on which his homily was written. He struggled to maneuver back out of the pulpit, and bend down to retrieve the paper.

Grant was impatient. *Come on, Jed.*

With the trace of a lisp, Pastor Raft began:

What the heck are we doing here?

This is strange, isn't it? Mourning the passing of a Roman Catholic Pope in a Lutheran church?

Any murder, of course, is a horror, a sin. But why have Christians from across the Church assembled tonight in St. Mary's Lutheran Church?

It's because Pope Augustine I was trying to spark the Church to become a voice for moral clarity in a world that desperately needs it...

Stephen heard the words. Raft hit all the right points. At any other moment in time, Stephen would have been engrossed, even touched given the circumstances. But things still felt distant. He was more observer than participant or celebrant. He found himself working to restrain the impulse to pull out his BlackBerry to check for messages from Paige.

* * *

"Please come in," said Bradley Barnett.

As Johns opened the door, slipped in, and closed it behind him, he said, "Your wife sent me this way. Said she needed to check on something in the kitchen."

"Good, no reason for her to be in the way." Barnett got up from his desk.

The two met in the middle of the library, and shook hands.

Barnett stared at Johns. A flash of recognition crossed the politician's face, and then a broad smile. "Simply wonderful. I know you, Mr. Johns. Or should I call you Roy Wallace, columnist for the *Philadelphia Sun*?"

"Guilty on both counts," Johns replied without emotion.

Barnett laughed as he moved back to his desk. "Well, given the dismal state of the newspaper business, I guess you have to make a buck somehow." He enjoyed his own joke, with an even deeper and louder laugh. "But as an assassin? Who would have thought? It's simply delicious. No one would ever suspect. And you're a Brit, right? Or, Wallace is a Brit, correct?"

Johns replied coolly. "Yes, he is."

"Brilliant," crowed Barnett. "Which is it really? American or British?"

"I'm sorry, Mr. Barnett, but I'll never tell."

"No, I'm sure you won't." Barnett stared at Johns with a smile, shaking his head. "Just wonderful."

"Could we get down to business?"

"Of course," said Barnett. He pulled a briefcase out, and placed it on the desk. "Given the three million you've already earned, I assumed that another $200,000 would be sufficient to clean things up with Tyler. This has been quite an expensive undertaking, but given the results and the problems that Pope Augustine was planning to make for such a wide array of people, it is all quite worth the price."

"I'm glad you think so," said Johns. He took the briefcase full of cash. "Two hundred thousand works for me."

"You don't want to count it?" asked Barnett.

"I trust you, Mr. Barnett."

"And you can trust me, Mr. Wallace, to keep your lucrative and dangerous secret. I am quite familiar with the need to keep secrets for people in, let's just say, questionable lines of work."

"Yes, I'm well aware of your family's involvement in organized crime."

Barnett raised an eyebrow. "Excuse me, but ..."

"Spare me any protestations," Johns interrupted. "Unfortunately, though, I simply cannot take the chance." He pulled the pistol from inside his jacket.

"If you truly know my family history, you would not dare." Barnett stood up. "You're not that stupid."

"I'm not stupid at all, Mr. Barnett. Quite the contrary. The police also know of your family's line of work. And they will see the professional nature of your murder and your wife's – by the way, she is dead in the hallway – and be working the organized crime angle."

"My wife..." Barnett went to move from behind the desk, but Johns trained the gun on him, and said, "Please do not move, Mr. Barnett."

Barnett stopped. The growing panic was clear on his face. His eyes darted around the room.

Johns continued, "Meanwhile, given the reality that I will leave nothing behind of use to your mob friends, they will be at a loss as to who should be the target of their retaliation. Besides, I don't think they're going to work too hard on this one. Those wise guys loved your father, but from what I understand, they don't like you very much. In fact, no one seems to like you, Mr. Barnett. At least, that's the word in media circles."

Barnett pleaded, "You really do not have to do this. You know where I am, so I'll never talk. I can get more money, if that's what you want."

"More money? Now that would just be getting greedy. And while you might try to keep your mouth shut, you also might try to use those mob contacts of yours to finish me off. And I obviously can't take that chance." Johns trained the gun.

"Drop dead, you son of a bitch."

"Not me, Mr. Barnett. It is you who will drop dead." Johns pulled the trigger.

The bullet entered Barnett's skull through his nose. He fell back into his chair.

Johns deposited three more shots into Barnett's chest, and left with his money.

* * *

Bodily, he was back at St. Mary's. He told himself, again, that this is where he needed to be. He told Tom and Ron the same thing after the service was over, even mentioning what Paige said. But Grant's attention and energy kept returning to those responsible for the Pope's murder ... and making them pay.

Stephen tried not to appear distracted while Ron and Tom lingered after the service in his office. They commiserated over the loss of Augustine, and wondered what might become of his "Public Mission of Mere Christianity." But he avoided offering the usual beers in the hopes of breaking things up early, and turned down Tom's invitation to come back to the St. Bart's parsonage.

Once they were out the door, Grant was on the phone with Paige seeking the latest information. She mentioned that an FBI team was looking for any kind of signature left by the creator of the poison. But there was nothing new.

What now?

He didn't head back to the parsonage. Instead, Grant spent the night in his office at St. Mary's. Part of the time, he trolled the Internet for anything that might provide an insight on the poison, or an overlooked bit of information from Pope Augustine's background that might provide some kind of hint. The other part of the night, Grant slept on his office couch.

When waking on Saturday morning, he washed up and changed his clothes.

Grant looked at himself in the mirror.

You need to get a sermon done, Pastor Grant.

He looked away. Returning to his office, Grant purposefully avoided looking at anything around the room – bibles, crosses, a crucifix.

He scribbled a note to Barbara Tunney, letting her know that he would be back in time for the Saturday evening service.

I'll wing it on the sermon this week. Forgive me, Lord. But I just cannot do this right now. Unfortunately, I'm not sure what I can do.

Grant went straight to the coffee table gun cabinet, unlocked it, and took out his Glock pistol and Harris rifle, along with accompanying ammo.

Chapter 79

"You've heard about our friend?"

"Yes. It hit the news late this morning."

"What the hell happened? Do you know?" Andre Tyler's voice was shaky, trembling. "Could someone have known? I don't see how. And even if somebody found out, why kill Barnett?"

"I don't know," said Johns. "I was going to ask you the same questions. We need to meet to figure this out, plan what to do next."

"Meet? You want to meet?" asked a confused Tyler.

"We're the only other two who know. If this has anything to do with our joint effort – and I do not believe in coincidences – one of us must be next. We need to figure out who this is, and then I can take care of matters."

"Of course." A sense of relief crept into Tyler's voice. "Where are you?"

"Once I heard, I got out of my house."

Johns said, "Makes sense. I'm still local, laying low. I was planning to leave the country early next week. Where can we meet? Somewhere private."

"How about my office at the university? There shouldn't be anyone around on a Saturday."

"Perfect."

Tyler gave Johns directions. They agreed to meet at 2:30.

*   *   *

Grant's frustrations were only growing.

Nothing came from the morning spent shooting at the sportsmen's club. But he was not really sure what was supposed to come out of it. On the one hand, Grant hoped to think through the entire situation, hopefully coming up with something otherwise overlooked regarding the murders. On the other hand, he merely hoped that his mind might be cleared.

Instead, neither goal was accomplished. All Grant did was use up ammunition.

After a late lunch, Grant pulled out his phone to call Paige to see if he could be useful.

*   *   *

Robert Johns parked in the student lot closest to the sterile cement building with dark windows that housed the university's small philosophy department. He slipped on latex gloves.

Johns used a staircase, rather than the elevator, to get to the third floor, and carefully moved among the deserted, dark offices. He passed through a set of double doors, and stood in the philosophy department – which amounted to eight office doors off a wide, dingy hallway.

Only one door was open, with the lights on inside.

Johns entered. "Dr. Tyler."

Sitting at a desk full of papers, Andre Tyler quickly looked up. He was startled. "Johns?"

"Yes. Lower your voice. Is anyone else here?"

"No."

"And you're absolutely sure you spoke to no one about this entire effort?" Johns circled behind Tyler, and lowered the shades in the office window.

"About Augustine?" said Tyler, twirling his chair around to face Johns. "Of course not. Do you think I'm some kind of imbecile? I could ask you the same question."

"You could. But you won't."

Johns unsnapped a right-leg pocket on his dark green cargo pants, and unsheathed a Kizlyar Korshun knife. All that the white-haired Tyler could do was raise his bushy eyebrows in shock. Johns plunged the knife into the professor's chest. He added eleven more plunges and tears in Tyler's torso. The grizzly killing looked like it was carried out by someone out of control ... the exact opposite of Robert Johns.

Johns pulled a large ziplock bag from another pocket. He deposited the bloody knife and the latex gloves inside the bag, sealed it, and stuffed it inside his dark jacket. He left the building without touching anything else with his hands, making sure to leave nothing behind from which any information could be derived.

As he strolled to his vehicle, Johns smiled at a young college woman dressed in denim shorts and a white t-shirt heading in the opposite direction.

She smiled back, and said, "Amazing how warm it is for late September."

"Must be 80 degrees. Very hot."

As she walked by, the girl glanced over her shoulder, and spotted Johns eyeing her behind. "Like what you see?"

"Like I said, very hot."

"You're a bad man," she called back while still walking away.

"Very bad."

The girl giggled.

Johns stared a bit longer. He took off the dark jacket, making sure not to expose anything hidden in the pockets. Then he turned towards the parking lot.

Chapter 80

Paige Caldwell apparently was too busy to take Grant's call, which increased his frustration.

He decided to try another person who might have some information – Sean McEnany. Grant called the cell number from the business card McEnany provided.

"Pastor Grant?"

"Yes, Sean. How are you?"

"Good. What can I do for you?"

"To cut to the chase, have you been looking into the Pope's murder at all?"

McEnany hesitated. "Why do you ask?"

"Well, a general feeling of helplessness."

"I understand. Are you free?"

"As a matter of fact, I am," said Grant.

"Why don't you come by the house? I'm in Hunter's Run in Manorville." He gave the street address.

"I'm five minutes away."

Grant pulled into the driveway of a modern, quasi-Victorian home. It was a large house by typical suburban standards – nearly 4,000 square feet – with a neatly manicured front lawn and a roomy, fenced backyard.

After Grant got out of his vehicle, he noted three dark bubbles strategically positioned at various points under the roof's overhang. *Security cameras.* As he took a few steps closer to the house, a German Shepherd quickly appeared at the backyard fence, protesting the stranger's arrival with loud barking.

Before Grant reached the front steps, Sean McEnany opened the door.

"Pastor, welcome."

"Thanks, Sean. And thanks for taking some time."

"No problem. Come in. Rachel and the kids are out."

Grant had never been to McEnany's home before, and only exchanged pleasantries with his wife and children as they exited church. Together, they seemed like a rather average family. But since he had a couple of beers with Sean a little over a week before, it was different now. In his previous career, Grant knew many spooks who, at the end of most days, left work for a rather average home in suburbia. But compared to their neighbors, they were not typical suburban husbands and dads, wives and moms.

"Let's talk. Follow me." He led Grant by a living room with pastels and plush furniture, through a glistening white kitchen, and down stairs to a finished basement sporting a billiards table, bar, and Las Vegas décor featuring a poker table.

Grant noted, however, that the area was much smaller than what the footprint of the house would dictate. He followed McEnany into a utility room that included the heating and water units for the house. Sean moved a shelving unit on rollers revealing a metal door, with a keypad and small screen on the wall to the right.

Now, this fits the Sean McEnany I drank beer with the other night.

"Panic room?" said Grant.

"Not exactly," replied McEnany, who did not seem to appreciate the stab at humor.

McEnany punched in eight numbers. The screen came to life. He placed his right hand against the screen, and a scanner read his handprint. Three seconds later, the locks on the door clicked open.

McEnany opened the door, and Grant followed. The 24x20 room centered around a 10-foot-long table with three desktop computers and three desk chairs in front of each. On the wall on the other side of the table hung a 72-inch high-definition video monitor.

"Should I know about this?" asked Grant.

"I can trust you. Can't I?"

"Maybe."

McEnany smiled at that one.

Grant took note of the small arsenal – handguns, sniper rifles, shotguns, and knives – hanging on the back wall next to the door, along with night vision goggles and gas masks.

"Do you play the Wii in here with the family?"

"OK, if you're finished. Do I have anything of interest regarding Pope Augustine I's murder? That's your real question, correct?"

"Yes."

McEnany sat at the center desktop, which came to life with one tap on the keyboard. Two more strokes and the screen on the wall popped on. McEnany spoke as he typed away on the keyboard. "We work with the Pentagon and other agencies on a variety of issues. In this case, since the murders, our forensics team has been working to spot a unique signature on the poison."

"Anything?"

"As a matter of fact, yes. Very early this morning, our people found something. It was engineered from yellow jasmine."

"Yes, I know that."

"But others have come across this engineered version, or at least something close to it. We know that the Brits, Pakistanis, Germans, and in particular, the Russians have all had experiences with this kind of poison being used on

prominent individuals inside and outside of government."
He flashed through various photos on screen. "No one
considered comparing notes until we started asking around
yesterday. And given that no one wants to appear to be an
obstacle to nailing those who took down a pope – not even
the Russians these days – all were quick to provide rather
extensive information on each case."

"And where did that take you?"

"No one had any idea of who did the poisoning, or who
engineered the substances. But when we lined up all of the
cases next to each other, each poison had trace elements of
the coca leaf. If it's about coca, number one on the
production front is Colombia, of course. And it turns out
that your former employer – the CIA – knew of a former
KGB chemical warfare expert who has been living
comfortably – though not ostentatiously – in retirement in
Santa Marta, Colombia, for about a dozen years now." He
put a few photos up on the screen of a skinny, bald,
sunburned senior citizen enjoying the sun, the beach, and
some icy, colorful beverages.

"Who is he?"

"Pavel Moroshkin. Colombians reported that he's a
great guy. No trouble whatsoever."

"Are the Colombians cooperating? Going to pick him
up?"

"They would be more than happy to do so. But from
what I've heard, they've been unofficially asked to look the
other way, while some of our people grab Moroshkin. Idea
is that we might be better able to persuade Moroshkin to
cough up his client list."

That's the play I would have called.

"Have you heard the status yet?" Grant inquired.

McEnany checked his watch. "Nothing yet. Things
should be happening within the hour."

"Interesting. Anything else that you can tell me?"

"That's all I have, for now. Besides, don't you have to be getting to church soon for the Saturday night service?"

It was Grant's turn to check his watch. *How did it suddenly become 5:30?* "You're right. Time flies."

"But I'll give you a heads up when I hear about Moroshkin, if you like?"

"Thanks. This is some set up you have. A secret computer and communications room in your basement with the latest security, along with a small arsenal. Seems a bit much."

"Not really when you consider the work I'm doing. And as I mentioned the other night, anything you need let me know."

It crossed Grant's mind to again protest that he was just a pastor and no longer involved with intelligence work, but then he realized what he was doing right now.

McEnany said no more about what he did and what kind of help he could provide, and Grant knew better than to press.

Unlike the people who came to Pastor Stephen Grant to talk about their lives and faith, and wound up telling all, Grant knew that McEnany was trained to only say what was deemed necessary. Grant, however, thought that McEnany provided greater access today than his superiors at CorpSecQuest, GovSecQuest, or whatever security agency Sean McEnany might be working for or with, would be comfortable with, Stephen's background notwithstanding.

* * *

The attendance of Jennifer Brees at the Saturday night service was the first time all day that Grant's attention was diverted from the murders at St. Ambrose's. Stephen noticed her entering the church while Pam Carter played the prelude.

Jennifer sat just a few rows from the front. She was dressed casually, in jeans, white sneakers, and a pink polo shirt.

As the service began, fewer than 20 congregants were in attendance. And everyone but Jennifer sat in pews towards the back. Grant felt like he was doing the service with only her. He maintained the thought, as it helped him to gain some focus on what he was actually doing.

Jennifer was the last person leaving the church nearly an hour later.

"Nice sermon, Pastor."

"Really?"

"Yes, really."

"Thanks."

"And I'm so glad that you can make it tomorrow."

"I can?"

She raised an eyebrow. "When I called earlier, Barbara said that you couldn't come to the phone, but that you would join a few of us at my house on Sunday afternoon for a kind of end-of-season pool party and barbecue. It's supposed to be warm again tomorrow, and besides, the pool is heated."

"Barbara said that."

"Yes, she did. You can make it, right?"

Grant looked into her warm, brown eyes, and any thoughts of not going evaporated. "Of course, I'm coming. Forgive my porous memory. This has been a week to forget."

"I'd say it's been a month to forget."

She looked at the floor, then up. Their eyes met again. Jennifer said,: "Well, 12:30 tomorrow then."

"Good. 12:30. Can I bring anything?"

"No. I'll have everything we need. Good night, Pastor."

"Good night, Jennifer."

Chapter 81

The late September weather in Santa Marta was not much different from any other month in the Colombian city – ranging between average lows of 75 degrees and highs of 90 degrees.

Strolling along the white sand beach in khaki shorts and a red tank top, Paige Caldwell looked the part of a tourist or local beachcomber, as did her fellow CIA agents. Each closed in from different directions on a small white home with big windows, a pool and decking looking out at the Caribbean Sea.

Paige came up a path from the beach. The rest of the team pronounced the house empty and secure through her Bluetooth earpiece. As she reached the decking, Paige alerted them that a slight, elderly, white haired man appeared to be sleeping on a chaise lounge poolside.

Paige queried, "Pavel Moroshkin?"

The Russian opened his eyes to see four guns trained on him.

He sighed. "Americans, I assume," he said in a Russian accent.

"Good guess," said Paige.

"Not a guess. The Colombians leave me alone, and no one else would care about ex-KGB quietly living out retirement years in the sun."

"Perhaps not so quietly. And actually, Mr. Moroshkin, there are a good number of people interested in you, such as the Brits, Germans, Palestinians, to mention just a few. Oh yes, even Mother Russia is curious. Seems like some very prominent people are dying, and your knowledge of chemistry, combined with this exotic locale, has drawn attention. Apparently one of those prominent deaths just happened to be Pope Augustine's."

What little color there was in Moroshkin's face drained away. "Shit."

"Let's go inside and talk, Pavel."

Moroshkin needed no prodding. After hearing that his poison had been used to murder the Pope, he shrank into a weak, little old man.

At first, Moroshkin pleaded, "I'll give you everything, if you just leave me alone here."

Paige laughed. "How about I put in a word that you cooperated, and you pray for some kind of miracle that they don't execute you? Three meals a day in a cell is the best you can hope for now. How nice the treatment is depends on which country's cell you wind up in. We've gotten some bad press in recent years, but I'd hope for the good old U.S. of A. if I were you. Fun in the sun is definitely done."

Pavel Moroshkin got even smaller and weaker. "You are right. It is over. What do you want?"

"Well, we'll take you up on the offer of everything," replied Paige. "But to start, this is the poison that killed the Pope."

He read the paper from Paige. "Yes, I thought it was him."

"Who?"

"Unfortunately, I do not know."

"That's not what I want to hear, Pavel."

"I know. But that is the truth. I have worked with this one for the past seven or eight years. No one is more careful in hiding his identity. I will give you all of the information. The account numbers for payment. Where and how I sent the products. The e-mail addresses. The names used. But they are always different. A few years ago, I did get curious. Had an old colleague – very good at what he did – try to figure out who this was. No luck though. I never heard from this colleague again. In fact, as far as I know, no one has. So, I quickly became disinterested in this one's identity."

Moroshkin's voice trailed off, getting smaller still.

Within an hour, all of Moroshkin's computer files had been transferred to Langley. His poison making lab and hard copies disappeared without a trace, as did Pavel Moroshkin himself.

Chapter 82

Grant didn't realize how much he needed an afternoon like this.

He was away from St. Mary's. But being with a few friends, his mind didn't have time to obsess over what was going on with the Augustine investigation. He spent a few hours swimming, relaxing poolside, talking baseball and movies, helping Jennifer with the barbecue, and partaking in some relatively harmless church gossip.

In attendance were Joan and George Kraus, and their two daughters, Glenn Oliver, and the unrelentingly upbeat and chatty Nicole Foreman, along with her reticent husband and well-behaved 10-year-old son and six-year-old daughter. Grant wondered if the rest of the family was so quiet because they couldn't get a word in with Nicole.

It was a peaceful, thoroughly enjoyable, afternoon.

* * *

Unfortunately, the afternoon was not so nice for one of Jennifer's neighbors.

A Ford Flex drove down the street, did a u-turn in front of the Brees home, and exited the block.

Twenty minutes later, Robert Johns casually strolled down the road in gray cargo pants, a brown t-shirt, dark sunglasses and a baseball hat pulled down low, with a large black backpack hanging over one shoulder. When arriving at the mailbox proclaiming "The Millers," he walked up the driveway, and around to the back of the house. Johns knocked on the door.

An elderly woman with a soft face and wearing a similarly soft sweater answered the door with a look of bewilderment. "Can I help you?"

"Mrs. Miller?"

"Yes, do I know you? And why are you knocking at our backdoor?"

He slipped the backpack off and placed it on the ground. "I brought some of the equipment your husband was looking for."

"Oh, you mean for the trains?"

"Yes, is he in the basement?" Johns picked up the backpack and pushed his way past the frail woman. He unzipped an outside pouch, and reached inside.

"Well, yes. What's your name, again? Jim didn't mention that he expected anyone."

Johns turned around, and said, "He wasn't expecting me." He raised his gun with the suppressor attached, and fired.

Five minutes later, Mr. Miller lay dead next to his model trains table, and Johns was unloading his backpack in the master bedroom on the second floor. At the southwest corner of the home, the bedroom offered windows looking down on the street, and over the hedgerow into the yard and driveway of the Brees home, with the inlet beyond.

Johns opened all of the windows in the room, and laid out his equipment on the bed. He positioned a rocking chair so he could easily view both the street and the Brees property. Johns sat, watched and waited.

* * *

When done swimming and eating barbecued chicken and steaks, the guests at the Brees home gradually changed out of their bathing suits and back into the clothes they wore when first arriving. Dessert was just being set out, with ice cream sundaes for the children, and homemade cinnamon coffee cake with coffee or tea for the adults.

Families with children led the way home. The Foremans were the first to go. And once Jennifer convinced Joan that she would not be needed for clean up, the Krauses soon followed.

Stephen, Glenn and Jennifer rounded up all of the glasses and plates left by the pool and on the patio, and brought everything into the kitchen.

Once all were inside, Johns, who had checked his weapons and holstered them at various spots on his body, grabbed the backpack, and moved downstairs, around the body of Mrs. Miller and out the backdoor.

After bagging the last of the trash, Glenn Oliver said, "Jennifer, sorry, but I can't stay to help with the dishes. I've actually got a poker game scheduled for tonight with a few buddies. Do you mind?"

"Mind? Of course not. Thanks so much for coming and helping with the clean up. Besides, all I have left is to load the dishwasher."

"And I've got that covered, Glenn," added Stephen, who already was putting plates into the machine. "Poker? I'm jealous."

"Really? I can call to see if we need an extra player, if you like, Pastor?"

"That's OK. Another time."

"Come on, I'll walk you out," said Jennifer. Glenn winked at Stephen while following Jennifer out.

Jennifer walking Glenn to the car, and me loading the dishwasher. Weird, but it feels ... right.

Grant whistled while loading the glasses, dishes and silverware.

As Glenn and Jennifer came out the front door, Johns found cover by the pool house.

He watched the two people exchange pleasantries. The black man got into his car, and drove away. The woman went back inside the house. He pulled the small, powerful cell phone jammer from the backpack, and flipped it on. It would block cell phone activity within a city block radius.

He tracked the overhead wires coming in from the street. They went down the north side of the house to a plastic control box. He merely unscrewed the cable and telephone wires coming out of the box.

The Brees home was cutoff from all outside communications.

Chapter 83

"The dishwasher is loaded, and the soap dispensed. Shall I turn it on?" asked Grant.

Jennifer just returned from sending off Glenn. "Absolutely. You're handy to have around. Do you vacuum? I hate vacuuming."

"It has to be a beltless, direct drive machine, and none of those annoying bags."

"Wow, both demanding and well-versed in vacuum technology."

"I don't take such matters lightly."

"I can see that."

Grant said, "Well, I guess I should be ..."

Jennifer interrupted, "Did you have any of the crumb cake?"

"No, I had some tea, but I couldn't extract myself from a conversation with Nicole in order to get a piece."

"Good. I want you to try something. That is, if you have a little time?"

"Sure. What is it?"

"Cut a couple of pieces of the crumb cake. I have something that accompanies it perfectly." She grabbed a corkscrew from a drawer and reached into the wine chiller, pulling out a bottle of Sutter Home White Zinfandel.

Stephen placed the two pieces of cake on the island in the middle of the kitchen, and sat on a stool. "White Zinfandel? I have to be honest. I've never been much of a fan."

As she undid the cork, Jennifer said, "Have you ever had it with cinnamon crumb cake?"

"No."

"Then you've never really tasted it."

"And how did you find out about this combination?"

"William Safire."

"William Safire? The dead *New York Times* columnist?"

"Yes."

"Did you know him?"

"Never met. But I read his Civil War novel *Freedom*." She poured two glasses of the wine, and handed one to Stephen. "And that is where I first read about cinnamon crumb cake and White Zinfandel."

"Well, if it's good enough for a late *New York Times* columnist, who am I to doubt it? Which first, the cake or the wine?"

"I suggest a bite of coffee cake first, then the wine."

They both proceeded as Jennifer instructed.

Before commenting, Stephen tried to put on his most contemplative face.

Jennifer said, "Well?"

"Hmmm."

"Oh, come on. How is it?"

He finally smiled. "Delicious."

Jennifer's face lit up. "I knew you'd like it."

Stephen could not help but stare. "You have a beautiful smile, Jennifer."

She blushed slightly. "Thank you, Pastor." She paused. "Stephen."

"And I have to thank you for something."

"In addition to the cinnamon crumb cake-White Zinfandel revelation?"

"Yes, it was at church last night." Grant took another drink of the wine. "With everything that happened on Thursday – the murders – I've been consumed with trying to figure out the guilty party. I was disconnected from the Friday service, and felt incapable of focusing on the real purpose for being at church on Saturday. But you changed that."

"I did?"

"I know it sounds strange. You sat in the front, and everyone else was towards the back of the church. And with that bright pink polo shirt, it was as if the others melted into the background. Somehow, that helped me – you helped me – concentrate on what I was doing. It was like you and I were the only two in the church, and that got me in the right state of mind."

Jennifer had been looking at the counter top as he spoke. She took a sip from her wine glass, and then looked at him. "I'm not sure what to say."

Stephen blurted out, "I know. I'm sorry. I should not have said that. It's inappropriate. After all, you're still married. Forgive me." As the words came out, Grant could not decide if he was asking for her forgiveness or God's. Either way, it didn't matter. If honest with himself, he was not sorry in the least.

"Forgive you? For what? Pastor Stephen Grant, I am going to confess something to you. When you saved my life, my emotions and thoughts were a mess. But the lone bit of clarity I had was a deep feeling of appreciation. The following days only grew more confusing, given that it increasingly seemed to me that Ted was treating this as a political event, rather than a near-death experience for his own wife. And then, of course, came the night that my marriage ended – the betrayal, the anger."

"I'm sorry, Jennifer."

"Please stop saying that, Stephen. Do you know what now stands out from that night and the next day in my mind?"

He shook his head.

"It's a gift of chocolate truffles, and a kind, gentle, strong person holding me while I was throwing up. Though that last part's a little foggy. More and more over the past few weeks, I've thought of being with you, but I pushed aside those thoughts given that my marriage just fell apart. And I thought that with you being a pastor and me a parishioner, that it just wouldn't be possible. And then you tell me this, beyond anything that I dared to hope."

They remained seated, looking at each other across the kitchen island.

"Aren't you going to say something?" she asked.

"It's been a very long time since I've come close to feeling this happy."

Jennifer's smile and moistening eyes worked on him as nothing else had before. It was like nothing he'd even felt with Paige years before. This reached deeper. He struggled to remain seated. If he stood up, he would move to kiss her.

Jennifer said, "What do we do now?"

"Good question. Well ..." Grant suddenly felt the pressure in his head and ears that signaled a red alert. *What the hell?*

"Stephen, what is it?"

"Nothing, I'm sure. But I have a funny feeling."

The backdoor leading to the covered patio burst open. Robert Johns had his pistol trained on Grant.

"Stay seated and do not move," Johns commanded.

But Jennifer sprang to her feet. "What is this?"

Johns calmly shifted his focus to her. "I said stay seated." He tilted his head slightly, fired the gun, and Jennifer fell back. She knocked over the stool she was seated on, and landed face first on the tiled floor.

Grant screamed, "Jennifer, no!" He sprang at the intruder, whose shot at Grant whizzed past his right ear. Grant focused on the midsection of the gunman, like a blitzing linebacker targeting a quarterback.

But the gunman went with Grant's momentum, falling backwards and allowing Grant to slide over him. By the time Grant got to his feet, the intruder already was up and had the gun trained on him. Then it hit Grant. He recognized the man. "Roy Wallace?"

"That's one name."

It immediately clicked in place for Grant. Wallace survived the poisoning. He either murdered the Pope, or was somehow involved. But why was he here? "What the hell is this?"

"I'm sure you've surmised that I killed Pope Augustine."

"Why?"

"A very nice paycheck. I've been in the murder-for-hire business for a good number of years now, but this was my most significant one-day paycheck ever."

"I don't understand. Why are you here?" Grant quickly glanced at Jennifer, but saw no movement.

"It's quite simple. I'm here for revenge."

"Revenge?"

"You don't recognize me, Mr. Grant. But just before the Barcelona Olympics, you killed my mentor, Boris Krikov."

"Krikov? But ..."

"I was there. Plastic surgery has since transformed me."

The height and build match. "How's your knee, Yuri?"

"Ah, so you do remember. Good. I never forgot. But at least we killed your partner, and he was our target. And so many years later, there you were, and a clergyman no less. I decided that after I carried out my job, a personal mission could be undertaken. I'm here to kill you for free."

"How did you find me?"

"Your church secretary was quite forthcoming with the information."

"You bastard, did you...?"

"Relax. She is unharmed. I simply called, told her I was an old seminary friend, and she volunteered that you were at the home of Jennifer Brees for a party. A few clicks of the mouse, and here I am."

"Who hired you to kill Pope Augustine?"

"Ah, the delaying questions. Hoping for an out, a diversion. It will not work. You are a dead man. But since it does not matter, I'll tell you anyway. Bradley Barnett and ..."

"Barnett, the politician?"

"Yes. He is – sorry, I should say – *was* from a mob family. And my other employer, also dead, was a professor named Andre Tyler."

Tyler? Tyler. The guy with Linda Serrano? Taught philosophy and the environment. Barnett a leader among the local political enviros. The greens didn't like Augustine's mission. And some didn't like it enough to hire this murderer?

Grant persisted, "Why kill those two?"

"I like my work in the newspaper business. In order to keep doing that, I decided to clean up any possible loose ends. It's an ideal set up – murder pays well, media credentials give me tremendous access, and I still get to write and spout off my opinions."

"Nice for you." Grant had to make some kind of move, or he would be dead momentarily.

"Now, Pastor Grant, it is ..."

"Jennifer?" Grant looked at her unmoving body, and Yuri's eyes moved that way as well. Grant thought of Coz, Pope Augustine and Jennifer, grabbed the bottle of Zinfandel off the counter, and plunged towards Yuri. A bullet ripped into Grant's left shoulder, but he kept moving, and swung the bottle with his right hand. It struck Yuri on the left side of his jaw, and sent the man reeling. But he didn't drop the gun, nor leave his feet.

Grant decided flight was the best option. Heading to the front door would take too long. Recalling Jennifer's office filled with medieval arms, he turned down the hallway. He heard Yuri's pistol fire off three shots even with the sound suppressor.

As he barreled into the office, he felt no shots land. But he did feel the numbness that had spread down his left arm from the earlier bullet giving way to burning pain. He grabbed a 17th-century German quillion dagger off the wall with his right hand and as Yuri entered, Grant slashed at the murderer's gun hand.

Yuri cursed in Russian as the gun fell out of his hand. Grant struck Yuri's jaw with the steel pommel of the dagger. That staggered Yuri, and sent him to his knees.

Grant tossed away the dagger, and picked the gun up from the floor.

Suddenly, it was as he had envisioned it hundreds of times over the past few days.

Jennifer's murderer. Augustine's murderer. Coz's murderer.

There he was before him on his knees. Grant had the gun trained on him. No one else was around. Hatred raged. Grant thought how this man had taken away so much, from him and from the world.

Yuri did not look at him with pleading in his eyes. Instead, it was pure venom.

You obviously deserve to die. You son of a bitch. Who could possibly deny that? No one. Who would know, after all, what went on here tonight, that I executed you?

Yuri spewed, "Do it already."

Grant centered his aim on Yuri's chest, and slowly began to squeeze the trigger.

Pull the freakin' trigger. Do it, Grant.

The pastor in him battled the former agent for control of the trigger.

Who would know? You know who would know. He knows all. He sees all. You can't play the game of cheap grace.

Grant took a deep breath. He said, "No, I'm not going to shoot you. But considering what you told me tonight, you'll eventually be executed for what you've done. And I'll be there to watch."

But Grant had been away from the game too long. He relaxed just bit, took his finger off the trigger, and lowered the gun ever so slightly.

Yuri's right hand moved with speed that Grant was simply no longer used to experiencing. The Russian PSM was tucked behind his back, and with one sweeping motion the gun came out and Yuri fired twice. The first bullet landed in Grant's left thigh and the second below his right shoulder.

He fell back and wound up staring at the ceiling. The gun had dropped out of his hand. In a few minutes, his body would give way to the shock, and he would slip into unconsciousness. But Grant knew it would never reach that point. Yuri Kamenev would kill him now.

Yuri stood over him with the gun pointed at his forehead. Yuri was talking. But Grant was no longer listening. He was praying.

Dear Jesus, please forgive all my sins and my many failings as a pastor and as a human being. And I'm sorry for my inability to protect Pope Augustine, Brett Buck, Devin O'Neal, and – oh sweet Jesus – for bringing this to Jennifer. That was all about my background leading to her death. I put all that I am in your loving, forgiving arms.

He could see the anger rising in Yuri's face as Grant ignored whatever the Russian was saying.

But suddenly Yuri's expression changed. A glimmer of surprise appeared. Then Grant saw the point of a sword emerge from the man's chest. Blood fell down onto Grant's face from the wound and sword. He continued to watch in amazement as Yuri's eyes rolled back in his head, and the sword was quickly withdrawn. Yuri seemed to linger a moment in mid air, and then he toppled to Grant's right. Stephen could not turn his head to see where Yuri landed.

Instead, a pale, drained Jennifer Brees came into Stephen's view. He noted a blood-soaked towel awkwardly tied around her right shoulder and under her left arm. The right side of her face was bruised and swelling. He decided to start listening again.

Jennifer spoke barely above a whisper. "Hey, we're even now."

"Sure are." Grant heard the weakness in his own voice.

She held up a sword. "This was just delivered on Friday. A short-blade, English, 17th-century hanger. Didn't have a chance to find a place for it in here yet."

"Lucky me."

"Cell phones aren't working, and the phone and cable lines are out," she reported.

"He cut off communications. There's a cell phone jammer nearby. Could be anywhere. See if you can reattach the landlines outside. If not, you'll have to take a cell and get out of range, or get to a neighbor's. Take my phone, and call the number for Paige."

"Paige?"

"Tell her, nobody else, what happened. She'll get a cleaner team here and medical help."

"Cleaner?"

"Trust me. Go."

"What about you?"

"Shot three times and judging by how I feel, it will not matter much" – he felt a cold chill accompanying the expanding pain – "if we don't get help very shortly, I'm done. And you don't look so great either."

Grant could see Jennifer summon added strength. "Don't you die on me, Pastor Grant. It turns out that I think I love you."

The last thing he saw was Jennifer's face fraught with worry. He tried to speak. "And I love ..."

Chapter 84

At 8:30 Monday morning, the receptionist at Hackling-Johnson Advisors burst into the partners' dining room.

"Mr. Johnson, Mr. Hackling, the FBI is here!"

Hackling looked up from his western omelet. "What do you mean, Patty, the FBI is here?"

A tall, slim FBI agent with neatly cut black hair followed her into the room. "Mr. Hackling? Mr. Johnson?"

The two men put down their forks, took the napkins off their laps and rose from their seats. They replied in unison: "Yes."

"I'm Special Agent John Smith with the FBI, and we have a warrant to search the premises and all materials and files – paper and electronic."

Johnson took the warrant from the agent's hand. "What is this all about?"

"Apparently, gentlemen, money that you raised wound up helping to pay the person who was hired to murder Pope Augustine I."

"What!?" shouted Johnson.

The color drained from Arnie Hackling's face. "Shit. Andre."

The agent reported, "Mr. Tyler is dead. But he helped fund the hit through the Our Children Our Planet Foundation, and your foundation – the Faith, Trust and

Freedom Foundation – helped fund Mr. Tyler's foundation."

Johnson was incredulous. "What the fuck are you talking about?"

Hackling seemed to be going over things in his head. Again he whispered, "Shit."

"Arnie, what's the deal with Tyler?"

That snapped Hackling out of his trance. "I don't know, and shut the hell up." He turned to the FBI agent. "This is a tragic coincidence. And nothing more, Agent Smith. Please, execute your warrant. You will have our full cooperation. Patty, please tell everyone to cooperate with Agent Smith and his team."

She nodded nervously.

Smith smiled. "I'm sure I will have your cooperation, not that your cooperation matters, Mr. Hackling."

The FBI agent left the room, as did Patty the receptionist, who closed the door on the way out.

Johnson looked at Hackling. "Dollars we raised were used to pay for the assassination of a pope. That's it. We're done. Can we avoid jail?"

Hackling sat down, and placed his cloth napkin back on his lap. He picked up the fork, and ate a morsel of his omelet. "This is barely edible. Another few minutes and it will be too cold."

"What?"

"We certainly are not going to jail. And we are not going out of business."

Johnson seemed not to hear his partner and continued, "And who will react worse? The Fred Gruber types? The Hollywood crowd? What about the Wall Street donors? Oh, God."

"This is politics, nothing more. We have the best lawyers, and a PR machine."

The panic and distress drained away from Todd Johnson's face. "Of course. You're right." He left the room, and returned within five minutes. "The lawyers and the PR team will be in conference room A in a half-hour. They'll have a draft press statement, and an outlined legal strategy to discuss. I've got Hart's team confirming every dollar raised and spent on the effort countering Augustine's public mission plans, as well as picking apart Tyler's group. And I have Melissa, Sonya, Emma, Veronica, Candace, Isabelle, Kirsten and Stacy doing the uncomfortable work of calling everyone who contributed to tell them the situation, express our moral outrage, that they will likely be getting a visit from the FBI today, and how they should handle those visits. Those eight are cool and very soothing on the phone, and they've had dealings with these contributors before."

"Perfect. Thanks."

"No problem." He took a bite of his omelet. "Oh, terrible."

"Told you," said Hackling.

But even before Hackling-Johnson could release their press statement, Long Island Congressman Ted Brees had already issued his own, declaring his shock and dismay, and that he was firing Arnie Hackling as his campaign manager. "Even the mere appearance of being linked to such atrocities is unacceptable."

Chapter 85

Over Three Months Later – New Year's Eve

"Hey, Stephen, where did you get this?" called Tom Stone. Ron McDermott, Tom and his wife Maggie were looking at a painting hanging on the living room wall in the St. Mary's parsonage.

Grant was pleased to excuse himself from another conversation.

He came over to the three, and whispered, "Thank you. I've spent the last hour either listening to Suzanne Maher complain or Nicole Foreman speak without taking a breath."

Stone replied, "You owe me."

Maggie rolled her eyes, and said, "Seriously, Stephen, where did you get this? It's striking."

The painting was of a dark-haired knight. He was battered, dirty and bloody. A red cross and white background dominated his tunic, which was dirty and torn. But there was strength and determination in his face. The grip on his sword appeared firm. And a light radiated from behind.

Grant seemed a bit sheepish. "A Christmas gift from a friend."

"Details?" inquired Tom.

"It's supposed to be a knight of the Crusades."

Ron added, "A Templar or Hospitaller? They were known as warrior monks, I believe."

"Yes," said Stephen. "There's also a great deal of bad history about them, including by various pop novelists."

Maggie observed, "Black hair, green eyes, and in a religious order. Is this supposed to be you, Stephen?"

"I plead the Fifth."

Tom asked, "Who gave it to you, if you don't mind me asking?"

"Would it matter if I did mind?"

"Of course not."

"It was from Paige Caldwell."

Ron, Tom and Maggie said at once, "Ahh, Paige."

Grant said, "You people can be very annoying."

"How is Paige?" asked Ron.

"As far as I know, she is doing well." He changed the subject. "Ron, I saw Pope Paul VII's New Year's message. He did a nice job, I thought, noting the leadership of Pope Augustine. But there was still nothing about carrying through on Augustine's proposed mission. A little surprising. I thought as Augustine's right hand man that Juan Santos was onboard the mission."

"I know," said Ron. "He has praised Augustine, but has been silent on this. We'll see."

Grant noticed the time. "It's 20 minutes until midnight. Who wants to help me hand out glasses and pour champagne?"

Neither Ron nor Tom said anything.

"Oh, please," said Maggie, feigning exasperation. "Come on, Stephen, I'll help."

"Thanks, Maggie. Is Tom this lazy at home, too?"

As they walked away, Tom interjected, "Excuse me, but I thought I just said that you owe me."

All of Stephen's guests had glasses of champagne, and the two-minute countdown to the New Year began on television. But Grant was distracted by the fact that Jennifer had not yet arrived.

I knew she was going to arrive late, but not this late.

There were some thirty people crowded in and spilling out of his living room. At 30 seconds before midnight, across the heads of friends and parishioners like Scott and Pam Larson, Glenn Oliver, Barbara Tunney, Everett Birk and Sean McEnany, he saw the front door open. Standing on her tippy toes, pulling off a snow-flecked hat and scarf, Jennifer scanned the room. Spotting Stephen, she smiled and waved.

Grant waved back. He now felt more at ease, happy and content.

The countdown in the St. Mary's parsonage grew louder. As the ball in Times Square touched down, cheers and "Happy New Year's" wishes went up.

Grant made his way through handshakes, hugs and kisses, as he tried to get to Jennifer. But as he was chatting and well-wishing his way through the kitchen, he lost sight of her.

He paused and looked around. Behind him, the bathroom door swung open, a hand grabbed the back of his sweater, and pulled him inside.

Grant turned around, the door closed, and he found himself pinned against it and looking down nose-to-nose with Jennifer Brees.

"Happy New Year, Pastor Grant."

"And Happy New Year to you, Jennifer Brees."

"Wrong."

"Excuse me?"

"You called me Jennifer Brees."

"You're not Jennifer Brees? Well, this could get interesting. Who are you?"

"I have a New Year's surprise for a certain pastor who has been unwilling to even fool around just a little with a separated, soon-to-be-divorced woman."

"Hey, this has not been easy on ..."

"Quiet, please."

"I apologize. Continue."

"Thank you. As I was saying, my surprise for this certain Lutheran pastor. Two days ago, I officially became a single woman."

Grant smiled. "Jen, that's ..."

"I said quiet, please."

"Again, my apologies."

"Later that day, I went to the Social Security office and reclaimed my maiden name. You are now uncomfortably close to one Jennifer Shaw."

"It's like being with a mystery woman."

"You have no idea, Mr. Grant."

Grant pulled her even closer, and kissed her deeply.

"Hmmm, apparently you failed to fully reveal your kissing skills," Jennifer whispered.

"Darn good yourself, Ms. Shaw."

"Does this mean we get to compare bullet scars after the party?"

"That sounds like something we can look forward to for the rest of our lives."

She leaned back and looked at his face in surprise. "Do you realize what you just said – rest of our lives?"

"I know what I said," replied Stephen.

"Are you serious? Are you proposing in the bathroom? What a romantic!"

They kissed again.

After a knock at the door came the voice of Tom Stone: "Excuse me, are you going to be much longer? There's a line forming out here."

About the Author

Ray Keating is a weekly columnist with Dolan Media Company (including *Long Island Business News* and *Colorado Springs Business Journal*), a former *Newsday* weekly columnist, an economist, and an adjunct college professor. His work has appeared in a wide range of additional periodicals, including *The New York Times, The Wall Street Journal, The Washington Post, New York Post,* Los Angeles *Daily News, The Boston Globe, National Review, The Washington Times, Investor's Business Daily,* New York *Daily News, Detroit Free Press, Chicago Tribune, Providence Journal Bulletin,* and *Cincinnati Enquirer.* Keating lives on Long Island with his family. This is his first novel.

Made in the USA
Lexington, KY
16 September 2011